PALOM

To Jack,

May you always have the courage to face your fears.

25.5.19

By L. L. McNeil

WORLD OF LINARIA

Book One: Moroda

Book Two: Palom

PALOM

BOOK TWO
WORLD OF LINARIA

L. L. McNeil

First published in Great Britain in 2018.

ISBN: 978-0-9957922-1-0
Cover by: Book Beaver
First Edition Print

Printed and bound in Great Britain by Clays Ltd,
Elcograf S.p.A

www.llmcneil.com

DEDICATION

For Pipkin, who has brought unending joy, happiness, and laughter to my life.

ACKNOWLEDGEMENTS

My writing group, Garage Fiction, has provided incredible support, critique, and encouragement since I shared my writing journey with them. In particular, I'd like to thank Olivia for her ceaseless patience and dedication in pushing me to complete this novel.

To anyone who purchases my book, I am eternally grateful. It would mean the world and more if you would be kind enough to review *Palom*.

SUMMARY OF MORODA

Moroda's home town of Niversai, the capital city of Corhaven, is burned by a dragon in an unprovoked attack. She and her sister Eryn escape on a sky pirate's airship, but the dragon follows, intent on burning them, too. They are saved by the unexpected arrival of a stranger who slays the dragon with little effort.

Moroda and Eryn find themselves thrown in with people from across the world of Linaria: Amarah—the sky pirate, Palom and Anahrik—two Ittallan trading partners, Morgen—an officer in the Imperial Guard, Kohl—the dragon hunter from an exiled race, and Sapora—the Varkain crown prince.

Aciel, an Arillian Lord, has the power of compulsion and can turn anyone to his cause with his voice and will. By slaying dragons and stealing their crystals—the very essence of their magic and power—he has boosted his strength enough to command a growing army and attempts to conquer Linaria.

The dragon which attacked Niversai was under a similar thrall to the rest of Aciel's followers. On discovering this fact in Berel, home of the greatest university in the world and city of Samolen mages, Moroda and the others seek a powerful dragon known as a Sevastos to aid their cause and stop Aciel.

They encounter Aciel's partner, Jato, and Amarah leads a heist to steal her ereven sphere—an ancient artefact that enables the user to scry for dragons—cutting off Aciel's eyes and hoping to slow his dragon hunt.

After their successful theft, they flee across the Sea of Nami to Val Sharis, home country of the Ittallan shapeshifters, and neighbouring country to Sereth, home of the Varkain. On arriving at the capital city, Taban Yul, the group is greeted by Princess Isa, Sapora's half-sister. She delights in her brother's return as he is due to become king when he reaches Sereth.

The palace throws a ball to mark the beginning of winter, and Eryn is keen to relax after their encounter with Jato and Aciel. Despite Moroda's wishes to use Jato's ereven sphere to find a Sevastos, the sisters and Morgen stay to enjoy the fine food and music.

When Sapora and Isa get up to dance, they transform in the middle of the song. Sapora's true form is that of a thirty-foot tall cobra—and he immediately kills those in the ballroom who aren't loyal to him. Terrified by the bloodbath, Eryn panics and flees into the snowy wilderness outside, pursued by Moroda, Morgen, and Kohl.

Jato and her elite Arillians ambush them, but before the fight begins, Kohl flees, abandoning the three to their deaths. In the ensuing battle, they are outnumbered and overwhelmed. Palom and Anahrik enter the fray at the last minute, wielding newly-forged, dragon-infused weapons: the *Valta Forinja.*

Despite driving off the Arillians, both Eryn and Anahrik lose their lives, and Palom swears revenge against Kohl for his betrayal.

The palace prepares itself against an all-out attack by Aciel and his army, so Amarah flies what remains of the group to the border between Val Sharis and Sereth in a hunt for any dragon who might be able to help. Sapora leaves the others at the border to claim his crown, leaving Moroda, Amarah, Palom, Morgen, and a scholar from Berel, Topeko, to follow the ereven sphere into a blizzard.

They reach a cave in the mountains and find an injured dragon inside—along with Kohl. He shows genuine remorse at the deaths of his old allies and reveals he cannot bring himself to harm Jato as she is his daughter.

Palom is angered, yet Moroda forgives him. With Topeko's help, they manage to move the magical power from Aciel's slain dragons to the wounded dragon, restoring her power and dealing their enemy a massive blow. In spite of their help, the dragon is not interested in aiding their cause and flies away, leaving Moroda and the others to face Aciel alone.

Meanwhile in Sereth, Sapora meets with his half-brother, Tacio, and their father Vasil, the reigning king. In Varkain tradition, he must prove his worth before he may take the crown and is subjected to several intense battles deep in the bowels of the earth against opponents of varying strength and numbers. Sapora is victorious, even killing a member of the Old Guard—one of the Varkain's greatest warriors strengthened by blood magic.

Following his victory, Sapora supersedes Vasil as king of the Varkain and—through Vasil's conquest of Taban Yul some twenty years prior—king of the Ittallan.

Even after proving his strength and ability, Tacio is reluctant to accept his brother as king. The rivalry between the two brews as Sapora takes his crown and sets into motion his plans for the Varkain.

Aciel attacks Taban Yul with an army of Arillians and warships, and a vicious battle ensues. Terrified she'll lose more friends, and with nothing to lose, Moroda steals Amarah's airship and flies back to the mountains alone to beg the dragon for help.

While the dragon again refuses to get involved, Moroda is able to reverse engineer the ereven sphere and summon the Sevastos to her. She wishes prevent any more of her friends from dying. Moved by her pleas, the Sevastos agrees to help and sacrifices himself. Armed with a crystal bursting with the Sevastos' power, the dragon flies her back to the battlefield.

Moroda wishes above all else to stop the fighting—not kill Aciel—and she uses the Sevastos' power to do just that, sealing Aciel and herself in crystal, breaking all compulsion and freeing thousands from Aciel's grasp, thus ending the war.

In Sereth, Topeko challenges the newly crowned Sapora for his inaction against Aciel and questions the Sevastos rumoured to be hidden in Sereth. Sapora exiles him in retaliation, saying he has bigger plans for the Varkain than getting caught up in Aciel's war.

Topeko returns to the surface to celebrations, but with Sapora and his plans, he fears it is the beginning of the end for Linaria.

'From dragon-flame begun. From dragon-flame undone.'

Chapter One

The dual bladed great-sword glowed blue in the firelight. Flames jumped from the roaring hearth opposite, sucked in by the enchanted metal.

Palom's bulk dwarfed the low stool he sat on. He rested his chin in his hands and leant on his thighs as he watched the flickering fire mix with the sword's light. His mug of black ale sat untouched on the table beside him, already forgotten.

Though he had forged the new *Valta Forinja*, he still didn't fully understand the weapon's power. Not this sword, not the twin dirks he'd crafted for his business partner, not the scythe for the sky pirate, nor the short-sword for the officer of the Guard. It had been a boyhood dream he'd fulfilled as the threat of imminent death spurred him on, and he'd ploughed through to forge the weapons without thought of consequence.

The original *Valta Forinja* had been used only once before, in the Great War some two thousand years ago. Those were little more than relics, locked in a University half a world away for study by the scholars of Berel. And now, Palom, hero of the Ittallan, had recreated them to devastating effect.

Around him, the tavern heaved with throngs of revellers dancing and singing in celebration of their victory over Aciel. The Arillian conqueror would have taken Linaria for himself, had it not been for the *Valta Forinja*. Palom had turned the tide of battle and stopped the Arillians in their tracks.

But he hadn't stopped Aciel—at least, not by himself. He was *not* the sole hero half the city claimed him to be. There'd been others with him, allies who'd stood firm together. In the end, Moroda had been the true victor, and she was gone.

Despite the elation that had coursed through the city for days, Palom couldn't bring himself to enjoy their hollow victory.

Sickness flared in his stomach as a woman smiled at him as she passed, her heady perfume lingering long after she'd moved out of sight. How could they be so happy when they'd suffered such losses? The palace had only just set up a guard around the crystal pillar on the edge of the battlefield beyond the city's walls, and all the violence of war had been forgotten.

Something crashed to his right, and Palom glanced up in time to see a trio of drunken Ittallan youths collapse on the floor, arms entwined. Their glass tankards smashed on the flagstones, and beer seeped into the rug in front of the hearth.

Palom growled at their lack of respect, but the three of them laughed as though they'd enjoyed a good joke. A handful of others stumbled to their aid, but with so much intoxication in the air, they all fell to the floor in a heap.

One managed to grab onto the mantle and pull himself to his feet. He had a freckled nose above a small chin coloured with day-old stubble, dark hair, and blue eyes that couldn't quite focus when Palom looked at him. He recognised him as a young soldier in the Imperial Guard, but wasn't sure of his name or rank.

'A toast to the hero of the battle!' The youth roared, picked up his cracked, empty tankard and lifted it to Palom. 'The great tiger who saved Linaria!' Cheers erupted around him as other Ittallan took up the cry, their voices bright with glee.

Already, tales of the battle had exploded out of control, as was so often the way with heroic stories. Palom had allegedly saved Taban Yul alongside a group of dedicated fighters with *Valta Forinja* at their control. Then it had escalated to saving all of Val Sharis. Now, it seemed, he'd saved the world alone.

Snow settled over Taban Yul as winter took the city in its grip, the tavern's windows half-obscured by thick snow drifts.

He sighed, trying to peer through the frosted glass.

Lathri was late.

In all the years he'd known her, she'd never been late.

He chewed the inside of his cheek, checking around him in case he'd missed her, though he knew full well she wasn't there.

His sword absorbed another tongue of flame, and he exhaled through his nose in irritation.

The main door to the tavern creaked open, snow blasted through the gap, and Palom spun round on his stool to see a new figure arrive. He was a lean man, bundled up in thick travelling furs and black leather boots. Men and women had been arriving and leaving all night, but this one drew Palom's attention more than most. Something about the smoothness in the way he moved, a calculated confidence that made every motion a little too perfect.

Palom narrowed his eyes, his attention away from his *Valta Forinja* for the first time in days.

The stranger closed the door behind him and shrugged out of his furs, revealing pale grey skin on a fine featured, youthful-looking face. Underneath, he wore a well-tailored coat, which he cleared of melted snow, wiping away the moisture with the back of his hands. His dark, reddish-brown hair had been slicked back with oil, and he took his time in removing gloves from his hands, displaying a number of jewelled rings in silver and onyx.

Another Varkain. They'd been slipping into the city with increasing regularity since their new king came to power.

The Varkain rarely left their tunnels in Sereth, but it seemed Sapora's ascension from prince to king had kick-started a mass exodus. What Sapora had said to undo millennia of cultural preference, Palom couldn't say. Seeing so many snakes in *his* city unnerved him as it would any Ittallan, but with his new weapon to worry about, a funeral of his friends and allies on the coming dawn, and Lathri due any moment, he couldn't bring himself to care why.

The new Varkain peered around, golden eyes darting from face to face as he took stock of his surroundings. His gaze lingered on Palom, who clamped down on his instinctive urge to flinch, and then he was gone—disappearing into the crowd.

Palom turned away from the rabble, his gaze drawn once again to his weapon as it flickered in the firelight. A pang of longing rippled through him, and he frowned.

As though listening to his thoughts, his sword flashed white and blue. The *Valta Forinja* mocked him. It didn't have a single nick or scratch, and it pulsed with power as though eager to fight again.

Palom had not escaped the battle unscathed—a number of new scars littered his body—but he wanted peace. That was supposedly what they had won, so why wasn't he allowed any of it? They'd lost too much to call it a victory.

He'd lost too much.

More than that, he'd sworn to protect his allies, and he'd failed. They'd fallen.

It was his fault.

It was always his fault.

He'd drank heavily the first night, losing himself in the numbness at the bottom of a barrel. When he'd regained consciousness, the pain of failure bit sharper than any of his healing wounds. Guilt smothered him, crushing his chest, while the Ittallan called him a hero.

He'd saved the palace. Saved the city.

But what did it matter if he'd been unable to save those most important to him?

Eryn.

Moroda.

Anahrik.

Imagining their faces brought overwhelming sorrow, and he'd moved from tavern to tavern, drinking them dry of ale, cider, even wine—though the headache and sickness it caused hardly seemed worth it—while around him the city celebrated.

No-one realised he drank deeply not in celebration, but to drown his guilt.

The Ittallan feasting and drinking had gone on for almost a week, but now the last of the battlefield had been cleared and the mass funeral loomed, things were reaching fever pitch. The palace was worse, with Princess Isa doing little to stem those wishing to honour him and his comrades. Though she meant well, he couldn't stomach her blanket acceptance of gratitude.

Amarah had basked in it, of course, and even Morgen had enjoyed the swooning before he and the scholar Topeko had flown back to Corhaven to sort out the damage caused by Aciel. At least Kohl had respect enough to avoid the crowds; but where Arillians had once been tolerated, they were now despised.

Kohl. *Betrayer*.

If it hadn't been for him, they'd not have lost so many allies to the Arillian army.

Palom left the palace in the end, driven away by the sickening, undeserving praise. But he couldn't return to the forge where he'd lived and worked before everything had started.

Anahrik wasn't there anymore.

That was a step too painful to take just yet, so he'd asked to meet with the only person he had left in the city.

The only one who could help him, who wouldn't judge…who would understand.

Now, waiting in the heaving tavern, desperate and hopeful, Palom couldn't bring himself to even sip his drink. His thoughts and worries threatened to overwhelm him so completely, he didn't notice anyone approach until a hand rested on his shoulder.

'I thought you'd join the celebrations. You always enjoyed your ale.' The voice was soft, yet somehow cut through the noise of the crowd as if she'd spoken directly in his ear.

'Lathri.' Palom choked. 'You…have not seen me for past few days. I have had too much.' His face darkened. 'I did not think you would come.'

He stood up to greet her, even though he towered over her by a good two feet. Palom bowed his head to shorten the distance, raised a hand to her cheek, and cupped it with his palm.

She was covered in snow, already melting in the heat of the tavern, her face flushed from the walk, and she looked as beautiful as the last time he'd seen her. His stomach knotted at his mistake, masking the sadness for a few moments.

'I'm not in the business of letting people down. I thought you'd know that by now. Isn't that why you wanted to meet? A messenger from the palace, indeed. How curious!' Lathri pressed her cheek into his hand with a coy grin and took her seat opposite him. 'I've ordered food. You look like you've not eaten in months.'

Palom shook his head and sat down, reaching across the table to clasp her hands in his.

'I have not eaten as I should,' he admitted stiffly. 'It is hard to eat when grieving.'

Lathri's eyes dropped, and Palom studied her face. She was much as he remembered her: long, blonde, almost translucent hair, high cheekbones on a smooth face, and stunningly vibrant orange-brown eyes. Her eyes hinted at her true form, and they glittered in the reflected firelight. She wore a brown woollen cloak with white fur and feathers lining the neckline and sleeves, and she'd removed her moleskin gloves to reveal thin, supple fingers. He'd always thought they were musician's hands.

'We've all been touched by Aciel's war,' she said after a respectable silence. Energy pulsed gently around her, warming his hands where they held hers, and his sadness eased, somehow softening around the edges.

He'd forever be grateful for her education at Berel University.

'Will you go to the funeral?' Lathri asked.

Palom nodded, grateful at the respite the healer brought him. 'I am part of parade.'

Her eyes widened, but she quickly masked her surprise. 'I thought the Imperial Guard—'

'Are under control of princess,' Palom interrupted. 'She has permitted me to carry…' He shuddered, fighting back the sobs that threatened now his emotions had been loosened by her touch.

Lathri rubbed her thumb along his. 'I know how much this means to you. You don't need to explain yourself.'

Palom dropped his eyes. He knew his skin sagged, that he was a shadow of his former strength, and hated himself for showing such weakness in front of her. But Lathri had never been one to judge, and she'd seen him worse off. That was a comforting thought.

A serving boy approached the table with a large platter. 'For the hero of Linaria and his beautiful companion,' he announced with a grin. Palom scowled at him and held a growl back, but Lathri smiled politely and passed him a few coins.

The smell of food overcame Palom's irritation, and for the first time in as long as he could remember, his stomach grumbled. Thick slabs of bacon cooked in butter and sugar lay across bread inlaid with wedges of cheese. Lathri had also ordered them a large pot of tea, its heavily-scented liquid steaming from the spout.

Palom winced. Moroda and Eryn's father had been a merchant of tea and coffee before he'd died. It had been why he'd offered to look after them in the first place. He tried to ignore the stabbing guilt picking at the back of his mind as he poured the tea.

'You were instrumental in stopping the war,' Lathri said, taking the knife to cut herself a piece of bread and meat. 'Many people have sons and daughters, brothers and sisters, who were part of that battle. If they weren't on the airships, they were on foot, or in the palace, or producing the weapons and armour.' She gave him a look.

'They don't speak like that to Imperial Guard.' Palom shoved bacon into his mouth. 'Why am I special?'

Lathri sipped her tea, it's heat reddening her cheeks where she held the mug close. 'You must know. The main reason is resting against the wall.' She raised her eyebrows and tilted her head.

Palom looked over his shoulder at the glowing sword and the few sober Ittallan who hung around it, eager for a peek at the famed weapon. He looked back at her with a huff.

'I can feel its power, even sat here. It's far too strong. It has just one purpose: to destroy, and that's what it's done. That's what it's doing now—to you. Surely you can see that? Feel that?'

He chewed his lip. Lathri was clearly upset, but the sword was the reason he'd survived the battle against Aciel's troops. The reason Aciel had lost. It had been a simple blade, a test weapon, and it had absorbed the power of the dragon-ore and transformed into something miraculous.

The sword hummed as though it were alive, and sent shivers up his arms, his *meraki* piqued. 'It…is…special…'

'You've made the stuff of legend, Palom. *You* are the stuff of legend, whether you want to accept it or not.' Lathri put her mug down and ate.

He felt her withdraw. He understood her hatred of the sword, fear, even, and somewhere deep down, he agreed with what she said.

But he couldn't get rid of it. Not after everything he'd gone through to forge it in the first place. He didn't know if it *could* be destroyed, even if he'd wanted to. He picked at his plate in silence, hunger squashed as quickly as it had surfaced, and he longed for her touch again.

'People have seen what you've made, seen you in battle. You know tigers are rare enough.' Lathri said after she'd eaten several mouthfuls.

Palom let her words hang in the air, remembering his first visit to the city when he'd been barely sixteen. The Imperial Guard had requested he joined them as soon as they'd learned what he was—not that he'd been in the right frame of mind to join, anyway.

Of all hunter Ittallan, tigers were one of the strongest. Aside from Mateli, of course—but he was an exception. Palom shuddered as the painful memory of Mateli's frenzied bloodlust floated, unbidden, in his mind, and he glanced to the *Valta Forinja*.

Palom had come to Taban Yul full of sadness, and Lathri had helped him. Now he was back in the same city under the same circumstances, and once more, he'd turned to her for help.

He took her fingers in his own and squeezed them, exhaling slowly as her magic dissipated the memories. A small weight in his jerkin pocket pressed against his side, and the faintest smile touched his lips.

A gift for her. A promise.

He thought of the best way to explain how he felt, preferably in a way that didn't seem selfish, but Lathri spoke before he had the chance to say anything.

'It is *emonos*, Palom. I don't care what you did to create it. I don't care what you've achieved with it.' Her warmth vanished in a heartbeat, her eyes cold and clear. 'You can't run forever. I've some friends I'd like you to meet tonight. We might be able to help each other.'

Palom withdrew his hand, all thoughts of his desires forgotten. 'What friends?'

'Eat, first. You need your strength.' Her smile was back.

Palom stared at the food and ignored its inviting smell.

Emonos.

That's what she'd called it.

Unclean.

Evil.

A word in the old tongue to describe the death of a traitor. It was a hammer blow to his gut.

Whether it was the word's meaning or the fact it came from Lathri, Palom suddenly wanted nothing more than to rid himself of his sword. But his fear of being too weak without it kept him from moving.

'Palom?'

He looked up, wincing at the obvious concern in her face. 'I am okay,' he muttered, and ate.

*

'Kylos and Aetos are from Tum Metsa. Do you know it?' Lathri asked as they pushed their way through the crowd. If anything, there were more people now than earlier in the evening, and while many patrons attempted to make way for the pair, most fell over themselves to shake Palom's hand or touch the sword at his back.

Palom grunted at those who stepped aside for them but ended up shoving more people out of the way than shaking hands. When they were finally across the room and clear, he thought of the towns in Val Sharis. 'Tum Metsa is in north? Near sea?'

Lathri nodded, casting a sympathetic look over her shoulder at the crowd that stared after them. She led him through a door to a passageway at the back of the tavern. 'That's right. They came to Taban Yul shortly after the ball. Word spread quickly of what Sapora did, of those who perished that night.' She looked away when she spoke, her hair masking her face.

He had the feeling she was choosing her words carefully and appreciated the care she took over his emotions. 'So, they have come for revenge? Knowing Sapora is in palace?'

'You know us Ittallan. We hold our grudges.'

He said nothing at that, immediately thinking of Mateli, and more recently, Kohl. Anger passed through him.

'Voulhrik also lost someone. His mentor,' she continued. 'One of the councillors had given him work in the palace. His name was Elafion, a stag. Unfortunately, Elafion disliked Sapora's claim to rule. Killing for loyalty is never the way to go about it. Voulhrik still works in the palace, though. A glorified messenger, really. But some of the things he's heard…' She shuddered. 'Better for you to hear it from him.'

Palom frowned. What did Lathri have to do with the palace and politics of rulers?

She strolled confidently to the unguarded door at the end of the passageway. Palom waited a few heartbeats before continuing—partly to ensure no-one followed them, and partly to enjoy the view and memories it evoked. She knocked once, opened the door, and walked through, Palom accompanying her inside.

The room was furnished simply, with six beds, a large round table, and several chairs. Three of the chairs were full, and all three occupants got to their feet, weapons grasped. When they saw Lathri, they relaxed.

Palom felt his sword flare with energy, and he took several deep breaths. He could tell two were hunters—a man and a woman, no doubt Aetos and Kylos—but the last man was taller and broader even than he was. He had to be Voulhrik. Fighting any of them would be a challenge.

No. He wouldn't need to fight.

These were Lathri's friends.

Conflicting emotions warred within him for a long second.

'Please, sit,' Lathri said, shrugging out of her cloak and laying it over the back of an empty chair. 'This, as I'm sure you all know, is Palom.' She ran her fingers through her hair and took her seat at the table.

Palom watched as a flicker of recognition appeared across their faces. He sighed, bracing himself for their reactions.

'Sorry about that. Never can be too careful, Lathri. The state the city is in…' the big man said, waving a long dagger before sheathing it and taking his seat. Palom disliked his thin moustache and beady eyes but tried to let it slide. He was here for Lathri.

'It's fine.' Lathri brushed down her long sleeves.

'Palom? The tiger?' The woman, Kylos, asked, still standing. 'So, you're the one the whole country is in love with.' Her black hair was long and smooth, tied back with gold clips. Her eyes were a lighter orange-brown than Lathri's, more yellow, but no less cunning.

Palom looked to the man beside her—he was half a head taller than Kylos, but with matching hair and eyes. The resemblance was clear. If they were friends of Lathri, he should have nothing to fear. But suspicion ran deep when allies betrayed you, and he didn't let his guard down.

'You must be… Kylos?' Palom asked her, eyeing the short, curved blade she sheathed at her hip. She nodded once, sharply, and sat down, her brother following suit.

'Things are getting worse, Lathri,' Aetos said, his voice scratchy, as though he didn't use it often. 'Everyone on the south side of the city has gone mad. People walking into the freezing river, jumping in front of moving wagons, or just disappearing into the forest. So many families have up and left their homes, some leaving full winter larders. Others have been found curled up, babbling to themselves, making no sense. Our medics can't help them. Most have died. I've never seen a sickness like it.'

'Who has died? People here? In Taban Yul?' Palom asked.

'Yes, most people on the outskirts. Whatever disease this is, whatever's causing this, it hasn't reached the inner city yet,' Aetos replied. 'No-one seems to know what to do. They say it's an omen with Sapora in charge now.'

'And of course, we've got the Varkain moving themselves in like they own the place,' Kylos added. She grimaced at the mention of the race. 'The snakes rarely come here. Never in winter, anyway. But, now…'

Lathri's brow wrinkled in concern. 'I know. It's a worrying sign.'

'Why don't you talk to Princess Isa if you have concerns?' Palom asked, sitting down beside Lathri at last. Though he hadn't been in Taban Yul for over half a year, the city was still his home. If his fellow Ittallan had problems, it was down to the palace to fix them. 'I know Princess Isa. Is that why you brought me here, Lathri? So that you could speak?'

'Isa's been compromised,' Kylos said quickly, folding her arms. 'With half the council gone thanks to her brother, there's no Ittallan left in Val Sharis who'd trust her. Talking to her alone would be ideal…but she's not stupid enough to meet strangers without an escort. Do you have that kind of influence?'

Palom shrugged. 'No. But Princess Isa still cares about Taban Yul.' The princess had been a little vain, of course, but she was royalty. It was to be expected. But compromised? 'I can take you to her after funeral. Then, you will see.'

'With Sapora listening to every word? Don't make me laugh. She's probably in league with the Varkain! She was at the ball, too, don't forget,' Kylos continued, clearly the most vocal of the three. 'This war isn't over by a long shot. We've just changed enemies.'

Palom sighed.

Lathri remained quiet, listening to the talk around her.

Aetos spoke again, 'The snakes can wait. They've been at our doorstep since Linaria had four moons. They won't go away any time soon. The problem is the sickness in the city.'

'The sickness may pass. Sapora and his Varkain are a bigger threat,' Voulhrik said, his deep voice rumbling.

'Then talk to Imperial Guard!' Palom said, exasperated. Whether there was a sickness in the city or they had concerns about the Varkain moving in, he didn't see how it was his problem—or theirs.

'The loyal ones have been killed. Those remaining in the Imperial Guard are in Sapora's pocket now,' Lathri said quietly. 'Perhaps even those in Niversai, as well. They've always been our allies, and if his snakes have their fangs into Corhaven's capital… Half the world could be under his poison.'

'Surely you saw they're under Sapora's thumb while you were swanning around in the palace?' Voulhrik said with a sneer. 'Or were you too busy counting your Varkain gold?'

The difference in behaviour from regular townsfolk to these three jarred Palom. 'I was not *swanning* around!'

'Voulhrik, I know you're hurting. Don't take it out on Palom,' Lathri said. Heat emanated from her, diffusing the tension in the space of a few breaths, and Voulhrik backed down.

She rubbed her eyes, suddenly looking tired. 'To answer your question, I'd hoped you'd join us. You know Sapora and his ways. You know the princess. You could easily get into the Imperial Guard—especially after everything you've done against Aciel—and help influence things away from the Varkain. Sapora couldn't refuse a fighter like you in his ranks. Voulhrik is doing what he can, but one palace worker isn't enough. If we had someone in the thick of it, someone higher up, who knew what Sapora's plots were…You could help find out what's happening in the city, what they're planning to do with the crystal now he has a guard set up there—'

'Moroda is inside there!' Palom bellowed, aware he was shaking but too angry to do anything about it. 'It is not some*thing* to look into. It is burial site. She made blood oath with Sevastos to save your skins. Amarah and Kohl left Taban Yul to find way to break her free!'

Lathri blinked, taken aback. 'But don't you see? That's why you should stay with us.'

Palom balled his hands as he fought to restrain his anger, fought against the urge to grab his sword. 'You have not said what is your plan to do.'

'Do you trust Sapora?' Aetos asked.

Palom shook his head. 'I don't trust any Varkain.'

'Exactly. At least Vasil kept the snakes to their tunnels. But this new king is young, a half-breed to boot, and more ambitious than any Varkain we've known. If he's planning anything, I'll bet a thousand crowns it's against the Ittallan.'

Knowing Sapora, it wasn't an unfair statement.

'There's been talk that Sapora plans to wipe us out. For good, this time.' Voulhrik said, drawing their attention. 'I've heard him talk of ancient powers, keys, seals…'

Palom swallowed and went very still.

'He whispers of it to the Varkain he has guarding him. His personal guards. Only a handful of them. Whatever he's cooking up, he's keeping it quiet.'

Palom's mind whirled. If Voulhrik was right...If those things had been mentioned...He shuddered to think what it could mean for the Ittallan.

'Isa is one of us more than he is. We'd hoped she would one day be our queen, but it looks like we'll be overrun by the Varkain before we can recover from Aciel's attacks and get her in power,' Lathri said, breaking Palom's thoughts. 'If it comes to it, we need to be ready for whatever Sapora has planned against us.'

Palom's sword pulsed at his back. Conversation exploded around him. Why was Lathri leading this? Had she forgotten what Sapora did to those he disliked? What he'd done at the ball was the very reason her allies were all here.

Panic swelled, rising from his belly to his throat.

'Lathri, stop this,' he shouted, slamming his palms flat on the table. The sudden yell reverberated around the room. 'You can't fight Sapora. Alone, he's stronger than any of you. Now he is ruling as king of Varkain and Ittallan. He is untouchable.'

Talk of ancient powers had changed things. Drastically.

If his fear was right, Sapora would ruin them all.

His heart pounded.

He had to get away. Had to get Lathri away. Before he lost someone else he loved.

'I thought you were supposed to be a great warrior,' Voulhrik said, sneering. 'You've won a single battle and now you want to run? Some hero.'

'I never said I was hero,' Palom said, rising to his feet, Voulhrik mirroring the action. 'I never asked to be one.' He drew the sword from his back and pointed it across the table. 'If it wasn't for Moroda, Aciel would have beaten us hundred times over. Sapora is worse than upstart Arillian. You want my opinion and knowledge on him? Trust me. He is greater threat. If any of what you say is true, we cannot stand against him.'

'Voulhrik. Palom. Please,' Lathri said, raising her hands. 'I said before that sword is too powerful. Think carefully about what you mean to do with it.'

Lathri's energy wrapped around him. Palom felt his heartbeat in his throat, sweat on his forehead. He tightened his grip on the sword's hilt.

All it would take was a flick of his wrist. A tiny, inconsequential movement, and Voulhrik's head would be severed. His world dimmed, Lathri's voice muffled as he focussed on his blade and the man who stood before it.

The weapon's desire filled his mind, competing with Lathri's magic, and his hand trembled.

'I do not know all of Sapora's power. I do not know if he is causing this...this...sickness in city. But I know enough to understand it is no safe place for Ittallan anymore. We should leave while we can. All of us. Now.'

'Leave the city? The capital of Val Sharis? There's no safer place in the world.' Kylos scoffed.

'With that snake here, it is now most dangerous place.'

Lathri's magic intensified, and the hairs on Palom's arms stood up. 'Palom, we have a duty to our people. We can't rely on the Imperial Guard as we have before. This sickness may not be Sapora. But we can't run, or we're handing victory to him. Aciel is gone thanks to you, but he's paved the way for the next conqueror. We've enjoyed peace for far too long. We must be ready. We can't turn against each other.'

It would take the tiniest movement.

'Please.'

Glaring at Voulhrik, Palom lowered his sword, and rested the tip on the table. 'Lathri. Aciel's war is over. Let Sapora rule. His father was king. By law, he has right to be here, even if we don't like this. Now, he might be planning to kill all Ittallan...Why put yourself in danger? People die in wars.'

'So, you won't help us?' Desperation edged her voice.

'Lathri, let's get away from... from... this.' He gestured to the table with his free hand. 'I fought Mateli when I was sixteen. It was right thing to do. I lost people. I fought Aciel for same reason and lost more people. I won't fight Sapora, too, or whatever darkness lurks in Taban Yul.'

His attention lingered on Lathri.

'I'm not asking you to fight if you don't wish to. But stand with us, Palom. You can't run forever,' Lathri pleaded.

Even with his *Valta Forinja*, Palom didn't know if he could take on Sapora and all his Varkain. He didn't want to come to blows with the snake, not if what he feared was true. He'd already been part of ending one war. Immediately starting another would be madness.

He closed his eyes.

'I can't.'

He turned away, ignoring their words as he left the room and exited the tavern.

It would be a cold funeral tomorrow.

Chapter Two

Frigid wind bit into Amarah's skin as she gripped the wheel of her airship, *Khanna*. She cursed, struggling to keep on course while besieged by the weather. According to her guide, the blizzard would keep her safe from wandering Arillians who might see her as a threat and attack, but as another wave of turbulence almost threw her from her feet, she pursed her lips in annoyance. The driving snow seemed more likely to pluck her from the sky than offer security. She scowled, adjusting her sails for the hundredth time.

He might have been at home in the snow and wind, but *Khanna* struggled.

Her guide flew ahead of her, only a few ship-lengths ahead and yet nigh invisible in the raging storm—a storm he created to shield them as they flew deeper into *their* territory. *They* were the enemy, and yet she was heading right into their midst of her own free will. It was nothing short of madness.

They harboured a deep magic, old as Linaria itself. Generally, Amarah had no time for such sorcery, yet this particular branch of magic held the smallest of potentials for her: a prize too tempting to pass up. Her guide had given her good reason to believe that this Arillian power could resurrect those lost from Linaria.

It sounded like foolishness, but any chance—no matter how slim—had to be taken, didn't it? It was how she'd made the most of the opportunities that had presented themselves over the years. Plus, if things turned sour and this old magic couldn't do what it claimed, she had her weapon, she had her wit, and she had her guide—Kohl.

The Arillians were a brutal race, full of storms and destruction, leaving a trail of devastation whenever they visited the mainland countries in Linaria. Two wars against Arillians had certainly not warmed Amarah to them. Plus, they were so far removed from the rest of Linaria that any stories which made it to the mainland were cast aside as myths.

No-one could *really* have half the magic and mystery as the Arillians claimed. A hidden paradise, eclipsed from the rest of Linaria, with secrets and treasures and—surely the biggest myth of them all—the protection of an ice golem army that kept any would-be invaders out.

No.

It was nonsense.

Amarah expected a barren rock, much like people who made up stories to sound important and wealthy but actually had nothing of value.

Peering over the side of *Khanna*, she saw a blanket of white mottled with grey spanning as far as the eye could see. Quite where the frozen sea gave way to frozen land, she couldn't tell; a thick layer of snow covered everything and attempting to discern the finer details gave her a headache. White and grey blurred together, and the wind forced her to squint. She could just barely make out the dark silhouette of some scavenging animals, a bear, perhaps, or maybe a fox.

In the far distance, just on the edge of her vision, the mottled grey gave way to a pair of large, bleak mountains rising from the flat land. An imposing darkness in an otherwise white world, they were twin gates to the Arillian settlement of Oren, part of the scattered islands at Linaria's northern-most tip. Amarah prided herself on her experience exploring the skies as a self-proclaimed and oft-hunted pirate—she boasted there was no land she had not visited, no secret place left to find, no treasure hidden from her eyes. Yet she had never travelled here before.

There was nothing here worth knowing, she would have said in defence to those who might have questioned why.

Kohl had warned her that Oren had never seen outsiders, and a warm welcome was unlikely. Amarah had shrugged. She'd stayed in the open, slept behind rocks, and even in a badger's set once when pressed for cover. Comfort was always optional. It wasn't a trip for pleasure.

Amarah looked at the state of her ship, at the charred wood and ripped sails, the way it lurched whenever a particularly strong gust of wind caught her. A year ago, she'd have never been seen in such a place. But now? She fought for someone else, for something other than gold, riches, and enhancing her own prestige.

It was what she told herself to justify being out in the middle of a frozen tundra.

Kohl slowed his pace abruptly, and Amarah glanced up at the sudden halt. She pulled a lever to fan out her sails and brake. She watched as he flew close, hovering above where she stood at *Khanna*'s wheel. 'What's going on? We can't be there yet?'

In a flurry of snow, Kohl landed gently in a half-crouch. Wind whipped around his feet and hat as his large, feathered wings brushed the floor. 'We're going to be inspected,' he announced. 'The golems have requested we halt.'

'Golems?' Amarah's heart pounded. 'They're…real? They're here?'

'Ice golems, yes. You didn't believe they're our guardians? They shouldn't attack you, not with me here.' He turned to face her now the wind had died down, his pale, leathery skin stark in the evening sun. Scars criss-crossed his cheek and a chunk of his lip was missing. She'd thought him fearsome when they'd first met and had seen him take down a rampaging dragon single-handedly, but in the same breath, she'd never known someone so averse to fighting.

Amarah knew he ached for his home yet avoided his kin. He'd been in the wars, literally and figuratively, though she didn't know the extent of his history. From their time together, he gave away very little, and Amarah wasn't one to pry. Dragons above, she liked her own privacy, and was perfectly content to keep as quiet on her past as Kohl chose to with his. But ice golems? Even among legends, they were myths.

Her weapon, a scythe forged with dragon ore and layered, lightened steel, was formidable against most enemies. Yet for all the weapon's famed power, it surely couldn't do anything against the

Arillian guardians. She had to trust in Kohl, much as she'd rather run.

Whether the golems were ice made living, a creation of the Everwinter so far north, or some other magic she couldn't hope to understand, Amarah didn't know. The strength of their defences was legendary. It's why their stories were dismissed. A power like that just couldn't be real.

'What do I do?' she asked, looking at the ground below for these creatures who had demanded she halt.

'Nothing. They will tell me when we may pass.'

With a huff, she scratched the side of her neck, caught her skin with her nail and drew blood. She swore at the pain. 'Hope they don't take long to decide. I can't afford another sail to freeze! It'll be night soon!' She knew fear drove her frustration but ignored the tightness in her chest.

'Patience.' He waved a hand, stepping away from the airship captain to the side of the deck. His cloak, brown and faded with age, was still now that he had halted the storm surrounding them. Kohl removed his wide brimmed, sagging hat, and dusted it off while he waited: a slow, methodical action she'd seen him perform many times.

It irritated her.

'Patience. Damn patience. Why can't I go now? They're on the ground, right? I can fly over them.'

Kohl put his hat on after adjusting it and looked back at her. 'I wouldn't risk it if I were you. They've stood guard here for eons. They allow only those who are worthy. It's why no army has ever launched an attack on my home country; why no outsider has ever entered without escort. They are as old as the ice here, created from it, and the power which gives them life is older than the dragons themselves. They cannot be moved, harmed, defeated. You will not be the exception if you try to thwart them.'

Kohl spoke softly, but Amarah shivered at his words. She pushed aside her immediate instinct to retaliate and exhaled through her nose, mulling over her choices. 'Older than the dragons? Hah. Rhea herself created Linaria, everyone knows that.'

All talk she'd ever heard of the golems had been from drunkards. She'd wondered, but not truly believed they existed. Their being real went against the lore of Rhea, dragons, and the very essence of Linaria's magic. Went against the creation story of how Linaria had come into being, went against what Berel taught. Everyone in Linaria knew how the world worked, including magic.

The golems just couldn't have been real.

And yet, here she was, and here they were.

She placed her hands on her hips to keep from pacing, her scythe a few steps away if she needed to grab it. Even if it would do nothing against the ice golems, just having it close made her feel safe.

'Of course Rhea created Linaria,' Kohl replied, closing his eyes. A sudden gust of freezing air blasted the ship, rocking it where it hovered. 'We can pass. Let's go. Quickly.' Kohl took to the air again.

Amarah had half-crouched, balancing against the violent shake, her eyes darting about for any hidden threat. 'You sure?'

'They've been known to change their minds. Let's not give them reason to,' Kohl replied, flapping his wings and flying ahead.

'I don't like all this damned sorcery.' She pushed the lever back in and grabbed the ship's wheel, turning it to follow Kohl.

A flutter of panic rushed through her chest as the gap between the two mountains drew near. She had killed Arillians in a battle half a world away only a week ago—brethren of those she would see soon. The troops whose lives she had taken were not themselves when she'd ended their pain; they were under Aciel's compulsion. Did that justify what she'd done? Did it matter who they were or what they thought when she'd defended herself? Would the survivors even remember what had happened?

Kohl had fought with her. And Morgen, an officer in the Imperial Guard, typically her greatest enemy—she'd spent half her life running from them. But they'd put aside their differences to unite against Aciel. Palom had fought as well. Then there was the Varkain Prince, Sapora, who'd slunk off to his tunnels before the fighting had even begun.

Damned snake.

She'd lost companions, too. Palom's business partner and brother in all but blood, Anahrik, had perished. And Eryn, a Goldstone from the city of Niversai. Amarah hadn't been surprised at that—the girl had never fought before. She had no place on the battlefield against trained warriors.

Kohl, however, was the reason they'd died: indirectly, by fleeing, abandoning them when ambushed, and directly, by fathering the Arillian General who'd killed them: Jato.

When he'd revealed his relationship to Jato, Amarah's anger towards him dissipated. She acted in her own self-interest all the time. Kohl was just doing the same.

But his actions had split the group. Betrayal clearly wasn't common outside thieves. She understood why he'd done what he had. Everyone was always out for themselves. It wasn't like he'd physically stabbed them in the back.

But in the same breath, a few days after the loss of their friends, she'd lost the one person who'd saved them. Eryn's older sister, a Goldstone with so much spirit and inner strength it had caught her by surprise. Moroda's determination to see the good in everyone, to bring an end to the fighting, to protect those she loved…It was because of Moroda's actions that Amarah was still alive.

And she hated being in debt.

The entire world had bowed, ready to break under Aciel and his army, but Moroda had sought strength and delivered. She'd sacrificed herself for it. Readily sacrificed herself. If Amarah felt any guilt for her way of life, of pirating and thieving, taking what she could without care for anything or anyone else, it was watching Moroda die without reaping any of the rewards herself.

The mountains grew as she flew *Khanna* towards them, her unease increasing the closer she got. Unfamiliar ground. She glanced to Kohl as he flew ahead, wondering whether he'd survive his return home. He'd said his kin had little love for him, which wasn't reassuring.

Amarah had lost countless friends and allies over the years. That's how life worked. But she'd found Moroda's loss hard to bear. She hadn't died, not truly—she was frozen in the crystal of the Sevastos whose power she had used to defeat the Arillian army—but she was gone.

It was as good as death.

That crystal pillar sat outside the walls of Taban Yul, watched over by Princess Isa and the Imperial Guard stationed there. She shivered again at the thought of it.

Kohl could well be the key to bringing Moroda back, so she turned away from Taban Yul, refusing the reward money from Isa for a chance to resurrect Moroda. In the aftermath, as the Imperial Guard counted the dead, and the survivors licked their wounds, Amarah saw first-hand the change wrought in Linaria. Certainly, her place in it had changed. She had a purpose now, a reason for surviving that bloodbath and dragon-flame.

And, perhaps, a chance to redeem herself in the process.

'Amarah, look below,' Kohl called. A sudden gust of cold air caught her square in the face, and she wiped her streaming eyes, pushing hair out of her face as she looked down. They were almost at the two mountains, seemingly the only landmarks in the frozen land.

At their base stood the silent watchers who monitored their presence; the great ice sentinels of Arillian creation. They remained motionless in their thousands.

In their hundreds of thousands.

She gasped, her mouth falling open.

Fallen snow piled up about their legs, half-burying them, making them seem more a part of the land than something which walked upon its surface. They were great grey-blue monstrosities, headless, four-legged, four-armed hulking chunks of living ice. In the failing light, their silhouettes merged together with the shadow of the mountains, so Amarah had no idea of their true numbers. They were intimidating and awe-inspiring in the same breath. Snow covered their shoulders, making their bulk seem all the greater, and she shuddered at the thought of that army moving toward her.

'I can see why no-one ever breached your borders,' she said, her humour feeble. Idly, she wondered why Aciel had not brought these with him on his conquest. Surely a handful would have overrun any defence the rest of Linaria mustered against them?

'It isn't too late to turn back,' Kohl said, as he swooped overhead to land beside her. 'You can always say my clan rejected you. None would question that.'

Amarah replied with a snort, adjusting her sails as the wind changed. She refused to show any fear and pressed on, passing through the valley of the mountains, their shadows stretched in the low sun. Another chill washed over her as she crossed the physical border into Arillian land, the golems still and silent far below.

'Long as there's something hot to drink when we get there, I'm fine,' she said. 'And no storms! Don't want anything to happen to this ship. I've been through too much with *Khanna* to lose her to a stray bolt of lightning from one of you lot.'

'You needn't worry.'

'Give me your word?' Amarah raised an eyebrow.

'Indeed.' He adjusted his hat again. 'We've passed the first test. The hardest part is over.'

'First? How many damned tests are there? You never said nothing about no tests!'

The corners of Kohl's lips turned upwards for a moment, the scars making his crooked smile seem disfigured. 'It's been so long…'

Accelerating forward, Amarah pushed *Khanna* across the tundra. She rolled her shoulders, emboldened now they were away from the golems. 'Jato gonna be there?'

Amarah saw the Arillian flinch, and she smirked.

'I… don't know. Perhaps.' He fiddled with the brim of his hat.

'Won't that be a brilliant father-daughter reunion,' she cackled. 'Now the love of her life ain't around to enforce your exile, she can't say nothing about you coming home. Who knows, maybe she'll have missed you! I'm sure she'll forgive you for killing Aciel.'

'Why do you do that, Amarah? Are you hurting so much all the time that you must inflict pain on everyone around you?' Kohl asked, watching her. 'Is peace too much to ask? Is there another reason you want to resurrect Moroda?'

The sky pirate snorted again. She didn't have to answer. Didn't have to justify anything she did or said. She saw him smile his crooked smile again and bristled. She couldn't even put her finger on why it agitated her and resigned herself to complete the rest of their journey in silence.

Kohl had other ideas, it seemed. 'Topeko had such patience with you. Why did you not listen to his teachings?'

'I don't see what's so good about those damned teachings of his!'

'You've been through hardship, I understand. You were shunned by your loved ones and forced to strike out on your own. As was I. Yet…I did not resort to thievery.'

His words stung. That was too close to home.

She picked up her scythe and brandished the blade at her companion. 'One more word. I warn you.'

Kohl raised his palms and stepped back. 'I meant no offense.'

She took a deep breath. He was her guide. Without him, she would not be able to pass safely, nor return. She couldn't let herself be riled by his every comment and jibe. At least he wasn't malicious. The complete opposite of Sapora.

She straightened her stance and lowered her scythe, though she kept hold of it. 'Fine.' Her breath formed in front of her face as she spoke. She thought to the practicalities that lay ahead, which calmed her. 'If your village don't get outsiders, where am I meant to keep *Khanna*? There's no dock at all?'

Kohl shook his head. 'No, we've no need for them. Our children can fly before they can walk. We carry them if we must travel. There will be a plateau for *Khanna* to rest, protected from the worst of the snows by a bluff.'

For all the times she had her rag-tag party on *Khanna*, Amarah had been beyond frustrated with their incompetence and inability to do as they were told. Now it was just her and Kohl, she almost missed her old companions. They had united and stood against a threat. Now everyone had split up, as was expected, she felt empty somehow. Perhaps she'd crew her ship with Arillians desperate to see the rest of Linaria? Arillians looking for adventure, glory, and riches. Perhaps.

That had certainly been her dream, once. Still was, in some regards. The glistening of gold was a hard thing to resist—collecting it meant guaranteed food, shelter, comfort, even a little luxury when times were good. Things were lean, now. She was on the last of her supplies and hadn't carried out a raid for the better part of a year, though she still owned a warship docked in Taban Yul, maintained among the rest of the Imperial fleet.

Perhaps she could undergo formal training and become a warship pilot? It would be under Sapora's rule, though, and she shuddered at the thought of that filthy snake commanding her. She wouldn't be able to fight back then, and all the money in the world wouldn't be worth that restriction.

She twirled her scythe as darkness coated Linaria. Her weapon was unlike any other—ultra-light, with a sharp, twin edged blade, and the strength of dragons emanating from its core. It was this weapon that had saved her during that final battle, and it was this weapon that would keep her protected now she was deep in Arillian territory. She'd thank Palom a thousand times over for forging it. *Valta Forinja*, he'd called it. Not that the Ittallan words meant anything to her.

If the Arillians took a disliking to her, she'd damn well make sure to take as many of them down with her as she could.

'We're here,' Kohl said, breaking her thoughts. The first moon had risen, and the sun slipped towards the horizon.

'What? Where? I don't see no town?' She looked ahead and squinted in the failing light, trying to make out any indication of a village: a torchlight, a flurry of movement, even shadows grouped together to form dwellings. But she couldn't see anything other than darkening, snowy tundra. 'Sure we're in the right place? This snow all looks the bloody same.'

Kohl smiled again and flashed a few teeth. 'Arillians are creatures of the sky, Amarah. We don't live on the ground.'

Eyes widening, Amarah took a step back and looked straight up.

The sight took her breath away.

The fog which collected in extremes of cold had masked them as she approached, but she could see them now she knew where to look. Right above *Khanna*, about a league high, were a collection of floating islands.

The bare, blackened rock underneath the islands hummed low and emanated power; an invisible barrier of some kind, which pressed against her face, slowly pushing *Khanna* away as it pulsed.

'It…they, how…do we get up there?' she stammered, catching her breath as she tried to collect her thoughts. She cast her mind back to all the rumours she'd heard of this place before, all the tavern stories and jokes. There had to be something to explain how to broach the islands.

'If you can't fly straight up, then I suggest a spiral approach, steep as you can,' Kohl replied, staring up at the islands with an expression Amarah could only describe as longing. 'I'll stay on *Khanna* with you. Guide you through the storm.'

Amarah looked back at him, 'Storm? I can feel that…that force. That's a storm?'

'In a way. The elders can move air, not as wind, but as a kind of pressure. Like a shield. It keeps the islands floating and anything unwanted away. A superb defence.'

She exhaled, 'With those Golems standing guard, do you even need that barrier to protect you?'

Kohl licked his lips. 'Let's go, before the light completely disappears.'

Amarah knew he was right. She didn't have time on her side. She clicked her tongue, adjusted her sails, and pushed forward on the throttle. *Khanna* would be the first ship to touch this undiscovered land.

That meant something.

As *Khanna* picked up speed, Amarah opened her large side sails and turned wide, curving around the perimeter of the bottom of the islands. Once happy with her speed, she pulled back on another lever, lifting the nose of *Khanna* and beginning her ascent. The force of air which shielded the islands grew stronger, shaking *Khanna* as she continued to climb, circling all the while.

Amarah saw Kohl raise his hands and then the chill of his power washed over *Khanna* as he unleashed his own magic to challenge the islands' defence. The force pushing against her slackened, as though he'd lifted the barrier, and she approached unimpeded.

Sweat gathered at her temples from the effort of holding *Khanna*'s climb, turn, and speed, and her arms shook at the effort of it. Through *Khanna*, she felt every touch of wind, every air current, every shift in pressure and temperature.

Some part of the hull groaned under the conflicting forces as Amarah pushed her ship to the limit. One of her already torn sails flapped wildly, and with a sudden screech, ripped away, lost in the darkness behind them.

Amarah knew if she let go, even with Kohl's aid, the strength of the islands' barrier would fling her off into the darkness, following her lost sail. She couldn't give up. Wouldn't.

Khanna groaned again, a low noise that vibrated under her. If Rhea existed, she prayed she'd keep *Khanna* held together. Her ship had survived hurricanes and storms at sea, the steepest of dives and the fastest, most strenuous of airship races. *Khanna* would pull through. She always did.

The air crackled in front of her, like sheet lightning, as the islands' magic fought against Kohl's, and she willed *Khanna* to go faster. It was no wonder no-one had ever come here before.

Amarah's fur-lined boots slipped on the wooden deck as ice formed underfoot—a by-product of Kohl's magic. She wore a double layer of gloves; lambs' wool for warmth and leather for hardiness, yet the cold at this altitude numbed her fingers, and the barrier's pressure threatened to throw her off the wheel.

'Don't let go, don't let go,' she growled, her teeth grinding together as the muscles in her arm spasmed. Wood splintered from somewhere behind her. She was balanced on the knife's edge, a moment's breath from being blown away into the tundra.

As beads of sweat trickled down her face, the force suddenly intensified. It whipped around her, along the deck, buffeting her body and pushing her from the wheel and her controls. She bent her knees, leant into the barrier, and closed her eyes to the stinging cold. She could faintly hear Kohl calling out, but the wail of the air filled her ears and throat, and she couldn't breathe.

'Don't…let...'

The effort was too much.

The wheel slipped from her grasp and the edges of her world dimmed as *Khanna* span wildly out of control, caught in the vicious force of the islands' barrier.

'Amarah!' Kohl's voice cut across the screaming wind, and she gasped for air.

Her world brightened again. The rush of wind had disappeared, and she found herself sat on *Khanna*'s deck, Kohl awkwardly holding the wheel with one hand and looking at her, his other hand outstretched.

'Amarah, we're here. Amarah?'

She shook her head, dizzy and sick from the forces playing with her body. She'd never been sick in the sky, not since she was a child, anyway. She breathed deeply, dazed. 'Ugh.'

'Take a minute to catch your breath,' Kohl said, his crooked smile gentle. 'That was quite the ordeal.'

Rolling onto her front, Amarah leaned forward on her hands and knees, grounding herself with the feel of *Khanna*'s deck under her. It didn't take long for the shaking to stop, and she pushed herself to stand. '*Khanna* okay?' she asked, looking around for anything else that might have torn off during the ascent.

Kohl shook his head. 'Look past your ship. Welcome to my home, Amarah. Take pride in being the first non-Arillian permitted here. We must have a greater purpose after all.'

Oren sprawled out under them, as well as other islands in the distance. Some were great rocks of ice, others were bare, others were covered with snow or grass, with mountains dotting most of them. Now they floated above Oren, Amarah realised the barrier had disappeared completely, leaving her to breathe in cold, fresh air.

She smiled.

'We're on the main island. There's four that make up the whole settlement. And other Arillian villages scattered about, too...But Oren is my home. Where I was born. I've...It's been a while. Ignore any stares, please. They will know you mean no harm for the Golems to have let you through,' Kohl said, his voice quavering as he took in the landscape before them.

'Oh, if Topeko could see this. He'd wet himself!' Amarah said, stepping up to *Khanna*'s controls and descending towards the main village. Her body ached down to her toes, but the elation of being the first visitor to breach this hidden world gave her renewed strength and vigour.

'Perhaps you'll return with him to show it off?'

Amarah thought it over. 'Or perhaps I'll keep it as my own secret and not tell him anything.'

Kohl shook his head. 'Do you feel well after the climb?'

'I'm fine, stop fussing.' She breathed deeply, trying to catch her breath after the ascent. This was her best opportunity yet.

Now she'd finally made it to Oren, she had the chance to learn all she could of the Arillians and get them to save Moroda.

Chapter Three

The heavy trudge of marching boots echoed across the houses and streets of the South Galeo district. Steel-capped toes scraped on the cobblestones where snow had been cleared. Thousands had gathered to one of the richest districts in Taban Yul to watch the procession as it passed by. Onlookers crowded along the edge of the main thoroughfare, countless more cramped in side streets and alleys, pushing and jostling with one another to catch a glimpse. When space on the ground ran out, people huddled on sloped rooftops and leaned off chimneys, gripping with one hand as they strained to see the column of soldiers who marched below.

The red and gold armour of the Imperial Guard glinted in the bright winter sun, carving a line of colour through the city's white and grey buildings. While Palom marched with the soldiers, he did not share their livery.

He, along with countless others, wore ceremonial armour as befitting the last of the outside world the dead would ever see. Long feathers dyed red to represent phoenixes and their rebirth cycle had been stitched into the lining of his armour.

The crest of feathers at his shoulders were bright, vivid red, but as they stretched along his back and down to his feet, they turned black and ashen.

His *Valta Forinja* rested on his back—he'd not let the sword out of his sight—covered by a thin, black robe that fell to his knees.

Palom and five others carried a litter on their shoulders, red fabric to match the armour of the Imperial Guard draped over the corpse. He'd tried to count the litters that morning as they got into position, but lost track after fifty. His stomach knotted at how closely death and glory seemed interlinked.

Somewhere up ahead, near the front of the procession, drums beat. The Imperial Guard marched in time to the rhythm, but Palom—and scores of others who were not trained soldiers—shuffled along as they tried to keep up, beholden to their task. Princess Isa had permitted the survivors of Aciel's war to carry the fallen to their final resting places alongside the Imperial Guard. Palom was grateful for that, even though Lathri had suggested he stay with her to lessen the emotional strain.

As the street slowly descended, an enormous building of white marble came into view. Its curved walls and domed roof reflected the sun like a mirror, the light broken only by intricate gold embellishments protruding from the stone. The decorative features were fashioned into animals, the true forms of prominent Ittallan figures from the past. Lions. Eagles. Peacocks.

The mausoleum.

Palom had vowed never to return to this place of death, had avoided the entire district for as long as he had lived and worked in

Taban Yul, but he couldn't avoid it now. He knew more than anyone else there was no way to bring them back—but seeing the final resting place of so many people was almost more than he could bear. A physical manifestation of his guilt and sorrow.

Names of lost loved ones flooded his mind, their faces flashing before him as he marched closer.

In Val Sharis, where hatred between the Ittallan and Varkain ran strongest in Linaria, anything underground—or linked to the underground—was not only immoral, but utterly unacceptable. The Ittallan dead were not buried in the earth where snakes lived; their dead were honoured in flawless tombs where sunlight flooded in through the day and bathed in moonlight at night.

The mausoleum in South Galeo was the largest in Taban Yul. Kings and queens from ages past were laid to rest here, as were councillors, decorated warriors, and others who were in the good graces of the current ruler. It was only fitting that those who'd given their lives to protect the city from Aciel's forces would be able to rest in this prestigious building.

Weeping and cheering from the gathered crowds broke through his thoughts, and Palom chanced a look around. His eyes met with others echoing his sadness. Suddenly Lathri's suggestion of remaining with her made more sense, and he had an urge to put the litter down, turn tail, and run back to security and comfort.

But he'd sworn to protect those he travelled with. Those he had failed.

Eryn.

Moroda.

Anahrik.

Even his *Valta Forinja*, for all its power, hadn't been able to stop their deaths. Couldn't bring them to life.

Its weight on his back grew heavy.

Moroda's body could not be recovered, but not for lack of trying. It seemed she truly was trapped in the Sevastos's crystal along with Aciel. The teal-blue stone, immovable and invulnerable to damage, sat on the outskirts of Taban Yul. A handful of soldiers had been positioned nearby as guards, marking the point where the Arillians had come so close to wiping out the richest—and arguably most powerful—city in Linaria. Palom imagined it would become a landmark, some tourist feature to point out to visitors.

She wouldn't get the respect she deserved.

He and five others carried the litter for Anahrik, his business partner—the one who'd introduced him to Taban Yul, who'd set up shop with him, helped teach him the common tongue and bring him into modern times. Anahrik, who'd introduced him to so many friends—many of whom lay in the mausoleum ahead.

His eyes stung.

After everything he'd been through with Anahrik, Eryn, and Moroda, for all his strength and power, the *Valta Forinja* he'd forged to turn the tide of battle—it was all for nought.

He had survived, but Palom would gladly trade places with them, if he could.

Now Lathri and her friends wanted to stir it all up again, getting themselves mixed up with Sapora and his plots.

Palom never had been interested in the power struggles of Goldstones and nobility. Wars were fought and lost on the strength of someone's claim to rule—be it over a plot of land or an entire country. Death followed in the wake of every ruler, and he didn't want to have any part in it anymore. He couldn't. Seeing his friends to rest was about all he could manage.

The drums stopped beating, and the air quietened, the procession coming to a halt several paces before the golden doors to the mausoleum.

Thick clouds swirled above, blocking out the pale sunlight. Palom strained to keep still, his leg twitching as though it had a mind of its own. His mind drifted back to the battle, to the swarms of Arillians and warships thick in the air. To the blood and burning, the flashes of lightning and constant thunder.

Every night, when sleep finally came, he'd relived those memories. Every night, he tried to save Anahrik, Eryn, Moroda, but they'd slip from his grasp, pulled away by the winged demons.

Sometimes it would be Kohl, sometimes Jato, sometimes Aciel himself. Mostly they were faceless Arillians that he cast aside with a wave of his sword. The worst nightmare had been when he'd seen his own face looking out at him.

The sudden crunch of the mausoleum door brought him back.

Palom took a deep breath. He'd been slipping into dark thoughts and memories more and more often and disliked his lack of mental fortitude.

Two Ittallan stepped onto the street from within the mausoleum, their long grey robes resting on the tops of their bare feet. 'The tombs are ready. Bring the dead so that they may rest,' the one on the right said, his head bowed.

Palom steeled himself and followed the others into the sacred building.

The scent of burning wood hit him as soon as he crossed the threshold. Torches burned low along the walls, their embers carrying the stench of stagnant smoke. Wrinkling his nose, Palom followed the orders of the other robed Ittallan inside, and helped carry his litter to its assigned location.

Dozens of chambers led off from the passageways, each filled with cavernous stone tombs. Runes and inscriptions hand-carved around the edges of each doorway by the shrine guardians. Most gave thanks to the deeds they had carried out in life, others wished them safe onward journeys. All were carved in the old tongue by the Ittallan who lived and worked in the mausoleum.

If the circumstances were different, Palom might have taken the time to return to pay his respects and admire the skill and care taken by those who made the mausoleum their home and work. But this place was nothing more than a reminder of those who'd lost, people who'd suffered, and the bastards who put them there.

He wandered past chambers he recognised from his life before Aciel. Most of the people resting in this mausoleum were put there by someone else—casualties of war and battles, those who lost their lives at someone's blade. Anger raced through his body for a moment as he thought to the person who'd filled over half the mausoleum.

Mateli.

A demon from his past.

'Now Aciel rivals you in filling this place…' he whispered to himself.

The place was death.

Memories and fear took hold, spurred on by the angry heat from his sword. It overwhelmed him.

He tried to straighten his back, but his sword pushed against him as though trying to force him to the floor.

When he blinked to clear his mind, the shrine guardians in ahead were speaking funeral rites before a large doorway.

Palom steadied himself from the plethora of emotions, ignoring the stares from the soldiers beside him as they waited before a southern-facing chamber on the third floor of the mausoleum.

'Palom…You okay?' A voice whispered to his right.

He turned his head slightly, catching the eye of the concerned-looking Ittallan, and nodded in what he thought was a subtle, reassuring movement.

'You do not speak in this sacred building!' One of the guardians snapped, hushing the others who continued to say the rites.

Palom bowed his head and sweat trickled down his nose. He watched as it fell from his skin and spattered on the floor, darkening the stone.

When he looked up again, the guardians had moved on, and he walked the litter through the door into the large chamber.

Eryn and Anahrik's final resting place. Their stone coffins empty and waiting.

He had no doubt Isa had seen to it they received highly honoured spots.

The six of them gently rested the litter on the stone floor and removed the fabric cloth. Each body had been individually wrapped in thick, grey linen, the same style as the guardians. Taking a deep breath, he lifted each body—their weight nothing to him—and lowered them gently into their waiting tombs, the heavy stone lids resting at an angle, so they could easily be dragged into place and sealed. Beside him, the other five did the same with the remaining bodies, the gentle sound of sobbing echoing across the cold, stone room.

When Anahrik was in place, Palom leaned forward and placed the younger Ittallan's twin daggers over his chest. He had no need for them now and wanted to bury the weapons with their rightful owner. If any of the Imperial Guard or shrine guardians saw, they didn't object.

Palom heaved the stone lid into place, sliding in with an almighty judder that shook the room. The chambers outside echoed with sealed coffin lids.

Palom stood beside Anahrik's coffin, head bowed, eyes closed. He whispered an almost-silent prayer to Rhea, for whatever good it did. One soldier clapped him on the back as he left, and Palom knew he could not remain where he was for long.

‘Brother. Forgive me. Please.’ He choked back a sob.

Mateli slipped back into his thoughts, and the sword at his back thrummed again. He took a step back from the coffins and lingered in the doorway. He wanted to say something important, hope his apologies carried over to whatever plane death held them. Repent for all the mistakes he’d made.

But nothing felt right. It all paled into insignificance whenever he tried to give his thoughts voice.

In the end, he had to leave. The shrine guardians approached, and he stepped out of their way, watching as they sealed the chamber and began to carve the next line of writing.

*

Taban Yul had always been beautiful, in any season, at any time. It was something Palom boasted about to every non-native he’d come across or traded with. Val Sharis’ capital was the jewel of Linaria, the place where everyone had to visit at least once. From the riches of the Upper Rails to the plethora of goods at East Cross, to the palace itself—constructed of white marble and gold—Taban Yul was unlike anywhere else in the world.

But in the bleak winter sun and gentle snowfall, his pocket full of gold as reward for his help in the war and friends either lost or dead, Palom wanted nothing more than to escape it all.

His feet carried him along well-worn paths, over bridges that crossed brooks and past houses and businesses still open for the day. The crowds thinned as he left South Galeo, but there was no shortage of people on the streets, with several darting forward to shake his hand or bow to him as he passed. They’d said how wonderful it was to see him in the streets of their beautiful capital, how honoured they were to have met him.

Palom felt sick. He was no hero. He'd fought and killed, yes, but that alone couldn't make him worthy of their praise?

When he stopped to gather his thoughts, he looked around, and realised he'd made his way to Little Yomal; a quaint residential district full of townhouses stacked on top of one another and crooked towers rising higher than they should, their balconies offering unparalleled views of the city. Waterfall flowers cascaded down many of the building fronts and brought touches of bright yellow and red to the drab grey. The snow fell more heavily here, and he shivered.

He'd stopped underneath a particular building, one with four floors, the top balcony full of flowers of all colours. He could smell the blue winter roses from the ground. 'I shouldn't…but…I must…'

A lump formed in his throat, and he walked through the building's doorway, ascending the stairs two at a time, until he reached the wooden door of the top-most house. He stood there a long while, contemplating whether to knock or leave. Before he'd the strength to talk himself out of it, the door opened, and Lathri appeared. Her eyes were tinged with red, her dark eyelashes clumped together— she'd been crying.

'Lathri, I—'

'I've been waiting for you,' she said, opening the door wider and beckoning him in. She wore a dress of silver and cream, her long blonde hair almost fading into the material in stark contrast to her eyes.

He cleared his throat and stepped into her home, goose bumps rising on his arms at the sudden warmth of the room. 'You were not watching funeral parade?'

She shook her head. 'Too much death and sadness. I don't want to see it up close, even though I think there'll be more to come with Sapora in charge.'

Palom turned to face her, and she opened her arms. He stepped into her embrace, tears falling freely once his skin touched hers. He couldn't remember the last time he'd cried.

'Anahrik was your brother. Now you've lost two,' Lathri said. 'You carried him to the mausoleum, didn't you? Fool. You should have stayed here with me. It would've been easier for you.'

Palom relaxed into her, allowing his emotions to seep out. She smelled of the flowers on her balcony, of warm sunlight, of clothes stitched and re-stitched over the years. He buried his face in her shoulder and closed his eyes, giving in to the sadness, anger, and guilt he'd carried since Moroda had given up her life and ended the battle.

'I felt him in there,' he said, finally pulling away. 'Mateli. He caused so much death. And, now…Aciel.'

Lathri walked through the door onto her flower-filled balcony and stood in the falling snow. She leaned on the railing and peered down onto the narrow street, unfazed by the chill in the air.

'And now Aciel.' Lathri repeated. 'You've been part of two people's wrath, here. Getting away from it all will do you good. Why don't you go home and comfort your family? Stay away from all these bloodthirsty warriors?'

Grateful she didn't mention his meeting with her allies the previous night, Palom said, 'I cannot return home, you know this.' He joined her on the balcony, feeling hollow now he'd cried. He steadied his breathing and shook his head again, embarrassed. 'I dream of fighting. Most nights.'

'Not helped by that sword of yours.' She raised a hand and touched the petals of the flowers near her, brushing off the snow that tried to settle. Palom didn't need to see her face to know she wanted to say more. 'What of your comrades? The ones who fought against Aciel with you. What are they doing?'

He scratched behind his ear. 'Morgen is in Imperial Guard. He returns to Niversai to help rebuild. Sapora sits in palace with Isa making up new rules and destroying old law. Amarah and Kohl fly north, like I told you before.'

'North?'

'To Kohl's people. He thinks...' Palom trailed off, unwilling to speak of the betrayer and his plans.

'He thinks what?' Lathri had turned to face him now, regarding him with her intense stare.

He forced himself to look away. Lying to Lathri was simply impossible. 'He thinks Arillian magic can...maybe...break Moroda free from crystal.'

Lathri contemplated his words for a long while, as though hearing them for the first time. 'I don't know anything about Arillians other than the destruction they bring. Is it true? Could they release her?'

Palom shrugged.

'Why didn't you go with them?'

'I wanted…' he trailed off and exhaled.

'...Comfort?'

Palom stared down at the street below, watching a small group of Ittallan saunter along arm in arm. Their gait was easy, and their laughter carried up to the balcony. He felt a pang of jealousy and looked back to Lathri. Warmth washed over him again.

'I can fight. I know how to look after myself,' he said, stepping over to her and wrapping an arm around her shoulder.

'Are you sure you can? There's more to looking after yourself than killing those who'd hurt you… Or running away from them.' She hesitated, opened her mouth to say something else, then changed her mind.

'I can survive,' he corrected. He didn't want to hear about her plans against Sapora, or what she wanted to get messed up in.

Silence gathered between them, an easy, comfortable silence despite the heightened emotion. Lathri had a talent for emotion, for providing sanctuary in the darkest of times, enhanced by her education in Berel. It was a safety unlike anything he'd experienced before or since.

'It isn't your fault. I know you think it is, but it's not,' Lathri said after a long while. 'You're not responsible for anyone.'

Palom turned his attention to the flowers, and brushed the petals of one with the back of his finger.

'War brings death. Suffering. That's how it's always been. You can't stop that cycle.'

'I know.'

'Then why do you drown in guilt?' She moved out of his embrace.

'Because I made mistake.' He grunted.

'Everyone makes mistakes. You can't blame yourself for everything that goes wrong in the world!'

'If I had killed Kohl—'

'Killing Kohl wouldn't absolve him—or you— of fault! It wouldn't make you happy! Wouldn't bring Anahrik back!' Lathri's voice had raised.

'If I had killed him earlier. Before things got worse. Anahrik and Eryn might still be alive!' Palom said, unwilling to give in.

'You're responsible for your own happiness. Killing wouldn't make you happy. You're not Mateli!'

'I know I am not Mateli,' he said, dropping his voice. Saying the name out loud made him shudder.

She pressed her forehead into his chest and wrapped her arms around him. 'First Mateli and then Aciel. Sapora will be the third, you know. After what he did at the ball.'

He felt her tense under his arm.

He'd been away from the carnage at the ball, forging his *Valta Forinja*, while the Varkain prince had slaughtered those who did not agree with his rule. It had kick-started the chain of events leading to Anahrik and Eryn's deaths.

'I think so too. Many times on our journey I stopped him attacking others. The snake has a taste for death and power. He should be away from Taban Yul. He should not be in Val Sharis.'

'Friends of mine lost family that night. If they weren't killed, they were chased from the palace, from the city.' Lathri's soft voice grew softer still as she spoke of her own sadness.

'I am sorry,' Palom said. A pang of guilt rippled through him. He'd come to her and dumped his own woes on her while she recovered from Sapora's slaughter.

'Yet he claims to rule. You may be visiting the mausoleum again, soon. I hope you are not the one being carried, this time.' Lathri sniffed and let go of him, turning to head back inside now the snowfall thickened.

She wiped the snow from her shoulders, and Palom followed her. It was just as things had used to be, before…He didn't want to leave her, not again.

After he'd travelled across the Sea of Nami to Corhaven with Anahrik, things had happened so quickly, he'd hardly realised quite how much he'd missed her. Being back in her home brought comfort and security, and he enjoyed the simple fact he wasn't fighting off waves of Arillians.

Now there was no Aetos, Kylos, or Voulhrik, he could speak to her plainly. Truthfully.

He couldn't stay in the city, there were too many bad memories. Now Sapora could be on the warpath, he knew he had to get away.

Had to get her away.

A lump formed in his throat. Before it was too late.

'Lathri. Close your eyes. I have gift for you.'

She faced him, a half-smile on her lips as she tilted her head in confusion. 'What…?'

'Please.'

She cleared her throat and closed her eyes as asked.

Palom reached into his jerkin pocket and withdrew a small, drawstring bag. Taking a deep breath, he placed it in her hands and clasped his over the top. He held her hands close for a moment, bracing himself for the worst, and then let go.

'Now you can open.'

She immediately flicked her eyes open and looked at the bag in her hands. 'Palom…?' She looked at him and then back to the bag, before opening it. Her eyes widened. 'Palom!'

He bowed his head. 'Please do not be involved with Sapora or sicknesses or palace politics. You'll end up getting hurt. Or killed. Sapora is too much of threat for you and your allies to cope with.'

In fairness to her, she listened without interrupting. He continued, before he lost the thread of what he was trying to say. 'You make me happy. You have always made me happy. Marry me, Lathri. Come with me, away from this, and I'll keep you safe from whatever Sapora does. Whatever Aciel and Mateli have done. Against any who'd stand against you. Against any darkness in this world.'

Tears formed in her eyes, and her brow wrinkled. 'Now the fighting's over, you want to pick up where we left off? How? Everything's changed.' Her voice cracked.

'I should not have left before. I won't leave you again.' He held his breath to keep from shaking.

'You want me to heal you, like before. You want help and safety again,' she said, suddenly unsteady on her feet. 'I can't help you. Not with this. There's a darkness inside you. A darkness sprung from death, from guilt, from shame. From that *sword.* That is a wound I can't touch. Can't heal.'

Palom swayed.

'You've been chipped away, slowly but surely, ever since you left home. You won't go back to Feoras Sol to see your parents! You've just run from place to place, running from those who've killed your loved ones! You won't even speak of Ta-'

'Don't!' Palom roared, his whole body trembling.

Lathri shook her head. 'See? It's been over twenty years and you still can't say your brother's name! You blame yourself in so many ways, for so much loss.'

She panted, trying to catch her breath after her outburst.

'But I am stronger now, and—' he started.

'No. You're not. You're weaker. For all your heroic deeds, all your strength in battle…You're more a kitten than a tiger. I asked you for help and you refused. You'd rather run away than stand and fight with me. How could I leave my friends and the people of this city? I'm not afraid of Sapora or his Varkain. Why are you being such a coward?'

The words sliced through him, and his legs threatened to give way.

Lathri held the gold brooch in her hand, rubbed a thumb over the blue jewels set deeply into it, and brought it to her lips. She kissed it once, gently, and returned it to the bag, holding it out to him.

Palom stood in silence, his world crashing around him, a flood of emotions coursing through his veins.

He didn't trust himself to speak.

With a shuddering breath, he took the bag from Lathri and left her home.

*

The scent of molten steel and melting silver never quite faded. It seeped into the floor, furniture, clothes, tools. It was the scent of the workshop, of the closest thing he had left to home. Palom knew the smell would remain long after it was burned to the ground.

He'd had once adored the scent. It was his work, his life. But now, the smell was grief and loss, emptiness and failure. Now, his workshop was another bad memory. Something else to erase.

Anahrik had been a brother to him. They had been through so much together, building their business from nothing and crossing continents to sell their wares to Goldstones and wealthy merchants.

But he had failed Anahrik.

Like he had failed Lathri.

Failed himself.

And all he could do was run.

Palom stood in his empty workshop, taking everything in one final time. A glint of silver caught the weak winter sunlight drifting through the window. Anahrik's silverwork. His finery brought something special to their weapons. A mark to differentiate them from all the other blacksmiths.

His heart and soul ached, and the sword on his back felt heavier than a battle axe. He couldn't continue in his trade. Not now. With another deep breath, he crossed the workshop floor and lit the bellows for the final time. The fires wouldn't be hot enough to work metal for some hours, but it was hot enough for the task at hand. Without hesitating, he tipped the growing flames onto the workshop floor and trudged out.

This would be the end of his life in Taban Yul.

He thought to Amarah and Kohl, of his claim that Arillian magic could be used to bring Moroda back. He knew Amarah had asked him to help fight whatever demons lay at the edge of the world, but he couldn't play along with Kohl. Not after everything he'd done.

Palom scoffed at himself. He'd screwed up too many things, let too many people down. Perhaps leaving was a cowardly act, as Lathri suggested, but he had no brother, no family.

No choice.

Grey smoke rose from the workshop in thick clumps, swirling around in the wind and spreading out across the wide, paved streets. A huge swathe of Taban Yul was dedicated to trade, with Palom's workshop right in the centre of it, near the eastern gate of the city itself.

He ignored the acrid scent as he made his way down Trader's Alley. The district was well named for what it was—a hub of shops and market stalls—and busier than ever now the city was recovering from Aciel's war.

At its widest point, the main street of Trader's Alley could fit six carts abreast, but even with the vast space at ground level, the buildings were cramped together— grey slabs of stone giving way to deep, rich, blue on the higher floors. Many had ornate gold or silver around the windows—the more gold on the building, the more gold it was assumed you carried in your pockets.

A group of blue towers flanked the street's head: hexagonal in shape, each with a roof of gold. The Imperial Guard would usually be in position beneath them, but considering winter had claimed the city, there was little need for their presence. That, and much of the Guard had been cut short following the battle with Aciel.

Palom thought briefly about returning to his hometown, Feoras Sol, which lay a few day's travel from the capital. But it would mean facing his father.

Fear bubbled in his gut.

It was very likely his family still lived in Sol, mining the Feor Mountains as they had done for generations. They'd be none-too-impressed with his return, he was sure.

No business.

No gold.

Leaving death wherever he went.

Palom wasn't sure he could stomach the shame of looking his father in the eye if it came to it.

He'd only seen him twice since his blood brother had died; once to tell him what had happened, and once more to tell him he was leaving.

To return after twenty years with his tail between his legs? The embarrassment would be too great. No. Perhaps he should keep to the wilds and avoid other Ittallan for the time being.

His thoughts were interrupted by a wooden cart crashing along the cobblestones a short way ahead. The wheels were large and thin, catching between misshapen rocks. Palom watched as it wobbled violently and thought it would topple over. The driver pulled up, cursing under his breath. He looked up as Palom approached.

'Ah, just the person I need! Would ye help me pull this old thing out the city, Palom? I need tae be in Feoras Sol in three days. There's not a chance I'll get there in time on me own.' He was short, balding, wearing a cloak far too big for him which kept catching under his feet as he heaved the wheel out of the crevice it had gotten stuck in.

'Not going that way. Sorry,' Palom replied.

'What if ye take me at least as far as the inn? There's one half a league from Sol. I'll pay ye, too! Three florins a day, and ye welcome to share me food. It's your hometown, isn't it? Sol? Who'd be better tae look after me?' He reached into his pocket and brought out a fistful of coins—florins and half florins—with smaller pennies spilling out onto the ground.

Palom stopped where he stood, considering.

'Five florins?' The trader asked, a hint of desperation in his voice.

'Just to inn...'

'Ye have a deal!'

Palom exhaled. He'd barely taken ten steps from Trader's Alley and already he was getting caught up in something he had no business being part of. He looked the man over again—he was slightly hump-backed, with a wiry grey beard and moustache, and grey eyes.

Fodder.

The cart itself was no better—completely wooden with two large rear wheels, and two smaller wheels at the front. It was slightly bowed at the back, he presumed from the large barrel it carried. High wooden slats made up the sides, with a small deck at the front from where it could be pulled or pushed along.

'Give me florins now and I'll pull it,' Palom said, making his way over to the trader and adjusting the sword on his back.

'Ah, dragons above, thank ye, Palom. I'll not soon forget this!' He handed over six silver coins, dark with age and use, but holding all their value. 'Oh yes, me name's Jekkin, but ye can call me Jek if ye want. Everyone knows ye, Palom! Not many weapon smiths gets tae live at the palace! Fewer still make swords like ye with that power. I must guess the whole of Val Sharis knows who ye are!'

Palom shoved the coins in his pocket and regarded Jek. 'I didn't live at palace. I was invited to stay after battle.'

‘Ah well, the locals all here think ye a bit of a legend now. What with Aciel and all that, ye know. See, we know ye one of us. And we know what with what happened tae the wee lass, eh… Moroda?’

‘We go, now. Or you’ll never get to Sol,’ Palom said, interrupting the barrage of words, grabbing the arms at the front of the cart, and hoisting them up to his sides.

‘Aye, let’s. But we all saw what happened tae ye. An…. An I’d like tae offer me condolences for your losses,’ Jek said, bowing his head slightly and closing his eyes.

Palom grunted. He couldn’t face more talk of those he had lost, not when he’d just been rejected by Lathri and burnt his workshop to the ground.

As Jek continued to chatter, Palom focussed on putting one step in front of the other, pulling the cart along at a steady pace. Though it was empty, something he could easily lift and pull as required, the cart felt heavier with every step he took from Trader’s Alley, until it was as though he dragged a boulder along behind him.

His breath grew ragged, and he realised it was the emotional burden just as much as it was the cart but didn’t know how to separate the two.

He’d hoped destroying the workshop would have brought him relief, but if anything, he’d made things even worse.

Chapter Four

Amarah was not used to being fussed over like some Goldstone at a grand ball. Even if she'd had a lifetime's experience, she'd never get used to it. The Arillians of Oren crowded around her, cooing and touching her back, dumbfounded by her lack of wings. Amarah quickly discovered that being a spectacle wasn't fun, but Kohl had explained almost no-one in Oren had ever left the village, much less the floating islands, and had never seen anyone who *wasn't* an Arillian. Her legions of new fans were equally impressed with her ship, and asked question upon question until Amarah's head span.

What was it made of?

How did it fly?

What storms did it bring?

Did it speak?

Did it move on its own?

She'd been exhausted after the first day, and hadn't been able to find out a single thing about their resurrection magic, or whatever power could supposedly release Moroda from her crystal prison. Every time she'd tried to ask anyone about it—because Kohl found her awkwardness amusing and refused to step in to help as they jostled to get near her—they'd ignored her questions and asked half a dozen of their own.

The children were worse, darting about in the air just above eye level, touching her back and shoulders then swooping off before she could do anything to retaliate, their wings sending ripples of wind over her.

The older Arillians shooed them away, eventually, but the whole experience drained her. They all wanted to know more about who she was, where she came from, how she lived.

What life was like on-ground.

Interestingly, not a single person mentioned Aciel, the war, or the intense dislike the rest of Linaria held for Arillians.

Amarah had docked *Khanna* on the edge of a low plateau, which was immediately investigated by the goats, birds, and other wildlife that made the remote islands their home. She spent a short while hunting a particularly scrawny goat while Kohl went off to make introductions, and when he returned with a handful of curious—or bold—Arillians of various status, all thoughts of food vanished as he thrust her into the midst of their society.

She'd found her first foray into the village full of surprises. Instead of being ignored, or looked down on with disdain, the Arillians were kind, generous, and exceedingly friendly. None of them carried weapons, either, which meant Amarah quickly relaxed despite the unfamiliarity with their culture.

A huge fire burned at the village's centre: roaring flames that never went out, Kohl explained, and as they approached, she saw Arillians cooking or warming themselves by it. Many flew up to greet her as she arrived, dozens and dozens of them, their wings ranging in colour from charcoal-black to straw-gold and every hue in between.

Kohl kept most of them at bay while Amarah marvelled at the flames. They must have reached ten feet high, and were so vast, she couldn't see through to the other side. Tall shards of smooth, greyish-black—yet somehow translucent—rock jutted from the ground, almost like a frozen waterfall, surrounding the base of the fire.

She'd reached out to touch the rock, and immediately withdrew her hand when her skin touched the surface.

They were burning cold.

'The same material as the Ice Golems,' Kohl had told her. 'They let us to see through our storms.'

He'd been about to say more, when the crowd of Arillians swelled, and Amarah decided to retreat to *Khanna* to rest.

Even sunrise here was bizarre, as the sun rose below the floating island, casting shadows from odd angles. But once it rose above the island's horizon, Oren seemed much the same as anywhere else in the day. From first light until nightfall, the skies were full of Arillians flying from one destination to another.

They'd carved towers and buildings into the sheer rock face and ice, giving the whole settlement a silver-blue tinge except during sunrise and sunset, when it looked as though the Oren had been built from melted gold. There were no curved walls or domes—everything followed the natural lines of the rock—and most buildings were tilted as a result. But the strangest thing was the lack of doors—most simply had a particularly large, glassless window somewhere near the top of the structure through which Arillians flew in and out.

In a way, it reminded her of Berel.

At ground level, Oren spread out over most the main island, which Amarah estimated to be about a third of the size of Niversai, though with fewer inhabitants. Kohl couldn't tell her their exact numbers, but suggested only a few hundred lived here, most of whom had been left behind by Aciel.

In fact, the majority of the Arillians in Oren were either very old or very young. Everyone else of fighting age had been swept up in Aciel's plots, and they were returning to the village in dribs and drabs.

That unnerved Kohl, Amarah noted. He spoke in hushed tones to several older Arillians, asking after their family and friends, but every time Amarah wandered over to get involved in the conversation, they'd hurriedly changed the subject, or flown away.

She hadn't been permitted to meet the few who had returned, either—a dozen or so—they'd been whisked off to recover from their injuries.

Supposedly.

While Amarah would normally accept their reasoning, she'd not seen any blood, not seen Arillians help carry them back. They'd arrived under their own strength, and that conflicted with the idea of having to recover from severe injuries.

When she'd wandered close to one of the many dwellings that housed some of the retuning Arillians to investigate for herself, the moans and wailing which echoed from within unnerved her to such a point that she'd raced off before she'd even peeked inside.

Even the children—who were happy enough to fly anywhere they liked—avoided the areas returning Arillians had holed up in to recover, and she wondered whether there was perhaps some strange illness they'd brought back with them.

They were, after all, outsiders to the mainland.

When it became obvious Amarah wasn't getting anywhere with learning about their magic while they were so excited to meet a foreigner, she decided to indulge them.

In fact, she couldn't remember the last time anyone had taken the time to talk to her—just talk—without an ulterior motive.

She even went so far as to say she enjoyed being fitted in some of their traditional dress: multiple robes of linen folded around her body in some intricate pattern she couldn't follow, and a simple bracelet fashioned from polished eagle claws and bits of animal bone she couldn't identify.

Snow-covered rock made up the vast majority of Oren; trees draped along the higher peaks, with winter shrubs and stiff, hardy grass shoots pushing their way through the ice where the land flattened out. In the very lowest spots, meltwater from the snow-capped peaks flowed down into pools, around which Arillians gathered at varying points through the day.

Here, there were no seasons. No summer warmth to melt the ice, no autumn leaves to paint the land in reds and golds. Here, the days were short and the nights long. Here, the Everwinter ruled, every day of every month; a vast, unchanging land of cold and snow.

To Amarah, it brought stability. But to many of the Arillians—particularly the young ones—it brought boredom. Tales of savages on the mainland were often told to entertain the children, though Amarah's decidedly non-barbaric nature seemed to clash with the more colourful parts of their stories, but despite the Arillian's thoughts about where she came from, the sky pirate found Oren peaceful above anything else.

Their food, however, was not to her taste.

It consisted chiefly of dry bread, roots, and vegetables that were tougher than any meat she'd ever eaten, no matter how long she cooked them for. Even boiling the water was nigh impossible at such high altitudes.

Lukewarm and tasteless was as about as best she could manage, and she thanked herself for stockpiling black pepper and cured meat.

Once Kohl was sure she was as comfortable as she could be, he'd disappeared, leaving Amarah with the crowds of sixty or so Arillians who made up Oren's core community.

She suspected he was going to see the returned Arillians, or Jato, perhaps. Or maybe any other family he still had. Come to think of it, she hadn't asked if he had a wife, parents, or siblings. The thought hadn't occurred to her, and Kohl had only explained about his link with Jato when he was on the threshold of being executed by Palom.

She assumed he had a wife, or at least knew the mother of Jato, but he'd never mentioned anything. Amarah knew what it was like to be shunned by those who were meant to love you. Her own upbringing had not been the easiest.

She blamed her rough start for getting involved in piracy. She'd effectively been exiled and had no inclination to return "home" and live in the desert country of Ranski.

Kohl, however, seemed to feel very differently about his home. She could see the pain in his eyes and hear the sorrow in his voice whenever spoke of his Oren, and she wondered what had caused his exile in the first place.

As darkness rolled in at the end of her second day in Oren, hunger pushed her back to her ship, so she sat cross-legged on *Khanna*'s deck, a pot bubbling away on a small fire, chunks of wild goat and vegetables floating in the broth. The flame was small and fierce, and came from a bottle—portable Samolen magic, about the only thing from her home country that she used—and offered warmth in the frigid land.

She stirred the pot and dropped in some cheese in an attempt to thicken it into something with taste, as a familiar, cool, breeze washed over her, signalling Kohl's arrival.

'Eating?' she asked, barely glancing up as he landed on deck.

'Oh, yes, thank you,' he said, removing his hat and stepping over to the pot. 'My tastes have grown used to ground-food. It's been so long since I've been here…'

‘Know what you mean. I took some vegetables to be nice, but it’s awful stuff.’ Amarah stirred again. ‘You see Jato, then?’

Kohl knelt down opposite Amarah and busied himself with picking at his hat.

‘She didn’t wanna see you?’

Kohl looked up, the light from the cooking fire catching his face. ‘She was…unavailable again, today.’

Lifting a spoonful of stew out of the pot, Amarah sniffed it carefully before tasting. ‘You never did say why you were exiled, you know. Was it that you spotted Aciel for the rat he was, and everyone took his side?’ She kept her eyes on her dinner, spooning out the dish into her bowl, and then into another for Kohl.

‘You really have no boundaries, do you?’ The Arillian asked, though he didn’t sound offended.

‘Not in my line of work,’ she replied, looking up at him with a grin. She handed Kohl his bowl of food before sitting back with her own and letting the steam warm her face.

The two sat in silence for several minutes before Kohl took in a deep breath. ‘I didn’t like Aciel. But perhaps not for reasons you might think.’

Amarah brought her bowl to her mouth with both hands, slurping at the contents and watching him carefully. She knew the tell-tale signals of liars. The twitch of a lip or the dilation of a pupil could signal fear, anger, desire. She waited for the signs.

Kohl said, ‘He admired Jato. Young love, it was. Lust, really. He wanted to be with her for a while, but he was too low in rank to be a suitable match for anything more than fun.’

'Rank? Don't tell me you Arillians have Goldstones and all that nobility rubbish.' Amarah wiped her mouth before gulping down more. 'Thought that was just Corhaven!'

'I was the leader of my people,' Kohl said, swallowing. 'My blood is old. I have the frost-touch, the same powers as my ancestors who created the Golems.' He took a deep breath, as though speaking for the first time. 'Fire burns bright and hot, and then it passes. Fades. Like the dragons themselves will fade, eventually. But the ice? The ice has always been here. It will always be here.'

Amarah narrowed her eyes. What he said conflicted with what she knew of Linaria. What she'd been taught. But he didn't show any signs of dishonesty, and he spoke so earnestly that she almost believed him.

Kohl continued, 'Jato was to follow in my footsteps, and she was expected to…choose someone worthy of that status.'

Amarah added another ladle to her bowl, her mind racing.

'Aciel is not a candidate. *Was* not a candidate. He is one of our lowest classes, with weak powers. He used his compulsion to have others do the work and labour he should have done. The match could never be agreed. He wasn't even from Oren! But Jato said the old ways were dying and they should die with me. Teenage rebellion, I think,' he chuckled, though his smile didn't reach his eyes.

'They saw each other in secret, and he convinced her of his...new way. His compulsion turned a lot of Arillians to his way of thinking. The old way—my way—had previously led to the destruction of most of our people, of our homes.'

'The Great War?'

'Indeed,' Kohl nodded. 'Though that was before my time, I suppose I'm a traditionalist. I wanted to preserve what we'd almost lost in that war.'

Amarah shrugged.

'As Aciel used his compulsion to bring more Arillians into his fold, I fought back. I called upon the Golems to intervene.'

'What? But… I… didn't you say they were to keep outsiders out? To keep your lands safe?'

'They do more than guard the gates. Through me, they...I can speak with them. Not control them, but as the leader, I could talk to them. Demand judgement. They heard my plea and came to my aid. They brought Oren to the ground to determine whether Aciel or I would lead the Arillians here.'

Amarah's bowl was forgotten in her hands as she listened to Kohl, not quite able to believe the things he described. How on earth could the floating islands be brought to the ground?

'Their action enabled Aciel and I to fight on even footing. I'd always been immune to his abilities, I suppose I have my strong blood to thank for that. I didn't want to kill him. I just wanted to make an example of him. I wanted him to be fearful of me…enough so he wouldn't push his luck or try and stir up dissention again. But he controlled so many people by that point. He had them fight against me, too, and the Golems couldn't tell the difference between them and Aciel himself. They don't have eyes, you see, and Aciel was the one making all the decisions. So, they didn't stop the fighting as Aciel's followers overpowered me.'

Kohl took another breath, shaking his head as he spoke, his own food untouched.

'Jato begged Aciel to stop. Insisted he'd won and that I'd submit. But Aciel wanted absolute domination. He told her *she* had to deliver the final blow to end our battle. She had to strike me down herself. Once he'd commanded her, she…she….' He broke away with a shudder.

'As she raised her hand to attack me, the Golems sensed the interference of an outsider and attacked her.'

'How did they attack her but not his other followers?' Amarah interrupted, an eyebrow raised.

Kohl looked at her, then dropped his eyes. 'She'd never been under his compulsion. The whole time, she went along with what he wanted and asked because…she was infatuated with him. Like me, she was immune. I guess it didn't make a difference in the end.'

Amarah sniffed. 'So, she survived the Golems' attack?'

'Our laws are unbreakable. They would have killed her. So…so I attacked them instead. The result is what you see of my face.' He tapped a finger to the scars on his leathery skin, still smiling his half-smile.

'They couldn't kill me as they are unbiased in our disputes. By that point, it was too late, anyway. I saved my daughter, but Aciel had won. Won her. Beaten me. Gained followers. Everything. On the Golems' command, I was exiled, their instruction carried out by Aciel, now the new leader, and Oren was restored to its place in the sky.'

‘Kohl…’ Amarah said, shocked at his admission.

‘Now that Aciel’s dead and the Arillians are leaderless, there isn’t anyone who can enforce the law of the Golems, so I’ve been permitted to return, it seems. We’re lucky.’

Amarah’s mouth hung open as she struggled to comprehend Kohl’s story. It seemed the magic which bound the Arillians was far stronger than anything she understood of the Samolen, whose blood she shared.

‘So, all this time, the Golems could’ve attacked you when we were flying here?’ Amarah said.

Kohl dipped his head to her.

‘And…and that’s why…when we were in Berel, you were so keen to find a book on compulsion that could have broken Aciel’s hold on his followers.’

‘In part, yes,’ Kohl said. ‘I’d also hoped there was some other string to his powers that controlled Jato. Something deep down that affected her differently to everyone else. I didn’t want to believe that she’d really…’ He trailed off.

‘Your food’s getting cold,’ Amarah said.

For all her hatred of authority, Kohl had ruled as the leader of the Arillians until Aciel had come along—and lost it all to save his daughter, who saw him with nothing but contempt.

‘If….If Jato was never under Aciel’s compulsion…She… must know what you went through?’ Amarah said, placing the remains of her bowl on the floor beside her.

‘Yes,’ Kohl said, drinking his dish and refusing to meet Amarah’s gaze.

'And she still—'

'Yes.'

Amarah poked her bottom lip out as she thought about it, frowning and scowling at the same time. There had to be something more to it than Kohl was letting on.

How could Jato hold such a grudge against him, even now? Surely, she had the sense to see Aciel had been a vigilante, no matter how in love she thought she was.

Kohl broke her thoughts. 'Jato also wanted power of her own, I suspect. Growing up in my shadow can't have been easy. She will not obtain my frost-touch or ability to communicate with the Golems, not until I die. Then the power in my blood will become hers. The Golems are not only the gatekeepers to our home, but to our history, our culture. They are our teachers and defenders.

I need to speak with them. Access our deepest magic, the magic that might be able to free Moroda. But as I am no longer leader, I don't have the strength to put forward such a request. Jato has been a temporary leader. She's been a General for years. The Golems haven't yet recognised her as the highest ranking Arillian, so I need to find a way to get the plea to them. Find out what they can teach and see if it can help.'

Amarah looked up as Kohl spoke again, thinking back to those great titans stood in the snowdrifts, and wondered what on earth they could teach. 'Sorry, Kohl.'

'Sorry? What for?' Kohl laughed.

Amarah shrugged, 'Seemed to be the thing to say. It's something Moroda would have said.'

'Indeed,' he agreed, bowing his head slightly at the mention of Moroda's name. 'Don't burden yourself with my woes. It is not your concern, and Jato is not your fight.'

'Is my concern if it affects getting Moroda back,' Amarah said, spooning another load of dinner from the pot to her bowl. 'But I don't care about Jato. I've got too many enemies of my own, too many battles to fight without adding your crazy daughter into the mix.'

Kohl smiled again, his lips twisting in a macabre way. 'Of course. There are legends of the great sky pirate Amarah and those who want her head. I imagine King Sapora will be near the top of that list.'

Amarah laughed, sitting back down and taking a long slurp. 'Damned snake!'

'You've always been spiteful to each other. What is it about him that you hated?' Kohl asked, his wings rustling.

'A game of questions tonight, is it?' Amarah grinned, downing the rest of her dish in one go. 'I hate the damned Varkain. You know what they did to me when I got to Niversai for the first time? When I was a kid? They ganged up and attacked me! Left me for dead!'

Kohl nodded.

'And that Sapora…always throwing his weight around. I tell you, I can't stand people like that. Because they've got money, or clothes, or talk a certain way. Fuck the lot of them! We don't choose where we're born, or who to. He's only important cause his daddy was important. He's just a maggot like the rest of them!'

Amarah ran her fingers through her hair. 'You know what? I thought of throwing him overboard a few times. Especially when we crossed the sea. But he's so fucking fast, I'd never get hold of him before he struck. Had to put up with him. And look—he turned tail and ran before the last battle!'

Kohl flinched and glanced away. 'I know I've let people down. It's hard not to, it seems. I must be cursed.'

'Oh shush, I didn't mean you,' Amarah waved her hand in his direction. 'Wouldn't expect you to kill your daughter. Sapora, though...We'd none of us still be alive unless he needed us for something. I tell you, the next Varkain I see, I'm killing.'

'An innocent Varkain who's done nothing to you?'

'They're not innocent!'

Kohl shook his head, smiling his twisted smile again.

'What's so funny now?'

'You are, Amarah. You just said yourself you can't choose where you're born, or who you're born to. Would it have been that Varkain's fault? You don't sound all that different to Sapora. Or even Aciel.'

'That's damned rude,' she said, glowering.

'Sorry,' Kohl said. His smile faded.

Amarah blinked, confused. She was used to people rising to every quip, spoiling for a fight. Kohl backed down and her rage ebbed away. She thought over what he'd said of family, that he'd only mentioned Jato and no other relatives. Perhaps she was his only true friend. Even Jato hated him. The other Arillians here, his people, were more interested in her and *Khanna* than the return of their former leader.

She couldn't understand it. To have status, prestige, and love and to lose it all because of an ungrateful child.

Amarah found she liked Jato less and less the more she heard of her. She'd only ever seen her briefly before, twice, once when she snuck aboard her warship and stole from her, and then on the battlefields above Taban Yul, when Aciel led his army to attack the city.

She hadn't liked what she'd seen of her then.

She wondered whether Jato would even remember her. Wondered whether Kohl would feel true grief if Jato were to die, or whether he'd simply be free from the exile he'd earned for being foolish enough to have compassion.

Amarah had no family, no children, no real friends— only those who used her and whom she used in return.

There was no love, no trust, no bond.

The closest she'd come to a friend was Moroda, and now, Kohl.

The strength of the emotions he felt was not something Amarah could fathom. Surely, it'd be simpler to cut all ties and seek his fortune on the mainland? The world was certainly big enough, and he wasn't missing much in Oren. The dull rock had little to offer, from what Amarah had seen and learned from the locals.

Why in Rhea's name did he feel such deep attachment to the place?

A sudden crackle of lightning and strong wind had her guard back up immediately. She rolled to her feet and grabbed her scythe, ready and tense before Kohl reacted.

Perhaps he was so used to the sound of his own kin, he didn't hear the approaching wings.

'Jato. Speak of the devil.' Amarah said, adjusting her grip on her scythe, giving herself more range.

Jato landed on deck a moment later, rattling the sails of *Khanna* and sending everything loose flying. She glanced at Amarah and her weapon, before turning her attention to Kohl.

'You've been summoned.' Jato said.

'At this hour?' Kohl said, getting to his feet.

Amarah watched as he lowered his eyes and hunched his back, all confidence gone as he faced his daughter.

Other than their body language, the resemblance between them was clear—both had the same grey eyes and blonde hair.

'Why else would I be here?' Jato snapped.

'To see your dad, maybe?' Amarah raised an eyebrow. 'We've been here two days, and—'

'I wasn't talking to you.' Jato said. She turned her head towards Amarah but kept her eyes closed, as though even looking upon Amarah was beneath her. 'Now, Kohl.' She crouched, wings raised.

'Excuse me?' Amarah said, rising to the insult. She aimed the blade of her scythe at Jato and the strength of the Sevastos ore within blasted a wave of blue light straight at her.

Jato deflected the attack with a flick of her wrist and brought her hand down, conjuring a bolt of lightning in the same movement, and sent it after Amarah.

'Jato! She is under the Golems' protection!' Kohl said, stepping between them.

Amarah yelped as the shock of the attack ripped through her body. She dropped her scythe and curled into a ball, a reflex against the searing pain.

'Kohl. Come,' Jato said, continuing to ignore Amarah as she took to the air.

Kohl sighed, his shoulders dropping as Jato vanished from sight. He walked across the singed deck to Amarah and offered his hand.

'Don't touch me. Go after your fucking brat.' Amarah spat, blood dripping between her teeth from where she'd been knocked to the floor.

'Amarah, I'm—'

'Sorry. Yes. Like you always are.' She coughed, getting to her knees and wiping the blood from her mouth. 'She just caught me by surprise. I'm fine. Run along now. Don't want to keep her waiting, do you?'

Kohl bowed his head, turned, and leapt from the deck to follow Jato.

Amarah spat blood again but was glad all her teeth were intact when she tapped her fingers to them. She wanted nothing more than to teach Jato some manners, especially after everything Kohl had done for her.

But it seemed Jato was an ungrateful, entitled, spoiled brat who had a taste for power and didn't want to let go. Gingerly getting to her feet, Amarah leaned on the side of *Khanna*, peering out.

In the distance, the village fire burned as it always did, the contrast of light and dark so bright that she couldn't see anything in the night sky.

Some leader Kohl was. At Jato's beck and call. And now the former lunatic General flouncing around like she still had Aciel's borrowed power.

Spitting the last of her blood overboard, Amarah picked up her scythe and slammed the bottom of it on deck.

She'd played nice for too long.

Tomorrow, she'd make the Arillians get whatever magic they needed from the Golems and get Moroda out of her crystal tomb.

Chapter Five

Sapora's task of assigning a new council in Taban Yul progressed slowly. Other than Tacio, Isa, and the raven—Koraki— who'd served in the palace for over sixty years, he'd picked a member of the *Cerastes*—guards—of Sereth: a grizzled old snake called Roke, who was missing an ear and his right hand, yet had the infallible ability to understand Sapora's moods and wishes without saying a word.

Sapora had also assigned a pair of lower-class Varkain who'd shown some aptitude in combat but were cowardly and lacked resolve. He knew they could not be relied upon, not truly: their own lives were more important than his, especially as they all longed to return to Sereth.

His people's affinity for the darkness and the comfort of their tunnels was their weakness. Sapora's Ittallan blood had given him the ability to enjoy the open air; he had no desire to hide and live in the gloom like his people.

Even Tacio—the boldest and most confident Varkain Sapora knew—wished to return to Sereth, though he knew Tacio remained in Val Sharis to save face rather than out of a desire to help on the surface.

Sapora was trying to set up a new order, a new regime, and even though he had been the crown prince and had always held a certain amount of power in Val Sharis, the strength of his rule was far less than he wanted.

The Ittallan in the palace feared Tacio more than him.

Sapora tried not to question it too much. His plans would come to fruition soon enough, and there would be none, not even Tacio, who could stand up to him.

He'd thought cutting out those who opposed him at the winter ball would have been enough, but it had merely stoked the fires.

Mere blades were no longer good enough.

He needed something more.

Some way to tap into the Ittallan primal fear and give him—and the Varkain—the respect they deserved.

Sapora stood in his antechamber and listened for footsteps in the passageway outside. Roke stood guard outside the door and should keep away any who decided to disturb him, but as much as he liked the Varkain's quiet obedience, Sapora rarely relied wholly on others.

He slid a shard of glass from his sleeve, remembering the runner's confused face when it had arrived with Morgen's letter. Voulhrik, his name was, Sapora remembered. One of the few who'd survived his cleansing of palace staff. Another quiet one, who bowed on cue and did as he was told.

The mirror glistened in his hands. Finally, he would have eyes across the sea.

The antechamber led to his personal rooms—both circular, like almost everything else in the palace—and held two armchairs, a table, and a large bookcase. A portrait hung opposite the bookcase: a portrait of himself in his true form.

It was a frightening depiction of the large, hooded cobra, long fangs bared in grimace. His scales had been skilfully painted in shades of black, brown, and green, and he actually quite liked the rendition. He enjoyed a little indulgence and examined it for several moments.

Sapora had not initially wanted the portrait, but when the idea came to him, he had it moved from the gallery and brought here, to his own quarters.

Now alone, he slipped a clawed finger behind the portrait and pressed it into the stone wall. With an almost inaudible click, the wall shifted and Sapora swung the portrait to the side, revealing a hole wide enough for him to walk through.

He stepped into it and slid the portrait back into place behind him.

Choosing to have his chambers in the older part of the palace had its benefits: the hidden stairwell led to a large basement which had once been home to a secret cellar. The smell of wine lingered in the stone itself, but the room now served Sapora's purpose.

Mirrors lined the walls in place of tapestries. Dozens upon dozens of them; many full-length, bordered in gold and jewels, others were round, or oval, bound in metal or wood. Most of the smaller mirrors—or shards thereof—connected him to locations around Linaria, providing him with eyes and ears in countless places across the world.

Bringing his mirrors from Sereth to Val Sharis had been a monumental undertaking—each had its proper place, each had to be carefully wrapped in layers of linen to prevent even a scratch across their surfaces.

Any imperfection could dull—or kill—the blood magic within them.

Sapora walked to the far end of the room, lighting wall torches as he went. The flames sprang to life, their light flickering and reflecting across the mirrored glass.

Once happy with the light, Sapora clutched the new mirror shard and checked it over. He picked up a small, thin knife from the table at the end of the room and drew it across the back of his hand. Blood flowed immediately, and he spilled it onto the shard, where it mixed with the drop of dried blood already present.

In a matter of seconds, the blood disappeared into the glass.

Power billowed from his hand onto the glass, and dizziness gripped him. The mirror glazed over and became opaque.

As his dizziness faded, the hazy mirror slowly refocussed into an image—but not of Sapora's reflection.

The image showed the inside of a castle.

'Well done, Morgen.' Sapora said. 'Now, I wonder where you are…' The mirror shard was scarcely larger than his hand—not ideal, but still useable. He needed eyes everywhere, and Morgen was in the best place for his eyes in Niversai.

Sapora stood motionless and watched the mirror. The stone walls of the room were definitely of Rosecastle—it looked like Morgen had made it back to Niversai. 'Such a good soldier…'

No doubt the room Sapora could see was where Morgen slept each night. Armour and weapons rested in the corner of the small room, and an uncomfortable looking bed had been shoved against the wall, the sheets in disarray.

In Sapora's room of mirrors, there were no windows; no way to mark the passage of time. Sapora shifted into stasis as he waited: his breathing and heart rate slowed to almost nothing.

His shallow wound stopped bleeding, and his half-scaled skin began to heal. Something moved across the floor—a spider, perhaps—but Sapora ignored it; his only focus locked on the mirror.

A flutter of sound echoed through the glass: heavy footsteps. Sapora roused himself in time to see the door open and Morgen enter the room.

'There you are,' Sapora said.

'What the—?'

Sapora smiled at Morgen's apparent confusion. 'The mirror, Morgen.'

Morgen whirled around and gasped.

No doubt it was a strange thing for him to experience—another person from another place in his mirror. 'Sapora…? How? How are you…?'

'A Varkain method of communication. Much faster than the messengers you all use up here.'

Morgen ran a hand through his hair and pulled a chair that had been out of sight in front of the mirror. He sat down and shook his head, mumbling something to himself.

'I can't hear you if you whisper, Morgen. Speak up.'

'Sorry, I…What's wrong with a messenger?' Morgen said, still bewildered.

Sapora sighed. 'I just told you. This is a Varkain method of communication. We live underground. Can't very well have horses down in our tunnels, can we? Our blood magic enables us to…tap into mirrors if we have a shard of the original.'

'What? You can watch me from my mirror?' Morgen shot up, his chair flying backwards. 'That's why you wanted me to send it to you?'

'It's more complicated than that,' Sapora said. 'Now, I appreciate you following my instruction to send the shard. Tell me. What's the situation in Corhaven?'

Morgen scratched his forehead and took a moment to absorb everything Sapora said. 'Dragons running rampant. There've been reports of attacks on small villages. We've been sent out a couple times, but the dragons don't stick around. They burn what they can and fly off. It's just damage control right now.'

Sapora frowned.

Morgen continued, 'Rosecastle isn't fully rebuilt and part of Niversai is still closed off after Aciel's attack. Rhea knows where the King is—he's not been seen since the castle fell! Everyone fears the worst.'

'What a pity.'

'They were grateful you promoted me to captain. We lost so many soldiers to Aciel. We need more people to help sort everything out. We're firefighting every day! If you could send an airship or two of reinforcements from Val Sharis…'

'I'll speak to my council about it. I'm trying to rebuild relations, so you'll notice more Varkain coming over. I expect you and your Guard will treat them well?'

'Oh. Right. I'll keep an eye out.' Morgen glanced over his shoulder, as if suddenly nervous. 'Shouldn't you have…an official liaison with Corhaven? Why're you having this conversation with me?'

Sapora blinked slowly. 'My kind are not best trusted in Corhaven, and neither am I after the winter ball. I need to speak to someone I can trust. Someone who won't lie to me.'

Morgen bit his lip and nodded.

'As I told you before you left Taban Yul, you'll be well paid for your report.'

'I appreciate that…' Morgen said. He glanced over his shoulder again.

'Is Topeko still with you?'

Morgen shook his head. 'He was. He's staying in town somewhere. I haven't seen him for a couple of days now. Told me I shouldn't use the sword Palom made me, so I've locked it up in the armoury. He might be heading back to Berel, soon.'

'And…what about the Varkain treasure…?'

Morgen shuffled back. ‘I can’t speak for long, they need me to help out. One of the bridges in Niversai is gonna collapse any day now.’

Sapora supressed his irritation. ‘Have you looked?’

‘Not had a chance. I don’t get any spare time right now! I can’t get to the castle library. Should I ask Topeko?’

‘No. Don’t get anyone else involved. Remember what I told you.’

‘Okay, if you’re sure…’ Morgen’s body language screamed suspicion, and Sapora decided not to push his luck. He could bide his time with Morgen.

Val Sharis was his priority.

How could he rule anything if the country burned?

No, he had to ensure the country’s protection.

Sapora said, ‘No doubt you have your duties to attend, as do I. We’ll speak again soon.’

He stood up and placed the mirror shard against the wall, facing the stone. There was no point in spooking Morgen any more than necessary. He ran a tongue over his fangs and considered the soldier’s words.

Sapora strolled to the other side of the room, where a half moon mirror hung just below a flaming torch.

At first, there appeared to be nothing but darkness on the other side, but small details flickered into view after a moment. It was the murkiness of a smooth tunnel carved masterfully into the earth, sconces trailing along its length.

He hesitated for half a heartbeat before calling out. "Vasil. It is as I feared. The dragons' destruction has not ceased.'

Silence responded for several long moments, until his father, the former warrior-king of the Varkain, walked down the tunnel.

Though Vasil was into his fifties, he still carried himself as if he were in his prime. He was all sharp angles and calculated cunning. 'I wondered when we would speak. Is this true of Corhaven?'

'It is.' Sapora nodded, fighting the urge to glance in the direction of Morgen's mirror. 'Small villages and outposts. It'll probably worsen if nothing is done. We need to prevent this before all of Linaria burns.'

'And what of your weapon? It left some weeks ago.'

'It's not here yet. I don't want to use it to clear up unruly dragons.'

Vasil smiled, his fangs glinting. 'Dragons can't burn tunnels, Sapora.'

'I'm not leaving the city. Hiding in Sereth for the danger to pass? What kind of leader would that make me? You had the Ittallan eating out of your claws when you ruled. I must get them in the same position.'

'Always so eager to impress, aren't you?' Vasil said, smoothing down his lapels. 'Monitor the dragons. Their rage may fade once they've had some revenge.'

The wound on Sapora's hand throbbed. 'I'll take measures to keep them under control.'

*

'The latest search party returned to Taban Yul this morning without anything.' The old raven said. He knelt on the cold stone floor, head bowed, nose almost touching the floor. 'These Ittallan are from the furthest reaches of Val Sharis. If any such treasure existed, they'd have found it, my liege.'

'They aren't looking hard enough.' Tacio said, slouched in his chair, holding a tall glass of clear, sparkling liquid, watching as the light from his jewels reflected through the bubbles.

'They've searched night and day. There's no treasure.' Koraki had not once lifted his face from the floor since entering the chamber of snakes.

Sapora could smell the salt from his sweat in the air, and his lip curled.

'Send out another party. They can't have covered the whole country in a week.' Sapora glanced over the healing cut on the back of his hand, his father's words playing in his mind.

He had to keep more than the dragons under control.

'My liege, Val Sharis is a vast, wide land, and—'

Sapora lunged at the raven's first word, his blade drawn, and a fresh line of blood appeared on Koraki's cheek—the fifth on his face. He enunciated every word slowly. 'You *will* find them. I *want* those treasures, and I am losing my patience. If you cannot find them, I shall find others who can serve me better.'

'M…my liege…' Koraki stammered, a hand to his cheek as he shuffled backwards and hurried out of the tower room, almost tripping over his robes in his haste to get away.

'Don't you get bored of terrifying him? He won't have a face left for you to cut if you carry on about it that way.' Tacio watched Sapora.

'They'll obey me, or they won't live at all. The same can be said of you.' Sapora snapped at his brother. 'I *need* those treasures. They'll enhance my strength tenfold. Yours too. You cannot ignore that. I'm not going to allow that strength to slip away.'

'You hole up here in your tower and pretend you're less of a Varkain than the rest of us,' Tacio replied, downing his drink. 'You're trying to arm yourself with weapons of a power that isn't yours, and you pretend it makes you better than those you want to rule.' He dropped his glass onto the table in the room's centre. 'I've told you before, and I'll tell you again. We should go back to Sereth. It's winter. We can rest until the fresh season. See how things are then. Let the Ittallan sort themselves out in the meanwhile. Not like you're doing the best job in ruling them, anyway.'

'And as I've told *you*, I cannot rule a country I'm not living in.' Sapora glared at Tacio's empty glass. His brother needed little encouragement to challenge him. With alcohol in the mix, Tacio's behaviour bordered on unbearable.

'Exactly. What of your followers? Your *true* followers, in Sereth?'

'They remain loyal to blood, as you keep reminding me. They can wait. It's the Ittallan I need to overpower.'

'Because you can't win fairly? Because you aren't fit to rule them?' Tacio's smug tone set Sapora's teeth on edge.

‘You’re walking a fine line, Tacio,’ Sapora hissed, narrowing his eyes.

‘I’m the only one able to tell you you’re going about this the wrong way. Threaten, maim, kill all the Ittallan you want, it’s not going to win their favour. They’ll be more against you now than they ever have been.’

‘I don’t need their favour, brother.’ Sapora stalked across the room to the vast bookcase. ‘I just need them to realise they can’t beat me. Then, they’ll follow. Even if they must be made to.’

‘Hah, you sound like Aciel, now.’

Sapora did not respond. He blinked slowly, scouring the volumes of books he’d had brought up from the palace library. He plucked a weathered scroll from between two tomes and placed it on the table, shoving Tacio’s empty goblet aside.

He knew the treasures were here.

Somewhere.

At least *one* of them had to be.

‘If they’re useful, they’ll remain. Otherwise I’ve no need to keep them in line. I shall simply kill them.’ He unravelled the map and smoothed it out.

Ink splats dotted the depiction of Val Sharis from 5,000 years ago during the height of the Ittallan-Varkain war. While the landscape was much the same, the cities weren’t. Many towns and cities that existed then didn’t now, and these sites were of the greatest interest.

He’d circled several previously, and following Koraki’s report, he crossed through them.

'Sapora…' Tacio groaned, getting off the chair and joining his brother by the table. 'I understand you want to be greater than Father—'

'I am.'

Tacio rolled his eyes but nodded. 'Yes, I understand that. But Vasil was a fighter. A hardened veteran with a thousand kills to his name. He united Sereth and Val Sharis under one leader. He ruled both, without doing the *ruling* part.'

Tacio jabbed his claw at the map depicting lands owned by Varkain and Ittallan. 'He sorted this out, ended all this fighting.'

'I know the story just as well as you.' Sapora kept his focus on the map. He looked over the locations he'd yet to test and thought about potential others.

Thought about where his treasures were most likely to be.

'You don't *seem* to understand. The takeover is what he's known for. His reputation. It led to peace for over twenty years! You can't hope to better that. What are you conquering? The land's already yours by right. Why intimidate and maim your people?'

'We are a laughing stock!' Sapora rounded on him. 'The Ittallan pretend to be respectful and polite to our faces, but you hear them as well as I do. In the shadows they call us worms and maggots, creatures worth less than nothing.

Vasil may have strengthened our forces with the Ittallan, he may have prevented war with the Imperial Guard, but I will ensure we are *not* mocked. Not laughed at. We will no longer be the sick, dirty race clinging on to the Ittallan's scraps. It's about time the rest of Linaria showed us some respect!'

Tacio smiled, all fangs on display. 'I understand. I'm here to help you reach that goal for the Varkain, but…its best to heed a little advice every now and then. You did want my counsel, after all.'

'I did.' Sapora's eyes glistened, and he panted after his outburst.

'So, take my counsel; stop maiming your servants.'

'The damned raven gets on my nerves. Perhaps a new messenger…? That Voulhrik isn't half as irritating…'

'Why do you hate him so' Tacio asked.

Sapora glared at his brother.

'He's like any old Ittallan. Frail and weak. Fodder.'

'I think you just dislike anyone who isn't you,' Isa piped up as she clambered through the window and into the room, having apparently scaled the tower. She was covered head to toe in hay, and immediately set to picking out the strands from her braided hair.

Tacio immediately went on the offensive, 'What's your explanation for… your appearance?' He gestured angrily.

Isa flopped onto the floor, cross-legged. Having cleared her hair, she rolled up her sleeves and picked out the hay which had found its way into her clothes. 'I was down in Trader's Alley watching the end of season pack up. Might've accidentally fallen into a cart for horses,' she shrugged. 'One of the workshops burnt to the ground. Don't panic, the Guard got it put out before it did any other damage.'

'Embarrassment is nothing to you is it?' Tacio folded his arms. 'And we were just talking about you Ittallan.'

Isa looked up, paused in her grooming. '*Us* Ittallan?'

'You know what he means,' Sapora interjected. 'Don't be petty.'

'Don't be petty? Really?' She stood up and flicked her hair out of her eyes, strands of straw still poking out from various places. 'Starting to think you two are no different to the old council, you know. You made so many promises, Sapora. I don't see you acting on any of them.'

'I need time,' Sapora replied.

Isa scowled.

He continued, 'Nothing happens overnight, even the best plans must have time to get off the ground. The wheels are in motion, I assure you.'

'This is beyond you, Isa,' Tacio added, still glowering at her appearance. 'If you bothered to clean up and be presentable, we could invite you to some of the new council's meetings.'

Isa narrowed her eyes. 'Well I'll let you two *snakes* carry on planning those meetings, then. Don't let an Ittallan like me slow you down.' Her scowl showed playfulness, but Sapora heard her heart pick up.

Adrenaline.

Anger.

'I came to tell you that more Ittallan in Taban Yul's southern districts have gone mad, babbling to themselves and behaving strangely. The rest of the city is blaming you, Sapora. I'm sure you can just execute them as well, when they come to the palace with pitchforks.' She whirled around and marched across the room, glancing over her shoulder briefly before leaving through the actual door.

Sapora glared at Tacio and his careless words, their stark differences plain enough. Tacio, Isa, and he shared the same father, but the influences of their different mothers were strong enough to result in the feud between the three.

It was only because Sapora was the eldest that he held the most power.

'All right, Tacio. Get some of your best Varkain together, ones you trust. I'll give you a couple of new locations. Let's see if you and your snakes are any better than the raven's Ittallan.' He pointed to a new location on the map, a huge swathe of trees that ran along the spine of the Feor Mountains on the country's eastern border. 'I'll give your Varkain some crowns if they're successful.'

Tacio raised an eyebrow. 'What do I get?'

Sapora clicked his tongue. 'I'll owe you a favour.'

Chapter Six

By the time they reached the outskirts of the Rio Neva forest, Palom had half a mind to leave Jek and his damned cart in the trees.

The man was not unpleasant—he had plenty of knowledge about what Taban Yul had been like during the height of Aciel's war, and he made an excellent fish broth—full of herbs and smoky garlic—but he talked, and talked, and talked, and Palom's patience dwindled a little more every time he opened his mouth.

They trundled along the main trade road as it wound its way through the trees, following the river's twists and turns on its course from the Feor Mountains.

With every step, though, a growing sense of apprehension gnawed at Palom. His *Valta Forinja* pulsed periodically, making him check over his shoulder to ensure they weren't being tailed by some forest monster.

As a boy growing up in these trees, tales of creatures lurking behind every trunk had been at the heart of many adventure stories he and his friends acted out. They'd save each other from overgrown roots and fight off imaginary foes that kept to the shadows, all under the eye of his older brother, who'd kept watch over them.

There had never really been anything there, of course. Plenty of wildlife made Rio Neva their home, from deer to boar to badgers, many of which influenced the *meraki* of the Ittallan in Feoras Sol, but certainly no monsters.

He'd happily stroll through the forest alone, unarmed, and never worry or fear anything in the trees. Never consider anything that lived here *could* threaten him.

But now, travelling with Jek, and a *Valta Forinja* under his control, the unease grew more than he ever would have predicted.

Palom dismissed the feelings as paranoia.

He glanced skywards now and then and looked back the way they'd come more times than he'd like to admit. The gleaming, white marble city of Taban Yul and its palace had filled the horizon until they reached the trees.

He'd hoped to see a white owl floating on the wind.

Perhaps she might have changed her mind.

He sighed.

Of course, Lathri would not be following him.

Palom hoped Sapora's guards were good at their jobs and Lathri wouldn't get anywhere near the king. The others, he didn't care about. If anything, their deaths might dissuade Lathri from the ridiculous idea of plotting against him.

Their sacrifice for the greater good.

He smiled at that, ignoring the morbidity of the thought.

He rolled his tongue over his teeth as Jek continued to talk about the quality materials from this part of the country.

Would he ever be quiet?

They rounded a bend in the road, and Palom suddenly recognised exactly where he was. This had been the end of where he'd been allowed to roam as a child—the edge of his village's influence, as marked by a tall, wooden way sign that towered several feet above him.

Or, at least it had when he'd been ten years old.

Now he stood taller than it by almost a foot.

Returning to his hometown was the last thing he wanted to do, yet here he was, now on its border and getting closer by the minute.

The thought of stumbling into an old friend or family member made his legs tremble, so he'd spent a good chunk of their journey obsessing over what he might or might not say were they to encounter anyone, which drowned out Jek's chatter for the most part.

Not that the older man seemed to mind talking *at* Palom instead of *to* him.

Palom suspected that Jek had spent such a large part of his life talking, that he reverted to making noise as a matter of course.

As night fell, the two of them set up camp several paces from the winding stone road. Its edges were overgrown with foliage and pine needles, and determined weeds pushed themselves through the gaps between the stone where it had cracked from lack of maintenance and use.

Other than a handful of inns, Feoras Sol was the only settlement of any size this far east: a mining town full of people who mostly kept to themselves. Few Ittallan had reason to travel this way, and the villagers of Sol rarely visited the capital.

It seemed things were much as Palom remembered, despite two decades passing since he'd last been anywhere close.

The backdrop of the Feor Mountains loomed through gaps in the evergreen canopy, and the skies remained a miserable, dull grey which threatened, then loosed, snow. They were a couple of hours' travel from the Waterside inn—where Jek had asked for escort to—and for Palom, that time couldn't come quickly enough.

A small fire sizzled by the cart, which Jek had parked between two trees. Palom sat with his back against one of them, his feet pointed towards the flame. He idly oiled his sword, the familiar hum of energy reassuring, while Jek boiled a pot of water for whatever supper he'd decided to throw together.

Palom always ensured his weapons were well-maintained, but oiling the *Valta Forinja* was now something he found himself doing to calm down whenever he became agitated—usually with Jek or the old cart. Twice one of the wheels had fallen off, and twice they'd been delayed nearly an hour as the old rat tried to reattach it.

He hadn't seen his companion's *meraki*, but he guessed Jek was some luckless creature that would no doubt be squashed in a heartbeat by anything with teeth.

Now, Jek was rabbiting on about how poor the winter had been for his trade—precious gems and jewellery. He would find the right coloured stones, carefully carve them into the appropriate shapes, and create the most ornate looking jewellery Palom had ever seen.

Jek only had a few rings with him. His plan seemed to be to obtain more stock of stones in the Feoras Sol and make it back to Taban Yul before the weather really turned.

'So ye see, this Varkain girl, she was so picky. Nothing was right. The stone was tae blue, that one was nae blue enough. Another was nae big enough….' Jek explained while chopping up a handful of carrots across a slab of slate he carried with him everywhere.

Palom closed his eyes, trying to focus on the crackle of the fire. He was sure if he wandered off, Jek would continue talking until he fell asleep, none the wiser.

His hands moved rhythmically over the blade, ensuring it kept its edge.

Ensuring there was no weakness.

A slight rustle whispered through the spitting flames. He opened his eyes and held his breath, holding himself as still as possible.

Jek continued.

The fire crackled.

The wind blew.

Somewhere in the distance, an owl hooted. Lathri?

He narrowed his eyes and turned to Jek. 'Sshh.'

'In the end, ye see, her mother had tae be convinced that the green was actually much better. Brought out the colour in her eyes, ye know?'

The owl stopped hooting, and goose bumps rose on the skin of his arms.

The energy of his *Valta Forinja* prickled, rushing through him, begging to be picked up.

The wind stopped.

The fire continued to crackle, and Jek continued to talk.

'Jek. Be quiet!'

The rustle was almost indiscernible over Jek's breathing, but Palom knew the sound all too well. Someone, or *something*, stalking through the undergrowth.

His skin crawled, but this was not an enemy to wait out—this was one who struck fast.

Grasping his *Valta Forinja*, Palom swung it in a wide arc as he got to his feet. The power surged from the blade before he'd finished his swing. A slash of blue light cut into the trees on the other side of the road and took great gouges out of the thick bark.

A Varkain fell forward through the underbrush and onto the path, his startled cry turning into a gurgle of pain as he clutched his arm. Blood spewed from his sudden wound.

'Trying to sneak up on Ittallan? Very foolish,' Palom said, walking over to the fallen Varkain, who writhed around on the stone path, screaming as blood poured from the gash in his arm. 'It is harsh lesson you have learned.'

The Varkain glared up at Palom, drawing his lips back in a hiss to reveal black gums and a double row of fangs. Sweat dripped from his forehead, and his clothes were so caked in soil that Palom couldn't tell what colour they were.

Palom looked back to Jek to check he was okay, but two more Varkain leapt from the trees and pounced on his travelling companion.

He growled and raised his sword to them, it's power taut, ready to be released.

The Varkain dug their claws into the old man's shoulders and glared at Palom as Jek cried out. They hadn't killed Jek immediately, as Palom would have expected.

He furrowed his brow.

Perhaps they weren't their intended targets?

Varkain were known opportunists, especially when they travelled in a group, but this was too bold.

Attacking Palom—a battle-seasoned warrior who stood a hair below seven feet tall and almost as wide as three men—was a ridiculous notion even for the desperate.

'Step aside, snakes,' Palom said, squaring up and holding the tip of his sword above the throat of the injured Varkain. 'I will kill your friend, otherwise.'

They hissed back and held their ground, showing no signs of surrender or retreat. They were also covered in dirt, though to a lesser extent than the injured one.

Mine robbers, he supposed.

Stupid Varkain.

'If you do not move in three seconds, this one dies. You understand, yes?'

They remained motionless, the silence broken by Jek's ragged breathing.

If they wanted to die, Palom would happily oblige. His sword would make short work of them, and three fewer Varkain would do Linaria plenty of good. 'One. Two…'

The Varkain on the ground cried out as he attempted to transform and attack. Palom leapt out of striking range and brought his sword down in the same, swift movement.

The blade sliced clean through the Varkain's skull, splitting it in two. Blood gushed onto the weapon and the pathway, but his focus was on the other Varkain.

Jek wasn't paying him for nothing.

His *Valta Forinja* buzzed in his hand, and delight surged through him.

'Now he is dead. Leave. Or you will die as well.'

He glanced at Jek, who nodded subtly. Palom tensed, seeing the nod, but unsure what it meant.

Jek transformed in a flash, shrank in size, and slipped out of the Varkain's claws.

Palom wasted no time.

He lunged forward, pulling the sword up in a fast side slash, catching the closest Varkain on his arm and back. The blade bit deep—had Palom swung it with any more force, he would have cut through him entirely.

Wrenching his sword back, Palom stepped away from the blood pouring out of the collapsing Varkain, who twitched as he died, and raised it to the third and final assailant.

'You leave. Now. Tell your allies not to bother with my friend and me. Or I will cut them in half, too.' He smiled at the thought and licked his lips. His sword flashed blue, brightening the path for several seconds.

Too frightened or too shocked to say anything, the third Varkain turned tail and sprinted down the path towards Taban Yul, not even bothering to hiss at them.

Palom kept eyes on him for as long as he could, and when he disappeared into the trees, he finally relaxed, looking down at his blood-stained clothes and sword.

He hadn't really thought getting into a fight would be a possibility and hadn't prepared himself for the likelihood of one.

He huffed. He'd probably be back again with reinforcements, and he resigned himself to a sleepless night keeping watch. Just what he needed.

Paying no mind to the dead Varkain by the campfire, he strolled back to the tree he had sat beneath and opened his bag for a clean length of fabric with which to wipe the *Valta Forinja*, silent for now, momentarily sated.

Another rustle sounded behind him, and Palom whirled round, ready to fight off another attacker, but calmed when he saw a small racoon cowering underneath the cart.

It had a few flecks of blood in its fur but seemed otherwise unscathed.

'Jek?' Palom questioned, pleased the trader seemed to be unharmed. 'These are dead. It's safe.'

Jek poked his nose out from under the cart, whiskers twitching as he sniffed the air. Palom sat down with his sword and began to wipe it, content to give Jek as much time and space as he needed to recover from the shock of the ambush.

'I am not sleeping tonight. You rest. I will guard.' He hoped that would reassure the old man.

The racoon crawled out from under the cart and took plenty of time to sniff the air and listen to their surroundings. After several minutes, he transformed into the hunched-back old man, and shuffled back over to his pot of boiling water—now overflowing.

Palom ignored it, methodically cleaning his sword.

Why had the Varkain attacked?

What had they been after?

If they had been digging around abandoned mines, why attack them?

If they were opportunistic thieves, they were very foolish—he was clearly armed. Why risk life and limb? They carried nothing of value.

'Thank ye, Palom,' Jek said, after he'd seen to the pot. 'I don't think…They would have…' He stammered and trailed off. He rubbed a hand over his balding head and pulled at his oversized collar.

'It is fine.'

'I think I…lost me appetite a bit after that,' he said, glancing at the bodies and pooling blood. 'Don't suppose you'd like tae move on? Sleep somewhere else?'

Palom shrugged. 'I am not sleeping. We can move if you want to move. Dead Varkain are no threat.'

Jek cleared his throat, as if desperate to fill the silence, and then busied himself with putting away the pot and kicking out the fire.

Palom's thoughts churned as he got to his feet and grabbed hold of the cart again. Jek clearly wasn't going to rest here, but Palom preferred it. The Varkain weren't likely to come near this place, not now their dead lay here.

He followed Jek, hardly watching where he was going, until the other Ittallan found a place suitably far enough away from the fight that he could set up for the night.

Palom thought back to before the attack. Nothing seemed off. The forest was as it had always been.

Had Lathri warned him? An owl had been hooting just before the Varkain struck.

Hadn't it?

Once settled, he pulled out the dirtying cloth and wiped the *Valta Forinja* again.

What if Voulhrik had been right?

What if Sapora really *had* found a way to wipe out the Ittallan?

What if…that was why the Varkain had been covered in dirt and soil.

What if they weren't there robbing mines at all?

*

The following morning, Jek thanked him graciously with a double florin, but refused to speak of the attack, which suited Palom well enough. From all Jek's talk, he'd never dealt with thieves before. No doubt being ambushed by three Varkain had shaken him.

'You'll reach Sol this afternoon,' Palom said, a short time after they'd set off. He'd promised Jek he'd let the Imperial Guard know when they reached the Waterside Inn to keep him quiet. In truth, Palom couldn't care less about a couple of dead snakes in the forest.

Jek stayed quiet as they walked, and while Palom found the peace enjoyable, he knew his companion was uncomfortable. They'd not even eaten breakfast—they'd just gathered their things and headed off. Whether he was shaken after the attempted ambush, or Palom's brutal method of dealing with them, he wasn't sure.

Although he knew a counter-attack wasn't unlikely, the night had been quiet, and Palom shrugged off the lingering fatigue with a quick wade in the river.

Disgusting snakes.

He had killed people before, but only in self-defence. Last night seemed different. Had he really enjoyed watching the Varkain suffer?

Had the war changed him so much?

Lathri's voice rang in his mind. '*Emonos.*'

He ignored it.

The sword had saved their lives. How could such a weapon be evil? It was just a sword—a piece of metal. It couldn't be good or evil. It just was.

Palom rubbed his nose. Emotions coursed through him: sadness, guilt, loss, rage, even hatred. He told himself he felt these things towards Aciel and his war, losing his companions, losing Lathri, and to the Varkain who dared attack him… but deep down, they were emotions he felt towards himself.

Much of the morning passed in a blur, his *Valta Forinja* quiet on his back, pulsing only when he thought he heard footsteps behind them. When he turned, the path and trees were invariably empty aside from the wildlife.

It took over an hour before Palom realised the background chatter he'd grown used to had vanished. 'Jek? Are you okay?'

'Oh, yes, I'm fine, thank ye, just fine,' Jek replied, adjusting the laces on his cloak and flexing his fingers a little. 'Good that we be there today. Best ye be off on ye way. Don't want me slowing ye down, now, do ye?'

Palom narrowed his eyes. 'Indeed.' There was no reason to lie, and he had no words of comfort for the racoon. 'Keep safe on your way back to Taban Yul after you leave Sol. You don't want more Varkain to find you alone.'

'Hmm? Oh. Yes. Yes, ye probably right,' Jek nodded, drawing up his cloak about him and glancing into the trees either side of the path.

'I do not know what they were after,' Palom muttered.

'Ye…ye do nae think they…might've…been looking for more of the dragon ore ye carry?'

'Dragon ore? I don't have this. Only what is in my *Valta Forinja*—you cannot take this out.'

'Well…the sword itself. It…Well, it's valuable, no? Everyone knows it's that sword that beat Aciel.'

Palom thought it over. He supposed his sword was rare—the only other *Valta Forinja* than those he'd forged were in Berel, across the sea thousands of leagues away.

They weren't going to be stolen any time soon.

Perhaps there was some truth in Jek's suggestion. After all, dragons were the lifeblood of Linaria. He *had* managed to harness that in his sword.

The mountains ahead grew larger and Palom's stomach sank at the sight. He could almost smell the iron from here.

The path split, marked by a small sign written in the old tongue. One way led to Feoras Sol, and Sereth beyond. The other veered north, through the Rio Neva forest and deeper into Val Sharis. The Waterside Inn sat a short distance from where they stood, along the northern path, half-hidden by foliage and a large water wheel churning merrily in the morning sunlight.

A sombre note to end their partnership on.

Palom pulled the cart right up to the split in the path and set it down gently. 'Will you be okay to get to Sol from here? It should be hour away. Maybe less if you walk fast.'

'Aye that I will. Thank ye again for all ye help, Palom. I'd never have made it if it weren't for ye. I'll be sure to tell everyone what happened.'

Palom swallowed. 'Is best if not. I…am keeping low profile. I am here to rest in country. Do not tell people I am back.' It wasn't convincing, and Palom knew it. He rolled his wrists.

Jek scratched the back of his head. 'Well, if ye sure? No good deed goes unrewarded…'

'You did reward me. We are even. I will tell Imperial Guard at inn what happened, so you do not worry. Good luck with your trade. Fare well.' Palom stepped back to allow Jek and his cart plenty of space to pass.

Though irritating, Jek wasn't stupid, and understood the dismissal. 'Right ye are. And the same to ye. Thank ye again, Palom. I'm honoured tae have met the legend of Taban Yul!' He hoisted the cart up and pulled it slowly down the road towards Feoras Sol.

Palom watched him head off and sighed, thoughts circling round once again to the Varkain attack; to the two he had killed and the third who had fled.

Would more attack Taban Yul?

Were they under Sapora's control, or acting on their own?

His sword flared again, a flash of blue light, and he let out a low growl at the thought of any of those snakes getting close to Lathri.

He should have killed the third one, too.

Shaking his head, Palom tried to push the thoughts out of his mind.

This was as close to Sol as he felt comfortable, and yet so close to the Sereth border, there were bound to be more Varkain passing through on their way to Taban Yul.

He was certain there wouldn't be many Imperial Guard stationed this far into the country, so the thought of staying here to hunt down any Varkain who put a claw out of line appealed.

He'd be able to patrol this part of the forest in case other Varkain tried to pick off unwary travellers, Lathri would be safe, and he could avoid seeing his father and the others in Sol.

Palom shouldered his bag, checked his sword, and made his way to the Waterside Inn.

It wasn't as if he'd be of any use elsewhere.

Chapter Seven

'An Ittallan, you say?'

'Yes, my liege, no question. A huge man with a sword that…it had this energy. It sliced the trees apart without the blade touching them.'

'Without the blade touching them?' Sapora raised an eyebrow.

'Yes, my liege.'

'What do you think, Sapora?' Tacio asked, looking from the young, dirt-covered Varkain to his brother.

'I am your king, Tacio. You'll address me as such.' Sapora's tone reflected his irritation at having to repeat the fact so many times.

'It must be Palom. Who else would have a weapon like that? Not like anyone would be able to steal it from him,' Tacio replied, ignoring his rebuke.

'You're *absolutely* sure about that sword?' Sapora asked.

'I am. It was less than a day's travel from Feoras Sol.' The young Varkain clutched at his hands, drawing his claws over each other, head bowed before Sapora and Tacio. He still panted after rushing to the palace as fast as he was able. Sapora could smell the fear on his breath.

Sapora exhaled. 'It must be Palom, then. And...the tunnel?'

The Varkain's pounding heart beat faster. 'We...we found a plaque, my liege.'

Sapora's breath caught, and he swallowed. He felt Tacio's eyes on him, but kept his attention on the sweaty, dirt-stained Varkain.

'Um...it...it was buried really deep, my liege. The ground wasn't stable. On the edge of where we dug. We saw the plaque. But we couldn't go any further. Everything else had been sealed off, the ground too compact for us to go anywhere else. We tried but—'

'What did it say?' Sapora asked through gritted teeth.

The Varkain's eyes darted from Sapora to Tacio, and back again. His breathing grew more ragged and he swallowed. 'My liege. It said, "Malashash".'

Sapora permitted himself to smile, a grin that bared teeth and crinkled his eyes. 'I'm grateful for this information. You are dismissed.'

The Varkain raced out of the council chambers like he'd been bitten and left a trail of muddy footprints on the stone floor.

Tacio grimaced at the dirt, but Sapora paid it no mind. The ancient histories had spoken truly. He knew it!

Such a treasure, such a power, could not have vanished from Linaria. Hidden, yes, but not completely lost.

Now he had the location of the first piece, he could move to defend Val Sharis and Sereth at his leisure.

It went to show what a waste Koraki was.

Palom, on the other hand, was an insignificant irritation that had to be dealt with sooner rather than later. When training an animal, a swift response could mean the difference between desired results and further unwanted behaviour. Sapora couldn't allow him traipsing around the countryside killing his Varkain when he chose.

Surely there was no way the thuggish Ittallan could know why the Varkain had been in the Rio Neva forest. He'd moved hundreds of Varkain to Val Sharis to cover his plan.

And yet, he couldn't risk Palom getting wind of it.

He ran his tongue over his fangs as he thought; the Varkain for his task had been under instruction to remain silent.

Strict instruction.

Tacio had picked the handful of Varkain himself, so they should have been able to follow simple orders.

Had it been an unfortunate coincidence?

A case of Palom being in the wrong place at the wrong time?

Isa had explained the tiger left the palace shortly before Sapora had arrived, partaken in the funeral procession, then left the city. Without Anahrik, Sapora supposed there'd be little left in Taban Yul for him. Perhaps he was simply reverting to his feral side.

Yes, that was probably right.

Palom had a temper, plenty of brawn, and little brain. Formidable, yes, but not capable of cracking into his plans—they'd barely begun, at any rate.

The Varkain must have simply been unlucky enough to wander across his path, and foolish enough to challenge him.

And Sapora had no intention of letting Palom get away with it.

The tiger might be a hero in the city, but as far as Sapora was concerned, he was a stupid brute with the weapon of a god at his fingertips.

Someone who could make things very difficult, if he chose.

'We don't need to worry about the tiger, do we?' Tacio asked. 'I can't believe they found Malashash's plaque. I thought it was folklore. I just went along with you because it's funny to see Koraki squirm.'

Sapora licked his lips. 'Tell me, how much progress have you made in the excavation?'

'No pleasing you is there?' Tacio replied with a huff. He fiddled with the numerous rings adorning his clawed fingers, twisting them so the bright red and purple jewels faced upwards. 'Progress continues. Like I told you before.' He spoke like a petulant child, and sat in a large, high-backed chair beside Sapora's, seemingly more interested in straightening up his clothes than assisting his rule. He picked at dust on the material and spent a good while ensuring his appearance was impeccable.

Far too long for Sapora's liking. Vain snake.

Winter sunlight shone through the tall, glassless windows of the Council Tower, and a bird called from somewhere in the distance. Sapora loved and loathed the city. Full of pompous Ittallan more used to fluffing themselves up than getting anything done.

He wished Vasil had visited Taban Yul more frequently. It had to have been over a decade since his father had last visited his wealthiest city. Leaving such luxuries to preening peacocks had left much of the palace in need of maintenance and a thorough clean.

He'd scoured his own rooms from top to bottom, ridding himself of the lingering scent of Goldstones and Ittallan. His assumption that Isa was influential had been gravely wrong, and it had taken the ball to snap the dozing Ittallan to attention. They had a conquering Arillian on their doorstep and hardly seemed to bat an eyelid.

Had he not woken the lazy beasts up, Isa wouldn't have been able to rally her airship fleet in time to defend the palace. Even the officers in their Imperial Guard had never fought a real battle, never followed orders in a timely manner.

When he'd arrived at the palace, Sapora had personally spent days—almost a whole week—straightening everything out.

Not to mention all of Sereth watched his every move—some from within Taban Yul, now. Isa reported over 1,500 individuals or families had crossed borders, and Sapora had allocated them a section of the city they could make their own. Not everyone enjoyed skulking in darkness and hiding from the world above, and he'd given them arguably the most beautiful city in the world to move to.

From the palace, he could watch and move the pieces for his wider plans into place. Bringing some Varkain to Val Sharis was just the tip of the iceberg.

'Oh. I meant to say. The one you wanted? Mateli? He's still alive. Imprisoned, but alive,' Tacio said.

Sapora grinned, finally a bit of good news.

'Fair warning, the dungeons haven't been kind to him.'

Sapora stood up. 'He wasn't executed? I heard he'd committed unforgiveable war crimes.'

'Executed? Of course not. The Ittallan aren't so cruel as to end a life for something like that.' Tacio grinned, his golden eyes squinting at the breadth of his smile. His skin was grey, the same as any Varkain, but it was pale and smooth, almost white, matching his ivory fangs on display every time he spoke or smiled.

Sapora appreciated Tacio's counsel and little else. Only by right of age had he been given the chance to undertake the trials and take the crown before his brother—though there were still many who felt Tacio, a pure-blooded Varkain, had better claim to the throne.

As he was rarely allowed to forget, Sapora was a half-breed, the result of a union between his father and an Ittallan Goldstone. While he looked as much a Varkain as his brother—though he lacked Tacio's finer features—he had far more to prove.

Now Sapora ruled, his lineage was never openly spoken of, but he knew in the shadows, Varkain and Ittallan alike sniggered at his weaker blood.

Once he found the other three treasures, no-one in Linaria would question his weaknesses again.

Vasil, had conquered the Ittallan by force almost three decades ago, and allowed the Ittallan to rule themselves with their own council, so long as they paid homage to him each year.

It meant Vasil extended no effort to rule them, reaped the benefits of their bountiful country with gold, food, weapons, and servants, and kept them in check simply from the fear of his takeover and infrequent, unannounced visits.

The taking of the palace of Taban Yul was a story all Varkain grew up on—how their warrior king overpowered a stronger, larger enemy with strategy and utter domination.

Vasil had struck first, leading the attack himself. He'd infiltrated the sewers and tunnels underneath the city, passed the formidable twin stone walls of the palace undetected, and crept up through servant's chambers and cook's quarters.

He and his Cerastes had killed everyone they came across, Ittallan or otherwise and slaughtered dozens before the alarm had been raised. By that point, the Ittallan had no choice but to surrender.

With the palace fallen, Vasil took the seat of power in Val Sharis. In a single night, Vasil had claimed Taban Yul, and the rest of Val Sharis, for the Varkain, ending the centuries-long war between the two races.

An uneasy truce grew between the Imperial allies of Corhaven and Val Sharis, and the Varkain of Sereth. Vasil had what he wanted; after enjoying the luxuries of the palace for several moons, he returned to Sereth, taking thralls with him.

As a child, Sapora could turn into his true form, a cobra befitting his royal bloodline, but the younger Isa was a wildcat, following in the lineage of her mother. She'd been forbidden from entering Sereth, and Vasil left her in Taban Yul to be raised by the Ittallan who never truly saw her as one of their own.

Isa lived on the outskirts, unable to be shunned due to her powerful father, but unable to leave by the same strength. Sapora, however, was welcomed home to Sereth as the king's oldest child and heir to the throne.

Unions with multiple partners had always been part of Varkain culture, and when Vasil subsequently fathered another child by a Varkain woman and gave him a half-brother, Tacio, Sapora knew he'd spend the rest of his life proving himself to the Varkain and Ittallan both.

He *would* be greater than his father.

In generations to come, they would speak of *Sapora's* victory in Linaria, rather than his father's brutish one.

Vasil remained in Sereth, rarely venturing from his country after conquering Taban Yul, save a few fleeting visits to his wives and Isa.

Yet, Sapora found his Ittallan blood pushed him to explore the world above and felt cramped and frustrated when he remained below ground for more than a few days at a time.

By his father's leave, he left Sereth on errantry—to roam Linaria for the two years before his ascension to the throne, learning what he could of the world to strengthen his eventual rule, and ensure he never came second to Tacio.

Sapora had visited the palace in Taban Yul frequently throughout his youth, often alone, sometimes accompanying his father, and had forged a close relationship with Isa. He knew she thirsted for power in the same way he did and had not been afforded the privileges she should have been through her royal blood.

The Ittallan sneered openly at her, her mother was shunned for having a child by a Varkain, and Isa had been ostracised.

She was an outsider, a prisoner, in her own palace.

It infuriated Sapora, who promised her power when he became king in return for her undisputed loyalty—something she'd willingly offered.

The first thing he had to do to achieve that was disband the old Council of Val Sharis and replace it with people he could trust beyond question. He wanted—needed—at least some Ittallan on his side and considered appointing several based on Isa's recommendation. After all, she'd grown up in the palace and knew the Ittallan Goldstones better than anyone else—but Tacio had suggested keeping it all Varkain, to keep the ruling line pure.

Sapora had bristled at that, for his blood was just as muddied as Isa's, though he understood Tacio saw him as a Varkain and Isa as just another Ittallan, beneath his notice.

If he was to comfortably rule both nations, he needed allies on both sides. Already, there were rumours he was worse than Aciel, which angered him more than he liked to admit.

At least Tacio followed orders, though his somewhat blasé manner contrasted Sapora's dignified, more structured approach, but he had little choice.

From what he'd learned during his errantry, Linaria was a world on the brink of collapse after Aciel's work. While he actually thought the Arillian had the right idea, building an army through falseness and hypnotism was never going to work in the long run.

Harnessing the power of dragons, though? That was clever.

Sapora licked his lips again, trying to keep the smile off his face.

Once Tacio finished the excavation, he'd have another of the world's greatest powers in his claws—a Sevastos.

Only Isa, Tacio, Vasil, Savra, and the few Varkain dealing with the excavation knew of his weapon, and he was keen to keep it that way. He expected some sort of revolt—a new regime was never going to be accepted by all, particularly when those at the top lost out—and he wanted to be as prepared as he could be for when they decided to strike.

The idea of Val Sharis and Corhaven teaming up again and unleashing the full force of their Imperial army concerned him, but that threat was precisely why he'd planted his own ally in the Corhaven capital.

Come to think of it, he hadn't heard from Morgen in days. Sapora wondered what was going on in Niversai.

Sapora strolled to the window, hands clasped behind his back as he stared out across the city. Smoke rose from a street some way into the terraced rows of white and blue stone. The sunlight faded, and lit torches appeared periodically, dotted about the streets.

He enjoyed surveying his kingdom, and never understood why his father chose to remain underground, in the gloomy depths of Sereth.

He thought to Palom again, and what might have driven him from Taban Yul.

He thought to Palom's former business partner, Anahrik.

He thought to Kohl and Amarah.

Uncouth criminal.

He thought to Eryn.

He thought to Moroda.

Her death had been unfortunate, but not unexpected. What *was* unexpected, was her actions halting the Arillian threat. He had been surprised and pleased that the nuisance Aciel had been sorted out. Especially because he thought he'd have had to reveal his trump card to get rid of him.

Sapora turned his mind back to the issue at hand: Palom. 'Well then, we'd best release Mateli and put him to use, hadn't we? I've some bother with a large cat I need to be rid of. I'm sure he'll be up to the job. Explain that I will return him to his former position in the Imperial Guard with full powers if he takes care of this task, plus an advance of five crowns for the effort.'

'Five crowns?' Tacio said, raising his eyebrows. 'Surely he should do it for the reward of being released. Why waste gold on him?'

Sapora ignored Tacio's questions. 'Will you see to it he understands the task?'

Tacio rolled his eyes, huffing as he got up from his chair. 'I'll see to it, Sapora. Once I've had something to eat. I'm starving.'

'You'll see to it now.' Sapora said, turning around to glare at his brother.

The two stared at one another, the room tense.

'All right, all right. No need to be so moody.' Tacio said eventually, turning away.

Sapora stood alone, staring at the mirror shard. He ran a claw across it and smiled to himself. At least now he could receive information immediately. Sending letters by ship or horse took far too long.

'Treasure hunt going well? I'm guessing that's why Tacio looks so upset?'

Sapora glanced up to see Isa strolling across the room to him. He hadn't heard her.

'Palom's been killing Varkain,' he said.

'That's upsetting. I thought he left Taban Yul?'

'He did.'

She walked past him, her hand trailing on the table and papers scattered on it. 'When I saw him last, he was...in a rage. Grief, mostly.'

'He did not take Anahrik's death well.'

'No. He really ought to manage those emotions. The guy is the strongest Ittallan I know.'

'I need your insight,' Sapora said.

Isa sat on the window sill and peered out. She wore common clothes; short sleeves despite the cool, with fur lined boots and her thickly braided hair tied back out of the way. Her golden eyes were the same as Tacio's, though hers were much brighter. She looked as pure an Ittallan as Tacio looked a Varkain, whereas Sapora was something not quite either.

He immediately resented his heritage.

‘What do you need to know?’ She picked at her nails with a short blade not unlike the one Sapora carried, and shared his disinterested, bored demeanour.

‘Mateli.’

‘The old hunter? What about him?’ She picked a glob of dirt out and flicked it out the window.

Sapora smelt her fear permeate and narrowed his eyes as she feigned indifference. ‘Everything.’

Isa looked at him, her face stoic, then slid off the windowsill and into the room. Putting the blade away, she paced.

She seemed to pace when she thought, Sapora had noticed. Always moving, always touching, always thinking. He’d grown used to it, though it irked him somewhat.

He felt most in control when keeping completely still.

He watched her as she paced, his full attention on her words, tone, and body language. He did trust her—for the most part—but was always sure to detect the first signs of untruthfulness. They shared blood. It was always possible she might act for her own gain.

‘He’s been locked up…hmm…must be seven years now. He’s a crocodile, the only one I’ve ever known about. Never knew where he came from. He tried to run a separate branch of Guard who worked just for him. They did a lot of stuff, took over some of the scummy districts in the city. Killed people to keep others in line. A *lot* of people. But the Council put a stop to that after a while.’ Isa shuddered. She folded her arms as she walked back and forth across the room. ‘He’d been a captain in the Imperial Guard. He scared a lot of the peacocks and fodder away though—one of them claimed he ate his cousin. That's when the Council had to step in and do something.'

'Mateli *ate* him?' Sapora leaned forward.

Her heart rate increased, not quite covered by her constant pacing. She spoke rapidly, spurting out facts to cover her obvious unease.

'There was never any proof, but…I think he did it. Sapora, he's something else. The Council were scared of him too. Everyone was. I don't know why they kept him around when he terrorised the city every day.' Isa ran her hands through her hair and licked her lips. 'I suppose because he was good at his job? Crime rates were the lowest in Taban Yul they'd ever been. So, the Council put him in charge of training up apprentices for the Guard. Something softer, y'know? But he ended up putting six of them in coffins, ten more in the infirmary in the first week. He liked to break them. You could see it. He's filled a lot of the mausoleums in the city. Hah, thinking about it, he's more a Varkain than—'

'Than…?'

Isa sniffed. 'Tacio?'

'Hmm.' Sapora replied, watching her closely. He smelled the drop of sweat on her brow, though he couldn't see it.

He mulled it over.

She gave him the information he wanted, but she was clearly uncomfortable about it.

Mateli sounded like just what was needed, and he was known to other Ittallan. He would be perfect for the message he needed to send.

'I've got Tacio having a word with him.' Sapora said at length.

'About?'

'Our old friend, Palom. He's been sighted near Feoras Sol.'

'Isn't that his hometown?' Isa said, as she stopped pacing.

She couldn't hide her shock, then. 'So it seems. But he killed two of my Varkain. Butchered them, from the report. I thought Mateli could correct that.'

Isa nodded, flicked her hair, and resumed pacing. The silence lasted several minutes as she chewed her lip.

'You don't agree?' Sapora asked, when it became clear she was not going to say anything.

She shrugged. 'Mateli scares me. The way he moves, thinks…Everything.'

'You are my sister. He owes his freedom to me. I doubt your fears are founded.'

'This is *Mateli*. How did you even find out about him? I thought the Council tried to quash all talk of him after everything he was accused of...after everything he'd done. Most of the city districts haven't fully recovered yet.' Her pacing sped up.

Sapora shrugged. 'The Council gave me a lot of information as I got rid of them—one had the audacity to suggest I wasn't half as much of a threat as Mateli. I was intrigued, so I had Tacio scour the dungeons himself.'

'It's a bad idea.' Isa walked past him to the window. She clambered up onto the sill, the wind rocking her where she crouched.

'You should leave Mateli alone. This is more than what you said you'd be doing. What you promised.'

'Watch your words, Isa.' Sapora replied, bristling.

She looked back at him, all smiles gone. 'You're going to release him whatever I say, aren't you?'

'I am.'

She looked like she wanted to say more but shook her head and bit her thumbnail. 'Good luck with Mateli. You're going to need it.'

She turned back to the window and leapt out of the tower.

Chapter Eight

Palom's plan to patrol the road looking for unruly Varkain had sounded fine in his head, but when it came to acting on it, the few Ittallan who lived and worked at the Waterside Inn and beyond had swamped him to the point he'd retreated to his room for the entirety of the afternoon.

His experiences with Jek and the Varkain, Lathri and her allies, and even the comrades he'd travelled with in autumn rolled around in his mind like a violent storm. What did it all mean?

What was the point of power if you had nothing to protect?

He wondered whether those in Feoras Sol knew there were Varkain digging around right under their noses? If he figured out what they were after, would that put him in their good graces? Would it be enough for them to forgive him?

As the sun set, anxiety his stress levels rose. Being cooped up inside had never been enjoyable, and the itch to get outside grew too strong to ignore. His *meraki* rumbled within, and Palom realised he couldn't remember the last time he'd transformed—he'd grown so dependent on the *Valta Forinja*.

Against his better judgement, he left his belongings in the room, including the sword—which he hid under the mattress of his bed—and left the room.

His room—the largest in the inn, of course—sat behind the open dining room, where patrons milled around as they tucked into their supper.

When he stepped into the room, a dozen faces turned towards him. He'd never get used to it.

Palom nodded to the young captain of the guard stationed at the inn and hurried out the front door before anyone could jump to their feet to stop him.

Within the first few steps, he felt lighter, freer. He quickened his pace to a jog and followed the river that flowed beside the inn and gave it its name. Settling into the rhythm of the jog, Palom let his mind empty.

He'd been too pent up. Had too many dark thoughts.

Palom veered away from the river and made his way deeper into the trees. He recognised patches of forest and landmarks from his childhood and smiled at the memory of simpler, happier times.

Dusk lengthened the shadows around him, and a haunting breath filled the air as day gave way to night.

It was the time of day Palom most cherished.

He was back in the place he had grown up, the woods and caves he had explored with his brother and friends as a child: the place where he had truly found himself.

He loved the wildness of the place. The raw scent of the earth from where his kin had mined, the free-flowing, rushing waters of the river which fed and nourished the land, the warmth of distant fires and those who huddled around them.

Palom longed for it—to be sat by the fireside with his family and friends. But he couldn't face it.

Not after what he'd done.

Not after twenty years of running.

The last words he'd spoken to his father were when he'd left Feoras Sol: "I am leaving. Goodbye."

Before he'd forged the *Valta Forinja.*

Thoughts of his brother dying in the accident flooded his mind; his screams from where the weight of the rocks crushed his bones, his breathing failing as he slowly suffocated in the depths of the mine.

Palom had been powerless to help—everything had happened so quickly. One moment he was heaving at a large rock lodged in the mine wall, desperate to reach the ore behind it, the next, the earth growled back at him, the entire shaft shook, and then the walls and roof caved in.

Palom survived without breaking a bone, though he'd been badly bruised.

Thankfully, he and his brother had been the only ones working that day—it should have been a day of rest near the end of the harvest, but the two had a quota, and knew between them it wouldn't take long to complete.

His brother had tried to transform to escape, but his broken bones and pain would not allow his *meraki* to be used. He had called out incoherently, a cry of distress and anguish.

Palom knew he should have left to get help, but he could not leave his brother to die alone: in *emonos* was unclean.

Cruel.

Only traitors died that way, and Palom couldn't allow that to happen to his brother.

And, of course, he'd been too afraid to leave.

Lathri's face flashed in his mind, lingering on the edge of the memory. *'You can't even say your brother's name, can you?'*

He was young then. Too young, at sixteen. He still had two years before he'd be able to harness his own *meraki*.

His brother, three years his elder, had a new born daughter. He had a family to look after. Palom had taken her father from them because he was too afraid, too weak, to do anything other than sit and panic and cry, hoping someone heard and came.

All the while his brother slowly slipped away.

Palom had been able to move some of the smaller rocks, but he couldn't move the sheer mass of debris by himself. He dug as close to his brother as he could, held his bloody hand for comfort, stayed with him in that dark tunnel, worried at any moment the rest of the ceiling would give way and bury them both.

He had wished many times that the rocks would have come down harder, and his brother died quickly?

But Rhea had not been kind.

His brother suffered for two and a half gruelling hours before succumbing to suffocation or exhaustion. Every moment that passed, Palom had wanted to leave, to get help, to get someone who knew what to do, who could save him.

But he was too afraid.

What if he died?

What if he couldn't remember the way back?

What if the roof collapsed even more, and they couldn't reach him?

But the tunnel held.

He knew the way back.

And his brother died.

Palom could do nothing to ease his suffering or release him from his tomb. Towards the end, when he could barely breathe, Palom couldn't even hear his last words.

A final sting for what he'd failed to do, and the catalyst for his decision to leave Feoras Sol and go to the capital.

Unable to think clearly with memories and guilt bombarding him, Palom tapped into his *meraki* and shifted, the transformation giving him strength and power.

In his true form, worries drifted away as his world shrank to what he could sense and taste, and his sadness dulled. It brought him a measure of relief from the self-inflicted torture for his past actions and consequences of his inactions.

As he strolled through the trees in his true form, the growing darkness creeping up around him, he breathed in deeply, taking in scents from near and far. He could hear the breath of the creatures around him, huddled together in their burrows as they sheltered from the tiger's path.

Palom made his way towards where the stream broadened, and the trees thinned. Bright moonlight lit the river bank, painting the grass and water silver, turning the once familiar landscape into another world.

Crickets sang from the thicker grass, but otherwise the world was still, holding its breath, waiting for the hunter to pass. Palom stopped as the river flowed across his path, tail twitching as he watched the timeless water flow.

He heard laughter some way in the distance. The sounds from Feoras Sol carried loud and clear along the water, and he sat down, listening to the noise of his village.

His senses were not so keen as he could pick out individuals, but he could detect a mix of low, deep voices, and the high-pitched, shrill giggles of children. He heard feet pounding on stone as they raced around, the heaving of solid oak doors being pulled shut. He turned his head slightly to the wind, picking up on the scents of a hundred people, covered in salt, coal, and dirt.

The wind blew again, from the north-west now, bringing even more of a chill with it. He opened his eyes and looked across the water. Already Val Sharis had experienced snow, but there was more to come. He wondered where he'd be when that happened.

He sat by the water's edge for a long time. Night took hold of the land while he sat, and the laughter and chatter from Sol died down until it felt as though all of Linaria was asleep.

He had been debating heading back, when the noise of approaching footsteps put him on high alert.

Each step was direct, and confident; not the footsteps of someone wary of a tiger nearby.

He got to his feet and looked along the river, waiting, straining to listen.

Four steps.

Pause.

Four steps.

Another Ittallan, on patrol?

He wished he'd paid more attention, wished he had his *Valta Forinja* with him.

The clouds broke overhead, and Palom saw a shadowed figure step out of the tree line and approach the river maybe twenty paces away. In the clear moonlight, he saw another hunter Ittallan: another large cat.

Did he know this one?

The smell was as familiar to him as everything else: it was his old home.

Could it be a relative?

A family friend?

The other looked up, spotting him. She froze, tail lashing. She was a snow leopard, her grey-blue fur camouflaged in the silver moonlight.

She pulled her lips back to bare large canines at him.

Palom took a step back but held his ground. He heard her growl, sensed her unease, but did nothing to aggravate it as he studied her features. She did not have his bulk, though her tail was as long as her body, and she stood at twelve feet nose to tip.

Though she seemed familiar, as did everything here, he did not recognise her. She was definitely not in his memories. She bared her teeth again, tail lashing, taking one step closer to him, then another, then another.

Suddenly, about five paces from him, she stopped.

Her demeanour changed, and she stood up straight, ears pressed forward, nose twitching. She looked him over and engulfed herself in light as she transformed.

'You…you're Palom, aren't you?' she asked, hesitant. Her short, dark hair hung in different lengths, and her deeply tanned skin was darker than his own—but she had the unmistakable green eyes of his brother.

Palom, too, transformed, and dropped immediately into a crouch once he had two legs again. 'Solvi? *Leil* Solvi? It…You…You have grown much.'

'I should have known it was you. Tigers are such a rarity,' she said, shaking her head, long, dangling earrings clinking together as she moved. 'I can't believe you've come back after all this time!'

Her words spoke of surprise, but her tone was still aggressive. He didn't know whether she was welcoming him or guarding her home from an outsider.

'Solvi…' he said, voice barely above a whisper. 'You were new born when I last saw you... Look at you now.' He stood back up and stepped towards her, hands outstretched.

'Don't touch me,' she jumped back. 'You left us! You left us!' She shook, tears welling in the corners of her eyes. She wore bracelets of thin silver, each covered with multi-coloured beads and jewels, around her wrists and ankles. Her feet were bare, and she almost danced on her toes as she avoided his touch.

'How is Manilo?'

Her eyes narrowed at the name, and her lips turned into a frown. 'Your *patera* lives. My *pali matera* does not. You didn't come back when we sent word of her death.' She turned away, threatening to race off.

'I did not know about my mother,' he replied, taken aback at the accusation. He raised a hand to his chest and shook his head.

She scowled. 'I'm sure *pali* would have something to say about that. Showing your face after everything you've done?'

'Solvi, please,' Palom said, his heart aching at her harsh words. Her reaction was exactly why he'd wanted to avoid returning to Sol. 'Do not be like this. What happened…what Manilo told you, may not be same thing.'

She shook her head. 'I know all I need to know. You're a coward for leaving, even *pali* says so.'

'Will you not listen to what I am saying?'

'No. Am I taking you to *pali* or not? I'll tell him I saw you, even if you don't come.'

Palom sighed and shook his head. Her reaction of surprise and loathing worried him, and he didn't want to make anything worse. 'Would it make you happy if I went with you?'

'No.'

'Would it make you happy if I left?'

She thought about it before shaking her head. 'No.'

'I will see him soon, then,' he said. He had no other options. He hoped he would not displease his niece, and at least by giving them both time to digest their meeting, it would help strong feelings settle and pass.

He could hardly believe the baby he'd seen was now a grown woman and with access to her own *meraki*. She was fierce and strong, light on her feet, and seemed every bit the hunter his brother had been.

How he wished to have seen her grow and blossom into who she was now. He'd been so preoccupied about his *Valta Forinja* and the idea of seeing his father that he'd forgotten about his brother's baby daughter—and how she might feel about him now she had grown.

Palom suddenly thought back to the attack. 'Have you seen Varkain here?'

'Varkain? No. They don't come near Sol,' she replied, tilting her head to one side.

'I met three on my way here, in an ambush. You should ask *Archigo* to set up patrols in pairs, for a while.'

Solvi nodded. 'I'll pass on the message.'

'*Asfali niji.*'

Her eyes widened as she turned to race off. '*Asfali,*' she called over her shoulder, and loped through trees, transforming as she did.

He watched her leave and listened as her footsteps faded away, until he was left with no noise but the rushing of the river water and the trees bending in the wind.

Chapter Nine

Amarah walked through the village a little after dawn, a small crowd of new companions trailing her. Most were children, who would race forward and beat their wings, swooping past her or overhead, before circling back to the rest of the group. The sun came up somewhere below their floating island home, bathing everything in soft, golden light.

'Give her some room, younglings. Poor thing hasn't been left alone since she landed!' Tymē, an Arillian a little older than Amarah, called to the group of children who flew nearby. They scattered into the air, giggling.

'They ain't doing no harm. It's all right.' Amarah said, though she appreciated having some space.

The Arillian's long, blonde hair was tied back, with the loose ends braided and threaded with bones and varnished pebbles. Her wings were almost white-blonde, matching her hair. 'Even so, it's better for them to leave you alone. I'm afraid they've only heard tales of on-ground. Oren is all they know.'

Amarah shrugged. 'Haven't they been down to see the Golems? Kohl spoke pretty damn highly of 'em.'

'Kohl certainly would. His direct ancestors created the ice golems—his frost-touch is ancient. Hah, it transcends the dragons, you know.'

Amarah wanted to ask her about the powers of the Golems, and whether they truly could free Moroda from crystal. However, having a little tact when getting people to give up information always helped. Better to not go for the jugular straightaway.

'Most people would disagree. The Dragon Goddess Rhea created Linaria. So…she and the dragons were around before the world was. The ice can't be older.' Amarah glanced away as the Arillian children flew around each other in circles.

'You'd be surprised what "most people" are wrong about. I've been on-ground before. I've spoken to people. In Val Sharis, they say the Varkain are a lost, sick people, split off from the Ittallan. The truth is the other way around. On the ground there has always been ice. Above ground, there have always been Arillians. Under the ground, there have always been snakes. The Varkain are the oldest race, you know. It is the Ittallan who split off from *them*.' Tymē laughed, loose feathers falling from her wings.

'Well that goes against the Samolen teachings.' Amarah said, hands on her hips. She was hard pressed to say whether she agreed or not with the "traditional" mythos in Linaria.

She knew dragons weren't to be messed with and could understand why they demanded such reverence. But to believe that one had actually created the world? It *did* seem a little far-fetched:

something to tell children when they went to bed. Some way of instilling a belief of respect of the land and animals who inhabited it.

If she thought hard about it, she didn't believe, nor did she really care to. Amarah had never believed in the Samolen magic, either, despite there being plenty of evidence for that: she had lost Moroda to some concoction of Samolen magic and dragon power, after all.

Arillians, though? Did their skills transcend the dragons? Their magic was ancient, powerful, tangible. There was no reading of spell books, or uttering incantations and silly chanting.

Topeko had told her the Samolen power came from the dragons: from their stones, created from water in the sacred lake.

Rhea's breath, he called it.

The Arillians were from another branch altogether—completely different to anyone she had encountered anywhere else—and their plight and troubled history with the rest of Linaria reminded Amarah so much of herself.

'Wrong or right, it doesn't make anyone any better.' Tymē continued, 'Aciel thought he was right. Thought it was time for Arillians to rise again. No-one listened, no-one wanted to. So, he used that secret power of his.' She shivered, her hair blowing in the sudden breeze. 'Hardly the way to change history, is it?'

Amarah and Tymē walked past a number of buildings through which children and adolescents flew in and out.

Khanna lay a short distance away, and Amarah had been keen to keep her ship in her sights every time she wandered the streets. After their initial curiosity, the Arillians had been happy to leave *Khanna* alone.

Khanna made Amarah think of her warship docked in Taban Yul; part of the fleet that had battled Aciel and those under his compulsion. It had been responsible for the deaths of many Arillians.

Amarah felt a pang of guilt—but when you had a weapon in your hand and there were people charging down on you, fighting back was the only option. 'Hardly the way to change history.' She repeated.

'And now we hide and lick our wounds. The survivors suffer.'

'Suffer?'

Tymē nodded and gestured to a large, squat building on the edge of the residences. Amarah squinted. The wailing she'd heard before had quietened, and she hoped it meant they'd healed, rather than died.

Tymē said, 'Those who were under Aciel's compulsion the longest…they... well.... Their minds are not completely theirs.'

Amarah followed her to the entrance, where she spotted a male Arillian sat against the rock, head bowed, muttering to himself.

As her eyes adjusted to the gloom inside the building, she saw others—young and old—acting similarly. Some shuffled around in circles, others picked at their wing feathers, and some sat and stared into nothing. Amarah swallowed. They all shared a blank, haunted look.

'Some are worse than others. A few have recovered, only to seclude themselves.' Tymē said, her voice soft and low. 'They only have the faintest memories of what transpired, even over the long months of Aciel's campaign. Isn't it terrifying? To know you weren't in control of your actions, or able to remember them?'

Amarah shuddered at the thought, Aciel's cool voice suddenly in her mind.

'Give me back the sphere you thief.'

She remembered, clearly, the heat of Jato's warship as flames enveloped the deck. She remembered the heist to steal the ereven sphere from Aciel, and she remembered him taking control of her mind for a few seconds, before Moroda broke the spell.

That had been a close thing. Sapora had kept them alive, of that she was sure. But she'd taken on Aciel himself—had him pinned down, nearly sliced his arm clean off with her scythe.

She wondered how much more death and destruction she could have prevented if she'd been able to kill him.

Amarah also remembered Jato's scream. Dragons above, she'd never forget that. Apparently in love with him and following him of her own free will.

'His compulsion is a rare talent, even among Arillians. There's no-one in all our history to have used his gift to such an extent—to have controlled so many of us. Who knows if they'll fully recover.' Tymē walked away, leaving the sick Arillians in peace.

'What a bastard.'

Tymē laughed and shook her head. 'Kohl did say you aren't one to hold back with your thoughts!'

'Why would I?' Amarah shrugged. 'No point in not saying stuff that needs to be said.'

'This is true. Though many struggle with it.'

Amarah had learned quickly that her preconceptions for Arillians had been mistaken—they weren't death-wielding, callous creatures who destroyed their land with wild storms and lightning. If anything, they were more peaceful than the Samolen.

Two devastating wars had made the divide between Arillians and the rest of the people within Linaria all the greater.

And yet Amarah was welcomed into their midst, offered food, drink, and shelter. They were curious about her and her life, about her ship, about her desires and hopes and fears.

If an Arillian came to a town, any town—even Berel, capital of the Samolen homeland—they'd be met with suspicion if not outright hatred.

She understood why they treated the Varkain as such—they were nothing but killers and did nothing to dissuade that belief—but the Arillians were something else altogether.

Everything was spoken: their language, their lore, their histories, their magic. They had no need of parchment or writing; everything was handed down through their words, in stories told to their children and grandchildren.

Amarah loved it.

Why couldn't the rest of Linaria be the same? Instead of the Samolen notion that you had to be huddled in libraries, poring over dusty tomes, trying to understand the black markings scratched onto the pages—which apparently taught you the greatest secrets of the world.

She had struggled to understand the writing of her teachers: shapes and words blurred together or leapt off the page, and her eyes and head hurt when she tried to read for too long. She'd been yelled at for not trying hard enough, or for deliberately failing to understand it.

It had infuriated her—why would she pretend not to understand? The beatings she received and the shame she felt would surely dissuade her from pretending.

Her family gave up schooling her. Instead, they sent her away to Berel—home of the university and greatest school in all Linaria—to study under the scholars there.

No doubt they'd hoped the scholars would straighten her out, as attempting to beat sense into her hadn't worked. Yet she was passed on from scholar to scholar within the school, from class to class, and none had any luck in getting her to understand the letters in their tomes, nor to harness her supposedly innate magical abilities.

Topeko was the only one who hadn't forced her, and the only one who had earned her respect. His approach was far gentler and understanding, and he only accepted two or three students at a time, so when she failed, she wasn't a laughing stock of the class.

She learned more about the Samolen and the history of Linaria with him than from anyone else, but she still could not use magic.

She'd undergone the ritual early, which sealed in her cheek jewel in the hopes that the power embedded in the stone would awaken her dormant powers.

The ritual had been long and bloody, and she'd hoped the pain would be worth it. Topeko refused to believe she had no abilities, and tried to help her day after day, night after night, without success.

Whether she was the wrong person in the right body or the right person in the wrong body, all she knew was that she was no Samolen.

She could not tap into the "innate" magic of her family, no matter how hard she had tried or what methods she used.

Amarah hated the country, the people. She hated being pushed away, shunned, and treated like an outsider over something she had no control over.

She'd had cried herself to sleep, begging Rhea for an answer, asking what she had done wrong to deserve this, but the Goddess was not forthcoming with a response. The books she was made to read did not help—even the little she could understand—and she thought there had to be more to life than being made to feel like this.

For years, Amarah endured her forced education, trying to please her estranged family, other students, Topeko, and his peers.

She'd failed.

When she realised she'd been backed into a corner with no way out and no way forward, she made a decision. She cut out her heritage—literally slicing the Samolen jewel from her cheek leaving her with a scar under her left eye—and struck out on her own shortly before her fourteenth birthday.

Ranski bordered its neighbour country, Corhaven, which was larger and busier, and full of towns and cities, unlike the few villages that dotted her country. Corhaven's capital, Niversai, had treasures and opportunities galore. Corhaven boasted a population three times as great as Ranski, and the idea of being a face lost in the crowd, unable to be singled out and picked on, appealed greatly to Amarah.

Stealing several artefacts from her university, she bartered a passage north, crossed Ranski's border and left the desert landscape far behind as she began a new life in Corhaven.

She stowed away on airships, moving from town to town in secret, hunkered down in engine rooms. She became familiar with the variety of airships as they flew around Linaria. She learned to recognise the engines which would ensure a smooth flight, and those whose journeys would be swift.

She became friendly with junior members of the crew, and it did not take long for her to learn of piracy, and those ships who flew unrestricted in the skies above the world.

Her network of friends grew slowly: some were legitimately employed on Imperial fleets or traders' vessels, others flew under black sails and their own banners, answering to none but their bellies. She found their way of life appealing, and it did not take long for her to grow attached to various crews.

The idea of going against the rules; against what was expected and demanded, was liberating. The skies offered the freedom she sought, and sky pirates kept to a code more than the established rules of the countries they flew in.

Despite the camaraderie, Amarah believed she was alone in the world and only she would be able to chart the course of her own fate. She kept allies at arms' length and expected to be betrayed at every opportunity. She sabotaged the engines of those who wronged her, and openly challenged others for power and dominance over the skies.

By the time she bought *Khanna*, Amarah's name was well known by people on both sides of the Imperial Guard, and her reputation only grew as she completed heists against well-known and respected Goldstones, getting herself involved in bloody skirmishes leaving their victims dead or seriously injured.

Numbers, she understood—she worked in money and had to know the value of what she was thieving—but words were beyond her.

Apparently, it made her somehow "less than" those around her, never quite good enough, no matter how hard she tried. So, after a time, she stopped trying. If she'd never be good enough in their world according to their rules, she made up her own. She took what she wanted when she wanted, and anyone who tried to tell her otherwise be damned.

But it was here, after spending time in Oren, that she thought perhaps she should have been born an Arillian. That, perhaps, she had found somewhere she belonged, without need for aggression.

She loved flying, after all, and the food wasn't bad once you got used to it. But their culture, history, and way of life had the sky pirate mesmerised.

'Amarah? Are you well?' Tymē asked, raising a hand to Amarah's forehead.

The sky pirate took an automatic step back and shook her head. 'I'm fine. Just thinking… Why on earth has Jato kept Kohl for so long?' Amarah asked.

'I don't know,' Tymē replied, taking a seat around a large fire in the centre of the village. 'Jato was a general, Kohl was the former leader. Perhaps it is a discussion of power?'

'What normally happens when you lose your leader?' Amarah sat beside her and gazed into the flames.

'The Golems decide if there is no clear leader. Often the new leader kills the old and takes his or her place. Kohl's banishment was the first in living memory.'

Amarah said nothing. The flames flickered, almost absorbing the morning sun, and glowed brightly. Occasionally it was coloured by a flame of blue or green, and Amarah was sure, for a brief moment, the palace in Taban Yul appeared. She blinked and rubbed her eyes.

Somewhere to her left, an Arillian grabbed the rock jutting out from the base of the fire and sent out a bolt of electricity. She felt the crackle race through her, and the flames changed colour with a *whoosh.*

This time, when Amarah blinked, the palace of Taban Yul appeared in full view, clear as if she was in Val Sharis. Snow fell around the palace, bathing it in an eerie blue-grey light. 'A blizzard?'

'Oh yes. It's how we see through storms. This rock enables us to channel our power, the power of storms. We can see anywhere in Linaria where there is one,' Tymē said. 'I suppose it's easier for you to understand if you see.'

'I s'pose…' Amarah murmured, transfixed. She could see every tower, every wall, every guard stationed in the grounds. The scene grew as she looked through the storm, to the streets of Taban Yul, the crowds gathered, and even the most minute detail of the buildings in the city.

Outside the city walls, she saw forests and wild land split by deep valleys, and a snow-capped mountain range in the far distance. A large wagon made its way slowly towards the city, surrounded by countless people. The sun reflected off them and Amarah guessed they wore armour.

A lump formed in her throat.

Sapora had moved to the palace—what on earth did he have on the way to him?

With another *whoosh*, the scene disappeared, and the fire crackled as before.

It *was* winter. Cities took in supplies at this time of year. There wasn't anything unnatural in that. But something about the guarded cargo made her stomach turn.

Moroda was still down there. Right in the firing line of whatever Sapora planned to do.

Kohl needed to get on with sorting the Arillian's magic, and she was done waiting around doing nothing.

Shivering, she got to her feet and patted herself down, wiping away her uncertainty and replacing it with impatience. 'I don't want to wait for them anymore. I wanna talk to Kohl.'

Tymē smiled and looked to the fire. 'I wouldn't advise disturbing them. Jato's temper is quite fierce, and she may attack you again.'

Amarah shook her head. 'If she attacks me, I've got my scythe. If I need to use it, I will.'

'They'll be in Jato's home, I suspect, to the far north. Look for the fire pit outside. It's wide and deep enough to house your ship.'

'Thank you.' Shaken by what she had seen in the fire, she strolled towards *Khanna*, intent on arming herself against another of Jato's rages.

She had no idea what Jato wanted from Kohl, but needed to know what he had planned if she was to have any chance of finding a way to release Moroda and bring her back.

Chapter Ten

Palom woke drenched in cold sweat after a nightmare-plagued sleep. Immediately, he reached under the mattress and pulled his sword out, the familiar pulse of energy coursing through his hand where he gripped the hilt. It reassured him.

Emonos.

He could still smell the Varkain blood on the blade, despite cleaning it.

He lay on his back and gripped the sword with both hands as he stared up at the ceiling, his mind reeling to last night's encounter with Solvi.

She'd been a few months old the last time he'd seen her.

Sunlight trickled in through the window. Pigeons cooed, songbirds trilled, and every now and then he heard the splash of river water as a fish disturbed the surface.

It should have been a peaceful, calm morning.

But his mind turned over and over, thinking of past mistakes, making up worst case scenarios, and working out how his situation could deteriorate.

Every time he thought of something going wrong, the *Valta Forinja* pulsed, as if ready to fight.

He hoped Solvi's confirmation that the Varkain hadn't approached the village was true. The thought of them skulking about his family made his stomach turn. It was rare that Varkain visited Feoras Sol—hatred between Ittallan and Varkain ran high there, so close to the border—but any of those snakes so close revolted him.

What was Linaria coming to, if they crossed borders so brazenly? Although Sapora was the new king, the Varkain had always been creatures of the underground.

Sapora would return to Sereth before too long, surely. Vasil had only ever stayed in the palace a couple of months at most, but Palom couldn't shake the feeling that something was going on with the snakes.

In years past, the Varkain would only ever really enter Val Sharis during the trading seasons, and during its peak, at that. They would often travel in pairs or small groups, conduct their business, then disappear back to their own country.

Had a new king emboldened them so much that they challenged armed Ittallan openly? If they were all similar in nature to the trio he and Jek had encountered, it would be no good thing.

Or was it all paranoia? A misunderstanding that he'd taken completely the wrong way?

Had he killed innocent Varkain?

The sword trembled in his grip, and he sat up, holding it to the sunlight now blazing through the window.

Emonos…

Chatter from the inn's patrons drifted through to his room—carefree laughter and the clinking of glass and plates as breakfast began.

No. The Varkain hadn't been innocent.

They'd tried to prey on Jek.

They'd tried to prey on him.

Thoughts of the Varkain spurred him into action—he didn't want to think of them near Solvi or the others from his village.

The chatter through his door grew louder as Palom dressed, and once he'd strapped the *Valta Forinja* to his back, he left the room.

For such a small inn, the place seemed to have grown a crowd overnight. He cursed inwardly, glancing at the Ittallan squeezed into the dining area. Had Jek's mouth run off and attracted half of Val Sharis?

'Palom!'

He looked over the heads of the crowd and saw the young Ittallan in Imperial armour waving at him from across the room.

'Over here, Palom!'

At his name, others turned to face him, and Palom glowered. He stalked across the floor, the crowd parting for him as he moved. 'Be quiet, captain.' He said, noting the Guard's helm—it boasted three prominent horns, a sign of his rank. 'I do not want for all Val Sharis to know I am here.'

'Oh, I'm sorry. I didn't realise you were keeping a low profile!' He handed Palom a mug of dark ale. 'I know it's early, but I didn't get a chance to talk to you yesterday. And you came back so late last night, I was off duty. Wanted to thank you formally for what you did.'

Palom's stomach knotted.

Did he know about the dead Varkain?

Had the king sent someone to arrest him? The Guard worked for Sapora by extension, after all.

He took the offered mug but didn't drink.

The man folded his arms behind his back, red sash clasped in gold and silver jaws on his shoulder. 'Everyone knows you here, Palom. There's nothing out this way except Sol. Any news travels fast!'

Palom glanced around at those in the inn; watched them look away when his eyes met theirs. This wasn't the reverence he'd been used to in Taban Yul.

Was it fear?

He swallowed, mouth suddenly dry. 'Thank you, sir.'

'Chyro.' He smiled brightly.

When he'd been in the rage of battle, and even after, he'd not cared about the consequences of slaying the Varkain. But now…?

His stomach tightened, and he put the mug on the table beside him. What was he supposed to say? To do?

'What brings you this way, Palom? Seeing old family? Coming back to a hero's welcome, I expect?' Chyro asked. 'You are from Feoras Sol, aren't you?'

Palom flinched and looked away. He had a good idea of the sort of welcome he'd receive when he finally entered Sol, and very much doubted it'd be one for a hero.

Not if Solvi's response was anything to go by.

'I was stationed in Cora Keb during the height of Aciel's war,' Chyro said, without waiting for Palom to speak. 'After the attack, the capital needed to replace lost numbers. My mother had always pushed me to join the Guard in the hopes I'd serve in Taban Yul one day. If only I'd been there to see you save the city. I can't thank you enough for what you did.'

Palom relaxed a fraction. Chryo *didn't* know about the dead Varkain. He took a better look at the young Ittallan—what little he could see through his oversized helm—and found young eyes which had not yet seen true battle.

No doubt there would be a spate of young captains forced to take the place of their superiors who had lost their lives in the battle against Aciel. Chyro couldn't have been much older than eighteen or nineteen.

Palom thought to Morgen and considered moving to Corhaven. Would it be safer there? Out of Sapora's reach?

The young captain carried on, 'Of course, I *thought* I'd be at the palace living a life of luxury. But the new king isn't much a fan of Ittallan Guard, it seems. He brought in a load of Varkain to watch him. So here I am, in the middle of nowhere, nothing to do!'

'Better to keep peace than fight in war.' Palom said.

Chyro laughed. 'You're right. Excitement in the Guard isn't always a good thing, is it? I'm sure you know—your experience of fighting is all anyone 'round here is talking about. You're a legend, you know that? My kids'll look up to you for years!'

Palom winced, and energy arced from the *Valta Forinja* in response. 'I…have lots to be doing,' Palom said, glancing around to see if anyone had noticed. '*Asfali.*' Without waiting for a response, he hurried out of the inn into the cold forest.

Palom's jog turned into a flat-out run, as he put as much distance between himself and the inn as he could.

He'd been so stupid.

Chyro had been a fan, like any Ittallan from Taban Yul.

It made no sense that he'd jump to such dark conclusions.

And the sword had…the sword had wanted to harm him.

Palom ran for several minutes, boots echoing off the hard, stone road. Trees, roots, and vegetation whipped by, and only when his eyes began to water did he skid to a halt, panting heavily, one arm leaned against a nearby tree trunk for support.

As he caught his breath and looked around, he realised with sickening familiarity that he'd reached the site where he'd killed the two Varkain.

Standing straight, he pulled the sword from his back and held it in front of him, ready for any threat that might dart out of the trees. Birds sang in the distance, and sunlight filtered through the canopy above, bathing the road in dappled light.

Exhaling slowly to steady his nerves, Palom forced himself to relax and think clearly. The forest clearing looked much the same as it had when he and Jek had been there.

A sudden snap somewhere above made Palom jump, and he raised his sword instinctively. He paused when he saw Solvi sat on a large branch overhead—so large it almost crossed the width of the road below. Her legs dangled over the side, her feet bare, jewelled anklets refracting the sunlight in a thousand directions.

'Following me, Solvi?' Palom lowered his sword.

'I wanted to see where you'd go. Didn't realise you were going to run away again.' She looked up to the sky.

'I am not running away.'

'Really? Sol's in the other direction.' She glared down at him with childish petulance. 'Proves you're a liar.'

'I am investigating Varkain I told you about. I want to know why they are here, so I can report to Manilo.'

Solvi tilted her head and looked down the path from her vantage point.

'I am here for you, Solvi. Always. Even if I am not in Sol.' Palom tried another way to reassure her.

'Hollow words, Palom.' She kicked her legs, swinging them in the air, perfectly at ease so high up.

Arguing with her would be futile, so he continued on, his sword held tightly. It continued to pulse, sending shivers of apprehension coursing through him.

The difference in response from his family, who he held most dear, and complete strangers like Jek and Chyro, was worlds apart.

Everyone else revered him or saw him as their hero.

His niece shot him scathing remarks and scowled.

Palom could hardly bear the thought of what his father's reaction might be. Lathri's suggestion to visit him seemed suicidal.

He stepped off the road and into the clearing, noting the tree he'd originally been leant against. It was an unassuming section of Rio Neva forest which flanked the main road between Taban Yul and Feoras Sol. There weren't any markets or shops; even the Waterside Inn was too small to warrant robbing.

Palom span in a slow circle, narrowing his eyes as he looked around him. The birds sang in the treetops, sunlight danced in the moving leaves, and a cold breeze blew. There were loose stones on the edge of the road, dead leaves littered the edges, a few thin vines trailed from the trees, but nothing that seemed out of place.

Palom wished he had Anahrik with him—his partner would often fly high above an area and could spot anything with his keen eyes. They'd shared everything, and for years they had worked as a team.

Now, searching for something hidden, with no clear idea what he was looking for, Palom believed himself a failure.

Even during his travels with Moroda and the others, none of them had been alone. They'd covered each other's weaknesses and worked out problems together.

If he couldn't figure out why a few Varkain were sneaking around his own homeland, then perhaps Solvi's notion that he was useless held some truth.

'Find anything yet?' Solvi stalked him through the trees above, following his progress from the canopy.

'Still watching over me?' Palom led with his sword, pointing it towards the bushes and waving it every so often in a feeble attempt to sense anything lurking in the undergrowth.

Solvi leapt off the branch and landed a short way behind him. 'What are you expecting to find? A nest of Varkain? They live underground, everyone knows that.'

Palom shook his head, cutting away some tall leaves and frowning when he found nothing. 'I do not know. Whatever it was, it was important enough for them to attack me. There are no treasures hidden here? Gold? Jewels? Weapons?'

'Nope,' Solvi said, shaking her head. 'Too close to the dragons.'

'What dragons?' Palom rounded on her.

'They nest in the Feor Mountains, don't they? So, we never keep anything valuable here. Just essentials. This whole forest is part of their territory.'

'When did you last see one?'

She put her hands on her hips as she thought. 'Before that battle you were part of. One used to live in a cave near here—I guess it must have been a mine at some point. It's abandoned now. Haven't seen any since before then.'

Palom thought.

The Varkain had been digging.

'Do you know where is this cave?' He asked.

She nodded.

'Take me there. Please.'

She considered his request for a long moment, and then gave in—perhaps to curiosity, if nothing else—and darted off into the trees.

He sheathed his sword and tore after her, closing the distance with huge strides. They settled into a comfortable pace—not a full sprint, and yet faster than a jog. Palom recognised parts of the forest as they hurtled along, the sounds of the river fading as they went deeper, and all sunlight disappeared—blocked out by the thick canopy.

Even in the winter cold, Palom was sweating by the time Solvi came to a stop.

Here, the Feor Mountains encroached into the forest, and a large rocky formation protruded from the earth. A gaping hole several feet wide opened in the centre of the rocks and led into the depths of Linaria.

Feoras Sol had mined here for generations, emptying the earth of valuable iron ore. When mines became too unsafe or had given up their bounty, the Ittallan simply left the forest to reclaim it.

In this case, a dragon had decided to make one its lair.

'I told you. It's abandoned,' Solvi said, glancing back at him.

Palom breathed through his nose.

All he could smell was Varkain.

Even the air above was empty, clear of the phoenixes which trailed adult dragons, and the soil underfoot was cool and compact.

'Have you been inside?' He asked.

Solvi shook her head. 'Nothing in there, now.'

Palom wiped his brow with his arm. Something had been of interest to the Varkain here, but what? He checked his surroundings once, before stepping into the cave's mouth.

Inside, it widened into a dark, cavernous space where his footsteps echoed. The place reeked of charred wood, melted stone, and blood, above all else. The ground was a mix of loose soil and rock, and he took care where he stepped to avoid a twisted ankle.

Grimacing against the putrid smell, Palom covered his nose with his arm and continued forward, walking deeper into the cave, feeling smaller with every step.

He held his sword before him and looked at it closely. He thought back to the teachings of Berel University. He tried to recall Topeko's words and Moroda's skill with her Samolen crystal.

'I…wonder…' Closing his eyes, he focussed on the blade, and on his own *meraki*—tapping into the powers he used when he transformed, but not giving into them completely.

Palom held the magic on his skin and pushed it out on the blade. Goose bumps rose along his arms, and his fingers lost their strength.

He dropped the *Valta Forinja* and opened his eyes, half Ittallan, half tiger. His vision blurred, lost in some part-transformation as the dragon ore which lay within began to respond.

'Palom! What is this?' Solvi gasped and leaped back.

The *Valta Forinja* glowed bright, vivid blue, bursts of light leaping from it every so often, colouring the cave.

Palom dropped to his knees, unable to stand as his power left his body and lit up the dragon-forged blade.

'It…is…some melding of… *meraki* and… Samolen magic,' he panted, struggling to stand up. 'It was how…Moroda found Sevastos…She used…her own magic…with Samolen's.' He smiled, weak. 'I cannot…hold this power…for long. Quickly, follow the…blade. It…maybe will show what…Varkain were here for…'

'Palom…' Solvi's eyes were wide as she shuffled towards him.

With a grunt, Palom heaved himself to his feet. His hands shook, and he struggled to lift the sword. Using every ounce of strength, he lifted the tip from the ground and immediately felt a pull. 'It is like compass…'

Solvi walked closer, watching Palom and the sword with something akin to awe, as he slowly took a step forward, then another, following the sword all the while.

'Gently…gently.' Palom said.

Sweat rolled down his cheeks. Even standing up was agony—without his strength, he had nothing. 'Look, look, you see it? Look! The light… is brighter this way!'

'I see!' Solvi said, darting away.

Palom hurried after her as quickly as his weakened body would let him.

Solvi shuffled forward a few steps at a time, looking back at Palom and the sword every few seconds. 'This is what the Samolen taught you?'

'A little.' Palom acknowledged, the pulsing sword sending burning energy up his arms. 'But…but I had never tried…this until now.' Excitement gripped him—of seeing a new magic work, and of what he might find.

The light grew brighter until Palom could hardly open his eyes to it. 'We are close. It is...here...somewhere here...' He looked left and right, squinting around the *Valta Forinja's* light.

They'd reached one of the cave's walls; it sloped away from them, stone giving way to soft, loose soil which had been recently stirred up. Solvi crouched and edged towards the wall as Palom watched.

Both Ittallan held their breath, listening intently. Solvi inched forward another few steps, before freezing. 'There is no dragon.' She looked back at Palom. 'But...there is an old nest.'

Palom's breath caught, and dropped the sword, shambling forward to her side. His eyes took several moments to adjust to the dim light, and his mouth dropped open.

In amongst the upturned soil and loose rocks, pressed against the cave wall, Palom counted seventeen dragon eggs—or what was left of them. Most of the shells were cracked open, some with large holes where hatchlings had presumably escaped.

'The dragon's last clutch?' Solvi asked, reaching out to brush the eggs with her fingers. 'Were the Varkain looking for eggs? Doing something with them? These are old, hatched years ago...'

'Maybe...' Palom knelt in the soil and looked over the nest. He had no idea if the Varkain had been after eggs or were here for some other sinister purpose.

'Palom! There's one still whole!' Solvi gasped.

He followed her finger. 'It did not hatch...'

'Why not?'

He shrugged. 'Many reasons why young do not survive.' He leaned forward to caress the egg with one hand, its roughness coarse against his palms. Though his *Valta Forinja* lay on the ground a few feet away, its energy rippled through him again.

Palom focussed on the egg, his world shrinking to a growing idea. He licked his lips and plucked the egg from its spot in the soil.

'Palom? What are you doing? You can't take it!'

'Why not? There is no dragon. It is dead. If Varkain are wanting it, I will keep it from them.'

He sat down, cradling the egg in his hand, and released his power from the *Valta Forinja*.

It flickered again, once, before the light disappeared, plunging them in the darkness of the cave. He took several shuddering breaths as the sudden return of his strength hit him.

Palom held the egg close, felt it hum in his hands, similar to his sword. Aciel had messed with dragons once before, and now Linaria was suffering their wrath.

He did not want to anger them further.

Chapter Eleven

Isa stalked away from the palace, angered by her half-brothers. Sapora was aggressive. Tacio was arrogant. Both were far too controlling.

Neither had her best interests at heart, it seemed, and she doubted they wanted the best for Val Sharis, either.

Sapora, she could deal with. He'd been there for her as much as he could throughout his errantry. Certainly more than their father ever had been. Sapora was the only one who'd seen her for what she was—a queen worthy of respect.

She knew he and Tacio were capable of horrific acts, of violence and killing. They were necessary, most of the time. But today, she had the feeling that *she* was just as much a pawn in their plans as Koraki, or Voulhrik, or the Imperial Guard, or anyone else in the service of the palace.

It had been just over a week since Sapora and Tacio arrived in Taban Yul with an entourage of Varkain, and while Sapora had made a number of changes, none of them were what she'd thought they'd be.

She bit her thumbnail as she wandered across the palace grounds to the surrounding wall, leaving footprints in the snow.

She trusted Sapora.

He wasn't like the other Varkain.

He'd never been like *them*.

Perhaps he spoke truthfully, that his plans really would take more time to implement. He still didn't have a new council, after all.

Releasing Mateli, though? That was a step too far.

Palom had been an ally to her, had taken part in the funeral procession, and given back to her city. To set the old War Chief on him didn't seem right.

If she was quick…She might be able to stop him before he left Taban Yul.

Isa clambered up the wall surrounding the palace and stood beside one of the many golden statues—this one an elephant—taking a moment to survey the alley below. Satisfied, she dropped from the wall and landed in the shadow of the palace. It was one of her favourite shortcuts—she could scale the wall and council tower in less than a minute if she really put her mind to it, and the return route dropped her just north of the heaviest tourist spot in the whole city.

East Cross was a maze of taverns and shops—not the fine wares you'd find in Trader's Alley—this was cheap garbage sold for great expense, mostly to tourists from Corhaven, but Isa loved the fact you could get lost in the crowds here at any time of day.

Never quite accepted and never quite shunned, Isa had lived half-in, half-out of high society all her life. It was supposed to change with Sapora's rule, but, if anything, things had got even worse.

Now he had dissolved the council, any "friends" she'd had had been forced out of the palace. People she would spend time with, confide in, or even enjoy the company of, were no longer there.

Several moved into the city's richer districts, but most went to live with friends and relatives elsewhere in Val Sharis, no doubt waiting for the Varkain King to grow weary of the surface and return to his tunnels in Sereth.

Isa didn't believe that was ever going to happen, and she knew Sapora better than anyone else in all Linaria.

It was funny, she'd not slept in her palace rooms for several moons—she much preferred to sleep outside under the stars. Isa seemed to be every bit the commoner the other Goldstones said she was.

She'd always been light on her feet, a trait that strengthened when she came of age and could tap in to her *meraki*, and she used it to full effect when travelling through the city. She slipped in between crowds and shadows, moving purposefully, quietly, listening all the while.

Isa made her way south using smaller paths and side streets, taking the most direct approach to cut through the snow-covered city.

Following the fire in Trader's alley, Taban Yul's East Gate had been sealed off to enable repairs.

The North Gate had been sealed since the battle with Aciel and was guarded night and day. Isa realised that Mateli would need to leave by the city's South Gate, and she hurried to catch him before he got out.

What exactly she'd say to him, she didn't know—the man scared her more than anything she could remember—but she couldn't stand the idea of him loose in Val Sharis, hunting one of her few remaining allies.

A shrill, piercing cry carried from the sky, and Isa looked up. Her heart sank a little at the lack of dragons. They'd once been a common sight, but after Aciel had stirred up everything, she couldn't remember the last time she'd seen one.

There were plenty of birds in the sky: a mixture of wild and Ittallan—including a black eagle that soared high above, no doubt the one who'd made the noise.

Sometimes she wished she had wings.

How easy life must be when you could just fly away?

Isa continued on, crossing over a bridge of semi-frozen water into the southern part of Taban Yul.

Ittallan and Varkain—now many of them had moved in—huddled in thick furs as they went about their business. It wouldn't be long until it was dark, and then the cold really would set in. She kept eyes on where she was travelling for the most part, but occasionally chanced a look at someone who stood nearby or walked through a shop door and out onto the street.

A small group of elderly Ittallan sat hunched around a table outside a tavern smoking pipes and the smell of hot sausage pie wafted across the street. She licked her lips as she passed, suddenly thinking to her empty stomach.

'Dirty people.'

Isa narrowed her eyes. A woman had spoken—spat, really—in her direction. She stopped and looked back.

Of the four Ittallan seated, three rocked where they sat. They all muttered to themselves, but the old woman's voice carried louder than her companions. 'Horrid. Dirty. Kill them. Kill them all.'

Now she had Isa's attention. She thought to the nearest patrol of Imperial Guard, how quickly she could rally them. But as she watched, the old woman turned to her companion and struck him with a fist.

The thin man didn't make a sound as he toppled from his seat, landing with a thud on the snowy streets. Blood trickled from his temple, tinging the snow pink, and still he said nothing.

'What…?' Isa muttered, her eyes drawn to the old woman who carried on her tirade of abuse.

'How dare they. How *dare* they!'

Isa's skin prickled in the way it did when she was being watched, but the quiet street seemed deserted save the group of Ittallan.

She carried a knife on her at all times, though she rarely needed it, but the woman's actions and voice were so unnerving that she fumbled to grab it, just in case. 'Excuse me?' Isa called out in an attempt to get the woman's attention, but her call went ignored.

'Ugh. *My* city. Full of…full of…poison…'

Isa approached cautiously, glancing to the woman's companions, who didn't move or speak. 'What's full of poison? Taban Yul?'

The arrival of so many Varkain so quickly had infuriated a lot of the resident Ittallan. Sapora's rule and changes had not been met with welcome. "Poison" was often used as a derogatory term.

Was she another conspirator?

Tacio wanted them all rounded up and killed or sent back to Sereth as fresh thralls. Sapora, thankfully, had stopped that. But it was hard to rule a city full of people who hated you.

The woman didn't seem to hear Isa, or simply ignored her question. She carried on rocking where she sat, her hands shaking violently as though she were on the brink of having a fit.

'Kill the poison…Cleanse the world…'

Concern replaced curiosity. Perhaps the woman had a fever. 'Are you okay?' Isa asked and reached out with her free hand to touch the woman's forehead. The moment her skin touched the woman's, electricity burst through her. Blinding pain surged across her skin, crippling her.

'Isa…'

A voice in her mind, a central point around which the pain revolved. An intense cold washed over her, filling her up. It drove the electricity out and felt as though she'd jumped into a frozen lake.

'Isa,' the voice repeated, irritation edging its tone.

She bared her fangs and closed her eyes. Her hand still rested upon the woman's forehead, but her body had been locked into place as if held by an invisible force.

'Isa.' The voice boomed this time.

A command.

A demand of her attention.

The echo of her name floated around her mind, the voice expecting an answer.

She refused to respond.

She was a princess.

No—she was a *queen*.

She obeyed no-one.

Isa forced her eyes open and found herself staring into the blank face of the old woman. Her mouth slightly agape, wispy hair blowing in the breeze, she looked minutes from death. Her eyes stared into nothing, and that terrified Isa more than the disembodied voice.

She strained to pull her hand away from the old woman's skin. She heard her name again but continued to ignore it. With a cry, she finally ripped her hand from the old woman and leapt back several feet.

Panting, she doubled over, her knife forgotten on the ground near the table. Whatever dark magic had claimed the old woman, Isa wanted no part in it. She shook, the remnants of her name's echo fading from her mind.

The woman's comrades certainly seemed to be under a similar spell, though perhaps not as advanced as hers. Whoever found it amusing to curse the vulnerable in the middle of winter needed imprisonment.

Perhaps she'd be able to get Mateli locked up again alongside whoever had done this to the people in her city.

A little shaken, Isa noted the street name and turned around, hurrying further south, kicking up snow as she ran. She needed to report the curse to someone in the Guard she trusted—but she couldn't risk losing Mateli. The curse could wait.

She had to stop Mateli now, before he left Taban Yul.

*

South Gate loomed ahead: a wide archway built into the taller inner wall of Taban Yul which stretched to the outer wall built thirty feet further out.

A gleaming showcase of marble and jewels, the city's entrances and exits displayed the wealth of the Ittallan. Other than the palace itself, the four city gates were marvels of architecture, manned by sets of four guards on either side of both walls. The bailey in between them was busy all year round—large stables to hold traveller's horses, barracks to house the Guard on rotation, and kitchens to feed everyone passing through.

Isa had spent much of her youth here—never leaving the confines of the city, and yet not cooped up in the palace, and was on speaking terms with almost every worker here, in the Guard or otherwise.

Or, at least she had been, until Sapora began replacing them with Varkain of his choosing.

Varkain who looked down on her as they did any Ittallan.

With Mateli's reputation, however, she didn't need to talk to the Guard to know whether or not he'd passed through. She simply needed to be patient and listen. Residents and workers of Taban Yul, or travellers from Val Sharis and beyond, would not miss the opportunity to gossip about the great Mateli passing by.

The walls surrounding Taban Yul were far taller than those around the palace, and she could not easily scale them. If she wanted to get in to the bailey, she had to do it the old-fashioned way.

Two members of the Imperial Guard stood on either side of the first archway, resplendent in gleaming golden armour.

Three were Varkain.

She sighed and produced a small onyx stone from her pocket, holding it up to them so they could see what insignia it bore.

'Ah, the cat princess!' One Varkain hissed, gleeful. 'Where are you off to, little kitten?'

Isa raised an eyebrow, screaming internally but maintaining passive composure on her face. She didn't want to give him the satisfaction. Years of weathering this type of condescension had given her a vast amount of patience to deal with it.

'Who is some snake to ask the business of royalty?'

'None at all,' he said, still cheerful. 'Only the great King Sapora has asked to be informed should you leave the city. I'd like to give him a valid reason rather than explain how secretive you were about it.'

Isa didn't believe that for a second. Sapora might have been controlling, but he had bigger things to worry about than how and where she spent her time. She shifted her weight and looked the Varkain straight in the eyes. 'My movements are none of his business either.'

Snickering, the Varkain looked at each other.

Isa had to put a stop to their behaviour. 'I think my brother would be more annoyed with some low-life snakes preventing me from doing as I wish. We are both *very* good at replacing people. You're only where you are because your predecessor met an unfortunate end during the winter ball. You aren't immune from our fangs.' She didn't smile when she spoke, didn't give them the satisfaction of knowing they got under her skin. 'Now, get out of my way.'

Their snickering stopped, replaced by a scowl that could have stripped bark from a tree.

'Run along then, kitty. We're watching you.'

Isa walked past them to the open gateway. 'And if you ever address me as that again,' she said, pausing. 'I'll make sure you never see your precious tunnels again.'

*

Isa combed through her hair with her fingers as she wandered through the bailey, watching movement but not really seeing people.

The voice from earlier sounded in her head every few seconds, and she struggled to squash it. She had more pressing business and needed to keep an ear out to ensure she was on the right track.

It didn't take long for her assumptions to ring true.

'…I tried to tell him the gate was shut, but you know what he's like! Shoved me out of the way. Bruised my shoulder!'

Isa darted behind a granary, watching a stable boy pull his arm through his shirt, so the gathered crowd could see his purpling skin.

'I only heard 'bout him from stories. But my mam kept a poster of his that I've seen at home and it's him! He's got a beard now but it's Mateli for sure.'

'Shut it lad. If Mateli got out the city'd be in uproar. Get back to feedin' the horses,' the stable master growled. 'No more silly stories fer turnin' up late fer work!'

'But it's not a story! It was Mateli. It was! I swear on Rhea herself!'

'I've had it! One more word and I'll dock your pay, lad.'

Isa kept still, hidden behind the granary opposite the stable hands. 'The gate was shut…' she repeated.

Dragons above, was Mateli going to force his way through East Gate?

She raced towards the stables and jumped, landing on the roof smoothly. She transformed in a flash, her wild cat form large and sleek, a coiled mass of muscle designed to jump and climb.

Isa leapt from building to building, gaining height until in one huge leap, she crested the outer wall of Taban Yul and landed upon it.

The wind at such a height caught her, ruffling her fur and whiskers, but she had no time to lose. She immediately raced along the top of the wall, hurrying to East Gate as quickly as her body allowed.

Trader's Alley had always been a recognisable part of the city. The hexagonal blue towers at the street's head rose above the drab buildings, a clear landmark below.

Isa powered along, extending her legs in between leaps, half-running, half-jumping along the wall. When East Gate came into sight, she turned and leapt across to the inner wall.

Panting, she stalked along the wall and looked straight down into the streets and alleys below. So close to the sealed East Gate, the streets were deserted. Isa had an excellent view from above, and it didn't take long before she spotted him.

Mateli.

He marched towards East Gate, following a maze of narrow alleys in a confident stride.

Isa hesitated. He wouldn't have seen her from this distance—not that he could do anything to get to her even if he had—but seeing the famed criminal in broad daylight, especially after her encounter with the old Ittallan and the Varkain at South Gate, Isa was far less sure of herself than she'd been that morning.

But if she didn't do anything, he'd kill Palom.

What kind of ally would she be if she let such a monster out of her city?

She had to do something. Had to.

Isa looked around again, but the streets were quiet, and only a handful of birds soared overhead.

It was now or never.

Bracing herself, she clambered over the edge of the wall, sliding down the smooth, marble side and then pushing off to land on the wide street a few paces in front of the sealed gate.

She transformed as she landed and took in a deep breath, waiting for him to reach her.

When he stepped out from the shadows, it looked as if he'd never left them—an aura of darkness followed his every step.

'Mateli. I can hardly believe it's you.' She said, pleased her voice didn't shake.

At seven feet tall, he rivalled Palom in height, but carried more weight in his shoulders and chest, with loose jowls and filthy, matted black hair and beard. His ashen skin seemed to repel sunlight, and he stank of stagnant water and grime.

Isa swallowed, wishing she had her knife, though she knew it would do little against someone like him.

'East Gate is closed. You can't come this way.' She relaxed her hands, let them dangle at her sides.

Mateli grunted, the noise a kind of growl. He waited on the road, watching her, his bulk blocking her view.

'Turn around, Mateli. There must've been some mix up with paperwork. You shouldn't be out for another fifty years.'

He smiled at that. Just the corner of his lips. 'You're the Kitten Princess? Tacio released me himself. Gave me money.'

Isa exhaled slowly, calming herself, controlling her breathing. She wouldn't be intimidated or patronised.

'I'm tracking the tiger. He's been murderin'. Snakes want him dead.' His grin deepened, and Isa saw something very reptilian in his expression. 'I'm doin' what I been told ta do.'

'You won't be doing any of that. Palom is an ally of mine, and Tacio doesn't hold any authority here.' A white lie. 'Do I need the Guard to round you up again or are you going to go back willingly?'

He grunted again, taking a few steps forward and leering at her, his stench growing stronger.

Foolish.

Why hadn't she brought the Guard with her in the first place?

'I ain't goin' nowhere little cat. I'll eat you for me supper and then I'll take on Palom.' He wiped drool from his lips and let his mouth hang open a fraction, his breath coming out as a low hiss that sent shivers up her spine.

Isa pulled her onyx stone from her pocket and held it out to him. 'This grants me anything I wish in Taban Yul. Anything. Anyone.' Pulling rank was her last chance to avoid bloodshed. 'I want you to go back where you belong, Mateli. Things have changed since you were free to roam the city. I am a queen. Disobey me, and your punishment will be worse than what you just escaped.'

'I didn't get a meal before I left. Not eaten in three days. I'm 'ungry, and you're definitely the nicest looking thing ta eat 'round here.' His fangs poked out over his lips as he rolled up his sleeves.

'Don't even think about attacking me!' She snapped, forcing as much determination into her voice as she could, desperately thinking to how Sapora, or even Tacio, would deal with someone like Mateli.

'Too late.' He approached slowly, stalking towards her, raw strength rolling off him with every step, until he towered above Isa.

There was no way she'd be able to beat him in a brawl.

He sniffed deeply, savouring what he smelled. 'Any last words, little cat?' His fetid breath washed over her.

Isa reacted on reflex, slamming her left elbow into his throat as he bent down to her. Her aggression seemed to catch him off guard, and she smashed her opposite palm up into his nose with as much strength as she could muster.

The satisfying crunch of cartilage breaking, and the subsequent spout of blood made Mateli stumble, and he dropped to one knee, his hands covering his face.

She should have run, then. Got away before Mateli could hurt her. But she needed to bring him back to the palace, otherwise Palom would suffer.

She stepped back, her breath coming in short gasps, unwilling to flee despite her instincts screaming at her to get away from him. 'You're coming with me now. Do as I say, and I'll save you from getting executed for attacking me.'

Mateli groaned, his body heaving. He lowered his hands and looked at his palms, snarling at the sight. 'You…'

'On your feet, Mateli. We're going back to the palace.' She turned around to lead him up the road.

Isa hadn't taken a single step when something wet grabbed her left arm and yanked her to the ground.

'You bitch!' Mateli roared, spittle flying in his fury, his blood-soaked hands suddenly on Isa's throat. 'I'll kill you!'

Air cut off, Isa raised her hands to claw at his, scrambling desperately to get out of his grasp, tears streaming out of the corners of her eyes.

As he squeezed, Mateli's fangs grew longer, dark eyes shimmering to a dull greenish-yellow, his transformation slow and laboured. His hiss shifted into a deep bellow that shook the ground. 'And then…I'm going ta eat you.'

Adrenaline fuelled her panic, and Isa thrashed around, trying to wrench her body away from him, heart hammering in her chest.

He leaned close, the stench of stagnant water masking everything else, even the fresh blood dripping down his face. With a growl unlike anything she'd ever heard, he opened his mouth and bit deep into her left hand.

Isa screamed, high and chilling, the pain terrifying her.

She couldn't move.

Couldn't get away.

'Ugh. You're a dirty snake.' Mateli spat out the mouthful of flesh he'd gouged from her hand and threw her to the ground in disgust.

She cracked her head and back on the stone road, stars dancing in her vision.

'You can rot here instead. I got a bigger cat ta hunt.'

Isa's whole body shuddered, overwhelmed by shock, adrenaline, and deep, burning pain. She watched as he marched away, heard the splintering of wood as he forced his way through the sealed gate, and passed out.

Chapter Twelve

Palom sat on the floor of his room and stared at the dragon egg. A fire burned in the hearth, and his sword rested against the wall beside it, sucking in flames every few seconds. He'd bundled the egg in one of his boots and raced back to the Waterside Inn barefoot.

He'd glared at Chryo with such force that the young captain had stopped in his tracks, and Palom had retired to his room unquestioned.

When safely away from prying eyes, he'd decided to do the only thing that made sense: he placed the egg in the hearth and withdrew his fingers as the flames licked his skin. Having spent most of his life as a blacksmith, he was no stranger to burns from his forge, but the sting was still painful.

He didn't know if it was even possible to rekindle the life within an abandoned dragon egg. But equally, he didn't want to leave it if he had the chance to save it.

For all the foreign magic now in his life, he knew the deaths of dragons would only cause more trouble. Perhaps saving the life of one dragon would redeem some of his failings?

The thought gave him hope; the smallest sliver of it.

For a long while, he watched the fire burn around the egg, licking at each of the scales, one question lingering in his mind: what were the Varkain doing in that cave? Had they been after dragon eggs?

He had to warn Feoras Sol.

Getting to his feet, he grabbed his *Valta Forinja* and sheathed it behind his back.

Lathri was right, he should have returned home as soon as Aciel's battle was over.

He owed his father an explanation, if nothing else.

*

The path to Sol was familiar, and yet strangely different. It had been the better part of twenty years since he'd last set foot in his village. His mother had been alive, then. '*Matera…*' He whispered as he passed under the shadow of the trees, dragging his feet a little to prolong his return.

Solvi's initial reaction had not faded from memory; surely the rest of the village would respond to his presence in kind?

The afternoon was late before he sighted the village outposts; platforms built high into the trees where scouts could watch for approaching danger.

A high, wooden fence ringed Feoras Sol itself. It served as a marker more than a defensive barrier.

Sol nestled deep within the Rio Neva forest, tucked up almost to the mountains themselves; the eastern-most settlement in Val Sharis, only a stone's throw from the Sereth border.

His sword thrummed on his back, sending waves of warmth and energy coursing through him. Palom took strength from it and straightened his stance as he approached the open gates to Feoras Sol for the first time in two decades.

He never once believed he'd return, not after all these years.

Unsurprisingly, it was Solvi who came to greet him. Three of the five *Archigo*—elders—of the village accompanied her, wearing vivid blue robes and silver torcs around their necks to mark their rank.

Palom bowed his head as Solvi reached him. She took his cheeks in her hand and raised his head. '*Kali*...Palom...I didn't think you'd come.'

'I must speak with *Archigo*. And...Manilo.' Palom said, glancing past her to the three who stood in front of the tall gates. Already several Ittallan had gathered to see the new arrival, their faces familiar.

Solvi withdrew her hand. 'You haven't forgotten us.'

'Of course not! How could I forget? This is home. I remember it every day!' Palom said.

'You have always been welcome here, Palom. Since the day you left.'

Solvi stepped to the side so Palom could see the three *Archigo*.

The one who spoke was the oldest by far: his back stooped and his hair thinned to almost full baldness, though he wore a long, grey beard flecked with white that reached almost to his knees.

Palom asked, switching into his native tongue to mirror that which the *Archigo* spoke. '*Archigo* Saltos. You are kind. I left in *emonos*. How can I return anything else?'

'You were not banished nor shunned from our gates. You left with the raw emotion of a man who lost his brother. You blame yourself and refused comfort from those who needed you most.' Saltos gestured to Solvi. 'She has grown up with her *pali* and *mali* and has done well. But she needed you. *We* needed you.'

'No-one could go after you! You'd got into a vendetta against Mateli, and then we lost you in Taban Yul!' One of the *Archigo* said—a woman with snow white hair, her green eyes hard.

'Then we hear your *meraki* flourished and bestowed you the strength of the tiger.' Saltos' brown eyes flashed yellow for a moment, a flicker of colour brightening his wrinkled face. 'Surely you would have joined the Imperial Guard.'

'Please, *Archigo*. May I enter Sol? May I see Manilo?' Palom said, trembling at their words. He had no desire to recount those early months after Sol.

Back then, nothing could ease the pain and grief. Fighting dulled it, and he regretted getting himself mixed up with Mateli, but nothing could ease it completely.

Until he'd met Lathri.

'As *Archigo* Saltos said, you have been free to come home as you desire, Palom. For all your fears, you return home a hero.' The third elder said, a man several years younger than Saltos, whose beard still held the colour of auburn.

He swirled his robes as he turned around and announced to the gathered crowd, ‘Feoras Sol welcomes home our strength, our tiger! The hero against Aciel! Manilo-son Palom!’

There couldn’t have been more than thirty villagers gathered, but the roar they made at the *Archigo’s* words must have been heard all the way in Taban Yul.

Palom cringed, and then allowed himself to smile.

All the fuss he’d escaped from Chyro and the inn appeared to be tenfold at Sol.

Never in his wildest dreams had he thought he’d be *welcomed* back to Feoras Sol.

They’d hated him.

Hated him for causing his brother’s death, hating him for running away, hated him for all the death he caused and mistakes he’d made wherever he went.

Hated him for being a failure.

Or so he’d assumed.

‘Manilo has waited so many years to see you again,’ *Archigo* Saltos said, his eyes wet with emotion. ‘Come with me and I shall take you to him.’

Palom followed without question, wishing he’d brought a gift of some kind to ensure he remained in his father’s good graces.

Manilo had been a loving father with a firm hand. He’d raised two sons and lost both when they’d been on the cusp of adulthood, and his wife soon after that.

Palom felt sick with fear at the shame he’d caused him.

To hear that after all this time, he'd missed him, still loved him, wanted him to come home?

His sword responded to his emotions; almost buzzing with power, and Palom ignored it as much as he could.

Familiar sounds and smells cascaded over him as he walked along the winding path through the village. Buildings had grown extensions, or been knocked down and rebuilt completely, the trees had grown taller, the pathways a little more worn.

Red seemed to dust everything—path or building—and the scent of iron carried thick in the air.

Home.

Palom was becoming used to the soft footsteps of Solvi as she trailed him, and more Ittallan joined her as he walked beside *Archigo* Saltos.

These Ittallan didn't care so much about his fight against Aciel, or that he'd forged *Valta Forinja.*

They were just happy to have a son of the village back.

Towards Sol's northern side, a row of single-storey stone houses huddled together, joined in a central, communal space where the families could meet.

Where he'd grown up.

Memories of playing in the courtyard in front of the houses flashed in his mind; of hot, humid summers chasing other children around, climbing up buildings, and digging in the woods for undiscovered treasure.

How he wished he could turn back time.

Manilo emerged from the stone house on the end, his face world-weary and much, much older than he remembered. He wore a torc of silver above teal robes lined with yellow.

Palom's world stilled, he couldn't look anywhere, move anywhere, his whole attention locked on his father's eyes.

Manilo's features were suspended between surprise, confusion, and joy.

Palom breathed, his body relaxing, and he ran across the courtyard and into his father's arms.

'My son…' Manilo said between sobs. 'You…you've come back! You've come home to me!' His voice choked with disbelief.

Palom felt his father's frailness underneath his heavy robes, felt brittle bones and lost muscle. He loosened his embrace to avoid injuring. '*Pali…*'

'Palom…'

'I am so, so sorry for leaving you. Leaving *mali*. I should never have left, never have abandoned the family.' His words came out in a rush, blurted out as he thought them. 'I have wanted to come home so badly for so long. I was afraid you'd hate me. You'd all hate me. The *Archigos*, everyone. I was afraid…I couldn't stop him dying, *pali*. I wasn't strong enough to save him.'

Tears fell now, real tears, not what Lathri drew from him when they touched. He didn't care that they stood on his father's porch in view of the rest of the village. 'I have wished so many times that I'd died instead of him. He had little Solvi to look after. He was the strong one, the clever one, the brave one.'

'Hush, hush,' Manilo said, shaking his head. 'We've all done things we regret. You cannot live with such guilt in your heart for your whole life!'

'*Pali*, please forgive me. I should have been there for you. For *mali*. For Solvi...'

'My son...'

Palom shook, his words halted. His father's dark mane of hair had receded, grey streaking through it, but he still held a fierceness in his eyes that Palom admired. 'I didn't know...any other way.'

'You were very young. Fifteen? Sixteen?' Manilo said, stepping back, arms on Palom's shoulders, as he looked him up and down. 'I thought you hated me.'

Palom blinked, shocked. 'Why? You hadn't done anything?'

'I thought I must have done something terrible for you to leave. Without saying why. You left little Solvi. She was a baby, Palom. Your brother's little girl!'

Anxiety built in his stomach. He'd hurt Manilo more than he'd realised.

'I...I'm sorry...' Palom repeated, dropping his gaze.

'It was wrong of you to abandon your family, your duty. I can't forgive you for doing that. But I understand why you did what you did. You saw no other way,' Manilo said. 'You should have come to the *Archigos*. Come to me. We would have helped you through it. We needed you.'

Palom shuddered, his voice gone.

All this time, he'd been so wrong about everything.

His desire to make up for failing his brother and Solvi had lent itself to a desire to protect those around him.

Lathri.

Anahrik.

Eryn.

Moroda.

'Come inside,' Manilo said, stepping back and opening his arms. 'There is so much I wish to know, of your life outside Sol—outside Val Sharis. Tell me everything.'

*

Several deer roasted on a spit, the wind blowing embers into the air. Palom sat on a thin rug in the courtyard—which had been cleared for their meal—Solvi on his left side, Manilo on his right. Others from Sol sat with them, including the three *Archigo*, and Jek, of all people.

The racoon had thanked him profusely again for his help on the road, and Palom had been pleased when the *Archigo* had taken him to one side for more questions and catching up.

From what Palom understood, most of them wanted to enjoy the wealth they expected came from the hero of Val Sharis in their village. They'd asked about his relationship with the princess, and whether or not some of the crown's gold could be directed to Sol—particularly now times were lean.

Palom had shrugged, unable to give any guarantees, which hadn't been to their satisfaction. Manilo had saved him from further embarrassment—those matters could be discussed another day.

Now was the time for celebrating his son's return, and the deer had been hunted, brought back, and skinned ready for a feast.

Mixed emotions flooded him. Relief that he'd not immediately been cast out, happiness at seeing his father again, anger for not realising his mistakes sooner.

He contemplated his past and the emotions he'd associated with his perceived failures, weighing up which were real, and which were mistakes. Palom ended up spending most of the evening sat in silence, listening to the talk around him, only picking at his food.

With so many years to catch up on, Palom wanted to savour the moment by simply observing, listening, and enjoying the warmth and familiarity of home.

'How is Taban Yul?' *Archigo* Saltos asked, tearing at a strip of venison between his hands. 'With the Varkain Sapora in charge?'

Palom thought. Clearly, he'd spent the better part of his life paranoid.

Claiming Sapora and his Varkain were up to something terrible seemed far-fetched now, even though Lathri had been the one to bring his attention to them.

He settled to explain what he knew from Lathri's allies. 'I have friends in Taban Yul who believe Sapora will bring ruin and devastation to the Ittallan. There are rumours of him doing something terrible.'

He stopped to drink from his mug.

Whether it was a case of snakes being snakes, or Sapora really was working up to unleash some ancient and terrible power over Val Sharis, he suddenly wasn't sure.

Manilo shook his head, taking another bite out of his venison leg. 'This is above us. Above Sol. Let the would-be kings and queens fight out their power struggles, if that's what they want. We've always been alone in Sol, always fended for ourselves. We don't get caught up in their plots. You did well to leave them in Taban Yul.'

Palom nodded, though he didn't agree.

'What is important to us— important to you—is the same as always. Family. Blood. Loyalty. Nothing else is our concern, it's how we've survived for so long, through civil wars and dragon attacks and the Arillian army.' Manilo said, and agreement rippled through the gathered Ittallan.

Palom sighed.

Sapora's plans would be bigger than Sol; surely the village should get involved at some point?

Perhaps when all of Val Sharis was threatened?

Or all of Linaria?

'Solvi ended up studying in Taban Yul, you know?' Manilo said, his voice rich with pride. 'Tell him. Tell him who you were with.'

Solvi blushed when Palom looked at her. 'Princess Isa…She's a few years older than me, but I saw her there. We studied in the same building. She had her guards of course, but she slipped away from them a lot of the time. Didn't realise we'd both be cats…'

'Wow.' Palom supposed that explained why she spoke the common tongue so well, where her confidence came from. Studying in the capital of Val Sharis was no mean feat. He beamed at her. 'That's amazing, Solvi.'

Her blush deepened. 'Thank you, *kali*.'

He raised his mug to her.

All this time, he'd missed everything. Missed his niece growing up, missed his father become an *Archigo*, missed his village—his home—grow and change.

Births.

Marriages.

Deaths.

How he wished he could have Lathri sat with him, wished she could see what he could be when he wasn't being so stupid.

The flames crackled merrily, and he stared into them, looking at the shapes they made as they danced and flickered. For once, his *Valta Forinja* was still.

Peaceful.

If only he'd had the courage to come back sooner.

He'd had so many chances, and he'd squandered them all until now.

'*Archigo*! A captain of the Guard!' The sudden cry snapped Palom's attention back as one of the village scouts raced over to them, kicking up snow.

The scout pulled a man alongside him—blood trickled down his face.

'Chryo!' Palom gasped.

The young captain's legs were soaked in red. Whatever wound he had looked to be deep.

'Get the healers at once!' Manilo's voice boomed as he strode over to the scout and Chryo. 'Take it easy. What happened? Who did this?'

Chryo's eyes rolled in panic, and Palom could see the whites from where he sat. The captain trembled like a leaf in his father's hands and shook his head over and over. 'The Waterside Inn…attacked…a…a crocodile…He slaughtered everyone.' Chryo's legs gave out under him, and he dropped—Manilo catching him as he fell. 'I barely escaped...He could be on his way…here…now! Get ready to fight…'

Palom was on his feet in an instant.

He didn't know of any crocodiles—none for a thousand leagues, at any rate. Except for….

Dragons above, it couldn't be Mateli…could it?

He'd been imprisoned years ago.

He couldn't be out.

Couldn't be.

The Valta Forinja shimmered, sending blue light crackling all around him, and thoughts of peace vanished.

If it had been Mateli…then the deaths of everyone in the Waterside Inn was on his head.

'*Archigo*. Lock Sol down. Everyone is to stay inside.'

He and Manilo nodded to one another, then Palom picked up his sword and followed Chyro's trail of blood through the trees.

Chapter Thirteen

Amarah's attempt to retrieve Kohl was met with little success. Jato's influence remained strong among the community of Oren villagers, and when the former General had requested not to be disturbed, even Amarah—the popular foreigner—hadn't been permitted entry. She had moved *Khanna* across the island to be closer to Jato's home, and therefore, Kohl.

Amarah waited for almost three days, before she reached the end of her patience. She'd learned a newfound respect for their culture and processes, and she'd never get bored of watching the Arillians fly around when they weren't throwing bolts of lightning at you. She even knew several by name.

The Arillians who lived close to Jato seemed as friendly and curious about her as the others, but when she'd pressed for details on how they or the Golems would be able to resurrect Moroda—trapped in the crystal of a Sevastos—they suddenly became distant and answered with vagueness.

Amarah hated being played for a fool.

‘What about Berel?’ She asked a male Arillian on the third day of waiting. ‘Magic is magic, ain’t it? Can’t you talk to the Samolen about your Golem magic? Work together to get Moroda free?’

‘Magic is not magic! Ours is ancient, without equal, and powered by the Everwinter. Samolen magic is dragon’s breath. Flame and destruction,’ he’d said, offended.

Unable to wield—or understand—either branch of magic, Amarah rolled her eyes. They claimed to be her friends, and yet were unwilling to lift a finger to help.

‘You Arillians are meant to be the sworn enemy of the mainland, aren’t ya?’ She said. ‘I’m here being friends. So what if we’re different? Can’t you do the same with the Samolen magic? I know one of the scholars. Topeko. You can trust him, work with him.’ She lifted the corners of her lips in the hope it looked like a genuine smile. ‘I don’t care whose magic I use, or how it’s done. I just want to free Moroda!’

The sniff she received in response put that idea to bed, and she folded her arms as he flew away, citing business he needed to attend to.

Why was it so damned hard to get a straight answer from any of the Arillians? What if they had a time limit and Moroda needed to be freed soon, or be lost forever?

Not to mention Sapora and whatever cargo he had heading to Taban Yul.

Bloody sorcery.

She glared at Jato's home as if it would somehow force the brat out, and she'd get a chance to talk to Kohl. Sitting around hidden from Sapora's wrath was all well and good, but Amarah had never been one to shy from challenge. Kohl might have been cowardly, but she wasn't.

In three days, she'd not seen Kohl—or Jato—leave her home once. What in Linaria could they be talking about for so long?

Amarah twirled her scythe, smacking the bottom of it against the icy rocks. If something didn't happen soon, the Arillians would have a front-row seat of the barbarous nature she and the other mainland Linarians supposedly had.

She'd put up with enough.

Things would get moving *now*, one way or another.

Amarah strode forward, past the enormous fire pit which sat in front of Jato's home and approached the huge tower of ice. It widened at its base, a large entrance carved into the rock almost ten feet off the ground.

'Kohl! I'm done waiting!' Amarah yelled as she reached the base of the tower. '*I* wanna talk now!' She slammed her scythe down again, the noise echoing across the tower.

No response.

A few Arillians flying near glanced in her direction, but otherwise ignored her.

'Fine, if that's how it's gonna be,' she muttered, grasping her scythe with both hands, the power within the blade building until her arms vibrated. She whirled it around, slashing at the air in front of the tower and sent a beam of blue energy crashing into the icy rock.

Several chunks of ice fell from the tower, falling to the ground and disintegrating into dust.

That would get their attention.

Amarah continued to twirl her scythe and waited.

Several Arillians swarmed near, many whispering, some yelling, at Amarah's sudden show of aggression, but she ignored them, her eyes only on the entrance to the former General's home.

She didn't have to wait long.

Kohl emerged, looking flustered, holding his hat in one hand and waving at Amarah with his other. 'What do you think you're doing?'

'Getting *my* audience with you, Kohl,' Amarah snapped. In her peripheral, more Arillians flew in. She ignored them all. 'Three days, I've been waiting. I ain't on holiday. I'm here to get Moroda out. If you can't do that, then I need to go.'

'Please, Amarah,' he said, landing by her in a flurry of freezing air. 'You can't start attacking people!'

'I'll do as I damn well please! I only knocked on the door.'

Kohl shook his head. 'This isn't like the rest of Linaria. You've been permitted here by the Golems! Don't squander that!'

'I'm getting what I came here for!' She snorted. 'Either give me your magic solution to get Moroda out, or if you can't do that, come with me to Berel. Maybe Topeko knows more than you damned birds. This is a waste of my time otherwise.'

'Amarah!' His eyes widened at the slur.

‘Or if you’d rather spent time with your brat, you can stay here, and I’ll go by myself. Your choice’

The gathered Arillians’ whispers turned to appalled muttering.

‘Well? What’s your answer?’ she snapped.

‘You can leave whenever you want. No-one’s making you stay here.’ The cool voice quietened the Arillians as Jato flew out of her tower, her dark brown wings stark against the white snow.

‘In fact, I think you’d be doing us a favour if you left and never came back.’

Amarah lifted her scythe and pointed it at Jato when she landed. ‘I wasn’t talking to you.’

Shock rippled through the crowd, and Jato glared at Amarah with cold, grey eyes.

‘Kohl. Are you able to help me or not?’ Amarah turned back to her companion, who looked the most flustered she’d ever seen him.

‘I’m sure we can help Moroda,’ he began.

‘Now?’ Amarah raised an eyebrow. ‘If not now, then I’m going. You coming?’

‘Amarah, I need a little more time. The Golems’ power isn’t as precise as the Samolen magic you know, and—’

‘I know where I’ve seen you before,’ Jato interrupted.

Amarah and Kohl turned to look at her.

The former General continued, ‘You were on my warship. With the snake and the girl…?’

Amarah rolled her tongue but didn’t bother to reply.

'I thought I recognised you…Your…scythe…You nearly killed Aciel!' Jato's voice pitched as the realisation hit her. She lifted her hands and immediately threw a bolt of lightning at Amarah.

Amarah brought her scythe up across her body, its power deflecting Jato's attack. 'You've got a shit memory if you only just realised who I am.'

Jato wasn't listening. She threw another bolt of lightning, then another, then another, the electricity crackling around her and melting the snow.

'Calm down!' Amarah yelled over the clap of thunder, pushed back as she deflected Jato's attacks.

'I can't believe you brought *her* here! To my doorstep!' Jato was screaming now, her electricity careening towards Kohl. 'After what she *did*!'

Amarah ran to her right, away from where *Khanna* sat, from the crowd of Arillians, and from Jato's tower. 'What *I* did?' She yelled. 'What about what you and Aciel did? How many people you killed, enslaved?'

Jato took to the air and flew after her.

'You loved Aciel, I get it—'

'Don't speak of him!' Jato screamed, sending another wave of electricity at her. The force almost blasted Amarah from her feet, but she gained her balance and stood firm, glaring up at her.

'We can't all get what we want, you spoiled brat!' Amarah goaded, holding her arms open as if to invite another attack. 'Looks like you're learnin' that the hard way!'

'Shut up!'

Amarah had already braced for the next blast, and her scythe kept her safe. She grinned, enjoying herself.

'You nearly killed him!' Jato shouted, gulping down lungfuls of air as she attempted to collect herself. 'If it hadn't been for you, he wouldn't have been sealed in that battle!' She flapped her wings to slow her descent, her hands pointing towards Amarah.

'And if it hadn't been for *you*, thousands would still be alive, and I wouldn't be here to put you back in your place!' Amarah flicked her scythe up, a wave of energy charging towards Jato.

Jato evaded the attack and landed, her sudden rage over.

'Nothin' to say to me?' Amarah asked, her weapon held tight, ready to use again.

Jato flicked her hair out of her eyes, all pretence of condescension gone. 'For what you did to my Aciel…I'm going to destroy you and I'll make sure there's nothing left.'

Amarah grinned, brandishing her scythe. 'Come on, then! I'm ready!'

Jato ignored her taunt, spreading her wings and holding her hands out wide, with fingers splayed. The island rumbled, and the wind picked up as Jato's storm built. Electricity sparked through the wall of wind, licking at the melting snow and heating everything to vapour.

Amarah waved her scythe again, but Jato's raging winds simply absorbed the energy. Around her, Arillians flew away, escaping Jato's storm as more and more of the island shuddered, the pressure shattering boulders nearby.

Amarah gulped.

'Jato! Please!' Kohl's voice was almost lost in the wind.

Amarah felt his frigid wind as he flew close, his cloak whipping around him as the wind shifted into a gale.

'Amarah, run! Please!'

'I'm not running from her!'

'Please,' Kohl pleaded. 'You can fight and brawl, but Jato served as a General. She'll annihilate you!'

Amarah slapped him away, trying to keep eyes on Jato. 'Go on. Fly away again. Abandon me like you abandoned Moroda and the others! Damned coward.'

Kohl shook his head, his hat lost in the violent winds. 'I still love her. She's still my daughter!'

A ball of lightning crashed into them, sending both Amarah and Kohl sprawling onto the bare rock.

Amarah staggered to her feet, and screamed, 'Jato! You see that? Your damned father still loves you, even though you're a brat! He doesn't want me to chop your head off!'

Jato swooped in, arms outstretched, and Amarah leapt to meet her, bringing her scythe up in a slash that caught Jato on her side.

'Stop, please! Both of you!' Kohl screamed above the wind.

But Amarah had fallen into the singularity of the fight—avoiding Jato's lightning attacks and attempting to get in a swipe of her own, when she could.

She danced back, leapt up, rolled out of the way. Jato absorbed or evaded most of her scythe's attacks, but the blade itself drew blood, and Amarah tried to get as close to Jato as she could.

She needed to clip those wings.

Suddenly, Kohl joined the fray—flying up between them and blasting the pair in opposite directions with his own wind.

Bracing against it, Amarah shivered as the freezing air rushed over her skin, shoving her away from Jato and halting her scythe's next attack.

'I said stop this!' He roared, cutting Jato's wind away and replacing it with his blizzard. 'Jato! Now!'

Jato whirled off, swooping away from his attacks, only to meet him in the sky again. Everywhere she went, he was there, blocking her path, keeping her away with a freezing gale that covered the bare rocks in ice.

'Get out of my way!' Jato shrieked, almost hysterical.

Kohl didn't reply, focussed only on preventing her from getting closer to Amarah.

'If you'd accepted Aciel to begin with, none of this would have happened!' Jato continued, hovering in the air and pointing at her father. 'Whose side are you on? You're no leader! Bringing that foreign snake here and protecting her!'

The two Arillians dropped out of the sky, both glaring at each other, neither willing to cede ground.

'The Golem's chose to let her in. I'm carrying out their will.' Kohl replied, his voice calm.

'Kohl, move, or I'll make you!' Amarah spat, trudging back towards them from where she'd been pushed away. 'I shouldn't have trusted you. Went against all my instincts! There's no magic here to get Moroda back, is there? You just used me as an excuse to get back and talk to *her*!' She pointed her weapon at Jato, and it shimmered blue.

'No!' Kohl said, turning to Amarah briefly.

'Get out of the way if you can't help Moroda!' Amarah sent another pulse of energy towards the Arillians, and Kohl deflected it away from Jato.

'I'm not going to hurt either of you! Stop this, now! You don't need to fight!' He tried again, desperate.

Kohl was becoming more of an annoyance than Jato.

Amarah flicked her scythe over and over, sending wave after wave of attacks at the pair of them.

She'd force his hand.

He'd fight back or move.

When she finally felt the freezing wind, she smiled. A reaction from the stoic Arillian.

'If I go down, I'm bringing you both with me!' Amarah yelled, but when she tried to lift her scythe in another attack, she couldn't.

Looking down at her weapon, Amarah cursed.

Kohl had encased the blade in ice, the weight too much for her to lift and wield.

'Argh! You bastard!' She kicked at the ice, sending a few shards flying, but unable to break her scythe free. 'So, that's it? Disarm me? Leave me defenceless for your brat to finish off?' She continued to kick at it, and chipped away at the hunk of ice.

‘That’s not it at all,’ he said, landing beside Jato. ‘I’m stopping this. Now. There’s no need for you to fight! We need to work together, not rip each other apart!’

‘How dare you stop me!’ Jato jerked away from Kohl and scowled at him. She summoned another ball of lightning and hurled it at Kohl, who deflected it easily.

‘Jato…’

She threw more balls of lightning at him, but none came close to harming Kohl as he stood, impassive, shielding himself from her attacks but making no move against her.

Jato snarled. ‘What a terrible father! You’re a weak, shameful Arillian! Aciel was right about you! Why couldn’t you stay in exile? Coming back here with a thief and the one who hurt Aciel! How much more shame do you want to bring to Oren? The ones you say you care for? The ones you say you love?’

Amarah watched as Kohl slowly bent to her words, submissive and afraid.

‘I do love you, Jato. Whatever happened before, whatever will happen now. That’s unconditional.’

He spoke softly, and Amarah had to strain to hear him over the wind and the crunching of ice as she worked to free her weapon. She couldn’t believe it. After all her vitriol, he still loved her, still stood by her?

‘Get away from me! Get out of my sight! I don’t want you anywhere near me!’ Jato screeched, hurling another bolt of lightning at him.

The attack must have been stronger than all her others, as Kohl raised his hands to defend himself from the resulting crash and was thrown back. Thunder filled the air, and Amarah's ears rang.

This was her chance.

Jato was so consumed with hurting Kohl, she'd stopped paying her any attention. Kicking away the last of the ice, she freed her scythe and charged forward, lunging at Jato blade-first.

The Arillian saw Amarah at the last minute and jumped into the air, but Amarah's blade caught her wings and sliced into the feathers.

Jato screamed, but Amarah didn't relent, and hacked away at Jato's wings in a frenzy. 'You. Ungrateful. Bitch.' She punctuated every attack. 'After everything you've done! Kohl still loves you!'

One wing fell to the ground in bloodied tatters.

'I would have given *anything* for a father who cared! For someone, anyone, who cared! And you throw it away? You! Spoiled! Brat!'

Amarah raised her scythe, her arms weak but fuelled on adrenaline. She brought her weapon down with both hands, and Jato screamed as she jumped out of the way.

The blade sliced into—and through—Jato's elbow, severing her forearm. 'Just like your lover,' Amarah hissed as blood poured. Her chest heaved, her fingers loose on her scythe.

Jato's scream turned into a snarl as she brought a knee up into Amarah's stomach.

Immediately winded, Amarah dropped her scythe, only to be knocked to the floor as Jato smacked her with her remaining hand.

Jato lunged, grabbing Amarah's hair and pulling her back up again.

'I said I'd destroy you!' Jato said, her voice weak and trembling.

She grabbed Amarah's face and squeezed tight, her index finger pressed hard against Amarah's forehead.

Still winded, Amarah could barely struggle as Jato's palm was replaced by bright, flickering light, and the unmistakable crackle of electricity whiting out her vision.

Chapter Fourteen

'Forgive me, princess.'

Isa didn't recognise his thin, scratchy voice. Didn't recognise his smell.

Why did she hurt so much?

She tried to move but didn't have the strength to even open her eyes. She gurgled in an attempt to speak, but her throat burned, and she couldn't form words with her lips.

'I know it hurts. Keep still, please.'

Who are you?

What happened to me? 'Urgh…'

'Don't try to move. I'm Aetos, by the way. You'll be safe soon. Mateli left you for dead.'

Mateli?

That name meant something…

Aware she was moving, but unable to open her eyes or work out where up or down was, Isa groaned again.

She couldn't focus, her mind flicked between dreams and darkness, and she hurt *so* much.

*

Warmth rushed over her, accompanied by a familiar crackle and spit.

A fire.

Isa opened her eyes and blinked rapidly. She saw a candle burning on the nightstand opposite, but she didn't recognise anything else—not the bed she'd been tucked into, nor the room she found herself in. The soft linens smelled fresh, and she wanted to close her eyes again and drift off to sleep. If she hadn't been in such a strange place, she probably would have.

Carefully, she lifted her head from the pillow she'd been resting on—full of goose down from the feel of it—and tried to get her bearings.

There was a distinct lack of gold and jewelled furniture, and the room was small and square.

Definitely not the palace—most rooms were circular there.

She smelled green tea brewing somewhere nearby, a comforting scent that reminded her of the palace kitchens.

The walls were rich mahogany, with heavy fabrics draped from the ceiling beams to cover most of the window. Through the gap, Isa saw night had fallen, and she gulped.

How long had she been asleep? What had happened?

Her left hand itched and when she moved to scratch it, she realised it had been bandaged.

'Gently, princess. You've been through a lot.'

Isa span on the bed to see a tall, blonde woman watching her from the corner of the room. 'Who are you?'

The woman dipped her head. 'I'm Lathri, a healer. You're in my home, in Little Yomal.'

Isa didn't recall her name or face, but she knew the residential district. At least she was still in Taban Yul.

She looked back through the window, trying to gather her thoughts and work out whether or not she was in danger. Lathri didn't *seem* threatening, but that didn't mean anything. 'How did I get here?

'One of my companions found you bleeding in the street and carried you here.'

Isa recalled the name. '…Aetos?' A man carrying her, telling her to keep still.

Lathri smiled. 'An eagle. He'd been watching you in case you got into trouble with Mateli.'

Isa glanced at her bandaged hand, the memory of her encounter coming back in bits and pieces. 'Mateli attacked me,' she muttered, more to herself than Lathri. Then she remembered seeing an eagle soaring overhead while she'd been stalking the criminal.

'Why are you watching me?' She stood, and dizziness washed over her, but she weathered it on shaky legs. Her bare toes stepped onto a plush rug and she found the sensation oddly comforting.

Isa relaxed a fraction, despite being in a stranger's domain. There was something bizarre about the woman with her pale skin and hair, and her orange-brown eyes that seemed to look through her.

Her throat still burned, and if there had been a mirror in the room, she had no doubt she'd see Mateli's fingerprints pressed into her neck.

She swallowed and immediately winced.

'How did you know about Mateli?' Isa asked, a little irritated she'd not received an answer to her first question.

Lathri studied her, as if weighing up whether or not she'd fall over, before glancing at the closed bedroom door. 'Voulhrik?'

Isa knew that name, too. From the palace.

One of the messengers?

The new Ittallan entered the room at Lathri's call. Isa had never paid him much attention before—she rarely took notice of the palace servants—but in the small room, she saw how broad he was, with wide shoulders, barrel chest, moustache, and dark, piercing eyes. He wore a hoop of gold in one ear and stooped so he did not hit the beamed ceiling. When he spotted Isa, he nodded stiffly.

'You're from the palace.' It was a statement, not a question.

He nodded again, eyes darting to Lathri, before returning to her.

'Why have you been watching me?' Why did she have to repeat herself so often? Getting answers seemed to be akin to getting blood from a stone.

'We were worried you were in danger,' Lathri answered, her voice as soft as silk.

Isa narrowed her eyes. 'Forgive my…suspicions…but I am sister to the king. What could I possibly be in danger from?'

Her throat hurt to talk, but she couldn't stand in silence. Not when she had so many burning questions.

Lathri's stared at Isa's hand. 'In the city right now…I think you're probably in the most danger of all. You'll forgive me for not speaking as freely as you might wish, but your brother's dislike of Ittallan is abundantly clear, and we've no desire to cause…a disturbance.'

'Dislike for the Ittallan? He's half one himself! As am I. There's no disturbance,' Isa said, tilting her head to one side.

'On the contrary, princess, there is quite the disturbance throughout the city,' Aetos said, entering the room and bowing to her.

Isa looked at each of them in turn, mind whirling.

Then it hit her. 'You're against Sapora, aren't you? You want to overthrow him. That's what this is, isn't it? A kidnapping?'

Lathri laughed and raised her hand. Isa's skin prickled for a moment, and then she immediately calmed. She shuddered, wondering where her panic had disappeared to.

'Nothing so sinister as that, princess,' Lathri said. 'We had the chance to help you, so we took it. But…we are all in agreement here that we would see *you* in power, rather than a Varkain.'

Isa struggled to follow. 'I am half-Varkain. The same as Sapora.'

'You're more Ittallan than he is. Your father might be a Varkain, but you're one of us. You've always been one of us.' Aetos said. 'You've lived here your whole life, you care about Taban Yul and the Ittallan who live here.'

'Of course,' Isa said, frowning.

'More than Sapora,' Lathri added. 'We want you to be our queen, and we're not the only ones who think that, I assure you.'

'What kind of king releases a terror like Mateli?' Voulhrik said, eyebrows raised.

'You took him on by yourself. That was brave,' Aetos said.

Isa scowled. 'More foolish than brave. I didn't stand a chance.'

'You tried. You saw what a threat he was, and you acted. I doubt Sapora knows what you did...?' Lathri asked.

Isa bit her thumbnail.

'Are you afraid of him?' She pressed.

'Yes. Who wouldn't be? I'm not a coward, but I'm not stupid, either. By Rhea's luck, I survived Mateli's attack.'

Memories of her struggle against the crocodile came flooding back in explicit detail now she was fully awake.

Isa shuddered.

She'd need a long, hot bath to clear his stench from her mind.

'You put yourself in danger for the good of the city,' Lathri continued. 'Aetos did the same, when he rescued you.'

Isa didn't reply for a long while. None of them seemed to be dangerous. They'd also told her what they wanted, and it was certainly along similar lines to what she herself strove for.

But how?

Lathri blinked slowly, watching her every movement.

Isa wasn't sure she liked being observed to that level of detail; there was something about Lathri's gaze that made her feel like the healer was able to look right into her soul.

'If you're asking me to betray my brothers, you're mistaken. I appreciate the support—and help—but the situation is what it is,' Isa said at last. 'I know that...if not for you, I'd have died alone on that road.' She nodded to Aetos. 'I won't tell them where you are...but I'm not going to help you, either. You're asking me to betray my family.'

Aetos's shoulders sank, and even Voulhrik looked uneasy.

Good. They knew she still held the power.

They glanced to Lathri, clearly in charge of the group, and Isa took a few steps forward, walking around the bed.

She slipped into her boots and stood by the small hearth, above which a teapot warmed. 'So long as you don't commit treason against my brothers, you're safe to continue to work in the palace, Voulhrik,' she said. 'You have my word. I'm not the cruel dictator that Sapora seems to be. You saved my life. You think the same as me. That means something. But I'm going to leave now...You won't stop me?'

'It's your city, princess. You can go wherever you wish. Might I take those bandages back?' Lathri asked.

Isa lifted her hands and allowed the healer to unbind them. Slowly, as each layer of fabric pulled away from her skin, Isa's fingers tingled. When her hand was freed, she gasped. Several small scars lined the back of her left hand—from Mateli's fangs—all of which had healed. Her skin wasn't even pink and puffy.

‘How…?’

‘I’m a good healer, princess. You know where we are, if you’d like to talk.’

A little unnerved, Isa backed out of the room to find herself in a lounge. Another Ittallan woman sat on the sofa, a hunter, with a striking resemblance to Aetos.

The woman nodded to her, and Isa hurried out of the front door, trying to think what she’d say to Sapora or Tacio if either of them spoke to her before she reached her rooms in the palace.

*

‘Mistake to trust that one. You brought her to your *house*?’ Kylos said, staring at the closed door as if Isa would charge back inside at any moment.

Lathri sat next to her and brushed down her sleeves. ‘Isa fears Sapora. Probably Tacio too. She just disobeyed their orders by going after Mateli. She won’t tell them our location.’

‘Why not? She could try and get back in their good graces by ratting us out.’ Kylos said, turning to face Lathri. ‘We need to be ready for a Varkain attack.’

‘We’ll be safe.’

Kylos huffed and looked to Aetos and Voulhrik.

‘When have I let you down before?’ Lathri asked.

‘I just think *your* claim to the throne is better than some half-breed who could leave us in the same situation as Sapora. Or worse!’ Kylos said, getting up to walk to Lathri’s balcony.

Lathri sighed.

She'd had this conversation with Kylos too many times, and it still hurt. The memories were still too fresh: the beautiful food, music, and gowns of the winter ball.

And the dancing, of course.

Oh, the dancing had been wonderful.

She'd watched her mother take her seat at the council table between the two leaders, Keros the Treasurer, and Elafion the War Chief.

Lathri had been so thrilled to see all six of the Council together after such a turbulent year with Arillians and devastation—supported by prince and princess.

The swan, Eala, with her jewels and trinkets, had been well into her cups before the dancing had begun. And the old vixen, Tring, looked more regal than usual in her flowing silks, the pattern typical of the south, somewhere near Gur Bano, perhaps.

But despite the exotic fabrics, the jewellery, gold, and gemstones, her mother had looked the most radiant by far in a gown of red and gold. As head of Laws for Val Sharis, Drutia was always away at this city or that country, and rarely spent time in the capital. Lathri could go months without seeing her and couldn't even send messages because her movements were too erratic.

Watching her from across the packed ballroom, the chandeliers casting beautiful gold light over the tables, was the most she'd seen of her in the whole year.

She couldn't wait to catch up after the ball, to learn of where she'd been and what stories she had to tell.

After they'd eaten, Lathri had only glimpsed her mother and the others through swirls of fabric and dresses as the music summoned them all to the floor. She'd waved, and Drutia had smiled and waved back, her gold earrings catching the chandelier's light.

Lathri had danced with many people. Ten, twelve partners, perhaps, all spinning and losing themselves in the vibrant colour and music.

She'd laughed and sang along, and when she realised she'd torn the edge of her skirts in her movements, Lathri excused herself to repair it.

Ten minutes had passed. If that.

Koraki had raced down the passageway from the ballroom, sweating and whimpering, and she'd had to press herself flat against the wall to let him through.

He'd always been a worrier, but his behaviour that night—his raw fear—set her heart fluttering.

She'd returned to the ballroom to witness Sapora's Varkain form coiled underneath the swaying chandelier.

The music had stopped, replaced by screams and feet slipping on the bloodied marble floor in their haste to escape.

And on the Council table at the far end of the room, five bodies lay sprawled in their finery, crimson splashed across their stomachs.

Lathri had kicked her shoes off and raced across the ballroom when Sapora transformed back and left the clean-up to his servants. She'd run faster than she'd ever thought she could, her feet hardly touching the floor.

Tears blurred her vision as she'd grabbed her mother. She'd flooded her body with healing magic, sealed up the wounds, and cried silently, desperately hoping her sorrow didn't alert Sapora to her presence.

But she'd been too late. They'd all perished.

Perhaps if Sapora had only poisoned them, she'd have had a chance to save Drutia. At least his fangs had given them a swift end.

Shaking, Lathri had darted from person to person, reviving those who still clung to life, healing those whose wounds would have killed them, otherwise. When she'd finally been forced to flee from the Imperial Guard, all her energy spent, her fingers had been caked in red.

No. She had no desire to rule or hold power of any sort.

She simply wanted her country to be one of peace, where they were ruled by their own, by one who cared about the Ittallan.

Isa would be that one.

'I have faith in Isa. You should, too. Else why risk so much against Sapora?' Lathri said, hoping that she'd not been lost in thought for too long. 'We have to be patient. Isa will come around, you'll see. Sapora may be her brother, but he's more Varkain than she, and Val Sharis is the country of the Ittallan.'

'When I grabbed the princess, I saw Mateli heading towards Feoras Sol,' Aetos said. 'He may have picked up Palom's tracks, or he may be going there first, in the knowledge it's his old home.'

Lathri sighed. She didn't want to lose him, too.

'I can go after him? Bring him down?' Voulhrik offered.

'It's too dangerous. All our strength combined might not be enough to take on Mateli.' She shook her head. 'Thank you for offering, but no. It's too great a risk. You're needed at the palace anyway, to keep your eyes on our princess. We don't want Sapora becoming suspicious of you, too.'

Voulhrik snorted his frustration. 'If only we had Palom with us. Isa would probably have listened more…'

'Probably,' Lathri admitted, and refused to speak more about her old flame. 'How is recruiting?'

'Slow.' Kylos called from the balcony. 'Too many Ittallan are afraid of Sapora. They won't say anything against him. Won't risk Tacio's Cerastes after them. I tell you, it's not going to be long before someone gives up our names or location.'

Suspicion was always healthy. Lathri found Kylos to be a little too suspicious, sometimes.

'Once word gets around of Mateli's release, I think you'll find more Ittallan are interested in our cause. But…Perhaps we ought to spread our wings a little further…' Lathri said.

'We came from Tum Metsa! How much further do you want to fly?' Aetos laughed.

'I'm thinking about finding allies in Corhaven. Kings aren't overthrown so easily. We have to find out what Sapora's plans are and disrupt them. Isa will need to be ready to seize power when the time comes. We have a new landmark in our city. A crystal, the only thing that's left of Moroda. Think to her, and what she stood for.'

Lathri would see peace restored to Val Sharis, whatever the cost.

Chapter Fifteen

The stench of blood filled the air. Palom's nose curled at it. He was no stranger to death, to battles, but the slaughtering of innocent people made his stomach turn.

Though the wind had stilled, and the silence of night was thick, the reek of death touched everything.

As did the unmistakable stink of stagnant water.

He thought he'd never smell that again.

The fear that stench created made Palom think of nothing else but survival against Mateli. Even his *Valta Forinja*, ever at the forefront of his mind, paled to insignificance as Palom left the road and approached the Waterside Inn from the trees.

When the building came into his sights, Palom crouched beside a particularly wide tree trunk, nettles brushing against his arms where he rested them on his thighs. Hardly aware of their stings, he surveyed the scene. What little moonlight broke through the canopy bathed the inn and river in silver-white light, lengthening the shadows.

He didn't need to see the blood to know it was there.

A dozen or so corpses were sprawled in front of the inn.

Palom sucked in a breath.

He'd hoped to never experience this again.

But *where* was Mateli?

For a long while, he watched and waited, listening for any movement over the river water and the leaves rustling in the trees.

He waited so long that by the time he dared move, his joints had stiffened, and his knees cracked.

Mateli's stench covered everything.

Whether he was still here or not, Palom couldn't tell, but he assumed so. Better to expect the worst and stay safe than to let your guard down and suffer for it.

When it came to Mateli, suffering for it would be the last thing he ever did.

Palom made his way down the slope to the back of the Waterside Inn, moving with as much stealth as he could muster. If Mateli didn't know he was there, he'd at least have the element of surprise.

The kitchen door had been left ajar, and he slipped inside, taking another moment to gather his thoughts.

So many dead.

Regular Ittallan who were going about their lives.

Palom grimaced and made his way through the kitchens to the large dining area, to find overturned tables and chairs, curtains ripped, and glasses smashed. A gouge had been taken out of the wooden floor, and blood pooled in one of the room's corners.

And everywhere, on every surface, Palom smelled Mateli.

'Chyro…' He said, shaking his head that one so young as the captain had managed to escape the attack. Palom wanted to move the bodies, get them away from the site, but he couldn't do it alone—not quickly, anyway—and couldn't risk leaving for Taban Yul. He had to sort out Mateli first and put an end to this senseless violence.

Like he should have done years ago.

Making his way through the dining room, Palom exited the inn from the front door and went back outside. Mateli had to be nearby, still. Had to be.

Already, Palom had counted nine dead, and hoped the crowd he'd seen that morning had already left the inn and wasn't part of a body pile Mateli had might put together in some sickening display of brutality.

Palom had never been great at tracking. That had always been Anahrik's speciality. Working alone had never been one of his strengths, and the fear of failure began to niggle at him.

What if…Mateli had already left?

Was already heading to Feoras Sol?

Was already *in* Feoras Sol?

He wandered along the path, looking out into the trees, but they yielded no secrets, no movements save their own leaves.

Palom breathed through his nose again.

Stagnant water.

He had to be here. Somewhere.

Running his hands over his face, Palom sighed.

Or was he being paranoid again? Had Mateli already moved on now there was no-one left here to kill?

Mateli had always derived a sickening pleasure from seeing others fall apart. Palom had first been drawn to his strength, his confidence, and his utter righteousness in everything he did.

As a weak-minded, grieving sixteen-year-old in a big city with no friends, Palom had immediately gravitated towards Mateli's group of wannabe fighters. He'd had a seat on the Val Sharis Council as War Chief back then, and he took no prisoners.

Palom wanted to prove himself after losing his brother, after running away from home, and joined the ranks of Mateli's unofficial troupe.

When he turned eighteen, Palom's *meraki* gave him the strength he'd been so desperate to achieve, and Mateli had taken real notice of him.

Palom finally had the recognition he'd craved, the realisation he wasn't useless, wasn't a failure.

That he could be worth something.

Mateli's unorthodox ways of working and ultra-strict punishments had never sat well with Palom, but as long as he could keep up with Mateli's training and didn't step out of line and earn himself a punishment, he didn't think too much about it.

When he met Anahrik, and later Lathri, he opened his eyes to the truth of Mateli's violence and realised what he was becoming.

The friendship—if it could be called that—turned into a terrible rivalry, which evolved into a vendetta that left most of Palom's associates dead or severely injured.

Lathri had managed to pull some strings to have those in power *happen* upon Mateli's latest slaughter, which Palom helped set up with Anahrik's help. With the eye-witness account, the Council imprisoned Mateli for life, and Palom hoped he would die in prison.

He never thought he'd see him alive and free.

Water splashed from the river and Palom whirled around, on high alert. When nothing happened, he relaxed.

There were plenty of fish and frogs in the water.

Anything could make a splash like that, and he doubted Mateli would give away his position in such a rookie mistake.

He backed away, facing the river.

Far too paranoid...

Rolling his shoulders to loosen his joints, Palom turned back to the inn. He'd give it one final look over, try and see if he could figure out where Mateli had gone—decide whether or not he needed to get back to Sol.

If the village had locked itself down, at least Mateli wouldn't catch them unawares. His ambush attacks had been what killed the majority of his targets. If someone knew he was coming, they had much more of a fighting chance.

Sol wouldn't be an easy target—too many of them, many of whom were excellent fighters—surely Mateli would stick to those he could pick off easily and not bother himself with a tougher opponent.

Satisfied, Palom made his way to the inn's side, circling it as he looked for any clues as to Mateli's location.

As he rounded the corner, he felt—rather than heard—a deep hiss that haunted his dreams.

Mateli was on him before Palom even realised what was happening, before he even heard the movement, wrestling him to the floor, hands scrabbling for his throat and mouth.

Palom could only grunt in response, bringing his arms up to block Mateli's, and push the bigger man away from him. Mateli had gravity on his side, and he shoved an elbow against Palom's temple, pushing him to the ground as his other hand swung punch after punch.

'I'm so happy Sapora sent me ta kill ya. Should've left his snakes alone!'

Palom could hardly react to the words before he felt his skin break, caught by a couple of the blows. He kicked out—using his knees and boots to push against Mateli and give him room to move and breathe.

Mateli laughed as he swung, drawing his hand back and extending claws from the tips of his fingers. Palom pushed back with as much force as he could, throwing Mateli back before he had a chance to rake his claws over his face.

Palom leapt up in the same movement, light engulfing him as he shifted into his true form, his *Valta Forinja* forgotten. He extended his own claws and pounced after Mateli, who rolled out of reach just as Palom landed.

Snarling, the tiger leapt again, unwilling to let Mateli get any ground, and swiped at the Ittallan with massive paws.

Mateli grinned, hissing as he got to his feet and met the tiger's next pounce head on.

Palom's front legs wrapped around Mateli's upper body, the force of his jump nearly knocking him over. Ears flat, Palom bared his canines and bit down on Mateli's head and neck.

But where he'd expected to pierce flesh and taste blood, his teeth scraped against the armoured hide of Mateli's transformed body. Scrabbling his claws and teeth against the crocodile, Palom slipped back and stepped away from the enormous reptile.

At twenty-seven feet from nose to tip, the crocodile was nine feet longer than he was—though much of the extra was Mateli's tail—but his thick skin made him practically invulnerable. Mateli opened his mouth and bellowed, the low noise echoing through the trees.

Palom hesitated, tail lashing. He knew if Mateli managed to grab hold of him, it'd be over.

Mateli jerked his head towards Palom, and took several steps towards him, the ground shaking under his bulk.

With a defiant roar, Palom charged forwards, darting out of range of Mateli's huge jaws and leaping onto his back. His claws struggled to find purchase, and pulled a few of his scales loose, before Mateli whipped round, tail thrashing as he threw Palom off.

Teeth snapped the air where Palom's head had been as Mateli immediately went on the offensive, and Palom had to avoid teeth and tail blows while he tried to find some weak spot in Mateli's armour.

Both sets of fangs lunged at another, and Palom gripped Mateli's lower jaw, biting down as hard as he could, while his front legs scraped along Mateli's throat and belly.

Mateli's top jaw clamped down on Palom's face and nose, teeth piercing his fur as it gripped.

Growling, Palom shook his head, trying to inflict as much damage as he could, but when he released his grip to back away, Mateli's jaw had him locked in place.

He pulled back again, pushing his claws deep into Mateli's belly, tearing at the soft scales and drawing blood, but still the crocodile did not let go.

Mateli took a step backwards and pulled Palom with him, then another, then another.

Palom dug his back legs into the ground, holding himself rigid, but the crocodile's strength overwhelmed him, and Palom couldn't pull free from Mateli's vice-like grip.

Palom heard the river and realised in a flood of panic that Mateli was dragging him to the water. He redoubled his efforts; pulling back and lashing out, trying to tear himself out of the crocodile's grip however he could.

Mateli jerked his head a few times, no doubt trying to speed his victory, but Palom made himself as hard as possible to drag along. Every breath was a snarl, every kick of his legs had claws drawn, until Mateli's blood stained the ground.

Palom heard the splash of water as Mateli's tail touched the river, shortly followed by his back legs.

In a last-ditch attempt to get away before they reached the water, Palom slammed his head to one side, the violent movement ripping a couple of Mateli's teeth off and sending them flying.

Palom continued the movement, rolling onto his back in an imitation of what Mateli did to drown his targets, twisting himself in Mateli's grasp and threatening to pull more teeth out.

Still the crocodile did not release him.

Bringing his back legs up, Palom slashed at Mateli's face with his hind claws, digging into the flesh around his face and—though sheer luck—slashed across his eyes.

Mateli released him and then immediately snapped to grab hold again. Palom was already back on his feet and out of range, and the two growled at one another. He bared his teeth and Mateli backed down, retreating back into the river and disappearing into the murky water.

Palom stood where he was for a long time, watching the river, looking for bubbles or movement, waiting for Mateli to resurface.

After minutes of waiting, when he'd caught his breath and could no longer smell Mateli, he relaxed, shifting back and falling onto one knee.

Blood poured from his temple, and his whole body ached.

There was no telling whether Mateli had swum upriver or followed it further down.

He heard leaves rushing and twigs snapping, and Palom looked up to see Solvi racing through the trees towards him. She leapt over the river without breaking stride and hurried over to him once she landed on the other bank.

'Palom! *Kali*!' She said, skidding to a halt.

'Solvi? You should not be here,' he said, trying to stand but failing. 'Why are you not in Sol?'

'I couldn't leave you to face him alone!' She looked him over, wiped the blood from his face. 'Palom…!'

'Solvi…go back to Sol. Mateli will be back. You cannot be here when…he gets back.' He felt blood trickle down his neck and struggled to stay conscious.

Damn.

He hadn't realised it was such a deep wound.

His vision dimmed, and fear ran through him like ice.

'I will be fine. Go back to Sol…I can finish him.'

'Don't be silly! I can't leave you!' She crouched to loop his arm over her and pulled him away from the river.

He hobbled along with her but collapsed to the ground on several occasions before Solvi managed to bring him inside and lay him on his bed in the inn. 'I'll get your sword,' she said, darting back outside to pick up his abandoned *Valta Forinja*.

The fire in his room had almost completely burnt out, and Solvi added more wood, letting the flames grow again around his egg.

'I'll stay with you while you recover,' she said, when she was happy with the fire.

'Solvi…When he comes back…You are no match for him.' Palom coughed.

She tore up the extra bedding in his room and slowly wrapped it around his wounds. 'Hold this here,' she commanded, lifting his hand to press against his bleeding head.

'Solvi...You are not listening to me...' Palom tried again, doing as she asked.

She went back to the fire and fiddled around with the firewood. 'I know. But...But I could fend him off. Keep him away from you while you heal.'

Palom sank into the bed. Blood trickled through the sheets, but he turned his head away, so Solvi wouldn't see.

He wished he'd never left home in the first place.

He'd never have got himself mixed up with Mateli, would have been there for Solvi as she'd grown up.

He could hardly believe how courageous she was in the face of danger.

Then again, if he hadn't left, he'd never have met...

He gasped, half in pain, half in excitement.

'Solvi. You can...you can help me,' he said, voice weak.

'What do you need, *kali*?' She was by his side in a moment, clutching his hands.

'My bag...' he pointed to his belongings by the side of the hearth. 'There is...inside there is...brooch. For a friend of mine...'

Solvi hurried over and rooted through his bag, eventually pulling out the small drawstring purse Lathri had rejected.

'This?' She asked, holding it up so he could see.

'Please, Solvi...Take this to...Taban Yul...There is healer I know. In Little Yomal...'

Solvi frowned. 'Taban Yul is leagues away!'

He coughed, blood spattering the sheets. 'Lathri is best healer…She…Please ask her…To come and help…The top house…The blue roses…'

'Palom, I can't leave you! What if he comes back?'

He coughed again. 'Then hurry. Use…your *meraki* to run fast as possible…Lathri can fly, but please…Give her that brooch…Tell her where I am. I am begging you, Solvi.'

She held the bag close and looked to the door.

'Solvi…' He closed his eyes, desperate.

'I don't like it. Sol is closer…'

He shook his head. 'Lathri is best…Please.'

With a sigh, she transformed, her grey-blue fur brightening the room. She picked up the bag in her mouth and gave him a pained look before she raced off into the night.

Chapter Sixteen

Isa made her way downstairs, pleased that she'd not been spotted by anyone when she returned to the palace the previous night.

She checked over her hand multiple times and could hardly believe the skill with which Lathri had healed her.

Lathri and her allies had made her think seriously about how Sapora and Tacio were running the city, about their broken promises and aggression. She was older than Tacio, and yet the Varkain still had more authority than she did—Sapora always turned to him for advice over her.

She swept around the curving passageway, glancing at the tapestries lining the walls. Sapora's no longer hung next to the others—a shame, she thought. The artist had really brought depth of colour to his scales, and it had complemented Vasil's portrait in the gallery.

A pair of Goldstones sat at a small round table in the dining room where the kitchen staff served breakfast and tea to the palace residents—as well as wealthy individuals who would happily pay for the experience and a chance to peek at royalty.

She smiled at the staff, helped herself to a platter of toasted bagels and butter, and walked through the double doors at the end of the dining room, where she breakfasted in private.

The Council—those in residence, anyway—used to join her, but now she found she ate by herself most mornings.

Her usual pot of tea waited for her on the table by the window when she sat down. The view looked out over Taban Yul, and she thought how much her city appeared to have changed in a single day.

Conspirators.

Curses.

Monsters.

She needed to report that old Ittallan woman, before she ended up hurting anyone else. Isa ate slowly and wondered whether the best thing for the city was indeed the best thing for her.

She'd finished her first mug of tea, and was halfway through her second when the door to her room opened, and Tacio sauntered in.

She scowled at him.

'Mind if I join you?' he asked, sitting down without invitation, his long necklaces jingling.

'What do you want?'

He smirked at her and brushed down his lapels with one hand, his other drumming on the table as though he were impatiently waiting for something.

She had plenty of patience, however, and sipped her tea while she waited for him to explain himself.

Eventually, he coughed and stopped drumming. 'Have fun on your little excursion last night?'

Isa kept her face impassive, half using the mug to hide her lips.

'No…?' He leaned forward slightly, pupils dilating.

'I can roam the city as I wish,' she said, emptying her mug and placing it on the table.

'Of course you can. I wondered what was so interesting *outside* the city? You didn't get back until very late…'

She moistened her lips with her tongue, giving herself time to think. How much did he know? Had she been followed? 'I don't know what you mean.' She shrugged, the epitome of nonchalance.

Tacio's grin broadened. 'I think you know *exactly* what I mean, Isa. Now…the fact you're hiding your reasons for leaving makes me *very* suspicious. You can understand that, can't you?'

She raised an eyebrow. It was like being a child again.

'You've got personal airships, you can fly out if you want to go anywhere. But you left on foot, didn't come back until the middle of the night, and you look like you've been in the wars.'

The Varkain Guard, she realised.

They were under Tacio, not Sapora.

Why was Tacio keeping tabs on her?

'Excuse me? Been in the wars?' She was irritated now.

Tacio grabbed her forearm and pulled her close to him.

'What are you doing?' She hissed and pulled away.

'This is what I mean,' he said as he held her fingers and yanked her hand close.

She flinched.

'New scars? Come, Isa. If we have an enemy, don't you think you ought to tell us…?'

Isa writhed in his grip, but he wouldn't let go.

'Tacio! Get off!'

His claws pressed into her soft flesh for a moment before he released her with another smile.

'Who do you think you are?' She got to her feet, her chair scraping back on the marble floor, one hand holding her injured one.

'I want to know what you're up to, Isa.'

She scowled. 'I could ask the same of you! How many times have you snuck back into palace at dawn? What do *you* get up to in the middle of the night, hmm?'

'Doing the dirty work our king commands,' he said, getting to his feet. 'Managing our Cerastes and the Guard. Weeding out conspirators. Making sure his rule is nice and easy…'

'And you think I'm making his rule difficult?'

'I'm just making sure you don't.'

She rolled her eyes. 'Releasing Mateli will make his rule harder than I ever could.'

'Precisely why Sapora has an ace up his sleeve.'

Something about the way his eyes glinted made Isa's heart pound. What ace did Sapora have?

'Come and walk with me,' Tacio said, offering her his arm. 'Let's go and see our brother.'

*

The gardens were more crowded than Isa had ever seen. There had to be fifty Varkain in Imperial armour charging around, clearing plants, fountains, and ornaments like their lives depended on it.

The last time she'd seen such behaviour had been when Aciel's fleet had attacked the city.

Sapora stood in the centre of it all, barking orders and gesturing like the conductor of an orchestra. Isa hadn't seen him flustered before, but she could tell Sapora was close.

'Things running nice and smoothly, I see,' Tacio said, eyeing the organised chaos around them. 'Looks like your delivery is coming in right on time.'

Sapora ignored him and rolled up his sheet of parchment paper. 'In future, Tacio, I'd appreciate a more precise arrival time than "soon,"' Sapora said. 'Less time preening yourself and more time being active.'

Isa supressed a laugh, her breath coming out through her nose in more of a snort than anything else.

'Mateli is out, now, anyway.' Tacio said, after the redness in his face faded.

'Good. At least Palom will be dealt with.'

Isa's stomach knotted.

'Any other killing orders, or are you having a break from that?' Tacio ventured.

'I'd suggest a break from that,' Isa interjected.

She was keen to change the subject and also let him know about the old woman in town. 'You've got bigger problems in your city to deal with. Curses.'

'Curses?' Tacio sneered. 'Oh, is this what you were up to last night?'

She cast a filthy look in his direction. 'While I was in the city, on the south side, there was an old Ittallan woman. She looked in a kind of trance. Blank eyes. Muttering to herself.'

'Senile Ittallan.' Tacio shrugged and looked to Sapora.

'I asked if she was all right and when I touched her, I heard someone calling my name.'

Sapora's eyes widened. 'Who?'

'Don't know. It was in my head. A…a man's voice, I think. Soon as I let go of the woman he disappeared. There was a whole group of them.'

Sapora turned away, as he often did when he thought. Isa bit her thumbnail. 'I thought she'd been cursed…It's this sickness that's in Taban Yul.'

'Could be,' Sapora said, putting his rolled parchment in his inside pocket. 'Could be something else, too.'

'Does it matter? Not like we need to worry now *it's* here,' Tacio said.

Isa hated being missed out of conversations, and she felt very excluded right now. 'Now *what's* here…?'

'An old power for the Varkain,' Tacio said, unable to resist rubbing it in her face. 'We've got a god in our claws.' His eyes flashed.

'What are you talking about?' Isa asked. There was only one thing that could be considered a god. 'A Sevastos?' She looked at the commotion in the gardens in a new light. 'How…Sapora…?' She stammered.

'That's right. Nothing in Linaria can stand against it!' Tacio grinned, his usual lazy drawl replaced by excitement. 'Which means nothing in Linaria can stand against *us*. We've got all the power now! We're invincible.'

Isa looked to Sapora, who had been silent during Tacio's outbursts. If anything, she thought he looked angrier than ever.

'*Gods* do not exist. Power does not exist. There is only leverage. Anyone—anything can be broken. Even dragons. Even…a Sevastos.'

Panic suddenly gripped her. What did he mean?

She remembered the voice in her head, speaking her name—demanding she respond.

It couldn't mean…It couldn't mean Aciel…could it?

From Sapora's stony glare, she guessed it wasn't outside the realms of possibility.

If it was true, how on earth could they stand against that if a Sevastos had failed?

Sapora said, 'Isa, I want you to oversee the loading of my cargo. They're bringing it in now.'

She blinked, surprised, but nodded.

'Once it's in, make sure the canvas is brought out. It has to cover the whole garden. Understand? Then dismiss everyone but the Cerastes I brought with me. Roke will keep them in line.'

'Where are you going?' She asked.

'I'm borrowing one of your ships. Tacio, I want you to come with me.' He charged back towards the palace.

'Wait, Sapora! Where are you going?' Isa called out.

But he was gone.

*

'I'm telling you, she's up to something,' Tacio said, for what had to be the thousandth time.

Sapora ignored him again as he had every other time Tacio had suggested Isa was traitorous.

Koraki flew the two out of the city and due east in Isa's personal airship—one of two she owned. Designed for personal use, the ship could comfortably transport only a couple of people. The three of them had been a squeeze, and Sapora had opted to stand for the flight instead of sitting beside his brother.

Now his Sevastos had found its new home, he had a little breathing space. But he needed to get his second piece on the board as soon as possible.

Isa's report sounded suspiciously like Aciel's compulsion—albeit a weakened version—and he'd hoped Moroda's plan would have worked indefinitely.

But it seemed his own words were true.

Even a Sevastos could be broken.

If that was true, the damned Arillian could be free to try his hand at conquest again. He had to have a defence in place, and a counter-attack.

What good was it ruling if there was nothing left to rule?

He'd been trying to save a country on the brink of collapse and all he got for his trouble were reports of conspirators and angry Ittallan that the comfortable life they knew might change a little. For the good of their country.

He had to protect them; against dragons turning against villages and Aciel potentially still affecting people in Taban Yul.

He rolled his tongue over his fangs. With such powers at play, the safety of Linaria was no longer down to the Imperial Guard, Cerastes, or even what was left of the Varkain Old Guard.

No. This called for far more leverage.

'Bring the ship down on the edge of the trees,' Sapora said, as the Rio Neva forest spread out below them. In the distance, he could still see Taban Yul.

He really could have made his way here alone, but he had no idea how much time he had before he'd be forced to act, so he had decided to use the resources at his disposal.

Koraki landed the ship at the top of a slope beside the road, the trees dark and foreboding just ahead.

'Stay with the ship. Tacio, come with me.'

Sapora leapt off the side of the ship, disliking how exposed he felt in the fields leading up to the trees.

Perhaps there was a little more Varkain in him than he cared to admit.

He hurried along, as quickly as he could, avoiding trailing vines and large tree roots, pulling out his map periodically to ensure he was on the most direct path.

'She's an Ittallan, Sapora. An *Ittallan*.'

Sapora followed the path into the forest, then at the first bend, continued straight into the trees, following his own route and using his map as a guide.

'Tacio, in case you fail to realise—or have forgotten—I myself am half-Ittallan, too.' He turned at a particular tree and carried on through the undergrowth.

'Yes, but...you're not really one. You're *Naja*. Not some damned house cat.' Tacio continued, several steps behind him.

'I really do tire of you discussing my lineage. I'm your king. That's as much as you or anyone else needs to know. Isa is my sister and has lived in Taban Yul her whole life. You'll show us both the appropriate amount of respect, or I shall send you back to Sereth.'

'Argh!'

Sapora whirled round, one scimitar already out and ready to strike.

'My...cloak...' Tacio said. A thin branch had snagged it as he'd passed, and he gingerly pulled it free.

Sapora sheathed his blade.

Tacio needed to spend more time in the real world as far as he was concerned. 'Be quiet. We're getting close.'

He jumped over a particularly thorny patch of vegetation on the edge of the Feor Mountains.

'A cave?' Tacio asked.

'A cave,' Sapora repeated. He licked his lips and walked into the mouth, his eyes immediately shifting as the darkness surrounded him.

He'd been planning this since he'd first arrived in Val Sharis, but now he was here, he wasn't quite sure where to go next. He'd thought it would be obvious.

Tacio shuffled in beside him, pulling his torn cloak tight.

The Varkain had said there'd been a plaque.

A plaque should be simple enough to find, he supposed.

He walked forward, eyes down, looking through the churned-up soil for some indication of the plaque.

'Mal…a…shash.'

Sapora looked across the cave to see Tacio stood by the wall, reading from a plaque nailed into the rock several feet above.

'This was the treasure? An Ark's resting place?' Tacio said.

Sapora grinned. 'This isn't some ceremonial gravesite, Tacio. This is the real thing.'

'Not possible.'

'Anything's possible when you believe it.' Sapora made his way across the cave to stand beside him. 'I'm going to write history.' He pulled out the small knife he kept in his sleeve, and dragged it along his palm in one, clean, slice.

Balling his hand into a fist, he let his blood trickle through his fingers before placing his palm against the soil, the tips of his claws touching the plaque.

For a moment nothing happened, and then, once the blood seeped out, the wall cracked.

Sapora felt his heart in his throat as the wall fell away to reveal a tunnel. It had to be four feet in diameter—a squeeze in his true form. 'Shall we?'

Tacio paced near the entrance. 'Down there? I'll...get dirty.'

'You've lived underground your whole life!'

'In spotlessly clean Varkain tunnels. This looks like a damned badger dug it!'

'I may need you.'

Tacio scratched the back of his head.

'Well. Just your blood. Don't you want to be part of the new age of the Varkain?'

Tacio scowled at him, and Sapora felt his increased heart rate, smelled the sweat on his skin.

'Just a little blood.' Sapora pulled out the knife and handed it to Tacio. The Varkain took it begrudgingly, cut his hand in a similar way, and handed back the bloodied blade.

'I hope that's worth it,' Tacio hissed, caressing his hand.

'Perfect.'

Sapora slipped the blade back into his sleeve and crouched down, shuffling into the tunnel.

'See you on the other side,' Tacio called down to him, but Sapora had lost interest in the irritating Varkain.

The walls closed in on him within a few steps as the tunnel narrowed, the roof sloping down. Sapora ended up crawling on his hands and feet, until suddenly the tunnel stopped.

He cursed, looking around—had he missed a turning? Reaching forward, Sapora pressed against the tunnel wall and found it quite solid. When he put his hand back on the ground, soil fell away under his fingers.

Shuffling back, Sapora dug with his claws, shovelling soil and unearthing a hole in the tunnel floor. When it was wide enough for him to fit through, he clambered through it.

Loose dirt and worms clung to his skin, clothes and hair, but he ignored it all, dropping several feet to a much wider tunnel where he could stand. Now in pitch dark, Sapora relied on his sense of smell, hearing, and touch to navigate.

He followed it, crouching when the roof of the tunnel sloped, and squeezing through gaps sideways when it became too narrow to pass otherwise.

The tunnel was nothing like Sereth—even the more remote parts. Spiders scurried out of his path, even over him, and loose rocks and soil fell away from the walls when he touched them.

Smaller, side tunnels peeled off, and Sapora wondered more than once whether or not he should try those. But the smell of dirty water and the squeaking of rats made him think otherwise.

Malashash couldn't possibly be near vermin.

The main tunnel dropped away suddenly, and Sapora lost his footing, almost landing face-first in the dirt. He cursed, picked himself up, and continued.

He shifted into his true form now the tunnel was wider, and progressed quickly, his tongue keeping him away from dead ends and warning him when the tunnel curved.

Minutes passed in silence.

The tunnel's walls grew smoother, and the ceiling sloped towards him.

Forced to transform back, Sapora shuffled along in a crouch, his back aching, but the tunnel didn't relent. The walls and ceiling pressed down on him, until he was on his hands and knees again.

He took deep breaths to calm himself, but found he inhaled bits of dirt and spider's web and coughed it all out again.

Still, the tunnel continued, narrowing again until he had to lay on his belly and pull himself along with his elbows.

He couldn't push through this for much longer.

A thump of soil falling made him freeze, and he felt a weight on his foot.

Damn the tunnel.

It couldn't cave in.

It couldn't!

Slowly, Sapora pulled himself forward another body length, careful not to disturb the walls or ceiling too much.

He desperately wanted to transform again but wasn't sure if it would help given how fragile the tunnel seemed to be.

The walls pressed against his shoulders, and he thought of turning back.

It must be the wrong way…if nothing could fit through here?

Sapora shuffled forward again, unwilling to give up, unsure whether he'd be able to back out and try another way before he needed to rest.

He could hardly turn his head as the earth pressed into him from all sides, and he held his breath to stop trembling.

Had…he been mistaken?

A whiff of something…stone?

Sapora swallowed.

Something other than soil?

He pushed forward, the weight of the tunnel threatening to collapse on his back.

The smell grew stronger, and he continued with renewed vigour, until he came at last to a circular stone lip, marking the edge of the tunnel.

Hardly able to believe he'd reached the end, Sapora pulled himself across the edge and fell into a wide stone chamber—the tomb of Malashash.

Chapter Seventeen

Solvi wandered the street of Little Yomal, scared and alone. She'd visited friends who'd lived in the district while she'd studied but had never roamed the streets at night.

Palom's instructions hadn't been particularly clear, and she knew she had to hurry.

Mateli could already be back at the inn, finishing him off.

Many of the townhouses were stacked high, three or four homes cramped in one tall building, but none seemed to have the blue flowers Palom had described.

She clutched Palom's small bag to her chest as she hurried up and down different streets, looking for anything close to a healer's home. She wished he would have let her go back to Sol—there were plenty of healers there—but she couldn't say no to his pleading. He'd begged as if his life depended on it.

Solvi hurried down another street, relieved when she saw a pair of Ittallan at the end. Surely, they'd know of a local healer named Lathri?

‘Excuse me! Excuse me?’ She called, running down to where they wandered.

They turned around to look at her, a man and a woman, and Solvi pulled up short. They swayed on their feet, leaning into one another and then stumbling away.

Had they been drinking?

‘Hi, I’m looking for Lathri. She’s a healer here. Do you know where I could find her, please?’ Solvi asked.

They stared blankly at her, and she cleared her throat. ‘Lathri. A healer in Little Yomal.’

Still nothing

She huffed. There wasn’t any time for this. Even drunks were usually more responsive.

‘Please can you help?’ She tried again, getting frantic. At this hour, there was hardly anyone about. No patrols of the Imperial Guard, no open inns. The residential area was sound asleep.

The couple stumbled into each other again and collapsed to the floor with a thud.

‘Never mind…’ Solvi sighed, turning away from them. She had to have been up every street in the district by now.

She had to hurry. Had to find Lathri before Mateli decided to try and—

The woman grabbed her arm, trying to pull herself back up to her feet.

‘Solvi.’

Electricity coursed through her, bringing her to her knees.

‘What are you doing here…’

The voice reminded her of *pali*, only colder somehow. 'I'm trying to get help…'

'Help? You don't need help.'

'Not for me…' She answered, and suddenly she was spinning in the dark like she'd just tumbled down a hill.

'No. No help for you. No help for anyone.'

She shivered, her body numbing.

'You need to get away. You don't belong here, do you?'

'I don't…?' She thought she knew, but now the voice told her otherwise, suddenly she wasn't sure.

'No. You need to die.'

A distant sensation somewhere on the edge of her fingertips. Fear. Sadness. Pain?

'I need…' Solvi began to repeat, and then the connection was gone.

Solvi blinked her eyes open, cold sweat running down her forehead. She was sat on the street, the couple she'd tried to talk to flat on their backs several paces from her, and a new Ittallan stood between her and them.

'Can you get up?' She asked, her voice harsh.

Solvi swallowed and tested her legs and found them responsive. She got to her feet, and suddenly realised she didn't have the bag anymore. 'Oh no!'

'What's the matter?' The woman asked.

'My bag. I had a small jewellery bag…'

'To your side.'

Solvi followed the instruction and gasped in relief when she saw the bag on the edge of the street. She grabbed it and checked everything was still there.

Her head span, a painful, cold pressure building behind her eyes. 'What happened?'

'There's a sickness in the city. Seems to take hold of vulnerable people. The old, the young.' The woman glanced to the two she'd knocked to the floor. 'Those no longer in control of their senses…Touch 'em and you'll get it too. But it takes a few minutes to take hold. You're lucky.'

Solvi nodded. 'Thank you so much. I'm looking for Lathri, she's a healer—'

'I know her. She's my…Well she's a friend of mind,' the woman said. 'Why do you need her?'

'My *kali*—my uncle—he's been attacked. He's badly hurt. He asked me to get Lathri personally. Please can you show me where she lives? I can't find the house with blue flowers?' Tears threatened as she thought to how much time had passed since she'd left him.

'Who's your uncle?'

'His name is Palom,' Solvi said. 'There's not much time. Please, please can you take me to her?'

'Sure. This is becoming quite the eventful night.'

It turned out that Solvi hadn't been far off—the woman only led her three streets away before she spotted the towering building, blue roses cascading off the rooftop balcony. The woman made her wait outside, which suited Solvi fine—she only hoped Lathri would hurry.

After a minute or two of waiting, the woman returned along with a man who looked just like her, and an older woman who seemed to glow white in the darkness.

She felt her energy like a mist that spread and grew, calming her, and Solvi immediately understood why Palom had asked to see Lathri and no-one else.

'Hello. Kylos tells me you're Palom's niece?' Lathri said.

She nodded, and held out the jewellery bag to her, 'I'm Solvi. He asked me to give this to you, and please, please, Lathri, can you help him? It was Mateli…I…I don't know if he'll survive the night. I came here as fast as I could.'

Lathri sighed, as though she were being given mildly inconvenient news, rather than someone who desperately needed her was on the brink of death.

'Did Palom kill Mateli?'

'No. He could be back any minute. That's why you have to hurry! Please! Lathri…?' Solvi asked, her panic and growing headache threatening to throw her manners out the window. 'Lathri, he's dying!'

The healer nodded, solemn. 'Where is he?'

'The Waterside Inn, Rio Neva,' Solvi replied immediately.

'All right, then. It's not too far.'

Solvi grinned, her eye twitching as her headache intensified.

'Aetos, would you mind coming with me? Eyes in the sky would help if Mateli is still nearby.'

'I'll take you back there,' Solvi said, getting ready to transform again, when a blinding pain burst through her head.

'Solvi?' Lathri asked, rushing to her side and resting a hand on her head. 'Oh dragons above, you poor thing. Kylos, would you bring her inside? Keep her warm. I doubt I'll be back before dawn.'

The woman crouched down and pulled Solvi into an embrace, then picked her up. Solvi squeezed an eye open. 'I'm sorry.'

'It's all right. Side effect of the sickness. You'll be fine with some rest.'

'Promise?' Solvi asked.

'Promise,' Lathri said. 'I'll go to Palom now. Don't worry.'

*

Dawn sun streamed through the window, and Palom grunted. He'd not slept at all since Solvi left—hadn't dared to—though his body screamed for rest.

He knew Solvi would have rushed to Taban Yul, and he could only hope that she'd found Lathri. Surely, she would come. If not…then, he supposed he'd meet his end when Mateli returned to finish what he'd started.

The wound on his temple still bled, but it had slowed some. Blooded linen littered his bed, and he'd struggled to rip apart the rest to create more bandages.

Palom wanted to crawl to the river and wash away his wounds but knew that would be suicide. The fire had burnt low again, and he hadn't the strength to pull more firewood from the store and place it in the hearth.

He'd failed the egg as much as he'd failed himself, Solvi, his father.

His *Valta Forinja* rested against the wall, and he cursed for not grabbing that when he'd had the chance. Surely it would have cleaved Mateli in two, and he wouldn't be in this ridiculous situation.

Palom had envisioned Mateli in his room more than once—sometimes charging him, sometimes leering over him, blood dripping from his fangs.

He shuddered at the memory.

If only he could pull himself from the bed…grab hold of the sword…

An owl hooted.

Palom hadn't imagined anything that time, had he?

He propped himself up onto his elbows and strained to peer out of the window.

It hooted again, louder, this time.

'Lathri…?' He couldn't yell, didn't have the strength to.

He looked around, saw only linens on the bed, nothing that he could shove or push to make noise. 'Lathri…' He called, weaker this time.

Please let her have heard.

His vision swam with the blood loss.

A flutter of wings, the tap of talons on the window ledge.

He looked up to see an owl fill the window-frame, its feathers a mix of brown and white, its eyes ringed with black feathers, making her yellow-orange eyes all the more striking.

He'd recognise the colouration and markings anywhere.

'Lathri…'

She opened her wings to glide into the room, where she transformed back. 'Palom…Why did you take on Mateli?'

He bowed his head, chest heaving as he struggled for breath. 'He killed…these people. I had…to protect…Sol.'

She scowled at him. 'It's not your job to protect anyone! You can live your life without protecting people! You're not a failure if you don't!' She lifted her hands, her energy filling the room.

Palom winced as a torrent of warm air covered him, his wounds tingling as they healed.

She walked closer to him, stepping around the bloody laundry until her fingers touched his face. Her magic flowed through him, filling him with strength and energy.

'You…you have saved me.'

She dropped her hand and looked more drained than he had when she'd arrived. 'I haven't done anything,' she said in a tired voice.

'You have?' Palom rested a hand on her shoulder. 'I was injured. Maybe dying. Now, I am strong again, thanks to you.'

He breathed in her scent, wished he could stay like this, with her, forever. He felt her tremble under him, wished her healing powers did not take so much energy from her. 'I heard you before, Lathri,' he said. 'Before Mateli. Before this. When I came to Rio Neva forest, three Varkain attacked me.'

'Palom?' She frowned.

'An owl hooted. Warned me of Varkain attack.'

'It wasn't me, Palom. Aside from now, I've not left Taban Yul,' she said.

He blinked. 'But…I heard…I thought…'

She shook her head, fought to stave off tears, but they spilled down her cheeks.

'Lathri? What…what is wrong?'

'Palom, I've done as much as I can for you. There's nothing else I can do. Physical wounds heal, but you've a darkness in you that you have got to address.' She rested her hand on his chest. 'It's in here. It's eating you. And that sword is the catalyst!'

'No, no. I listened to you! I went to Sol. I saw Manilo. He was happy. I have realised I have missed out on so many things.'

'There's more to it than facing your past.' She wiped away her tears. 'It's the first step. But you have to stop dwelling on your failures when the real war is all around us and building! I'm dealing with a plague in Taban Yul unlike anything that's gone before! Sapora is releasing criminals and Isa is lost in it all.'

Palom took her hands in his. 'Then run away, Lathri. Run with me. We will find safe place away from all this sickness and despair. It's not your job to fight these battles.'

Lathri pulled her hands away from him. 'I'm not running away from my country's problems! I'm staying to fight! You're a tiger! Why aren't you acting like one?'

'I was tiger last night!' He said, raising his voice. 'Against Mateli, I held him off. Drove him back. He will not be attacking Sol now, because of me!'

'He wouldn't be anywhere near Sol if you hadn't run away from the capital!' Lathri yelled back, her emotions fuelling her anger.

'So, it is okay if Mateli is in Taban Yul? Attacking you? Attacking your comrades?'

'All of my allies and you? Together, Mateli wouldn't dream of attacking! You've come out here, to the middle of nowhere, alone. You're vulnerable! He *knows* that! Sapora knows that!'

'I am not fighting Sapora!'

'You *are*! He is fighting us! All of us! That means you! You can't run from that!' Lathri was almost screaming now. 'I may not be able to get to you if you run again! Farther into the wilderness. You can't expect me to drop everything and find you every time you get into trouble!'

He growled. 'I am sorry for…for…*inconveniencing* you…' He struggled around the word, but he could think of no other to make his point clear.

'You want to be with me? You want to get back together, to how it was before?' Lathri asked, her voice a little calmer.

'You know this is what I want.'

'Then come back to Taban Yul. Stand by my side. Fight with me.'

He knew she'd ask that.

He knew he'd have to say no when she did.

'My answer is same as before. I cannot.'

She trembled. 'Then there's nothing left for us.'

He stood silently for a moment, waiting to see if she'd say anything else, and not trusting himself to respond.

When she transformed back and flew out the window, he roared into the hearth with a cold fury that scared him a little.

She was wrong.

She was so wrong.

He wasn't a coward. He had fought.

He'd pushed through twenty years of fear and denial to return to his village; he'd met with his father, talked to him, eaten with him.

Solvi now saw him as part of her family.

He'd fought his greatest enemy and kept him from harming Solvi or the village.

Rage boiled up in him, and he roared again, screaming until he had no air left in his lungs.

What was the point of it all if Lathri couldn't see what he'd done? Didn't care what he'd done.

What was the point of any of it?

He grabbed his *Valta Forinja*, its power pulsing, and slashed it at his bed, the walls, the floor. It carved into the wood, splintering it and sending the linen flying.

He'd tried!

Rhea knew, he'd tried.

And it still wasn't enough.

Why wasn't it enough?

He threw the weapon through the window, the blade careening into the forest, sending sparks of energy in all directions, slicing through the trees and burning the ground until it came to a stop.

He collapsed on the floor, head in his hands, and wept.

Everything he tried, he failed in.

Even when he tried to make things right, he still messed it up.

What good was a tiger without a purpose?

How could he be worth anything to anyone?

Everyone he'd tried to protect had died, fuelling his desire to defend even more.

A vicious circle that he had no way to escape.

Palom decided to leave.

He couldn't stay here, in this place of death and mistakes.

He'd do just as Lathri suggested—go deeper into Val Sharis, lose himself in the wilderness of winter.

Perhaps then he'd figure out what it was all for.

As he stood to grab his belongings, the smallest of noises caught his attention. A chirp, like a bird. A tiny one.

He looked out the window, but the damage caused by the *Valta Forinja* had cleared the area of any wildlife. Palom strained to listen, when he heard it again—behind him, this time.

The hearth.

Eyes wide, Palom watched as the once dormant dragon egg twitched, rocking ever so slightly where it sat on the dead embers. A tiny crack appeared, then another, then another, all along the top of the egg.

'You are alive…' Palom said, too stunned to react in any other way.

He watched as a tiny black talon protruded from the gap, and the hatchling within took its first breath outside the egg.

Chapter Eighteen

Cold. So damned cold.

Amarah shivered.

'Why…why's it dark?'

'You were badly injured. I had to cover your eyes.'

Kohl's voice.

Where the fuck was Jato?

'Take off the cover. I feel fine. Where's Jato hiding?'

'She's gone.'

His voice seemed quieter than usual.

She lifted her hands, felt around her face, and picked at the fabric wrapped around her eyes.

Kohl moved somewhere to her left, sending a cold breeze over her.

Amarah shivered again and yanked the fabric off over the top of her head, the static sending loose hair in all directions.

She blinked.

Something wasn't right.

Firstly, she appeared to be sat on the broken floor of Jato's tower—somewhere she did *not* want to be.

Secondly—and this was the main problem—why could she only see out of her left eye?

Amarah brought her hands up to her face, felt the swollen skin, felt scabs over her wounds. Her fingers trembled. 'Kohl...'

'I got there as fast as I could,' he said, still not looking at her 'A few seconds longer and she'd have killed you. Jato's so strong...'

She heard what he said but couldn't process it. 'Kohl. Tell me...what the fuck happened.' She touched her brittle hair, and clumps of it came away in her fingers.

Then she smelled the burning, like a fire left as embers for too long. Her Arillian robes had been singed, the edges of her sleeves burned away.

'It was a direct hit, Amarah,' Kohl continued. 'Not even that scythe of yours could absorb her attack.'

Amarah stormed over to him, grabbed his shoulder, and turned him to face her. 'I'm alive, ain't I?'

He pulled away from her, and Amarah grabbed him more forcefully. 'Kohl, look at me!'

'You've been unconscious for nearly a week. I...I didn't think you'd survive.'

That stopped her in her tracks.

It felt as though she'd been fighting Jato only five minutes ago. How could she have been out for a week?

She traced her fingers over her face again.

That explained the scabs.

But her vision…?

She closed her left eye, and her breath caught.

Nothing.

She could see absolutely nothing.

'What did she do?' Amarah screamed, her hands running over her face. 'Where is she?'

Kohl just watched as she cried out, and that angered her even more. Why wouldn't he tell her?

'Amarah…I'm sorry…'

'Tell me where she is! I'll find her! I'll hunt her across Linaria!' She didn't care that she only had one eye, didn't care that flying *Khanna* would be hard.

She could fly with her eyes closed if she had to.

'Where's my scythe? I'll get her back for this, mark my words, I'll get her back!' Spittle flew in her rage, but Kohl still looked like a kicked puppy. 'Fine. Don't tell me. I'll find her myself. I'm used to hunting down things that are hard to find!'

Amarah saw her scythe leaning against what was left of the entrance to the tower. She took a step forward, the rock uneven underfoot, and wobbled.

'Be careful, Amarah. Your balance without both eyes…'

She stumbled, flailed, and grasped at the air as she fell. She caught her knee on the rocks, grazing it, and cursed again.

'Amarah, you…you can't…'

'Don't give me that "good father" rubbish, Kohl!' She heaved herself up and pressed on, using the wall to balance as she moved towards her scythe.

'It has nothing to do with that. You *can't* follow her,' he said, fluttering his wings to catch up to her. He landed beside the tower's entrance. '*Khanna*...*Khanna*'s destroyed. Jato...She...Her attack...'

Amarah wobbled again.

'I'm sorry. There's nothing left, there's only splinters...'

She dry-heaved. 'You've got...that's a sick joke. You still love her but...I'm going after her. Don't come up with pig-shit to...make me not.'

He rested a hand on her shoulder. 'I'm not making it up. Amarah, I'm sorry.'

She coughed, began to hyperventilate. 'Don't joke! Don't you dare joke about Khanna!'

'I'll show you...' He said, taking her hand and leading her out of the ruins of the tower and onto the snowy field.

Amarah recognised the fire pit—the flames now extinguished—and a small crater beside it. The dip in the ground was full of snow, and when she peered over the lip of the crater, tears streamed down her face. There were only a few wooden boards and a bit of fabric from her sails left.

She tried to swallow, spat it out.

Coughed again.

'*Khanna*...What have you done to my *Khanna*!' Amarah collapsed onto her knees, fists pounding the ground. 'I trusted you, Kohl! What a damned mistake that was! I should have gone to Berel! Should have gone to Topeko!'

Kohl sat on the edge of the crater and said nothing.

'What a fucking waste. Came out here to do some good and look what happened!' She cried, letting out her grief.

What was she going to do without *Khanna*?

She'd been through everything with that ship.

Khanna was her freedom, her life.

Khanna was as much a part of her as her arms and legs. 'And I'm stuck on this damned rock without a ship to get away!' She sniffed and shook her head.

It would be funny if it wasn't so bloody depressing.

She sobbed for a while. A handful of Arillians flew overhead and looked down at her.

She didn't need their pity.

Or were they afraid she'd attack again?

When her tears dried, and her nose ran, she sniffed and wiped her face. She didn't care about her eye, her skin, her hair.

She was angry at herself for coming out here on the strength of Kohl's promises.

Amarah sat back on her knees and looked at him. 'Be honest with me. Could you ever have helped? Your Arillian magic? The Golems? Would any of it actually worked?'

'I think there's a chance. But I needed Jato to work with me to ask them, to use her leadership to try…' he said.

'So, she'd rather mope about her dead boyfriend than do anything about it.' Amarah sniffed, wiping the last of her tears from her face. 'Great, just fucking great.'

'I tried to convince her.'

Amarah licked her lips. 'You haven't got a hope of convincing that one of anything.' She shuddered and looked up, trying to halt the sudden wave of tears which threatened. 'So, where'd she go?'

Kohl sighed. 'I don't know. There are still Arillians who're loyal to her. She took them and flew off. She wants revenge for what happened to Aciel…She…She holds a deeper love for him than she does for me.'

'I could've told you that,' Amarah said, suddenly feeling empty.

He shook his head. 'I'll never speak to her again…'

'You're better off. Trust me.'

She slumped where she sat, dizzy from her compromised vision, and half-raging, half-grieving over the loss of *Khanna*. 'What a bloody wasted trip.'

'I'm sorry,' Kohl said.

Amarah shrugged. 'I should've known it.'

This put her back to square one—how to get Moroda out.

Without an airship.

While blind in one eye.

'What else is stronger than a Sevastos?' She asked. 'Other than your Golems, which are about as useless as the ice they're from.' She raised her hands, then let them drop to her thighs with a slap.

Kohl didn't bother to rise to her insult. 'Nothing, as far as I know. Rhea herself, if you believe in her.'

Amarah didn't much care for gods and fairy stories.

She pinched the bridge of her nose, thinking. She'd always had her ship to get out of whatever mess she'd found herself in.

Always.

'If a Sevastos sealed Moroda. Maybe another one can break the seal?'

'I…I suppose?'

She bit her lip, thinking. One of those ereven spheres would be nice. That'd help her track down another Sevastos same way Moroda had.

'You're good at hunting dragons, aren't you? Maybe you can make up for this fuck up by offering to help track a Sevastos for me.'

Kohl frowned. 'I wouldn't have the first idea how to find a Sevastos.'

Amarah rolled her eyes. 'Dragons above, use your brain! How did you track normal dragons before? What can you take from that to apply to a Sevastos? Come on, Kohl, I know you're upset. Damn, so am I—like you wouldn't believe—but sitting on this icy rock moaning about it ain't gonna change anything!'

She saw him wince. 'What else were you gonna do? Sit here and hope one day Jato would come back and hug you? I tell you know, she ain't like that. The sooner you move on, the better.'

She was doing it again. Covering her fear and pain with anger. Pretending she was stronger than she felt.

'Amarah can you just…can you just *not*? For once?'

She pushed herself to her feet. 'No! I'm not sitting around waiting for you to stop feeling sorry for yourself. If Jato's on the warpath again, people will die. I'm here to sort out Moroda. Are you gonna sort out your daughter?'

He covered his face with his hands, rubbed at his eyelids.

'I came here for one reason. That's blown apart, so I'm looking at my options, doing what I can.'

'Amarah, you don't even have a ship. How are you planning on finding a Sevastos?' There was a bite in his tone.

'I don't have my *Khanna* thanks to your brat,' she huffed. 'Wanna know what I'm gonna do about it?' She put her hands on her hips.

'...What?'

'I need a ship. I'm going on an old-fashioned treasure hunt, 'cept it's a dragon I'll be hunting. Lucky for me I've got allies who know a thing or two about treasure hunts.'

'You have allies?' Kohl raised an eyebrow.

'I have friends in all sorts of places,' she said. 'I'll see if I can call on some of my old pirating partners. See if we can strike a deal. You gonna help me out on this hunt? Pay me back for destroying my ship?'

Kohl looked at her, incredulous. 'You just said you didn't trust me?'

'I don't need to trust you to benefit from you. Right now, I could do with someone who hunted dragons for a living. An' you owe me a ship. So, if you feel bad about this,' she pointed to her right eye, 'you can call it paying me back.'

'Amarah, I don't...' Kohl hesitated.

'You told me you were a leader once. Lead, damn you!' She hobbled back to the remnants of Jato's tower and picked up her scythe. 'Or don't. If you'd rather sit here and mope, I can't stop you. I'll get another Arillian to help me. They want me gone. They'll help me get off this bloody rock.'

She wanted to cry again. Wanted to scream.

Khanna destroyed because of his damned daughter. Why couldn't he see how toxic she was? That Linaria would be better off without her? The he would be better off without her?

Amarah widened her stance, twirled the scythe a little slower than usual. She'd have to push through—somehow.

'I'll come with you,' Kohl said. 'But you should rest. You've been hurt, badly. Heading to the mainland is too much—'

'I'm not waiting,' she snapped.

He raised his hands defensively. 'Okay. Sorry for having consideration.'

She cackled at that. 'Don't make me laugh. The only thing you care about is Jato.'

'I used to. There's nothing left for me here, now.'

She frowned. 'Look, you're actually listening to me now!'

'Could it…could it be a chance at redemption? You and I have a second chance to do something right?'

Amarah rolled her eyes. 'It's taking opportunities when they come along.'

'I…Have I been on the wrong path this whole time? I wanted to save Jato. Even if she didn't understand, didn't want to be saved.'

Amarah trudged away, leaving Kohl to mutter about his change of heart. He'd said he'd help her, that was all she needed. So long as he got her away from Oren, she didn't care what else he did.

She'd find her allies, get a new ship, and free Moroda.

Then she'd hunt down Jato and cut her into so many pieces even Kohl wouldn't recognise her.

'Amarah, hold on!' Kohl called, flying after her when he'd realised she'd headed off alone. 'I'll carry you back to the others. You'll need supplies if we're to be on foot down there.'

She considered for a moment, then nodded. She didn't even mind the indignity of being picked up and flown by Kohl. Anything to get moving faster.

*

'I think it is best that you're leaving,' Tymē said when Amarah told her what she planned to do. 'Things with Jato are still unsettled. Those under Aciel's compulsion are still unwell. It may be years before they come back to their senses. But so many loved the prestige he won us, and that's why they follow Jato.'

Amarah huffed. 'I don't care why they follow her. They're idiots to think she's gonna get them any respect.'

Tymē shook her head and handed her the bundle of robes and furs that Kohl had asked if she could provide. 'These are all we can spare. I have never walked to the mainland, but you know how long it took to fly…'

'I'm not worried,' Amarah said, wrapping the linens around her and pulling on a new pair of fur-lined boots. 'Kohl will fly me as much as he can. I only need to get to Tum Metsa.'

'She is very optimistic,' Kohl said to Tymē.

'I know. Goodness knows we could do with a little positivity.'

'Will you be okay?' Kohl asked.

Tymē shrugged. 'We've been on our own since your exile. I'm sure we'll manage.' She smiled sadly at him, and Amarah sensed a longing in her body language.

With a bag full of cold meat and vegetables, about the only food that would last, and bundled up in thick clothing, Amarah finally felt ready to return to the mainland.

She'd spent far too long on the floating rock. 'No more secrets, Kohl,' she said. 'Don't let me down this time.'

'I won't,' Kohl said. He'd managed to procure a new hat, whether that had been from Tymē or another Arillian, Amarah didn't know. Somehow it didn't suit him – she was so used to seeing the old, faded one.

'Perhaps I should go first,' Kohl said. 'Find an airship, have it brought back up here?'

'Don't start any of that. I'm going. Now. I'll be able to cope! I don't expect you to carry me the whole way back,' Amarah said.

Tymē leaned forward and wrapped her arms around Amarah. 'Good luck on your journey. If you see Jato…Be gentle with her.'

Amarah patted Tymē's back but said nothing of what she'd do were she and Jato to cross paths again. Amarah liked Tymē and didn't want to antagonise her.

Kohl hugged Tymē next, and Amarah rolled her shoulders. The world looked so different through one eye, off-centre, somehow. At least she'd have time to get used to it before she could fly an airship again.

A crowed of Arillians had gathered again as they stood near the edge of Oren. She supposed nothing much ever happened up here, and she'd created all sorts of entertainment for them.

As much as she felt welcome among Linaria's outcasts, she wouldn't miss the place. 'Whenever you're ready, Kohl,' she called, and the Arillian reluctantly pulled away from Tymē.

'We have to pass the Golems again,' he said, walking over to stand by her side. He looked down, expression grim.

'You got me past them before. If we're leaving, should be even easier.'

'Ever the optimist,' he sighed.

'Let's go.'

Kohl picked her up, one arm around her back, the other under her knees. Amarah wrapped her arms around him, scythe clutched tight. She took a deep breath.

Flying was easy when you had a ship under your feet.

With Kohl, the descent would essentially be a freefall.

He raised his wings and leapt, and Amarah bit down on the urge to scream.

Wind rushed up around them, stinging her skin as they descended. Her hair whipped around her face and Amarah squeezed her eyes shut – partly to lessen the stinging, and partly so she wouldn't see the ground rushing up to meet them.

She gripped onto Kohl rightly, her fingers digging into his cloak. Going down was so much scarier than coming up.

Finally, the wind quietened, and she opened her good eye.

They were greeted by the two mountains she'd flown through, and at their base, the Golem army.

Beyond, the snowy tundra went on and on into the distance.

Gently, Kohl set her on her feet. 'You all right?'

'I'm fine.' In truth, she thought she'd vomit at any moment.

Amarah patted herself down, pulling loose fabric that had been blown around during the descent back into place. By the time she'd finished, the initial wave of nausea had passed.

'The Golems await,' Kohl said. 'Shall I carry you again?'

'I'll walk for a bit,' she said. 'Get my bearings, y'know.' She gestured to her eyes, and he nodded.

Her first few steps were shakier than she'd have liked, and she bumped into Kohl more than once, but eventually she fell into a kind of rhythm, and the two of them walked across the snow to the Arillian guardians.

From such a distance, the Golems looked like toy figurines. Amarah knew her sight was playing tricks on her as it was, but it felt like all of a sudden, they appeared before them, taller than anything she could have imagined.

She had to tilt her head back as far as she could and even then, she could barely see the tops of them. 'What…what would they actually do if…If they attacked?'

'They'd move,' Kohl said. 'If they're still, they're happy.'

Amarah puffed her cheeks out and exhaled. 'Good to know. If they stepped on us, we'd be dead!'

Kohl smiled. 'Pretty much.'

They cautiously moved forwards, past the enormous ice sentinels as they stood guard silently.

Amarah bit her lip, held her breath, tried to walk across the snow as quietly as possible. It was silly, really. From what Kohl had said, the Golems knew she was there. But she couldn't help but try to make herself smaller, quieter, and hope she could slip past them undetected.

It took the better part of ten minutes to walk past them, creeping forward step by slow step. Kohl had fluttered his wings once, the movement making her jump, but otherwise the Golems remained impassive to their presence.

'We're okay…?' Amarah asked, when they were finally in front of the Golems.

'Yes. We've a long way to go until the mainland,' Kohl said, and she heard the relief in his voice. 'I'll fly us as long as possible.'

Though she didn't like it, Amarah knew what he said made sense. He could fly much faster than they could walk, especially while she was still unsteady on her feet. 'Okay. But not too high. Dragons above, I don't like flying with anyone else in charge.'

Kohl attempted to hide his smirk at her words, and she resigned herself to being carried for the next little while.

'A shame those Golems of yours couldn't help,' she muttered, looking back at them as Kohl flew off. 'Would've made losing *Khanna* worth it.'

'I am truly sorry.'

'She's a spiteful one,' Amarah replied. 'I just hope this other Sevastos helps. If not, I'll be in debt for the rest of my life, and that just don't sit well with me.'

She sighed, resting her chin on Kohl's shoulder, as they flew towards the mainland, and her hope of resurrecting Moroda.

Chapter Nineteen

Palom had little experience with babies—of any type—and spent the best part of an hour simply watching the dragon hatchling as it explored its surroundings of the hearth and the remnants of Palom's room.

He knew he needed to leave, but he wasn't sure what to do with the hatchling now it was here. He'd taken the old egg to look after it more than anything, he hadn't actually thought that a dragon could still somehow be alive and hatch.

The young dragon's scales were a smooth, sea blue, with a pale underbelly, white, downy mane, and sharp black talons. It watched Palom, curious, with bright golden eyes.

About the size of a house cat, it followed Palom as he walked around his room, investigating his belongings and sniffing at his sword when he picked it up.

Irritated at his new "shadow," Palom lit the fire again and watched the hatchling settle happily into the flames as if it were a bed.

Content that he'd have peace—for a little while, at least—Palom continued to gather his belongings and what supplies he could find in the Waterside Inn.

Flies had gathered around the corpses, and Palom held his breath as he walked back through the dining room and into the kitchen, where he helped himself to whatever food hadn't gone mouldy.

He had no real idea of where to go or what he would do next, but he knew it would take him a long while to figure things out.

From the inn's stock, he plucked an apple and munched through it as he moved from room to room, taking what he needed, no longer caring what he did. He knew it was ransacking, but as Amarah would say, the dead didn't need their things.

It didn't matter, anyway.

Nothing mattered anymore.

Palom carried his haul to the inn's entrance, bundling up what he could in a large bag. It would be midday before long—he needed to get going soon, so he could cover as much ground as possible while he still had light.

Clouds had gathered through the morning, and they threatened to unleash more snow over Val Sharis. 'Is fitting weather…' Palom muttered to himself, knelt by his bag as he tied it up.

Now he just needed to grab his *Valta Forinja* and decide what to do with the baby—

Palom thought he'd been hit by a boulder.

He crashed into the side of the inn, a booted foot pressing his chest down to keep him pinned, knocking the breath out of him.

'You recovered quickly,' Mateli hissed.

Palom looked up and saw him properly for the first time.

Heavier than he remembered, Mateli seemed to have broken his nose some time recently, and his jaw had been shredded to ribbons.

'You…should be…in prison,' Palom wheezed as Mateli pushed down harder on his chest.

'You should be dead,' Mateli retorted.

Palom grabbed Mateli's boot with both hands and shoved him back. He got to his feet in the same movement, wishing he'd had the foresight to bring his sword outside with him.

They leapt at one another, punching and kicking, kneeing and grappling. The threw each other around, grabbed hold of each other and wrestled, with neither the stronger one.

Palom landed a strong punch to Mateli's chest, felt ribs crack under his knuckles. He fought on instinct, on reflex. Dodging attacks and landing his own when he could.

The very act of killing Mateli to protect his family seemed completely unimportant now.

'No more friends to help you out?' Mateli asked with a sneer, when they'd parted for a moment. 'I'd have had ya last night if that girl hadn't turned up.'

Palom glowered. 'I can beat you by myself.'

'Sure, sure. That's why I always kicked the shit outta ya when ya mouthed off to me as a kid,' Mateli grinned, as though relishing the memory. 'We would have changed Taban Yul! You and me. Woulda kept everyone in line. We'd have been kings of the city!'

'You are monster. Even Sapora is better king than you would be.'

'Anyone is better than a snake!' Mateli spat.

Palom laughed, mirthless. 'You are worst kind of scum, Mateli. It was mistake to follow you for so long. Sapora made mistake to let you out.'

They grappled again. Palom grabbed at Mateli's long hair and pulled the man's face into his waiting knee.

Mateli grabbed Palom's legs and pulled him down with him, both kicking snow and dirt into each other's faces.

Mateli snarled, shifting form, and Palom responded in kind.

Palom wouldn't let Mateli grab hold of him again, and there was no more Lathri to help if he got injured.

That thought fuelled Palom's rage as the two of them came together, slashing and biting at one another.

Kill Mateli.

Kill him, and then he could get away.

Snow began to fall, slowly at first, just a snowflake here and there, and then a flurry soon masked Palom's vision.

Their roars echoed through the trees, and Palom lunged again and again, trying to land a bite or swipe at Mateli's eyes or nose—the only weak spots in his armour-plated body.

He considered running inside, grabbing his sword.

But then he could bring Mateli onto the hatchling, and he didn't want to do that—the young dragon had only just emerged.

The crocodile snapped faster than a creature of his size had any right to. Even with his bulk, his tail delivered a strong blow when it landed, and Palom felt his muscles bruise.

Though refreshed from Lathri's healing, Palom's mind had yet to rest. He'd not slept all night and became aware of his reactions slowing down.

He struck Mateli in the face with his right front paw, and Mateli took a few steps back.

Palom panted, the explosive energy he'd had at the beginning of the fight all but gone. He couldn't afford for Mateli to wear him down. He needed to bring the fight to an end, one way or another—and there was only one way he'd be able to do it.

He approached Mateli from the side and withstood two blows in quick succession from Mateli's armoured tail. He leapt and landed on Mateli's back, immediately clawing his way along Mateli's body.

Mateli bellowed again, the sound as deep as a pit. Even under his *meraki*, Palom's blood turned to ice, and the crocodile rolled.

Palom dug his claws in and held on, but the sheer weight of the crocodile almost crushed him, and he cried out in pain.

Mateli whipped his jaws around, snapping them inches from Palom's face as he leaned out of the way and pulled himself free from under the crocodile.

Immediately, Mateli charged forward, putting on a burst of speed that brought him within striking range. Palom bared his teeth, snarling and snapping at Mateli's jaws.

He leapt again, straight up and over Mateli's teeth to land on his back. Palom turned and lunged forward, sinking his teeth into the back of Mateli's head. His front canines pierced the crocodile's skull, and he bit down as hard as he could.

The half-scream, half-roar that Mateli produced was deafening, but it faded to nothing as the crocodile finally stopped struggling.

Breathing heavily, Palom staggered off and transformed back. It was over.

He'd beaten Mateli—and he hadn't used his *Valta Forinja* to do it!

He'd been strong enough alone.

Hardly able to believe it, Palom sat for a moment in the falling snow, watching at the crocodile slowly shifted back, revealing Mateli's glassy eyes.

If he'd done one good thing recently, Palom knew it was this.

Once he'd caught his breath, he limped back into the inn and his old room. The dragon chirped happily at his return, flapping its wings and snapping its tiny teeth. It had no idea that Palom had been on the brink of death just a few minutes ago.

He smiled a little, then picked up the gold brooch that Lathri had returned to him, kissed it once, and put it back on the mantle.

He grabbed his sword and turned to the dragon. 'Are you coming or staying here, little one?'

The hatchling growled, then leapt out of the flames to follow Palom as he left the inn.

He shouldn't have been surprised, really.

He suspected it might be hungry, but Palom didn't have any meat, and any he'd found in the kitchens had spoiled.

'We will go hunting soon. You will find life can be hard. You may be hungry a lot.' Palom wasn't sure why he was talking to the hatchling, but it felt better than ignoring it.

The snow was coming down heavily now, and from the looks of the grey clouds overhead, it would be snowing for at least the rest of the day.

He sighed.

'Farewell, Lathri. I am sorry I failed you.'

He turned away from the inn and started up the stone path, towards the north of Val Sharis. He'd barely taken ten steps when he heard boots slapping on the stones, and stopped to look back.

Chyro was running up the road. He looked like he'd recovered a little, but the healers of Sol were nothing to Lathri's standards.

'Chryo. Why are you here?' Palom asked, raising an eyebrow as the young captain reached him.

'I wanted to help you against the crocodile,' Chryo said, one hand on his chest as he caught his breath.

'I told you to stay. Is everyone in Sol okay?'

Chryo nodded, still too out of breath to speak.

'Good. It was Mateli who attacked you and Waterside Inn. He should be in prison. Looks like King Sapora released him early for good behaviour. You can clean up this, yes?'

Chryo swallowed and peered round Palom, his eyebrows lifting when he saw Mateli's body on the ground. 'Y…Yes. I'll need to get help from Taban Yul, first,' he said.

Palom picked up his bag. 'This is good. I am leaving now. Stay clear of Varkain, they are trouble.'

'Wait, wait! Palom!' Chyro called after him. 'Where's Solvi? Please tell me Mateli didn't get her? I told her not to leave Feoras Sol, so did your father, but she wouldn't listen…'

'Solvi is in Taban Yul,' Palom said, trudging along the path, his boots already crunching in the settling snow. The young dragon bounded after him happily. Every so often it would dart forward and nip at his boots, but Palom ignored it.

'How come she's in the capital? Why…is that a *dragon*?'

Palom glanced over his shoulder as Chyro hurried through the snow to catch up with him. 'Yes. It…Is long story.' He sighed, unwilling to recount the details to the overenthusiastic Ittallan.

'Wait a minute, Palom! Please?' Chyro asked again.

With a sigh, Palom turned to face him. 'What do you want, Chyro?'

'What I just asked! Why's Solvi in the capital? Is she hurt? I can ignore the dragon for now,' he gestured to the hatchling, who hopped between Palom's feet as though it were some kind of game.

'What about your father? Manilo? The *Archigos*? The rest of Sol? Are you leaving them again?' Chyro pressed.

Palom regretted stopping for him.

If he left now, he didn't have to explain anything.

Didn't have to think about what he was doing—rightly or wrongly.

'I am leaving because it is better if I go.'

'Better for who?' Chyro asked. 'You just protected Feoras Sol—no, this whole region—from Mateli. And now you're *leaving*? I'm sure you could be rewarded for that!'

Palom sighed.

Considering Sapora had been the one who'd released Mateli, he highly doubted the king would reward him for slaying the crocodile.

A fact seemingly lost on Chyro.

Naïve boy.

'I am not interested in rewards or gold or…or…people telling me I am hero!' He felt his rage build and his *Valta Forinja* pulsed again. 'I am danger to people. I am threat. I am causing problems and deaths everywhere I go!'

'But—'

'No! I am done. People do not need me, apparently. So, I am going. Now.' He took another step along the path.

'Going where?'

'Away!' Palom bellowed.

He was angry now. Or was he upset over Lathri? Over Mateli?

It didn't matter.

Nothing mattered anymore.

'I don't understand. You've just come back into Solvi's life and now you're leaving…' Chyro tried again.

'She has you. She has Manilo. Archigos. She has everyone she has always had. I have not been there for her before. She can live without me now.'

Palom wouldn't speak of it anymore.

It was just too painful.

'What am I going to tell Manilo?'

Palom shrugged. 'Tell him what you want. The truth. A lie. It does not matter. At least Mateli is no longer problem for him.'

He continued up the path, afraid that if he stopped again, he'd never leave.

He had grown fond of the captain. 'Goodbye, Chyro. *Asfali.*'

'Palom…' Chyro stopped trying to call him back, trying to bring him back into conversation.

He hated it. Hated what he was becoming.

If Lathri was right—and she was rarely wrong—he only had the sword to blame for it.

The dragon leapt at him, grabbing hold of his leg with its claws and scrambling up his back to sit on his shoulder.

Saving a dragon couldn't be wrong…could it?

He glanced at the hatchling and adjusted his hold on his bag.

No. The sword might have more powers than even he understood or could control, but it allowed him to find the egg. Allowed him to save a life.

It couldn't only be a weapon of destruction if that had happened, surely.

‘I guess I am not completely alone, then,’ he muttered to the dragon, who chirped in response.

Before Palom reached a bend in the road, where the trees grew even thicker, he glanced back to see Chyro stood in the falling snow, watching him leave.

Chapter Twenty

Sapora sat on the floor, his back against the stone, panting. The stale air was thin and tasted disgusting, but it was sweet relief after almost losing himself in dirt. He wiped a handful of it off his chin and used his forearm to clear the sweat that had gathered at his hairline.

Sapora squinted in the dark, trying to make out the room's features, but all he could tell was the chamber was circular, and made of stone. He ran his hand along the wall beside him, and saw ancient writing carved into it. A Varkain tongue, he thought, recognising a few of the symbols.

An old one, for sure.

It made sense. Malashash had to be five thousand years old at least.

He grinned.

Once he'd recovered from his excursion through the tunnel, Sapora got to his feet and walked forwards, he steps echoing all around him, highlighting how cavernous the crypt really was.

Sapora shuddered a little at the cold, or was it leftover blood magic that caused the chill?

He approached the centre and felt the stone shift underfoot.

He glanced down and saw narrow channels carved into the stone—six of them, and all deep. Sapora crouched and put a claw in one but couldn't feel anything of significance.

Did he…Did he need more blood?

He stood up again and frowned. He certainly hoped not.

Thralls he could rustle up from Sereth, but getting *so* many down here to fill those channels…?

No. There had to be another way.

Sapora followed the channels in a straight line until he reached a plinth, upon which sat an enormous stone statue. It looked to have been carved by a master stone smith—every scale, every piece of armour had been fashioned perfectly, and in such exquisite detail.

'As though the real thing simply turned to stone…' Sapora hissed, his pupils dilating.

He glanced down to the base of the plinth and saw a shallow dish—like a deep platter.

He reached forward with his bloodied and dirty hand and rested it against the stone statue.

At his touch, the wall sconces surrounding him immediately burst into blue flame. The crypt had been so dark, Sapora hadn't even known sconces had been mounted to the wall.

When he looked back to the statue, Sapora saw Malashash staring back at him with deep green eyes.

Sapora swallowed and took a reflexive step backwards, his scimitar clutched in his good hand.

'Malashash,' he said, regaining his composure after a moment.

The eyes didn't move, didn't blink, their green the only colour in the stone body.

Sapora pulled his small knife from his sleeve and placed it in the dish in front of the plinth. What little of Tacio's blood had survived the tunnels dropped to the bottom of the dish.

The fires in the sconces flickered, hardly noticeable, and then continued to burn.

Sapora narrowed his eyes.

He'd brought the blood. His and another willing to partake in the ritual. The fires burned.

Why hadn't Malashash responded?

He checked the dish again—plenty of Tacio's blood there…

He looked around the room, looked for some clue as to how to get Malashash free.

Was there something in the sconces?

On the floor?

The plinth itself?

Sapora stalked around the room, feeling for anything out of place, any lever he needed to activate, stone he needed to move.

But the crypt gave away nothing.

He cursed.

'*Naja…*'

Sapora whirled around. Malashash hadn't moved. The word echoed off the stone—or had he imagined it?

Too long underground, without fresh air to breathe?

He scowled. There had to be something obvious that he'd overlooked. Something he had to have done or said.

Some kind of key…?

Sapora pulled the map from his inside pocket and held it up by one of the blue flames. The coloured light threw shadows across the parchment, but Sapora narrowed his eyes, trying to look past the abstract shapes and movement.

But the map revealed no secret, not hidden password to access Malashash and reverse the stone imprisonment.

He cursed again and transformed.

His coils filled the stone crypt and circled Malashash in the centre. The flames licked his scales, but he was too large to avoid their touch.

Sapora moved as close to Malashash as he could, lowered his fangs until their tips brushed the stone. He allowed a drop of venom to fall down.

It hissed as it touched the stone, and then disappeared, absorbed by it.

Still nothing.

Sapora flicked out his tongue, tasting the air for something, anything, that he'd missed in his weaker form.

He must have overlooked something.

None of the Arks had ever been freed—he was deep in the unknown. The histories had hinted at what happened, guessed at their locations, and he'd filled in the blanks.

He knew how they'd risen, what their strengths were.

But bringing them back?

Uncharted waters.

It made sense that it wouldn't be as simple as a drop of blood.

He transformed back, knelt on the stone floor in front of the plinth. 'Forgive my haste, Malashash. It won't be long. I swear it.'

*

Isa thumbed through the books in Sapora's Council tower. He and Tacio spent most of their time holed up here, flicking through one book or another while Koraki and Voulhrik carried messages for them.

She'd done what Sapora had asked—she'd overseen the arrival of the Sevastos into the palace grounds and arranged for the canvas to cover the width of the gardens, covering it from anyone flying overhead.

Now, she needed to figure out where Sapora and Tacio had charged off to in such a hurry.

Without telling her.

Lathri's words replayed in her mind. Sapora's dislike of the Ittallan. He's a Varkain, not one of them.

It was clear that she and he were on different pages. He didn't trust her as much as she claimed, otherwise she'd be privy to his secrets.

And Tacio didn't trust her at all.

She huffed, shoving reams of paper across the table as she tried to find what had obsessed Sapora for so long. For what might explain his sudden disappearance.

The tomes he'd been reading were histories. Ancient histories. From the Ittallan-Varkain war, mostly. She snorted. Why was he reading those if he supposedly had the Ittallan's best interests at heart?

Her stomach sank.

Had she been naïve all this time? Believing him to be something better than he was?

He'd shown her respect, kindness, compassion, when no-one else had. Even the Varkain today still belittled her.

But did that mean Sapora was good?

Of course not.

He acted in his own best interests.

She bit her thumbnail, shoved books out of the way with her free hand, and unearthed a ream of loose parchment. 'Maps?'

Come to think of it, Sapora had been studying maps more than books recently.

She grabbed the nearest one, pulled it close. As to be expected, it was a map of Val Sharis dating back an estimated 4,000 years. A little after the war, then.

As she studied it, Isa noticed ink marks—recent ones—splotched all over the country at random intervals. He'd written and crossed over the words, circles blank spaces on the map—where Isa knew there to be towns now—and had also circles towns which no longer existed. He'd sectioned up the Feor Mountains, Rio Neva forest, the snow plains to the far north and the estuaries and lush meadows to the south and east.

What was he looking for?

What had he *found*?

She cast the map aside and looked at another, smaller version. It depicted Val Sharis some 6,000 years prior and had even less detail.

Footsteps outside. Isa glanced up, holding her breath.

She hadn't been expressly forbidden from being in here, but it was an almost unsaid rule that no-one entered the council tower without Sapora himself being there.

The footsteps disappeared, and she relaxed, dropping her shoulders. Probably Roke looking to report.

She had to be careful.

At least she could escape through the window when she needed to get away.

Isa made her way to the bookcase next. They books had been arranged relatively neatly, and she glanced over the spines.

Histories.

Geographies.

Law.

Studies of Arillians.

Wait…Arillians? The book seemed out of place, so she plucked it from the shelf and opened the cover.

It seemed to have been read and re-read as there was a crease in the pages, and Isa let the book naturally open to them.

A passage had been marked in the same ink that was all over the maps:

The Ice Golems of the floating isles have a power unlike anything else in Linaria. They are landscape made living and have shaped the Arillians' cities in a way that hasn't been seen since. Many have attempted to recreate their power, with little success.

Isa scratched her head. Was Sapora trying to create some kind of super weapon? But he already had a Sevastos.

She paced, mind reeling. Thinking to all the conversations she'd heard him have with Tacio. All the talk he'd had with Roke.

She went back to the big map on the table, looked to the far north, where the Arillian islands were. She'd ignored them at first because no-one considered their land as part of Val Sharis, but now she looked, she saw Sapora had written four very distinct names:

Malashash.

Brahm.

Veynothi.

Karekis.

Isa swallowed. She knew those names.

She picked up one of the history books, just to be sure. Isa thumbed through the pages, eyes scanning, looking for just those names and nothing else.

Her breath caught.

The Arks.

Sapora wasn't trying to make a super weapon.

He was trying to bring them *back.*

Panic rose in her gut. It was no wonder Sapora kept referring to the treasures. If anyone knew, anyone believed that was his goal…

She had to tell someone who would appreciate the magnitude of her discovery. Someone she could trust.

'Lathri,' Isa whispered to herself. She shoved the books back as she'd found them, transformed into her wild cat form, and ran straight for the window.

*

Isa pounded on the door. She didn't care who saw her, didn't care if anyone thought her behaviour didn't fit royalty. 'Lathri! It's me, Isa! Please, open.'

She heard the door unlock, chains slide across, and then Kylos answered the door. 'Please, princess…There are sick people in here.'

Isa swallowed. 'I'm sorry, this is urgent.'

Kylos narrowed her eyes, and Isa saw her look past her.

'I've come alone. I swear,' she said. 'Can I come in?'

'Lathri isn't here, she had to see to someone late last night. She isn't back yet.'

'That's fine. I'll wait.' Isa took a step forward, but Kylos blocked her.

'I'm afraid I can't let you in, princess. Not while Lathri's not here.'

Isa frowned. 'I knocked on the front door to be nice. If I wanted, I could climb up the building and come in through the balcony. I thought you wanted me on your side?'

Kylos considered for a moment. She sighed, and then stepped back, holding the door open for her.

The lounge was much as Isa remembered, though there were blankets on the sofa that hadn't been there before. Isa suspected she'd woken Kylos up. 'When will Lathri be back?'

The woman shrugged, running a hand through her hair. 'I don't know. Hopefully soon. She only went to Feoras Sol.'

Isa's eyes widened. Healing those in Mateli's wake?

She didn't want to pry.

'Kylos…Who's there? Is Lathri back…?'

Isa looked over to the bedroom open bedroom door, through which a young Ittallan woman stepped through, and rubbed sleep from her eyes.

'Solvi, you shouldn't be up yet. Lathri said you had to rest until she could look at you,' Kylos said, stepping over to shoo her away.

But Solvi's eyes were locked on Isa.

'P…Princess Isa…?' She stammered.

Isa blinked and nodded.

'You're…I…' She turned a bright shade of pink. 'I used to…We went to the same school together and…'

Isa smiled. 'I remember.' She didn't, but it was kind to pretend with these kinds of people. It was rare anyone knew her as anything other than "the kitten princess."

'Really!' Solvi asked, her face lighting up with a wide smile. 'I mean, I only ever saw you from afar and…And we're both feline Ittallan, and…'

'Solvi! Back to bed!' Kylos pointed.

Isa couldn't help but grin as Solvi struggled, caught between obedience of Kylos and reverence of Isa. It certainly made a nice change.

Kylos won in the end, physically pushing her back into the room and closing the door. 'She's sick,' Kylos said by way of explanation.

'It's okay. What's wrong with her? She looked fine to me?'

The woman licked her lips, and Isa had the impression she was choosing whether or not to be truthful. 'Something's happening with the Ittallan in Taban Yul. Some kind of trance. If you touch them, you get sick too. Even if you regain your senses, you can be ill for quite a while. Lathri and the other healers have been working flat out to control it, but…'

Isa swallowed. She had an answer for that too.

Sapora had a Sevastos, was on his way to bringing one of the Arks back, and now Aciel somehow had influence in her city. Couple that with the dragons attacking villages and it seemed Linaria was on the brink of collapse.

She'd been about to say more, when a shrill cry pierced the air, and Kylos hurried to the balcony. 'They're back!'

Isa followed Kylos, and looked up just in time to see the black eagle from before dive for the balcony. He transformed in a flash of light a few feet above—his vast wingspan dwarfed the small balcony—and Aetos landed a moment later.

He looked tired, and Isa wondered if he'd been flying all night and day. Aetos came inside, making room on the balcony for an owl of stunning white and brown plumage swoop in. She was much smaller than the eagle, and landed on the balcony railings. After setting her wings and feathers right, she, too, transformed, and Lathri slid off the railings to stand on the balcony.

Any relief Isa felt at seeing the healer vanished when she saw her face. If Aetos looked tired, Lathri looked utterly exhausted. Now there was no question—they had to have been flying all night and day.

'Lathri? Dragons above, you need to rest, woman!' Kylos scolded, taking her by the arm and leading her inside to sit down.

'It's been so long since I've flown so far,' Lathri said. 'Palom's wounds were severe. I doubt I'll be of much use to anyone for a while.'

'Palom?' Isa said, stepping forward.

'Princess Isa? You did come back, then,' Lathri smiled. 'Yes. Mateli had tracked him down and torn him half to pieces.'

Isa looked away. That had been her fault. 'Palom is…okay though?'

'Oh yes. He has that damned sword,' Lathri said. 'Whether it'll keep him alive just to kill him more slowly though…'

'Is everything okay, Isa? I didn't expect to see you back so soon,' Aetos said, smoothing down his clothes.

Isa couldn't think of an easy way to put anything to them, and she didn't particularly want to with Lathri looking so weak, but she had no choice. 'Tacio no longer trusts me. He suspects conspirators, so I warn you now, any of you may be being watched by his Cerastes.' She let that sink in for a moment, ensuring the seriousness of her words was understood.

When they didn't object, Isa continued. 'Early this morning, a large wagon arrived at the palace. This contained…a Sevastos.'

'What?' Aetos and Kylos said in unison.

'I didn't know either. Despite being his sister, he hasn't shared...much with me,' she said. She wanted to bite her thumbnail but resisted the urge. 'Shortly after its arrival, Sapora took Tacio off in one of my personal airships. I'd never seen him so distressed.'

'Off on a hunt?' Aetos asked.

'I considered it. But I went to the council tower, looked through the books he'd been studying to work out why...after obtaining the most powerful creature in Linaria—a god by all standards—did he desperately need to head off?'

'What did the books tell you...?' Lathri asked.

'I think...I think Sapora's gone off to find Malashash.'

Lathri, Aetos and Kylos immediately began talking over one another. Cries of outrage and huffs of disbelief.

'...Who's Malashash?' A quiet voice from behind Isa.

She turned around to see Solvi peeking out from the half open door.

Kylos stormed over to put her back in the room, when Lathri halted her. 'It's all right, Kylos. She's well enough to stand. She's old enough to listen.'

'I'm eighteen, you know!' Solvi said, though her manner reminded Isa of someone much younger.

Lathri ignored it. 'Malashash...is an Ark.'

Isa closed her eyes. Hearing someone else say the words somehow made it more real than when she'd thought them.

Solvi came out of the room completely, and approached the group. 'What's...an Ark?'

'You're from Sol, aren't you?' Lathri asked. Solvi nodded. 'What do you mine there?'

'All sorts,' Solvi said. 'Iron, mostly.'

'Iron. A mineral that can be turned into incredible defences and fortifications. Armour, right?' Lathri asked.

'What's that got to do with the Ark?' Kylos asked.

'It has everything to do with Malashash. Did you ever wonder why Sol, of all settlements along the Feor Mountains, had mines so rich in ore that they became famous for it? Became wealthy for it?'

Kylos shrugged.

'It's not because they're particularly skilled. It's not because they're any better than the other miners who work the mountains. It's because Sol was built practically on top of Malashash's burial site. Malashash was the Ark placed to defend Sereth from any aggressors during the war. He was known for his ability to shield those around him. At his peak, he was utterly invulnerable. His defensive powers seeped into the very soil and rock…and Sol has reaped the rewards ever since it was built.'

Isa swallowed. She hadn't known *that*.

'I still don't know what an Ark is…' Solvi said. 'Something to do with the Varkain? If one was defending Sereth?'

'How do you know that, Lathri?' Aetos asked.

'From my studies at the University of Berel. To be a healer of the standard I wanted, I needed to learn the histories of illness and injury. What the Arks did to people…did to the Ittallan? Countless books on that.'

Isa licked her lips and paced. Though the lounge was small, she couldn't bear the thought of standing still.

'The Varkain created the Arks about 5,000 years ago. Four of them. And they used the Arks as weapons against us during the height of our races' war. They were…they were Varkain, once. Twisted by their blood magic and with powers that could level a town in hours. Malashash defended Sereth, and the other three savaged Val Sharis. All our attacks on them failed—they were immortal creatures. Nothing could stand against them…It was death and destruction on a level never seen before.' Lathri's voice trembled.

'Immortal?' Solvi gasped. 'Where are they now?'

'They disappeared near the end of the war. One of Linaria's greatest mysteries,' Lathri shook her head. 'The Ittallan claimed to have thwarted them, and they scrapped all knowledge of the horrors they'd brought to Val Sharis. Even their burial sites were guesses at best.'

'And Sapora has found the first one,' Isa said.

'He's going to ruin Val Sharis!' Kylos said.

Isa continued to pace. She couldn't look at them right now.

'Sapora set Mateli on my uncle!' Solvi said, her voice adding to the others. 'I hate him for that! *Hate* him!'

Sapora was her brother. Her blood.

The only one who'd ever stood by her.

The only one.

But she couldn't stand by him if he had decided to bring such an ancient threat to the world.

'More than that,' she said. 'Aciel is still here.'

'What?' Lathri said. 'He's been sealed by Moroda and the Sevastos!'

'He has. But…somehow his influence is spreading through the city. I touched an old Ittallan woman yesterday. I heard my name being called. Heard him calling it. Trying to order me. It's not like the compulsion when he was alive, but if so many people have been affected by it, it's not far off.'

Lathri heaved herself to her feet as Aetos and Kylos began talking again. Isa watched as Lathri walked to her, her arms coming up to hold her by her shoulders.

'Princess Isa. You understand our plight. You can see what Sapora plans to unleash upon us…'

'Yes…' Isa's voice was soft.

'Help us. Use your influence. We cannot save Val Sharis from one dictator to hand her to the next. We need more allies to stand against Sapora. I've exhausted my influence here, but yours stretches farther than mine.'

Isa thought. What allies did she have in any kind of power? Allies who didn't ridicule her?

'Morgen…' she muttered.

'Who?'

'He's a captain in the Imperial Guard. Stationed in Niversai…'

'Princess Isa. The time to act is now. Can you contact him? See if he'll help? There's no tiptoeing around it—he needs to know what's at stake. Aciel. A Sevastos. The Arks. Everything.'

Isa bit her thumbnail.

She didn't know if Morgen could send the kind of aid Lathri needed.

That would be treason, no question about it.

She couldn't betray her brother.

Tacio she couldn't care less about, but Sapora…?

'Please, Princess Isa,' Solvi said. 'He tried to kill my *kali*. Released Mateli!'

Isa looked away. She felt everyone's eyes boring into her.

Could she really betray him?

For the sake of Val Sharis?

A Sevastos was one thing. Malashash was quite another.

And through all this, Sapora hadn't once thought to consult her. He'd ignored her when she'd told him not to release Mateli.

He was acting by his own code. A Varkain code.

The Arks were a step too far.

'All right.'

Chapter Twenty-One

Amarah slogged through the snow.

She realised she hadn't actually spent a huge amount of time wandering around on foot—at least, not since she'd bought *Khanna*. Her situation was made worse by her poor vision—things were so much easier with both eyes.

Kohl had flown them across the short channel of frigid Northern Ocean, which separated mainland Linaria with the Arillian scattered lands.

When they'd reached the other side, Amarah had felt his arms trembling. But he hadn't complained once and hadn't demanded she walk.

Despite his chivalry, she couldn't afford for him to collapse with exhaustion. 'Kohl. We're on the mainland now,' Amarah said.

'Yes,' he replied, lips tight.

'Let's walk for a bit. You don't have to carry me the whole way,' she said. 'I must weigh a tonne with all this fur!'

Even worse, the mittens she wore were so thick, she could hardly grip him—or her scythe—anymore. She didn't think he'd drop her, but now he was trembling, Amarah didn't want to risk it.

Kohl descended slowly, landing as gently as he could, and placed Amarah on the now. He tried to hide it, but she saw how tired he was, and she suddenly felt bad for yelling at him earlier.

Through it all, Kohl was doing the best he could of a pretty awful situation. At least he didn't complain to the same level as some of her old allies.

And, though Jato still lived, Amarah supposed Kohl was grieving, too. He'd only just realised he'd lost his daughter, and he was clearly struggling to come to terms with that.

'Do you wanna stop for a bit? Have something to eat?' she asked, rolling her shoulders and stretching out her arms and legs to ease away the numbness.

'We…can do. There's not really anywhere we can use for cover.' Kohl looked around, sceptical.

They were surrounded by icy fields, covered in snow. To the east, she could see the edges of a vast forest, and to the south, the ice fields continued until the settlement of Tum Metsa, the most northerly-town on the mainland. West and north—where they'd come from—was semi-frozen ocean.

'We can use those trees.' Amarah pointed. 'Don't look too far. That okay?'

Kohl nodded and walked off without complaint.

*

When they reached the shelter of the trees, Amarah was quite sure her feet would fall off. Her thick furs and layers of robes kept the cold out—but coupled with the constant walking, she thought she'd boil inside them.

There may have been a path through the forest at one point, but the trees were so numerous, and the snow was so thick, that she couldn't make out any details. The only hint to a path ever existing was an old, bronze sign nailed into one of the broader tree trunks.

She couldn't read anyway, and with only one eye, focussing on the letters was nigh impossible. She could make out only the first letter: K.

Or, was it an R?

She couldn't tell.

Not that she needed it, anyway—she knew roughly where she was, and where she had to go next.

The thick snow looked like it hadn't been disturbed for centuries and pulling herself through it had been hard going. So, when they finally reached their destination, Amarah stumbled to the ground in exhaustion.

'You should have let me fly us,' Kohl said, sitting down beside her. 'Much faster.'

Amarah waved a hand at him, too tired to retort. She knew he made a good point, but she never liked relying on anyone, and he'd looked about ready to drop from exhaustion, anyway.

She had to let him carry her down from Oren, and across the sea out of necessity, but now they were on the mainland, she'd resolved to get by on her own as much as possible.

Like always, she'd get herself where she needed.

Amarah loosened her furs a little and gave herself more room to breathe. She sniffed and glanced around, wiping at the snot that dribbled and froze on her upper lip.

So far north, the days were short, and the nights were long, and she doubted they'd reach Tum Metsa while they still had sunlight.

At least under tree cover, the snow wasn't as deep, and she didn't sink into it.

Even so, she wished she had *Khanna*, and wished she'd beaten Jato into the ground…

But the Arillian had been too strong.

It was as Kohl said—Amarah could brawl. But taking on an elite Arillian who had years of training and battlefield experience?

That was a completely different scenario.

Even when she'd been aboard Jato's warship, with Moroda and Sapora by her side, the only reason she'd managed to hold Aciel off for so long had been due to the element of surprise.

Dragons above, even Sapora hadn't been able to kill her—though it certainly hadn't been for lack of trying.

She leaned her scythe against a tree beside her, the blade pointing up to the canopy. It was a fantastic weapon. The best she'd ever used. Probably priceless.

Yet that hadn't been enough either. Unless…maybe she just wasn't as good as she'd thought.

Dammit, was she losing her edge?

The wind blew, colder than she liked.

How did she find herself here? Sat on the edge of a forest in the snow, without her ship, having lost an eye. Amarah bit her lip to keep the emotions off her face.

She was done crying.

Khanna.

She'd become who she was on that ship. It was her everything—her home, her work, her life.

Kohl hadn't known where Jato had flown off to, but Amarah knew it wouldn't be long before reports of Arillian storms would sweep the country.

Then, she'd track her down and get her own back.

She hoped Traego would come through for her. He'd never let her down before—usually for something in return—but right now, she didn't have many options.

Amarah scratched her left wrist. Her unblemished skin gave away no indication of the mark she'd carried there since she'd been fourteen. In over twenty years and countless arrests, not a single member of the Imperial Guard had found it.

She smiled to herself. That had been another of Traego's tricks. So many parts of Samolen magic could be tweaked and moulded to fit a pirates' use, if you had the knowledge, skill, and patience to form it.

Or just deep pockets.

Of course, her whole plan rested on Traego being this end of Val Sharis.

If he was in Estoria, it could be weeks before he'd get to her, especially with the winter blizzards to navigate.

Traego didn't often come this far north, and she'd not seen him in years. She'd been out of the loop for so long now and hadn't visited Estoria in a good few seasons.

Considering the risks in their line of work, it was just as likely that Traego was imprisoned somewhere, or dead.

Failing that, she'd need to get all the way to Estoria herself—on the other side of the world. Kohl certainly wouldn't be able to fly her the whole way there.

She ran a hand through her hair, thankful that less and less came away every time she touched it.

Amarah had always been an opportunist. She prided herself on it. But even she had to admit it was hard to keep going with the odds stacked against you, and her luck on the turn.

She glanced at Kohl, who seemed sat in quiet contemplation. He was someone she struggled to understand.

Jato belittled him, insulted him, and still he tried to stay on her side, tried to do right by her.

Even when it wasn't wanted.

Or deserved.

She couldn't get her head around why he behaved as he did, why he allowed himself to be beaten so low. What kind of leader—or father—let himself be treated like that?

If he'd been a sky pirate, the others would have kicked him out or turned him into their sport.

Amarah wondered how Morgen and Palom were getting on. She'd asked the Ittallan to come with them, but he'd not forgiven Kohl.

She admired his physical strength but wasn't sure he had the strength of mind to cope with forgiveness and patience.

Amarah had seen another side to Palom's nature in his raw fury when Anahrik had died.

Come to think of it, following her encounter with Jato, it was probably for the best that Palom hadn't been with her.

Another cold breeze, from Kohl this time.

She sighed. 'Might as well get a fire going.' Amarah leaned forward to rest her arms on her knees. 'Must be weird for you? Bein' grounded?'

'A little,' he agreed. 'At least we can see for leagues here.' Kohl looked out across the fields, the view uninterrupted.

Amarah shrugged and grabbed the bag tied securely around her shoulder. She pulled out a small glass vial—her Samolen magic—un-stoppered it and tipped the dark red liquid onto the ground.

It immediately melted the snow, steam rising as it sizzled.

A few moments longer, and with a small *whoomf*, the flame emerged.

'That's what you cooked with, wasn't it?' Kohl asked, intrigued.

She nodded and put the vial back in her back. 'Little trick from Ranski. Damned Samolen are good for some things, at least.'

Amarah pulled her mittens off and held her hands near the flame. 'Can be lit pretty much anywhere. Won't go out until I put it back in the vial. Kept me from freezing to death more than once, let me tell you!'

'Incredible. No smoke, either?'

She shrugged. 'It's good.'

The small, fierce flames quickly warmed her fingers, and she relaxed somewhat.

The Samolen fires had always seemed to calm her.

'Food?' She reached into another compartment of the bag and grabbed some of the goat meat the Arillians had wrapped up for her.

Amarah handed Kohl a couple of pieces and started to chew on hers when a lone howl echoed across the ice fields.

She and Kohl glanced at each other.

'Plenty of snow wolves up here,' he said. 'Bears, too.'

She carried on eating. After everything she'd dealt with, a few overgrown dogs wouldn't give her much cause for concern.

A returning howl called out from somewhere in the trees, followed by another, then another, until a chorus of wolfsong carried in the evening air.

Shivers ran down Amarah's spine, and she shuffled closer to the fire. 'Damn…Gives me chills.'

Kohl made to stand up, but Amarah grabbed his sleeve. 'No point. We're fine. I've got my scythe. You can fly.'

'True. But I don't like the idea of being hunted.'

'Hunted? They could be after deer. Aurochs. Boar. Anything out here that they normally eat.' She took another bite out of her supper and refused to be afraid.

Kohl drew his cloak around himself, covering his wings.

Aside from the crackle of the flames and distant howling, their small camp was quiet.

Amarah closed her eyes and listened.

She heard footsteps in the snow, dozens of them.

Perhaps they were curious. Wolves were sociable, intelligent animals. They probably just wanted to see who had appeared in their territory.

'Amarah…' Kohl whispered.

She opened her eyes and jumped. Though the sun had almost set, she saw movement in the fields before them. Eight wolves, all loping across the snow as though they had winged feet.

Their fur seemed to meld with the ice—a blend of white and grey, red tongues lolling.

Despite her earlier confidence, seeing so many of them crossing the snow unnerved Amarah. She reached for her scythe with one hand, keeping her eye on the wolves as they came towards them.

'I can…' Kohl said, raising his hands, the wind picking up.

'Wait,' Amarah said. 'Let's not…be too hasty.' Her fingers wrapped around the handle of her scythe, and the familiar buzz of energy coursed through her arm.

Now, she was ready.

The wolves slowed their approach as they drew near.

Thoughts of them simply being curious went out the window when Amarah saw their expressions. There were no playful parks, no wagging of tails.

These wolves were not happy they were there.

They stopped several paces from the fire, and Amarah and Kohl got to their feet.

It had been a long while since Amarah had last been so far north—and she'd been on her ship, at any rate—so she hadn't realised the true size of the snow wolves. Their shoulders were almost as tall as she was, their bodies at least ten feet long.

The largest of them stepped forward, its muzzle a dark grey. It watched them both for a while, and then a low growl rumbled from its chest.

Kohl responded with a short blast of freezing air, but the wolves closed their eyes, lowered their snouts to the ground, and weathered it.

Amarah threw the last piece of her goat at its enormous paws, but the wolf ignored it, and took another step forward. 'Looks like they *really* don't want us here.'

Three smaller wolves broke off from the others, racing around them and into the trees.

'They're trying to surround us,' Kohl said. 'Grab your fire. Let's go. We don't want this to escalate.'

Amarah grimaced. She didn't want to leave the shelter of the trees, but she didn't want to attack the pack, either. Kohl's peaceful approach made the most sense.

With no choice, she pulled her vial from her back and scooped up the fire.

The wolves who had entered the trees stepped out behind them, growling, and driving them away from their camp.

Amarah looked back to the big wolf, who stepped aside, as if allowing them to leave.

'Maybe they've got cubs nearby?' Kohl said, looking from the wolves behind them to the others on the edge of the field.

'Maybe,' Amarah said, shouldering her bag and sighing. She didn't like the idea of being forced away, but she didn't want to take them on.

Nor did Kohl, from the looks of it.

Her companion raised both arms suddenly, and two rows of icicles shot up from the snow, blocking the wolves from their path.

Amarah jumped at their sudden appearance but didn't waste time. She ran between the two rows of icicles, the wolves' distorted faces eyeing her through them.

When she cleared the last of the icicles, the wolves had to be at least thirty feet from her, and yet they were so enormous it looked like they were sat right beside her.

Amarah shivered, but they made no move to follow.

'Definitely guarding something in the forest,' Kohl said.

'What I would give for a ship right now…' she muttered, and Kohl slumped. 'Won't be too long,' she said.

'I can carry you to Tum Metsa,' Kohl offered, glancing back every now and then to make sure the wolves weren't following.

Amarah shook her head, stumbling a little in the low light. 'I'm fine.' She didn't want to become dependent on the Arillian carrying her around. As an afterthought, she added, 'thanks.'

'What's in Tum Metsa, then?' Kohl asked. 'I wondered why there, not somewhere else? Somewhere in Corhaven, perhaps.'

Amarah scratched her nose. 'For one, it's the nearest settlement to Oren. On foot, we don't have much choice where we can go. For seconds, it's the haunt of one of my pirating buddies. He and I go way back.'

Kohl nodded. 'Another one you use but don't trust?'

Amarah cackled. 'Don't be naïve. Some of my best friends have used me just as much as I've used them. "Mutually beneficial", they call it. Just how we survive.' She shrugged.

It sounded cold.

Maybe it was cold.

But it was freedom, and freedom always came at a cost.

'I trust him enough to know I'll get what I need. Doubt he cares much about Arillians, so you don't have to worry.'

'Look at me, getting mixed up with thieves and pirates.' Kohl shook his head, a little humour in his tone.

'Treasure hunters,' Amarah corrected. 'Or dragon hunters, now, I s'pose. You had any thoughts on that? I wanna get going as soon as I've got a deck and a wheel.'

'Well, an ereven sphere would help,' he said. 'Otherwise it's a case of tracking phoenixes. They'll always lead us to a dragon. The more phoenixes, the bigger the dragon.'

Amarah nodded, wondering whether she should detour to Ranski to see if she could get an *actual* ereven sphere.

'But Sevastos are known to you all as gods for a reason. They don't usually come when called. I still don't know how Moroda did it.'

'The best treasure never does. You just need the right talent to spot the signs,' Amarah said, catching herself before she stumbled again, her sense of balance still out of sync.

'Here, let me—'

She slapped his hand away. 'Kohl. Stop it. I told you, I'm fine.' Amarah wiggled her foot in her boot, giving herself more grip. 'You just concentrate on hunting dragons. I'll make sure I've got a ship to come with.'

Kohl looked at her a long while, his expression caught somewhere between admiration and offence.

'And stop with the damned puppy-dog eyes. You're making me feel bad.'

He laughed out loud at that, and Amarah rolled her eyes.

She was definitely going soft.

As darkness fell, the two of them trudged through the snow towards Tum Metsa.

Chapter Twenty-Two

Palom's days and nights merged into one, snow-filled blur.

He traipsed north through the Rio Neva forest, following the line of the Feor Mountains as they cut the continent in two. Much of the path he followed disappeared through overgrown trees, fallen rocks, or lack of maintenance. With so few settlements on this extreme landscape, Palom hardly encountered another soul.

His *Valta Forinja* kept him out of any danger, flashing whenever anything threatening approached him—Ittallan or wild animal—and he tried to keep from killing when he could, but the sword was hard to resist.

A quick slash and almost guaranteed to perish.

Emonos.

He sighed.

The dragon hatchling, however, followed him throughout it all, quite happy to perch on his shoulder or trot along after him when Palom slowed down.

He shared meat with it and wondered what on earth he was going to do now he had a baby dragon following him all day and night.

He was not going to be the best guardian for it.

He didn't know the first thing about their needs.

Palom decided the best thing to do would be to try and find a wild dragon, and hope that somehow it would take on the hatchling, so he didn't have to worry about it—or messing up—anymore.

It was foolish thinking, really.

Dragons were a rarity after Aciel.

Even if he were lucky enough to find one, he was more likely to be incinerated by it than be able to give it the hatchling.

But for all his recent mistakes, he hoped that saving the young dragon and finding it a permanent home would mean he wasn't a complete failure.

His thoughts drifted to what he might do after bidding farewell to the hatchling, as they so often did.

How his life had changed in the past few months.

The Arillians had been the trigger for everything.

If not for Arillians, he'd never have met Kohl and been betrayed, lost Anahrik, Eryn, and Moroda.

If not for Arillians, things may have worked out differently with Lathri.

But…if not for the Arillians, he'd never have been able to forge the *Valta Forinja*. Would never have travelled to Berel to learn the secrets of the ancient weapons, would never have had the pressure or incentive to create them.

If the sword really was *emonos*, though…Perhaps he'd have been better off living out the rest of his days as a mediocre blacksmith.

He missed Anahrik.

Badly.

The other Ittallan always had an energy and enthusiasm about him that was infectious and kept them going even when things seemed grim.

Palom had needed to reign him back from time to time, but otherwise their business partnership had been fun from beginning to end.

Despite a seven-year age gap, despite the fact that their two types of *meraki* didn't often gel, they were friends.

True friends.

Friends who would do anything for one another, even—as it happened—die for one another.

Brothers in all but blood.

Anahrik hadn't wanted to get messed up in Aciel's war, in the fighting. He'd agreed to help Palom forge the *Valta Forinja*, to see if it could be done, and then he'd wanted to go north and stay with his cousins until things calmed down.

But Jato's Arillians had killed him before he'd had the chance to return.

Palom hated himself for that more than anything else. Anahrik's dream of peace snatched from him while he tried to help and protect their friends.

Of course, had Kohl stayed to fight, the outcome of that battle could well have been very different.

Anahrik and Eryn might have survived.

Moroda may not have been pushed to use a Sevastos's power to seal herself and Aciel away.

Palom shook his head.

So much had happened, and it all came back to the damned Arillians.

It always came back to the Arillians.

There was a reason their brutal race had been exiled, why they were only known for their storms and devastation.

His sword sparked, sending another ripple of blue light into the clearing.

He'd hunt them to the ends of Linaria, if he could.

Maybe he needed a ship to chase them out of the skies. A warship, one with plenty nets to trap them.

At least his anger and hatred could be fuelled into something productive.

The dragon nosed at his bag and chirped. Palom frowned. It always seemed to be hungry.

'You have eaten all food. Do not be greedy, *Leillu.*'

Little one, in the old tongue.

The dragon licked its lips and shoved its head into the bag, front claws scrabbling for purchase.

'No. No get out. No!' Palom clapped his hands.

With a surprised squeak, the dragon jumped away.

'You are not allowed in there,' Palom said with a scowl. He pointed to his bag in the hopes the dragon would understand what he meant. 'You will have to wait until tomorrow if you are hungry.'

The hatchling sat down and turned its attention to grooming itself, nibbling at the scales on its tail and tiny horns.

Palom sighed. 'At least you listen to me. A bit. Everyone else tells me how I am failure.' He held out his hand, palm up, and the dragon immediately darted over to him. It clambered onto his fingers and rubbed its head against Palom's skin.

He sighed again.

The dragon was dependent on him, but only took its share from what he hunted for himself. It would be years and years before it had grown enough to look after itself alone—and that was even assuming Palom could keep it alive until then.

'*Leillu*, I like your company. But I do wish you were bigger.'

The dragon yawned in response, showing off a range of razor sharp teeth, before curling up in Palom's palm, and looping its tail around itself.

His *Valta Forinja* had found the dragon. He couldn't just leave it in the wilderness to be eaten by the next biggest thing that found it.

No, he had to find it a home. Had to find other dragons for it to live with.

Without a map, Palom had no way of working out how far north he was. The forest had begun to thin, and the mountains grew even steeper, but he could be anywhere between Gal Etra and the northern shore of Val Sharis.

He'd seen a few airships fly overhead—trading vessels from the looks of them—but in such a remote part of the country, the days and locations blurred into one.

Palom hoped to see more dragons flying around, particularly now he was on the outskirts of Ittallan civilisation, where few people could disturb them.

He worried he'd underestimated the impact Aciel had had on Val Sharis's ecosystem.

The fires he built were small, barely enough to cook his food, much less keep him warm. There was simply too much snow, and he daren't risk travelling deeper into the forest where there was less snow for fear of stumbling into other Ittallan and his *Valta Forinja* taking control.

Palom pressed on. For all the days he'd been travelling, all the soul-searching he'd tried to do, he was still no closer to peace. He didn't feel any better about his past mistakes and hadn't yet stopped grieving over lost friendships and relationships.

He'd only just come back into Manilo and Solvi's lives and had abandoned them.

Again.

He was sure they were better off without him, as they'd always been. Manilo would have wanted him to return to Feoras Sol on a permanent basis, and the other *Archigos* wanted money from his status as a hero of Val Sharis.

Even if he'd believed it was all true, Palom didn't think he could return to mining or a quiet village life. He could set up a new forge, he supposed, but with such few Ittallan coming to Feoras Sol to trade, it would be a waste of time and resources.

Taban Yul had been the best place for that, and he'd already squandered his chance there by destroying his old workshop.

So, where did that leave him?

A nomadic traveller looking for his purpose in the world?

Trying to find a family of dragons for the young one he'd somehow managed to hatch?

He'd refused to get involved with the politics of war, had refused to stand with Lathri and her allies against Sapora.

He'd managed to shake off one very real demon from his past—Mateli—but his nightmares still haunted him as if the crocodile were still alive.

Lathri's words rang in his mind as they always did when his thoughts circled back to this.

What was he good for?

It certainly wasn't protecting people.

He sighed, picking his way along the narrow mountain trail as it wound its way above the treeline. Snow threatened to fall the higher he travelled, but he shrugged off the cold and kept moving.

The trail broadened, and the treeline fell away to reveal open sky beyond. Somewhere high above, so high Palom almost couldn't see, a pair of dragons soared.

On his shoulder, the hatchling looked up as well, chirping and flapping its wings. Whether it could see the dragons, too, or it was just having a stretch, Palom wasn't sure.

He watched them a long while, weaving and darting around one another, as though youngsters in play.

Not a care in the world.

One swooped lower, hovered for a moment, and then unleashed a torrent of flame into the distance.

Palom blinked.

Even with his keen eyesight, he could not see what the dragon had breathed fire at.

Its companion joined in, diving down and adding its fire to the first dragon's. For a long time, they hovered, sending fire into the air, before they suddenly whirled around and flew towards the mountains at top speed.

Palom crouched down, covering much of himself behind the rocks on the lip of the trail, and watched. His sword pulsed, ever-ready, and he unsheathed it from his back. 'Get down, *Leillu*,' he murmured to the hatchling, shifting his position to block it from view with one leg.

Both dragons flew past him, heading up towards the tops of the Feor Mountains. He looked back into the distance and squinted.

Nothing.

And yet…

His *Valta Forinja* buzzed with an energy Palom hadn't felt since Aciel's attack. Unsure whether to hide or flee down the mountainside and into the forest, Palom lurched where he was, gripped by a sudden sense of apprehension.

Then he heard thunder rolling through the clouds, and his gut told him what he feared.

Arillians.

From the sheer volume of noise, there had to be at least a dozen of them. Sheet lightning lit up the dark clouds, and another bout of thunder pealed across the sky.

The force of it shook the mountain and sent loose stones careening over the cliff edges. The young dragon trilled and clambered up Palom's leg onto his back, where it hunkered down.

'Do not worry *Leillu*,' he said. 'They might just fly past.'

Flashbacks of Aciel's battle flooded his mind along with memories of his nightmares.

He exhaled slowly, trying to calm his nerves.

Palom held his breath and steeled himself for another battle when the sky exploded with Arillians careening through the air. Their wings beat powerfully, and they shot lightning in all directions.

'Dragons above…' Palom whispered.

His earlier estimation that there'd been a dozen Arillians had been way off.

This looked closer to fifty.

Several Arillians clustered around something—or someone—in the centre of the group, but they were too far away, and he couldn't make out the details.

They plunged out of the air—feathered wings of different colours shimmering in the reflected light of their electricity—and charged towards the mountains.

Palom's eyes widened.

Were they after the two dragons?

He thought Aciel had been the only one after them—had they forgotten the terrors he'd brought to Linaria?

The loss he'd caused their kind?

He snarled and stood up straight as the whole flock of them flew overhead, either paying him no mind or too focussed on the dragons to notice him below.

If they so much as laid a finger on those dragons, he'd never forgive himself.

'Hold on, *Leillu*. I think we are going climbing now.'

Palom faced the sheer mountain as it rose above him. Wherever the dragons and Arillians were, it was much, much higher.

Scaling it would be nearly impossible, and he couldn't—wouldn't—leave the dragons to their wrath.

He looped his bag across his chest and under both arms and rested the *Valta Forinja* hilt-up against the rocks he'd been hidden behind.

In one, fluid movement, he transformed, the dragon clinging on all the while. Palom grasped the sword between his teeth, and then leapt up onto the rocks above.

He climbed upwards, jumping when the rock face became too steep even for a tiger's claws. With every step, he felt the sword hum, and his desire to avenge his fallen comrades and slay the Arillians grew.

Before long, Palom heard the crackle of electricity as the Arillians threw it about, heard the dragon's roar and whoosh of fire as they breathed it, and he quickened his pace.

As the mountain plateaued, Palom saw a handful of burned logs—the charred remains of whatever trees once grew here—in a wide, roughly circular clearing.

It was clearly the dragon's nest, but everything was in disarray. Bones and branches littered the ground, and above it, Arillians swirled in the sky, terrorising the two dragons.

Palom watched, creeping forward, using several of the larger logs for cover. The hatchling still clung to his fur, its small claws digging deep.

The Arillians swarmed like bees, rising and falling on the wind, trailing the dragons, blocking off their escape, and somehow avoiding the plumes of fire both breathed with worrying frequency. Black smoke filled the air where the flames licked the ground or caught an Arillian who was too slow to avoid it.

Palom wanted to help.

Wanted badly to save the dragons under attack.

Wanted revenge for his lost allies—whether these were the Arillians responsible or not.

The sword flickered, an arc of blue light flashing from the blade, and he dropped it onto the ground.

He was afraid he'd turn into a butcher again, like he had for those two Varkain near the Waterside Inn.

That seemed like a lifetime ago.

Leillu trilled again, and Palom knew it was afraid.

So much movement, so much electricity.

Thunder shook the ground and echoed into the cloudy sky.

He was not the hero the Ittallan of Val Sharis—or Feoras Sol—claimed him to be.

He'd beaten Aciel's warriors with his friends by his side, a fierce determination pushing them on.

He couldn't hope to match up to that on his own, now, could he? Not against so many Arillians.

Another plume of fire.

Another scream from the dragons.

Another Arillian storm.

Leillu fluttered its wings, though it still had its claws embedded in his fur.

Palom shifted back, gently slid off his jerkin, and pulled the baby dragon into his arms where he cradled it.

He wasn't a monster.

He wouldn't allow himself to become one again—regardless of Lathri's thoughts towards the *Valta Forinja*.

'It is okay, *Leillu*.' He looked up as the Arillians continued to attack the dragons, their lightning storm intensifying all around him.

The ground shook, the air felt thick and almost tangible, and the hatchling's breathing increased.

'You are safe. I am here,' he said, continuing to reassure the young dragon, but its eyes were locked on the sky above.

The tiny, brave little creature writhed in his hands until it turned to bury its head in the crook of his arm.

Palom could no longer sit around and watch and do nothing.

He could no longer let Linaria's wars and power struggles slip by him while he lost himself to darkness.

He would no longer be a bystander.

Bundling up his jerkin by the log, he wrapped the fabric around the dragon's body, concealing it as best he could. 'Stay still *Leillu*.'

Grasping the *Valta Forinja*, he took a deep breath.

He would be in control of the weapon, *emonos* or not.

He would not give in to its desires.

Palom took aim, the power in the sword building, until he unleashed the energy in a display of bright blues and teals that flashed in the dark sky.

Arc after arc, wave after wave, Palom pulled on all the strength of the *Valta Forinja* and cut open their ranks.

When the Arillians reformed, several turned their electrical attacks on him, sending bolts of lightning and waves of burning wind to the ground.

His *Valta Forinja* responded, a dome of energy shielding Palom from their attacks, deflecting the electricity harmlessly away.

The Arillians screamed at him and yelled at each other over the wind, the two dragons forgotten. He couldn't make out the words over the rushing wind and rolls of thunder, but it was clear from their behaviour that they were shaken.

Their ranks thinned as the sword sent another crest of energy upwards, cutting off those on the edge and splitting the Arillians.

Palom took several breaths, the weight of his attacks draining him, and watched, waiting for a counter attack or rebuke—but none came.

They circled several times, a towering vortex of storms and electricity, before they broke away from the plateau, some unsaid instruction to flee before a greater opponent.

Their thunder faded, and the ground stilled, as they disappeared into the dark winter clouds.

Palom swallowed.

He'd done it.

His *Valta Forinja* hadn't taken over and let him slaughter anyone!

The skies darkened as the two dragons descended, blackened and burnt by the Arillians, but both alive.

Palom dropped down to a crouch, hoping they didn't see him as a threat an attack—he did not want to bring his sword upon them.

They landed with a crunch, their talons scraping against the rock face, sending bones and small rocks flying.

He was no expert on dragons, but both were far larger than the young drake from Niversai. These two had to be adults—both easily sixty or seventy feet long, with long serpentine necks and spiked tails. Their scales shifted in the light, bronze with flecks of orange, and vivid yellow-gold.

Now on the ground, they flexed their wings, as though testing for breaks or tears, and Palom squinted in the force of the wind they caused.

He took a step back as they checked themselves over and glanced over to where he'd set his jerkin on the ground. The young hatchling was still wrapped up in the fabric, and Palom bent down to grab both.

A low growl caught his attention, and he turned to find both dragons crouched before him, their eyes locked on his. They rested their chins on the ground, and Palom was able to look both creatures in the eye.

'I…mean you no harm…' Palom said, though he was unsure whether holding a hatchling dragon helped or hindered his chances of being eaten by the enormous creatures.

Slowly, he held out his hands, the hatchling clutching his fingers. When the hatchling didn't budge, he shook his hands and stepped back, and the young dragon leapt from his hands to the ground.

It looked up at the two dragons before trotting back to him and sitting by his feet.

'No…You go with them,' he said, shoving it forward with one boot. The hatchling chirped loudly, and Palom looked up at the adult dragons, half expecting to be roasted.

They studied him a long time, smoke rising from their nostrils in puffs of black every time they breathed out.

Palom tried to look away—staring any predator in the eyes was a recipe for disaster—but struggled to break the contact. So close, they were breathtakingly beautiful.

The dragons were a primal power, ancient and mysterious as the goddess they represented. Even sharing the continent with them, Palom had never been close enough to touch an adult dragon.

After what felt like a lifetime, they turned their heads away from him, and Palom breathed a sigh of relief. One lingered longer than its companion, and it took several seconds for Palom to realise it wasn't looking at him—it was gazing at the *Valta Forinja*.

Did it know the sword had been forged with ore from a Sevastos's crystal?

The elder dragon they'd met before Aciel's battle had known.

In fact—she'd been the one to warn him about the cursed creation. He'd dismissed it then, but now accepted the notion warranted thinking about.

The dragon snarled and unleashed its fire onto the sword and rock against which it sat. Palom jumped back, startled by the sudden ferocity, the hatchling held close to his chest.

When the flames died down, the dragon stomped off after its companion—mate, probably—and Palom shuffled over to the burning rocks to check over his sword.

Despite the intensity of the dragon's heat, the sword seemed unscathed. If anything, it looked brand new—like it had just been cleaned.

He looked back to the dragons, who were busy digging in the centre of their nest, breathing small bursts of fire into the ground, and decidedly uninterested in him.

'What was that…' Palom muttered aloud.

The hatchling clambered up his leg to sit upon his shoulder, quite content.

'You are staying with me then, *Leillu*?'

He pressed the back of his hand to the hilt of the *Valta Forinja*, and realised it was cool enough to touch. Picking it up, he felt the familiar energy buzz through him—somewhat lessened following its use—but nothing different than he'd experienced before.

He frowned and glanced back to the dragons.

Had it breathed fire in annoyance?

Had it seen the sword as a threat?

Or was this some kind of acceptance ritual among dragons?

And now Arillians had returned to the mainland.

At least Sapora would have a chance to prove his worth as king against the aggressors.

Chapter Twenty-Three

Sapora stalked through the palace grounds, the Varkain on guard giving him a wide berth. Even Roke, the grizzled Varkain who seemed unfazed by anything, kept his distance and trailed him from no less than twenty paces away.

Sapora knew he was in a foul mood.

He just didn't care.

He'd been back in the city almost a week, spent half of it locked in the library, and the other half in his room of mirrors.

Morgen had vanished, and that irritated him.

He checked before dawn, checked in the middle of the day, and checked again at night, but Morgen's room in Rosecastle was always empty.

Sapora knew Morgen had to sleep at some point. But after three days in semi-stasis, watching and waiting, the door to Morgen's room hadn't even twitched.

On the third day, when his own stomach growled, Sapora had to presume Morgen had abandoned his task and ceased reporting for some reason he didn't know.

There was no chance the young soldier had caught wind of his plans—not that he could do anything about them anyway.

Morgen had always been loyal, obedient.

Sapora had hoped after his failure to revive Malashash that Morgen would provide him with favourable information about the hunt for the Arks in Corhaven.

But the captain's lack of response had only served to anger Sapora even more.

Topeko had travelled with him to Niversai. It was quite possible they spoke often—perhaps even daily. The damned Samolen's peace talk could well have put Morgen off Sapora's task.

Silly lamb.

Sapora had even sent a message the slow way—with a physical piece of parchment on a messenger ship through Voulhrik in the hopes that even if Morgen chose not to reply, at least he knew what Sapora wanted. He'd included twenty crowns as well—money always got people moving when you wanted them to.

So, Sapora had returned the palace library, dug up ancient texts from the basement levels and dungeons—texts which hadn't seen daylight in centuries—and continued to study.

He'd been through every book in the library, scoured over every leaf of paper, and found nothing.

Even Tacio had avoided the council tower while Sapora pored over maps and tomes, looking for some way to break the seal, some way of actually restoring the Arks.

His entire plan for the Varkain—for Linaria—hinged on bringing back the Arks.

All of it would be for nothing if he couldn't even do that.

They'd been sealed by a Sevastos.

He controlled that Sevastos.

Surely, he'd be able to unseal them?

Of course, he was trying to do what had never been done before, had never been conceived before.

It was no wonder there were no books with detailed instructions.

And Tacio had insisted that Isa was a spy for some Ittallan who were conspiring to dethrone him.

Sapora had held himself back.

Isa was essentially the queen she'd always wanted to be.

What more did she want?

Tacio had never met Isa before he'd moved to Taban Yul, and Sapora had been arrogant to assume he would understand her and get along with her as he did.

Their conflicts wore away at him.

He needed as many allies on his side as he could get.

Sapora decided to get some fresh air—too long stuck inside staring at writing by candlelight and he thought he was going half mad himself.

Perhaps he would try and speak with the Sevastos again.

It obeyed his orders, certainly. But speaking?

That was proving a difficult nut to crack.

From what Isa, Morgen, and Topeko had said, the dragon they'd found in the Feor Mountains had been an elder who spoke the common tongue.

A Sevastos would certainly be capable of this as well—and yet it hadn't said a word to him, or Roke, or any of the other Varkain he had guarding it.

Sapora supposed being disturbed from a 5,000 year-long slumber would put any creature in a bad mood.

Smiling bleakly at his terrible humour, he crossed the palace gardens towards where he'd kept the Sevastos.

It had been snowing heavily for some days now, and his Varkain were flagging. There was a reason they lived underground, and forcing them to stay outside, active and on duty, was a tall order for most of them.

Roke had reported a day or two after he'd returned from failing Malashash that Mateli's body had been found by a young Ittallan guard stationed in the Rio Neva forest along with nine others.

Sapora wondered whether the old crocodile had found Palom or whether he'd chosen to attack a group of Ittallan and they'd all perished in the ensuing bloodbath.

While his Varkain had confirmed Palom had passed that way, it appeared the tiger's trail went cold shortly afterwards, and the entire forest was simply too vast to mount any kind of effective search.

Sapora hadn't wanted to let Palom get away with murder, but he had to choose his battles carefully, particularly with the Arks out of reach and Aciel's will seeping through Taban Yul.

In the end, he'd settled to put a bounty on Palom should the tiger ever return to the city.

Until then, he had bigger problems to deal with.

As Sapora made his way towards his Sevastos, he spotted Isa sat atop the palace wall. She glanced down at him with the disdainful look she'd recently picked up, and Tacio's accusations echoed in his mind.

'Is it true, Sapora?' She asked once he was near. 'Mateli's dead?'

'You do have the best ears in all Val Sharis,' Sapora said, though his voice lacked mirth. His pride still stung from returning to the palace covered in dirt, sweat, and blood, without an Ark.

Isa shook her head and looked away. She never looked him in the eye anymore.

'I'd have thought you'd be happy. You didn't approve of Mateli, did you?'

'I just…' She bit her thumbnail and kept her gaze on the middle distance.

'Isa…?' Sapora hated seeing his sister like this. She was strong, proud, and fearless. Since he'd moved to Taban Yul, she seemed more of an emotional wreck than anything else.

'What if…what if this isn't right…'

Sapora narrowed his eyes. 'Excuse me?'

She turned to face him, nervous. 'Moroda wanted peace, not power.'

'And…what is it you think I'm trying to achieve?' He asked.

Isa shrugged. 'The Arks…?'

'How do you know about that?'

'Why didn't you tell me that's what you were after? You kept going on about "treasures" without telling me the truth! I had faith in you. So much faith. You were better than the Varkain who came before us, better than the Ittallan who sat in this marble palace preening and looking down on us!'

'Why don't you have faith anymore?' Had she learned of his failure to revive Malashash? His pride stung.

'I'm a prisoner again, Sapora.' She tilted her head back and looked up into the sky. She was trying not to cry, he assumed. 'Tacio hates me. His Varkain follow me everywhere I go. I just…I just…I wish I could turn back time. I would've done things differently.'

Sapora blinked. 'How so…?'

'Killing so many people wasn't the right way to go about it…'

'It was the *only* way to go about it. We discussed it. We agreed! Those peacocks and swans, who treated you like you were the scum of Linaria! I put them back in their place for you!'

'I know, but…'

'There is no going back. We make decisions, we carry them out. That's what good leadership is.'

'I want my home back.'

Sapora shook his head. 'What are you talking about? Half the palace is yours. You have two ships, the run of the city, you can go where you like, eat what you like, where what you like. Call yourself the queen if it makes you happy.'

She trembled slightly, her heart fluttering. 'It wouldn't…'

'Isa, you're not weak. Do *not* act like you are. You've more power now than a year ago. I'd have hoped you wouldn't be ungrateful.'

'What do you want from Val Sharis? From the Ittallan? From me?' She'd raised her voice, now.

Panic.

He spoke slowly and kept his voice low so as not to intimidate her. 'I am bringing in a new age, Isa. The age of the Varkain. Getting rid of the fear and stigma which plagues us and ensuring Linaria treats us—all of us—with the respect that we deserve!'

'And you need a Sevastos to do that? A god?'

'The Sevastos is an animal. Like any other beast you'd find, and it can be trained. Why wouldn't I use the resources I have?'

'And the Arks?'

He licked a fang. 'Aciel is influencing the city. Somehow. What if he is able to break free? Dragons are already terrorising the cities in Val Sharis. If he manages to escape, who do you think is going to stop him? The Imperial Guard? They did such an *excellent* job of stopping him before.'

She swallowed.

Sapora continued, 'I have no intention of giving up what we have—what we've worked so hard for—to an upstart Arillian with a bit of magic behind him!'

'But, the Arks…' She bit her thumbnail again.

'My liege!' Roke screamed from the other side of the gardens. 'A fleet of warships!'

Warships?

Could it be Morgen sending aid?

He and Isa shared a look before darting off to the nearest tower, clambering up the stone staircase and out onto the walls where his Cerastes guarded.

Though the sky remained thick with grey clouds, he could see as clearly as the other Varkain—and he warranted Isa's vision was even better—the six large warships floating over Taban Yul on their slow approach to the palace.

They bore Imperial colours.

'Must be from Corhaven,' he said. 'Where's Tacio?'

The Varkain on the wall collectively shrugged, most of them awe-struck by the enormous airships drawing near. He supposed hardly any had spent much time above ground, much less outside of Sereth. 'Find Tacio, now!' Sapora snapped, and a handful of them darted off.

If his brother had been summoning allies to their cause, Sapora wanted to know why he'd been left in the dark.

'Are these ones here for the sickness in the city?' Roke asked, lingering to Sapora's left.

Sapora didn't bother to reply. If he admitted to not knowing, that would show weakness.

The Varkain preyed on weakness.

He dropped his voice to a little above a whisper. 'Isa. How many warships do we have on our fleet here.'

'We lost most of our ships against Aciel. Probably three or four?'

'Three or four?' Sapora snapped.

'You've been busy hunting your Arks and Tacio's been busy hunting me!' Isa snapped back. 'You cared more about your damned Cerastes than you did with what remained of those who fought Aciel!'

Sapora scowled.

Something felt off.

No official notice of their arrival. Koraki nowhere to be seen.

His stomach tightened.

They had to be less than a league away, now.

In the pale sunlight, canons and ballistae glinted from their decks.

Brazen bastards.

'Cerastes! Imperial Guard!' Sapora shouted, making Isa jump beside him. 'Battle stations, now!'

'B—battle stations?' Isa gulped.

He heard her heart pound, but he didn't have time to focus on her.

'Get the palace secured. If our fleet can mobilise, get them in the air. We're under attack.'

Isa raced off, and Roke followed him as Sapora darted along the wall, scaling the stairs of another tower, and getting to the higher points on the palace.

A handful of Varkain joined him as he reached the top of the tower. Isa had often used its flat roof to land or take off from one of her ships, but here, it gave Sapora vantage across most of the city.

'Well, well, well, today has just got interesting.'

Sapora rolled his eyes at the drawl.

'Challenging you so openly. I *told* you they were against you.'

'*They* were unhappy Ittallan in the city. These ships are the Imperial Fleet of Niversai. I wonder whether Morgen knows about this. Maybe that's why he went quiet…'

'What do they want?' Tacio asked.

'Want?'

'Aren't they meant to make demands before they attack?'

A whirring sound filled the air, followed by a whistle and then the sudden impact of stone crashing against the palace walls.

Sapora gasped in shock, wobbling as the tower trembled and one of the numerous golden statues toppled. It landed with a deep thud at the bottom of the wall, and the Cerastes atop it hissed in defiance.

'Tacio. Control them.' Sapora said, his eyes locked on the ship who had fired first.

'Your commands…?'

'Kill them all.'

Tacio nodded and descended the tower's stairs to get his Cerastes into formation.

The other warships fired their ballistae, and Sapora braced as their projectiles slammed into the palace, walls, and towers over and over.

Sapora bore the brunt of every attack, holding his ground as the palace shook, and the warships grew closer still—their attacks stronger with every blast.

One ship, the first that had fired, flew over the palace walls and hovered in the gardens. Handfuls of men and women leapt from the ship or clambered down on lowered ropes; Ittallan and Humans both.

The Varkain on the ground immediately rushed up to meet them, swords slashing as battle broke out when they collided.

A second ship followed the first, another few scores of people clambering off to join their comrades.

Sapora watched eagerly.

The aggressors were a mix of fighters and citizens, it seemed. His Varkain cut down their attackers, but it didn't take long before they were overwhelmed.

Sapora had never kept a full complement of Imperial Guard in the palace, and even the Cerastes who'd come with him from Sereth hardly filled the barracks.

Battle cries turned to screaming as blades cut into flesh, people were knocked down, and more ballistae fired onto the palace. Everything descended into chaos—blood and snow kicked up as the palace gardens became a killing ground.

When the third ship hovered over the palace walls, and his aggressors leapt onto the Varkain stationed there, Sapora hissed in anger.

He watched, calculating, darting from fighting groups to individuals, to those fleeing the carnage.

Was anyone trying to break into the palace?

Were they there to kill him?

Were they a distraction for some other, greater threat?

Sapora weighed each option in split seconds as the fighting increased. A few more steps, and one group would be at the bottom of his tower.

If it was him they wanted, he'd make them regret it.

Pupils wide, he selected his targets and decided on a route to carve through to cross the gardens quickly to interrupt the fighting.

Roke stepped up beside him and lingered by his shoulder.

He didn't need to say a word.

When another huge crash shook the palace, taking a chunk out of the wall, Sapora leapt from the tower—drawing his scimitars in one movement—and landed feet first on an unsuspecting Ittallan. He plunged his weapons into the Ittallan's back, and drew them out again, blood arcing from the metal.

He leapt again, slashing one scimitar, and then another, dancing and weaving and avoiding the swords, axes, and hammers they'd brought with them to fight.

So slow.

They might as well have been standing still.

He lunged forward, dragging the tip of his scimitar along an unguarded throat. He dodged a shield thrust in his direction, and the metal smashed into the face of the Ittallan behind him. He spun around and drove his other scimitar into the shield-man's neck.

Blood gushed, sweat poured, and the whole garden stank of fear. It caked the ground and the air, and Sapora relished it.

All around him, his Cerastes danced the same dance, their fighting prowess pushing back the aggressors, and yet still more poured from the warships.

Fifty.

One hundred.

Two hundred.

They were storming the palace, and for all the Cerastes' abilities, they would not last forever against an enemy that had greater numbers.

They were used to fighting in tunnels, underground, where they had the advantage.

Sapora glanced up at the wall, saw more bodies charging into each other, and through all the blood he could hardly pick out who was who.

'Sapora! You killed my mother!'

He looked around at the mention of his name, his gaze drawn to a pale, blonde woman stood in a sea of red.

'I've killed a lot of people's mothers,' he hissed.

She held out a spear, its tip pointed directly at him. 'Drutia. Her name was Drutia.'

Sapora licked his fangs. This one he would enjoy killing.

Screams and roars sounded all around him, but he'd switched his focus to this Ittallan woman.

He wondered how many more like her he'd encounter.

How many more with personal vendettas against him.

He shouldn't be surprised, not really.

'And the daughter of Drutia...Her name is?'

'I am Lathri, and I'll kill you for what you did to her. What you're doing to Val Sharis! How dare you bring the Arks back.'

Sapora's eyes went wide.

Someone in the palace had let out his secret.

He scowled and tightened his hold on his scimitars. It made no matter, now. If the Ittallan were in open rebellion, the fear of the Arks would put them right back down at the bottom of his shoe.

Sapora exhaled, summoning strength and speed.

He'd only be able to strike so many times before it drained him. He bent his knees, focussed only on his target, and then moved.

Sapora appeared behind her, one of his blades to her throat, the other to her back. 'My dear Lathri...It will be my pleasure to reunite you with Drutia.'

The palace shook again, part of the wall crumbling completely as the ballistae shattered the marble.

More Ittallan and Imperial Guard charged in, screaming their fury and waving their weapons.

Sapora narrowed his eyes from across the gardens, and then turned to Lathri. He unhinged his jaw, both rows of fangs extended as he leaned forward to bite.

'Snake!' A man screamed, rushing up to Sapora and hacking away at him with a short sword.

He leapt back to avoid his strike and found himself in the middle of Lathri's entourage. Sapora hissed, whirling around to count them. He was surrounded.

‘I’ll kill you,’ Lathri said. ‘But you won’t be going near my mother. There’s no afterlife for you. *Emonos* Varkain.’

In unison, they surged forward, claws and weapons outstretched.

Sapora rolled to the side, an axe blade slashing along his back as he moved out of the way, drawing blood.

He hissed in anger, coming up a few feet away, and darted off. He’d fought more opponents in his trials and come out victorious.

He didn’t need to prove himself again.

And they would burn.

Sapora raced across the gardens, away from the fighting, several Ittallan trailing him, as he ran to the space covered by a large fabric canopy.

*

Isa trembled, watching the battle unfold from behind the safety of the dining room windows. She’d felt Lathri’s warmth before she’d seen her and had fled back into the palace.

What would Lathri think if she saw her in the middle of the fighting? Working against her?

What would Sapora think if he saw her working against him?

Caught between two opposing sides, she’d retreated to the safety of the palace—but with one of the walls already coming down, she had no idea whether the palace really was safe.

She considered getting to one of her small ships and flying away, but she had no idea where she would go to.

Lathri and her Imperial Guard reinforcements seemed to have the upper hand. Six warships and a surprise attack, and Sapora's Varkain were swiftly falling.

If Lathri won, Isa would get what she wanted.

Wouldn't she?

Behind her, all was chaos as servants and staff rushed around, bringing injured Cerastes inside and trying to repair the damage to the palace.

She was about to help them out when a thunderous roar rooted her to the spot in fear.

Even when the shadow of the Sevastos' wings passed over the window, Isa could hardly believe the sheer size of the dragon rising into the air from the gardens. It dwarfed the biggest dragons she'd seen by a magnitude of ten—all horns, wings, and teeth.

These creatures were considered gods for good reason.

Others joined her at the window, their mouths hanging open, their tasks forgotten as Sapora's Sevastos flapped its wings and shook the palace with its roar.

When it opened its mouth and breathed a flame so bright and hot Isa could feel it through the window, she knew Lathri was done.

There was nothing, nothing in all of Linaria, that could withstand such an enormous power.

The next plume of flame burned brighter than the first, and it engulfed two of the airships still floating—as well as half a dozen streets and buildings from the city below.

Did Sapora not care about the citizens?

The Sevastos' flame continued, unceasing, as it circled the palace, lighting up the streets below and turning everything to ash as it passed overhead.

Isa swallowed.

What had Sapora done?

What was left of the airships plummeted. They crashed into the city, the shockwave shattering the windows she peered through. It gave her a clear view of the thick smoke rising from Taban Yul as the Sevastos still continued to breathe flame.

It disappeared to the other side of the palace, but Isa still heard, still felt, the intense heat it radiated with its attack. She looked down into the gardens and her heart sank.

All the snow had melted, vaporised instantaneously in the wake of the Sevastos' rise.

What remained was blackened, ashen earth, and the charred remains of Lathri's followers who had not escaped in time.

Sapora, Tacio, Roke, and the other Cerastes and Varkain stood atop the palace towers or wall, watching as the Sevastos circled the palace over and over, cutting it off from the rest of the city in a wall of flame.

Chapter Twenty-Four

Night had fallen by the time Amarah and Kohl reached Tum Metsa.

It had started snowing as the last of the sun's light disappeared, and she was grateful for her thick Arillian furs by the point they reached the outskirts. Had it not been for the Arillian's help in Oren, she was sure she'd have frozen. It wasn't as if she could carry her portable fire while they crossed the ice fields.

Thankfully, they didn't need to go too far into town—not that many people would be outside in the night in the middle of winter anyway—but it was always good to not attract unwanted attention if you could help it.

Attention always led to questions, and she didn't really have a cause to be here.

She hoped to connect with an old colleague who didn't actually live there—wasn't even from Val Sharis—and so far north and remote, the Ittallan here weren't the friendliest of people.

Better to avoid them, if she could

Especially while travelling with Kohl.

After Aciel's war, and if Jato had passed by, she doubted Arillians would be looked upon favourably.

Of course, Kohl had spent many years in exile and was used to covering his wings with his cloak. Only the remarkable colour of his eyes gave him away as an Arillian.

In Corhaven, most people would probably assume he was an Ittallan, but here, in Val Sharis, he didn't have the same luxury.

Tum Metsa was a small settlement, even by her standards. Always covered in snow, the northern-most city in Val Sharis—perhaps even the world— could hardly be called a "town".

Traego used Tum Metsa to stash excess treasures, mostly. Or, sometimes he'd come all the way out here to hide and wait for the Imperial Guard to lose his trail.

It made sense.

Tum Metsa certainly wasn't the best location for a sky pirate's permanent base. But it had its uses.

Several outbuildings sat in the snow on the farthest reaches of Tum Metsa—mostly for food storage, as Amarah had learned in her youth—and most were sealed to lessen the chance of scavenging animals breaking in and helping themselves.

One building—it had to have been a barn at one point, she remembered—lay off to the side, hidden from view. Except to her.

It was harder still to spot it in the dark, but the tell-tale haze, almost a light mist, floating above the snow gave away the Shroud.

Her own personal inn, invisible to the eye.

Unless you knew it was there, of course, or could recognise a Samolen Shroud.

She enjoyed watching Kohl's confusion as she strolled towards it. Amarah exhaled, her breath forming in front of her, as she bent to slip underneath the Shroud as though it were a blanket, and she'd squeezed through a small gap underneath it.

She turned back to Kohl and held it open for him.

'Come on. Quickly.'

He hurried to catch up, crouching underneath as he passed through and then they were both as invisible as the barn.

*

Dust covered everything.

Amarah supposed sky pirate stashes weren't ever meant to keep things clean—they were meant to keep them safe. She wondered whether Traego actually had anything of value here, or if it was as barren as the rest of the far north.

'So…remind me again how this…friend of yours…ally…' Kohl began.

'Traego,' she said, clearing the floor of boxes, broken furniture, and ripped tapestries.

'…Traego can help?'

Amarah focussed on her task more than Kohl's question, but the Arillian patiently waited for her to answer. 'We ran a crew together for a few years. One of my first…acquaintances…when I came to Corhaven.' She shrugged, remembering. 'We struck up an accord. He took me on the ship he worked on and the rest is history.'

Though those times had been hard, perhaps her hardest after running away from home, Amarah always had fond memories of them.

She and Traego thought very similarly, and she'd always respected his opinion and judgement.

What a wake-up call that had been.

Five years, it had been since she'd last seen him.

'If he's from Corhaven, why would he be here?' Kohl helped her carry a broken wooden table top and rested it against the wall of the barn. 'I know you all have airships, but I didn't realise you crossed continents.'

Amarah thumbed through a handful of old ledgers. The parchment had yellowed over the years and the black ink had faded to silver-grey. She could still make out a few numbers and scrawled text underneath it. She had no idea what it meant, but she supposed it could be important.

She dropped them in a stack on top of a barrel near the door and strolled back to the centre of the room to clear more space. 'Not as many pirates in Val Sharis. Better pickings. Imperial presence is stronger here, I guess, but Traeg's a sly one. I'm sure he's doin' just fine out here.' If anyone could keep the Guard off their tail for so long, it would be Traego.

Most pirates' careers were over within a handful of years.

Memories of old allies came rushing back. Others on Traego's crew, or the first few who stood with her when she bought *Khanna* and became captain of her own airship.

How many people had she lost? Either to the Guard, other pirates, Goldstones with private security? Amarah slumped.

'You sound like you used to be very close,' Kohl said, sending a cool breeze fluttering through the musty room which picked up dust. 'What happened for you to part ways? You've mentioned him before.'

She glared at him, uncomfortable with what Kohl implied. 'No-one's business what I do.'

'Amarah...'

'What?' She whirled around.

Kohl raised an eyebrow. 'I know it's not my business. But...if we're to be working with him, I'd like to know the history. I'd rather not find out at a critical moment that you attacked his sister or something like that, or there's some terrible debt between you.'

Amarah held his gaze and then burst into laughter. 'Dragons above, nothin' like that! I wanted to do things my way. He wanted to do 'em his way. Nothin' bad. We never worked against each other. If he found out I was after something, he'd bow out. I'd do the same.'

'Sounds like a rarity among thieves. I thought you all tried to get your hands on whatever treasure you could find.'

She shrugged. 'I suppose so. Of all the allies I have, Traeg's the only one I come close to trusting. He saved my life once. He gave me a chance on his ship. All anyone wanted to do was take advantage of me. Traego was the one who saved me from the Varkain. So, I stuck around. Saw what I could learn from him.' She smiled a little.

She'd been so damned young and naïve, then.

The Varkain attack had been terrifying, of course. She'd been way in over her head, all full of hot air and no bite.

'You know, Amarah,' Kohl said, sitting down on an upturned crate now they'd cleared the room enough to be comfortable. He removed his cloak, laid it beside him, and stretched his wings out. 'You always pretended you were a loner. I did the same.'

She pulled off her outer layer of furs and busied herself with folding them up.

She didn't trust herself to reply.

Kohl continued, 'You remind me so much of myself, you know. We can both fly, in a manner of speaking. Having that in common is nice outside of Oren. But you shoulder a lot, perhaps unnecessarily. Just like me.' He paused and scratched the side of his head while he considered his next words. 'Don't think I've ever heard you talk like that about anyone. Even Topeko.'

Amarah rolled her tongue. 'Maybe. Linaria's a lonely place when no-one wants you around.'

'I know that feeling.'

'You had a family, though? You meant something to people.' She scratched the old scar under her eye.

'Maybe. Two hundred years is a lot of time to spend with them. It hurt to lose all those memories when I was banished.'

Amarah blinked. 'What? Two hundred...You're two hundred years old?'

Kohl smiled. 'Two hundred and four, actually. The last year has been my exile, of course.'

Her mouth hung open. She'd heard Arillians were long lived, but over two centuries? 'How long do you birds live?'

Kohl flinched at the slur. 'If we don't meet an untimely end at the hands of other Linarians,' he said. 'Three hundred and fifty, maybe four hundred years? Some of the very oldest made it to just shy of six hundred before passing, but they'd spent the last eight or nine decades in deep meditation.'

'That's why there's so few of you, isn't it?' She remembered thinking Oren had a small population for one of the only Arillian settlements, despite a large chunk of their numbers flying off with Aciel.

'By your standards, I suppose.'

Amarah whistled. 'How old's Jato then? And Aciel?'

'Jato is ninety-seven. Barely more than a youth. Aciel I'm not so sure—he wasn't from Oren. I'd guess mid-way through his second century? One hundred and thirty or forty, maybe?'

She couldn't believe it. 'All this time I thought you were in your late forties, early fifties.'

'Goodness me. I'd barely be out of school at that age!' Kohl laughed, relaxing into it and letting his true mirth show.

'Dragons above. Guess I didn't learn all that much about you Arillians.' She knelt down on the floor, pulling her bag with her, to light another fire.

Though it was warmer inside the barn than outside, she was still practically in the middle of nowhere, and needed heat.

'I'd say for the first visitor ever to come to Oren, you did pretty well,' he complimented.

She smirked, wanted to retort about how it had been a good trip until Jato ruined things, but didn't want to upset the mood.

She didn't think she'd ever seen Kohl laugh properly and didn't want to spoil that.

'I didn't do much. They listened. Nice change from being looked down on here.'

Kohl smiled. 'Don't forget, we've been looked down on all our lives. It will be the same for our children and grandchildren.'

'So why don't you do somethin' about it?'

'Aciel did try.'

'Something better than that psycho!' Amarah replied, shaking her head.

'What would you suggest?' Kohl leaned forward. 'Considering anywhere an Arillian goes, they're met with disdain, suspicion, and fear.'

It sounded like people's reactions to her—especially when she docked at a town on her ship. She hadn't been able to figure out a way around it. That's why she'd been so willing to take what she wanted from people.

If they wouldn't play nice, neither would she.

She supposed Aciel's drastic approach wasn't completely unwarranted.

If she really thought about it, she might have behaved similarly. She may not have led the conquest, but she'd probably have tagged along with it, compulsion or not.

And if all of them were hundreds of years old…that was a lot of time for a grudge to build and become something more akin to hate.

And yet…And yet the Arillians she'd met—even those on Jato's side—had all been friendly and welcoming to her.

Even kind.

'Perhaps if you didn't have that stupid shield that prevented anyone from coming to Oren, you'd start to change people's minds. If you don't let people in, no-one's ever gonna think differently of you.'

Kohl sighed. 'And what about those who come to Oren with ill intentions? The Golems let them cross the threshold, we lower the barrier, and then we have no way of getting rid of them again.'

'You can defend yourself if they attack you?'

'True. But what news will return to the mainland? The visitors will report we aggressive, destructive Arillians are just as people always thought. You know how negative stories fester and spread.' He looked away, bitter.

Amarah knew the truth of that more than anyone.

'Enough of that,' he said. 'How will Traego know you're here? Will he fly here on his own?'

'He might do,' she admitted. 'But I can't sit around and wait for him to check up on this place. Could be a year before he turns up.'

'Then, what?'

'A little Samolen trick Traego uses to keep in touch with all of us,' she said. 'Normally it's so new members don't run off with gold and jewels, but it'll work fine for this.'

Kohl leaned forward, intrigued.

Amarah supposed the Samolen magic did have its uses, even if she couldn't summon it as Topeko and her parents had wanted.

Her grin soured as she remembered how Moroda had picked it up so quickly. Damned Goldstone.

'All right,' she said.

Amarah wrapped her hand around her left wrist, her thumb and middle finger touching. She held her wrist for almost a minute, when her skin darkened as the Thief's Ink tattoo slowly appeared.

'What is that?' Kohl asked.

'Traego's the captain of a lot of pirates. He had a Samolen carve a map of Linaria into the wall of his cabin on his ship, *Otella*. Our tattoos are all on his arms, as well, so he can see where anyone is, anywhere in Linaria.'

Amarah watched as her tattoo darkened, a swirling mass of symbols that she'd never understood, but had grown fond of.

'But it works the other way, too. If we need to get away. We activate the tattoo, the matching one on his body lights up, and he can use *Otella*'s map to find us.'

'Ingenious!'

Amarah released her hand, her tattoo pulsing slightly. 'Simple but effective. Like the Shroud that hides us.'

'I'd never have thought sky pirates were so…so…sophisticated.'

Amarah cackled. 'Traego is the only one. The rest of 'em are thuggish brutes.'

She sat on the floor by the fire and warmed her hands.

'And now…we wait for him to receive your message?'

'He'll have the message. Now we just wait for him to come.'

'And if not?'

'He'll come,' Amarah said, staring into the flames.

Kohl didn't argue, and Amarah sat in silence. Traego would know where she was. She never called for help, so she hoped his curiosity would bring him to her.

Otherwise, she'd have a *long* journey down to Estoria.

She couldn't wait to get a ship under her feet again, then she'd be able to go after Jato.

Amarah grabbed her scythe and ran a finger over it, her tattoo already beginning to fade. She'd need all the help she could get to take on the former General.

For all the scythe's power, it hadn't been enough to take her. The blade itself hadn't been damaged in the fight, didn't even look slightly worn.

She sighed. The flames crackled and spat, warming the barn and turning her cheeks pink.

Amarah waved the scythe, feeling its lightness. Jato must have just got lucky. Nothing could really stand against it, could they? Even if Jato had years of training.

Holding it above the fire, she smiled as the scythe threw blue light rippling across the barn walls and ceiling. 'Nice light show,' she muttered, glancing to Kohl, who watched with amusement.

But when Amarah looked back to her scythe, she saw Palom floating just above it.

Startled, she jumped to her feet, but Palom vanished as soon as she moved. 'Kohl, did you see…?

'I saw!' The Arillian gasped, getting to his feet.

She looked at the blade, but couldn't see anything inside it, couldn't see anything different to a few moments ago.

'The fire?' Kohl suggested.

Amarah held the weapon out, allowing the flames to lick at the blade.

Palom appeared again. He was surrounded by snow, his cloak whirling around in the wind. It looked like he was in the middle of a blizzard.

Beside him, away from the snow, two dark shadows floated.

It was just the same as Arillians watching Linaria through their storms. She supposed Palom had forged all their weapons with dragon-ore, and dragons were all connected.

Had Palom made some way to communicate? To see across the world through the sibling weapons?

If so, the shadows had to be Morgen and Anahrik.

She'd figure out the details later.

'Palom!' Amarah called.

The Ittallan jumped as though he'd heard a ghost.

'Palom, can you see me?' Amarah called again.

'I…I hear you…' Palom said, looked all around.

'Your sword,' Amarah suggested.

He frowned, then unsheathed the great-sword from his back, and held it out in front of him. 'Amarah? How…?'

Amarah cackled. 'You tell me! You're the one who made these weapons!'

Palom blinked and shook his head. 'I did not realise…Where are you?'

'Me and Kohl are in Tum Metsa.'

'Amarah…What happened? Your face? Your eye!'

She sighed. 'Might have got into a fight with Jato. Lost *Khanna*. I've got allies coming here.'

Palom gaped, as though trying to speak. The snow buffeted him, and he crouched into it. 'Did Arillian magic work? Can you free Moroda?'

She glanced to Kohl and shook her head. 'No, but I've got another plan. Can you get to Tum Metsa? I could use some backup.'

'I…' Palom said, bracing himself against the blizzard.

Amarah narrowed her eyes as she saw movement somewhere at Palom's feet.

Something small, with scales.

'Palom is that a dragon?'

'Yes,' he said, yelling over the wind.

Amarah couldn't believe it. What in all Linaria had Palom been doing the past few weeks?

Another surge of snow, and even though she was nowhere near, shivers ran down her spine. He had to be somewhere in the north, she could see the Feor Mountains beside him, but considering how vast Val Sharis was, he could have been one league away or fifty.

'Why do you have a dragon? Palom?'

The blizzard filled her vision, and she heard thunder in the distance. Her heart pounded.

‘Palom, Jato’s in Linaria with some Arillians. Fuck knows what she’s after but stay clear of her!’ She didn’t want Palom hurting her—Jato was hers. ‘You hear that, Palom? Keep away from any Arillians!’

But the connection died, and Palom vanished.

‘Palom?’ Amarah called and received no reply.

‘That was incredible,’ Kohl said.

Disappointed, she lowered the scythe to the floor. ‘I had no idea my scythe could do that!’

‘Do you think Palom will join you?’

‘Why not?’ Amarah shrugged.

Kohl swallowed. ‘He…and I…’

‘Oh *that,*’ Amarah waved her hand. ‘Surely anythin’s better than wandering around in a blizzard?’

‘I’m not so sure…’

‘We’ve probably got a bit of a wait until Traego turns up, anyway. If Palom comes too, that’ll help in our little dragon hunt!’

She grinned.

If Traego came through and Palom joined her, she’d have no trouble at all tracking down Jato and cutting off her head.

Chapter Twenty-Five

Lathri's screams echoed through the palace dungeons. The stone muffled her piercing cries if you were in the main palace, but anything from the basement level below, and your ears would ring with the noise.

Sapora relished it.

His victory over the rebel movement had been undisputed, and his Sevastos had kept the fires raging around the palace afterwards, ensuring no-one could approach without his express permission.

He'd sat at the top of the palace towers, watching the enormous dragon, enjoying how Ittallan cowered before it, fled from its fires. The beast was utterly under his command—if he wanted it to fly, it would fly, if he wanted it to retreat, it would retreat.

For the first time since arriving in Taban Yul, Sapora had the respect he desired.

He had no intention of giving that up now.

'I will do tenfold to your rebels what the Varkain did to the Ittallan during our war,' he said to Lathri.

Battered and bloody, the woman remained defiant.

'I will bring back the Arks. All four of them. If your rebels even consider a new attack, the Arks will commit the same atrocities upon them as they did to your ancestors.'

He felt his physical façade slipping, his inner Varkain threatening to reveal itself.

Tacio hovered to his left, enjoying the spectacle.

'If you tell me what I want to know, then I'll make your death swift.'

She panted, the strain of her bonds sapping her energy.

'Who is your contact in the Imperial Guard? That's all I need. Just one name, and I'll stop your pain.'

She closed her eyes, pulled against the chains trapping her against the dungeon wall. Her feet gave way under her, and she collapsed to the stone. Her arms were chained above her head, ensuring she couldn't use her powers.

When Tacio had discovered she'd been healing the other prisoners, Sapora had taken drastic measures to keep her away—now she remained in a separate cell, her hands shackled to keep her from healing herself.

'Well, Lathri? Don't you miss your mother…?' Sapora said, grinning. 'I can take you to meet her. All I need is a name.'

The Sevastos' victory had given him enough of a confidence boost that he didn't care he didn't know how to free Malashash. He could be patient.

Surely, Aciel couldn't break free from his crystal prison so soon after being sealed.

And even if he did, somehow, he had his own Sevastos to keep him down.

The dragon would be powerful enough to keep any threat down—at least until he figured out how to break the Arks' seal.

'Your king has asked a question, Ittallan,' Tacio said, stepping in to address Lathri. 'You'd be wise to reply.'

Sapora slunk back, happy to let Tacio take the lead in Lathri's questioning. His brother had helped him round up a handful of rebels who'd managed to avoid his Sevastos' flames.

A couple had died of injuries sustained earlier in the battle, but most were fit enough to be arrested. Unfortunately, none of those arrested had been in the Imperial Guard—it seemed they'd all turned to ash when his Sevastos attacked.

A pity.

Tacio and his Cerastes had taken control of the Imperial Guard in Taban Yul and had been slowly infiltrating the ranks across Val Sharis.

Corhaven was across the Sea of Nami. Away from Sapora's eyes and influence, it would be much easier to mount an attack on his right to rule.

But who had orchestrated it all? Who had brought those warships together, stocked them, manned them?

Tacio had mentioned Isa again, but their sister had been in the palace when the attack came. He'd been talking to her.

If she had arranged for the Imperial Guard to attack, then staying in the middle of the target would have been suicide.

No. It couldn't be Isa.

This Lathri had a vendetta against him.

As did many other Ittallan.

He needed to understand who was at their centre. Who gave information, funds, bodies.

Then that person would be his Arks' first target.

'He…is no king of mine…' Lathri said, blood dripping from her cheek where she'd grazed it against the stone walls.

'Whether you accept it or not, he rules Val Sharis,' Tacio said, gleeful that Lathri had finally bitten. 'And he doesn't have to be your king for much longer. The name, if you please. Then we'll let you re-join your mother and your rebel friends.'

'The Arks will ruin Linaria,' Lathri said.

'I think they'll help the Varkain get back on top. But what we do with them isn't your concern. What is our concern is the Imperial Guard you've dragged to your cause.'

Sapora smirked and left the dungeon. Tacio would be able to get the information out of her, he was sure. If his brother failed, he'd try and get back in contact with Morgen, or fly to Corhaven himself.

Wouldn't that be a sight?

Arriving in Niversai on the back of his Sevastos, bringing terror and submission to any who saw him.

He'd make them all bow.

The thought amused him as he left the dungeons and made his way up the winding staircase to the main palace.

He heard Isa before he saw her, lingering in the hallway, pretending to stare out of the windows.

'Sister,' Sapora greeted. He closed the door behind him and nodded to Roke and the other Cerastes who stood guard. 'Hoping for a chance to see our prisoners? I'd give it a while. Tacio is down there.'

Isa looked away from the window. 'Sapora, is this really the best way…?'

'I thought of killing them,' he said. 'But Tacio convinced me that a question and torture session might prove useful.' He shrugged.

Isa scowled. 'You've changed things already. You have a Sevastos, you're on your way to releasing the Arks. Do you have to bring more misery to the world?'

Her words spoiled his good mood. 'Not this again…'

'Yes, this again! The Arks are worse than Mateli! Dragons above, I think Tacio is worse than Mateli!'

'Those rebels would have destroyed the palace, slain Tacio and I. Slain you! This is about striking back, harder and faster than they can. You and I have always lived by this. Why are you changing now?'

'You won't stop, will you? You won't free them?'

'Of course not. They're my prisoners. You would do the same if you were attacked, surely?'

Isa bit her thumbnail.

'I get the impression you always wanted to rule, but now you've the opportunity, you're not up to it. That's fine. Climb your towers. Jump in the hay. Enjoy the city. I will keep the country under control,' Sapora hissed.

Isa looked at him, hurt, then turned away and raced down the hallway without another word.

*

Tears squeezed out of Isa's eyes as she pelted down the darkening streets of Taban Yul. She'd grabbed a dark, cotton shawl and wrapped it around her head and chest as she left Sapora.

The Sevastos had finally lowered its flaming wall surrounding the palace, and perched atop the walls, watching the city with glowing eyes as if daring anyone to attempt another attack.

Ittallan had evacuated the city nearest the palace, and even those who lived in districts further out had opted to leave, despite the poor weather.

The few Imperial Guard stationed in Taban Yul who weren't Varkain had helped with the evacuation, while also helping any citizens unfortunate enough to have been caught up in the Sevastos' flames.

Isa smelt burning everywhere she went.

Every street, every alley stank of ash and death.

Some of the roads had been so badly burned by Sapora's dragon that the stones had melted, filling the air with an acrid stench Isa could taste at the back of her throat.

She desperately wished for snow to cover the death and destruction but knew that was cowardly.

Why cover up what Sapora had done?

It needed to remain in view for everyone to see what he'd done. What he'd become.

What she'd allowed to happen.

Isa hurried along, the streets eerily deserted.

She supposed that was a good thing. Anyone so close to the palace—and Sevastos—had to be mad.

Her heart pounded as she ran through the streets. She'd wanted desperately to leave once the Sevastos attacked but had to stay in the palace for her own sake. Tacio didn't trust her as it was, and if she'd left the moment the battle ended, it would have been even more suspicious.

Were Aetos, Kylos, Voulhrik, and Solvi okay? Had they all been in the battle? Did they have friends and family with them?

Lathri's Ittallan had suffered many losses—the amount of ash choking the palace gardens and surrounding streets was testament to that—but what were they to do next?

At least the cold of night kept most of the Varkain off the city's streets. They'd never been able to withstand the chill for very long.

She had a small window of opportunity, especially if Tacio was busy in the dungeons with Lathri.

Isa swallowed.

Poor Lathri.

And yet, Sapora hadn't killed her. Not yet.

If she didn't give them any information—and Isa had no reason to believe she would—would Tacio advocate for her death anyway? Or would she be kept alive for sport?

She shuddered at the thought.

Isa had never been to Sereth, but she knew how they treated their thralls. Sapora had told her plenty of stories that had made her blood turn to ice.

There would be nothing stopping Tacio from bringing a similar practice to Taban Yul.

Even though she had been the one to send the message to Morgen requesting aid against Sapora, Isa felt she'd betrayed Lathri more than her brother.

She'd been safe in the palace while Sapora's Cerastes had cut everyone down.

She'd watched from the side-lines as the Sevastos had risen and attacked.

She'd been safe while her allies had died.

And now Lathri was a prisoner of the Varkain.

Koraki had reported more dragons attacking towns in the far north of Val Sharis, and a group of Arillians seemed to be behaving in kind.

Her country was falling apart.

Dragons killed Ittallan because of the Arillians. Arillians killed more dragons in vengeance. On and on it went, with Ittallan losing out the most.

As a princess—as a queen—she should have done something. She had just as much right to rule as Sapora.

Now, with Lathri's words motivating her, she would do more. She would save Val Sharis from Sapora.

Quite how, she wasn't sure, but she could no longer sit back and watch as the Varkain took over.

She mulled over her options, picking out possibilities, as she approached the bridge that would take her into Little Yomal.

Isa spotted a young boy attempting to climb up the sides. He couldn't have been older than seven or eight, and Isa pulled up, wondering where his parents were.

So far from the palace, the streets were covered in snow, and ice had formed across the bridge.

'Wait! Stop! You'll slip!' Isa yelled, darting over to him.

But the child ignored her, intent on clambering up onto the bridge.

'Oh no, don't tell me Aciel has got you, too?' She sighed, when the boy continually ignored her. 'No-one is safe in Taban Yul anymore. Burn to death by the Sevastos or have your mind controlled by Aciel.'

The boy scrambled to the top of the bridge's side and walked along it, teetering slightly as he kept his balance.

Isa gulped.

He wasn't going to…throw himself off, surely?

She couldn't risk it. She darted forward and leapt at him, elbow out. She collided with his side, sent him flying off the wall and onto the bridge where he landed on the ground with a smack.

Isa hated herself for hurting him, but she wouldn't have been able to live with herself had he done the unthinkable. 'Are you all right?'

He brought a hand to his head, clearly in a daze.

'Hello?' Isa tried again.

The boy looked up at her, his blank gaze disappearing into curiosity. 'Princess Isa...'

She exhaled in relief. 'Where are your parents?'

He glanced around, confused. 'How...did I get....here?'

'You got into a bit of trouble. It's okay though. Where do you live?' She said, helping him to his feet.

'Little Yomal,' he said, patting himself down as if to check he was really stood in the middle of the bridge.

'It's just there,' Isa nodded. 'Come on, I'll help you.'

'My mum was packing up things. We was gonna leave the city,' he said, and took her hand.

'Smart thing to do,' Isa said. She walked him back over the bridge and into the residential district.

Her mind whirled.

How was Aciel controlling the people of Taban Yul? How exactly could that control be broken? It wasn't as if she could shove everyone over, so they whacked their head on the ground.

She half-listened as the boy talked about his parents and their plans to move further south to Tannon Sona.

When he recognised where he was, she let him race off to his home, while she continued on towards Lathri's townhouse.

Dread welled in her gut as she approached, and she smelt blood and burnt clothes from two streets away.

Kylos opened the door, as if expecting her.

'May I come in?' Isa asked, head bowed slightly. Even if she was royalty, she knew how to be respectful.

'Not like I could stop you, could I?' Kylos said.

Isa smiled weakly and stepped inside.

'Welcome, princess,' Solvi said. She was sat on the floor near the door to the balcony, her arm in a sling.

All around the room, Ittallan sat or lay in various states of distress. Some she recognised as palace workers, others she'd never seen before.

'Don't suppose you brought any medical supplies? Without Lathri, we can't do as much,' Kylos said, following her in. She knelt by her brother, who had a particularly large gash on his forearm, which Kylos continued to bandage.

'I barely got away,' Isa said. 'It would have been suspicious if I'd grabbed anything first.'

Kylos clicked her tongue but didn't reply.

'How is Lathri? Will…will she get a funeral?' Aetos asked, grimacing as Kylos tended to his arm.

'Lathri's alive,' Isa said. 'She's in the dungeons, along with everyone else who's been arrested.'

'Captured more like,' Kylos muttered, securing Aetos's bandage and standing up to face her. 'We lost so many people. Our one good chance to strike.'

Isa looked around and stepped out of the way as other healers and medics looked after the injured Ittallan crowded into Lathri's' small home.

'How many people?' Isa asked.

'Everyone left on the warships. At least twenty on each,' Kylos said. 'Over forty to Cerastes or Sapora himself,' she continued, 'and other than the eight people here, the rest are unaccounted for.'

'Probably ash,' Aetos said bitterly.

Isa swallowed. 'There are twelve in the dungeons, including Lathri.'

'I hope they meet a swift end instead of whatever poison lurks in Sapora's fangs,' Kylos said. 'Voulhrik died. Didn't have a chance against the Sevastos. Nothing goes. Lucky for you that you had the palace walls to hide behind.'

Isa scowled but didn't rise to it. None of them were unscathed, and she knew there'd be resentment because she'd been outside of the fighting.

'If Lathri is alive, can't we just free her?' Solvi asked.

'Tacio's guarding her himself. It'd be impossible,' Isa said.

She knew she'd be in more danger now than ever before and could only hope that Sapora was more interested in getting information from Lathri than suspecting her.

'If he didn't have that damned dragon,' Aetos muttered, wincing as he shifted how he sat.

'Attacking him again and freeing Lathri would be the easiest thing in the world,' Kylos sighed.

'There's got to be a way to break his hold on that Sevastos. I've never heard of anyone, even a Samolen, with that kind of power.' Aetos said. 'Isa, do you know how he does it?'

'I wish I did,' she sighed. 'I didn't even know he had one until it turned up at the palace!'

‘Well at least Sapora doesn’t have the Ark he said he would have,’ Aetos said. ‘He wouldn’t have left any of us alive if he had.’

Others joined in on the conversation.

Some wanted action, to press forward while Sapora felt victorious.

Others wanted to wait out the winter.

Others still wanted to seek new information elsewhere before deciding their next move.

Aetos and Kylos attempted to reply to everyone’s concerns.

But trying to calm and control a group of grieving, gravely injured Ittallan was not easy, and the discussion descended into a squabble, and then into a furious argument.

‘We need to focus on freeing Lathri. We can’t manage things without her,’ Kylos said.

Isa was inclined to agree. The healer’s peacekeeping abilities certainly kept everyone’s tempers low. ‘Security at the palace, especially now…It’ll be nigh impossible to even get into the palace unless you can climb very well. Or fly.’

‘That’s fine,’ Aetos said. ‘Nothing’s broken.’ He prodded his arm and tried to hide his wince. ‘It’s a risk, but we need our leader. I doubt Sapora would expect it, either. That gives us the advantage.’

An advantage over Sapora. Isa had never thought she’d hear those words. ‘You won’t succeed unless I help. I’d need to distract Tacio, get him away from Lathri somehow. You can’t all charge in, either. If there’s a large group, the game will be up before you cross the palace grounds. A stealthy approach would be best.’

‘I’ll do whatever it takes,’ Kylos said.

‘Any other volunteers?’ Isa asked.

‘I volunteer.’ Solvi stood up, fierce determination in her eyes. ‘I wasn’t hurt too much in the battle. But I’m used to hunting silently, used to ambush.’

Kylos smiled at the young woman. ‘I can’t say no to that.’

Isa nodded. The three of them would be enough—she hoped.

‘I’ll be our eyes above the palace. Give me a bit of time to rest and I’ll fly.’

Isa breathed. Good. She’d need time to prepare as well.

‘Tonight, then,’ Kylos said. ‘As late as we can leave it.’

‘Tonight…?’ Isa replied. The sun had set, and the first two moons had already risen. ‘You mean in a couple of hours?’

‘Strike while the iron is hot, isn’t that the saying?’ Kylos asked.

From everyone’s stares, Isa knew she couldn’t win this argument. She sighed.

She was in too deep to back out now.

‘Okay. Listen carefully while I tell you the best way into the palace, and the route you’ll need to take to the dungeons. I’ll focus on keeping Tacio and his Cerastes out of your way.’

And with that, Isa knew she could not rescind her betrayal of Sapora.

Chapter Twenty-Six

Patience, Amarah realised, had never been her forte.

While she knew Traego had received her message—how could you miss a tattoo on your body lighting up—he could have been anywhere in Linaria. Thief's Ink was not a two-way communication system, so she had no way of knowing how far away he was, or how long she'd end up waiting in the snow for him.

On the third day, Kohl had asked how long she planned on waiting, and at her shrug reply, had promptly disappeared, citing he wanted to stretch his legs in town.

When he returned with a proper eyepatch for her, Amarah had been moved almost to tears. 'You didn't have to do that!'

Kohl had smiled. 'Local seamstress was able to whip up something that I thought might work. More comfortable for you! How does it fit?'

Amarah adjusted the strap around the back of her head. 'Fits fine. Thank you.'

Perhaps the Arillians were kind, helpful people who had simply been misjudged all these years.

Well. Except for Jato, of course.

But there were bad apples in every society.

If Kohl could keep his old emotions towards his daughter locked up, then he'd be an asset.

'I don't know how long it takes your ships to cross the country,' Kohl said. 'But if you have to travel elsewhere for a ship of your own, hadn't we better get moving?'

Amarah had to admit he had a point. It could take her the rest of winter to get down to Estoria. And yet she didn't want to be too hasty. Traego could turn up at any moment, today or in a week's time.

How long was she prepared to wait in a small barn hidden from view until she could leave?

She huffed.

Not much longer at the rate of her boredom.

'I'll give him one more day,' she said after thinking it over for a while. Four days was enough time to reach Tum Metsa from almost anywhere in Val Sharis.

If he'd been out in Corhaven somewhere, then she'd have a much longer wait.

'One more day,' Kohl echoed. 'Been able to talk to Palom?'

Amarah shook her head. 'Nope. Wherever he is, I think the blizzard's too strong for any connection. But he knows where we are. He might come.'

'Sounds like there's a lot of hoping and waiting,' Kohl said, rubbing his eyes.

Amarah rolled her tongue.

Too much, as far as she was concerned.

But what choice did she have?

She had no idea how most people dealt with life without an airship. Walking just took so *long*.

'A shame that Thief's Ink of yours only works one way. It would be easier knowing whether or not he was on his way.'

'I know, I know.'

'I'd offer to scout, but from the conversations I picked up on in Tum Metsa, Jato and her followers are causing quite a stir in Val Sharis.' The dejection in his voice almost made Amarah wince.

She couldn't sugar-coat her response. 'I expected as much.'

'Taban Yul was attacked as well,' he added.

That caught her attention. 'Sapora's there, isn't he? Who in their right mind attacked *him*?'

Kohl lifted his hands. 'No-one's quite sure. He put down the rebellion, anyway. But that's not the surprising thing.'

'What is…?' Amarah wasn't sure she wanted to know.

He ran a hand through his hair.

'Kohl…?'

'And they called me the betrayer…' He muttered.

Amarah stamped the bottom of her scythe on the floor of the barn. 'What was the surprising thing?'

The Arillian looked at her, and Amarah swore he had more creases in his skin than when she'd seen him that morning.

'He…I don't know how, or if it's true…but everyone seems to say this….'

Amarah took a deep breath.

Whatever revelation Kohl was trying to say clearly had a huge impact. 'Just spit it out. Whatever it is, I can deal with it.'

Her mind raced. What tricks could that dirty snake have up his sleeve?

Kohl shrugged his shoulders again. 'They're saying he has a Sevastos. That it flew up from the palace grounds, destroyed their ships, and burned half the city along with them.'

It took Amarah several seconds to process the enormity of what he'd just said. When she was able to form a coherent thought, she said, 'How…how can Sapora *have* a Sevastos? They're not cats or dogs? They're not pets!'

'I know.'

'And if he had one all this time, why didn't he say anything when he knew we were looking for one to stop Aciel?'

'I know.'

'Flying from Berel to Val Sharis! We could have avoided the fight with Jato for her ereven sphere if he knew exactly where one was!'

'I know,' Kohl repeated a third time.

'Moroda might not have…Eryn and Anahrik…'

Kohl nodded. 'I wonder how Palom would feel if he knew.'

Amarah slumped onto a crate, gobsmacked. Everything that had gone wrong on their dragon hunt, every loss, every death…All of it could have been avoided if Sapora hadn't been so damned selfish and told them he knew about a Sevastos!

Explained that he had one under his control.

'I don't believe it. I don't fucking believe it.'

She smashed the bottom of her scythe on the floor again. 'And now he brings it out to burn some ships because his rule is so fucking terrible!'

Rage swirled within her. If he'd have told them earlier, none of this would have happened.

She wouldn't have had to go to Oren.

She wouldn't have lost *Khanna*.

She wouldn't have lost her eye.

'That foul fucking maggot!'

'Easy, Amarah,' Kohl said.

'No! All this time he had the key to solving our problems and he runs away and hides in his tunnels?' Amarah was shaking with rage now. It boiled up within her, from her gut to her throat, and she thought she'd vomit. 'I knew he was a dirty snake, but…'

'He had his own plans for that Sevastos, it seems,' Kohl said, but Amarah dismissed his words.

Right now, her target had switched from Jato to King Snake.

What an absolute bastard.

And he'd said *nothing at all.*

Let them carry on, knowing all the while he could have saved them.

Slimy, selfish snake.

'What about Isa?' Amarah asked.

'No idea. No-one mentioned her. Well, why would they? When they have a Sevastos to talk about.'

She shook her head, unable to even speak.

But then…if her next hunt was a Sevastos…and Sapora had one…?

Amarah looked at Kohl, who must have been able to guess her train of thought, because he immediately shook his head. 'I know what you're thinking…'

'What am I thinking?'

'You wanna go after Sapora. Get his Sevastos to free Moroda.'

'Why not? I know what I want. He has it. I'll take it.'

'This is Sapora we're talking about. Sapora who used this Sevastos to burn a fleet of warships! You'll burn just as well.'

She twirled her scythe. 'I won't. I won't let him.'

Kohl sighed, backing down.

Amarah was about to add another justification to her plan, when she heard footsteps crunch in the snow outside. 'Sshh!'

They were getting louder. She raced to the window and peered out. 'It's Traego!' She'd recognise his *Otella* anywhere, and he'd landed it flat on the snow fields a quarter of a league away.

He had two youths trailing him like hungry dogs, and Amarah rolled her eyes. She'd forgotten about his penchant for "saving" the needy and desperate.

She stepped back to make room for Traego and his companions as he slipped through the Shroud and into the barn.

'Well, well, well, if it isn't a face I thought I'd never be seein' again!' Traego said as soon as he entered the barn. 'I lost count o' how many years it's been!'

She shook her head, a smirk on her lips. 'Five years, Traeg. Not that long.'

Kohl stepped forward, took off his hat, and bowed low. 'A pleasure to make your acquaintance, Traego. I'm Kohl.'

'I'd never have pegged you travelling with an Arillian!' Traego said, eyes glinting. 'Nice ta meet ya, Kohl. I guess Amarah's told ya all about me, right?'

'Enough about you,' Kohl replied.

'Who've you picked up, Traeg?' Amarah asked, nodding her chin towards the two youths who were eying up the barn.

'Oh. Where are me manners? Carav,' he put a hand on the shoulder of the young woman, 'and Oris.' He dropped his other hand on the young man.

Both had to be in their late teens and looked grubby. Oris seemed to have drool leaking from the corner of his mouth.

Amarah wrinkled her nose and looked back at her old ally.

He hadn't changed a bit since she'd last seen him.

The same easy grin, the same laid-back attitude.

She'd missed it.

'Only five years and it looks like ya been in the wars,' Traego said, peering closely at Amarah. 'Patch suits ya.'

'Thanks...' She muttered, suddenly feeling self-conscious.

Kohl cleared his throat. 'Did you travel far, Traego?'

'From Lavonn in Corhaven. Little fishing village right on the east coast. But when I got here I couldn't see *Khanna* anywhere...'

Amarah dropped her gaze. 'Well that's why I asked for help, Traego. I need some gold to get a new ship.'

'Dragons above, what happened to her?'

'Same thing that happened to this.' She pointed to her eye. 'I'll hunt her down, don't worry.'

Traego grinned. 'Would never think anythin' less of ya. But gold you need, then? How much?'

'Twenty double-crowns.' It was a lot. She knew it was a lot.

Traego let out a long whistle. 'Tell ya what Amarah. Cause I'm a nice guy. I'll give ya the money…'

She raised an eyebrow. 'If…?'

He grinned and looked from her to Kohl and back again. 'If ya come on a little *treasure hunt* with me, first.'

'Traeg, I don't have the time…'

'Ah well then ya're welcome to find the gold yaself.'

She huffed. 'All right, all right. As long as it's quick. You know where you're goin'? What you're after?'

'I got it all listed out.'

She really didn't have much of a choice. 'I've got another ally on the way here, an Ittallan. He's got the most powerful weapon you've ever seen.'

'Where is he?' Traego asked.

'We're not sure. We hoped he'd have been here by now,' Kohl said, concern edging his voice.

'There's more Arillians than you in the skies above Val Sharis right now,' Traego said. 'If he ain't here yet, he ain't comin' here. My hunt's kind of on a time limit, so we need to get back to Corhaven now.'

'You were on the hunt when you came for me?' Amarah asked.

'Yep. I'd like ta get back on it.'

She felt bad that he'd abandoned a hunt to come and help her out. Traego also knew how she felt about debts and owing people.

Whatever his hunt was, he needed more people.

She sighed, wishing that he'd only come to help her out of the kindness of his heart, but she knew that wasn't the truth. When she thought about it, she really did miss the old hunts. She needed a ship – or money for one – and Traego was a secure offer. At least she'd be one step closer to getting Sapora back for everything he'd done – all the pain, hurt, and torment.

Not to mention getting towards freeing Moroda.

'Kohl, you in?'

He fiddled with his hat again, picking at the fluff and smoothing it out.

Amarah could tell he had second thoughts. 'Jato could be anywhere in Val Sharis, and we're crossing the sea. You had your chance to get back in her good books and she threw it in your face. Not like you have anywhere else to go, is it? Come with us outcasts and you'll find we're a better family than anything Jato could give you.'

Like Traego, Amarah knew Kohl had only helped her for his own gain.

Hoped to win his daughter back, hoped to protect his people and his village.

'My plans are bigger than revenge. This is about Linaria now. Don't regret not doing anything now.'

Kohl closed his eyes and sighed. 'I'll come with you.'

'Great ta have ya on board, Kohl,' Traego grabbed his hand and shook it vigorously. 'Chop, chop, kids, back ta the boat!' He clapped his hands and Carav and Oris hurried ahead.

'Like old times, isn't it?' Amarah said as they walked through the snow to Traego's warship.

'Except we're older an' wiser now.'

Amarah wasn't sure she agreed with that second part.

'So, what's this treasure hunt of yours? Corhaven ain't got much these days,' she said. 'What you after this time?'

Traego stopped at the base of Otella as Carav opened the hatch to get in. 'Ya ever heard of an Ark?'

*

The blizzard raged solidly for leagues on end.

Palom had lost his bearings more times than he could count, yet through it all, his young hatchling remained by his side.

'Brave one, you are,' Palom said when they'd woken up one morning to find their camp covered in four feet of snow.

Palom could navigate by the stars, but when the sky was blocked out by thick clouds and unrelenting snow, even he couldn't figure out which way was north.

He'd found Amarah's sudden communication shocking more than anything else. It went to show how little he truly knew about his *Valta Forinja*. What other secrets were his weapons capable of?

If Lathri knew it could communicate, perhaps she'd be less fearful of it? Less determined to see only the negativity.

All swords were designed to kill, after all.

The *Valta Forinja* was simply efficient in its duty.

It had been at least three days since he'd spoken to Amarah and had made the decision to join her cause shortly after the blizzard took hold.

He'd strongly considered tracking down the Arillians and cutting them down one by one. His sword was certainly capable of that, and it would give him some twisted pleasure.

But another part of him had abhorred the idea.

He'd saved the dragons they'd been hunting. By chasing them down, he'd be lowering himself to their level, and that thought sickened him.

Besides, *Leillu* had been shaken by the encounter, and he didn't want to distress his companion.

He could hardly believe that *Khanna* had been destroyed. He knew it was Amarah's greatest love, above anything else – gold, fame, notoriety – and yet she was carrying on, after losing the most important thing to her.

What was he doing?

Running away…?

But to where?

Joining with Amarah would reunite him with one of his last true friends, would give him a purpose.

Would stop him being such a coward.

She'd asked him to come to her aid, as well.

Her request had given him a strange sense of pride.

'What do you think, *Leillu*? Do you want to join sky thief?'

Leillu looked up at him and chirped, nostrils flaring.

'I take that as yes.' Palom smiled, aware of his sword pulsing at his back again.

At first, he'd used the sword as a sixth sense for danger.

But as he grew more determined to help Amarah, the more Palom found the sword frustrating. It was like a weight on his mind he couldn't shift—always there, pushing him to act a certain way.

They'd sheltered in the trees and dug themselves out of the freshly fallen snow. Thankfully, the blizzard appeared to be over – only a little snow fell, and there was no more biting wind driving him to the ground.

He remembered seeing a way sign the night before, and it took him a moment to get his bearings in a sea of white powder.

Gal Etra – Quarter League

Maybe it was time to re-join civilisation?

Leillu darted around his feet, jumping in the snow—almost swimming in it—perfectly at ease in the cold.

Palom remembered the crystals all dragons had in their chests. It gave them their fire.

Clearly it made them immune to freezing temperatures, too. He supposed he'd be the same if he could breathe fire at will.

'*Leillu*, it is time to go.' Palom said, forcing his way towards the path in the direction of Gal Etra.

But the young dragon was more interested in having fun in the snow and ignored his calls.

'*Leillu*? If you do not come now I am leaving you in forest,' Palom said.

Still the dragon refused to obey.

He watched as it tunnelled into a particularly large heap of snow, its blue tail disappearing, and didn't resurface.

Palom watched a while, before hurrying over to where he'd seen the young dragon disappear. '*Leillu*! *Leillu* I am here!'

He shovelled snow out of the way with his huge hands, shifting heaps in seconds, until he finally found where the young dragon had dug to.

'What have you found, *Leillu*...?' He whispered, gently lifting the dragon from the frozen ground so he could see.

There were several small holes, each about the width of his thumb. He frowned, unsure, when he heard a loud squeak.

Leillu bounced up, a mouse grasped between its teeth.

'Ah, you are hunting for yourself now.' Palom grinned. 'You are watching me and learning. Well done.'

The young dragon shook the mouse violently, before swallowing it whole and immediately sniffed around for more.

Palom sat down and waited as *Leillu* hunted three more mice. He pulled out his *Valta Forinja* and inspected it.

With the sword, he'd been able to talk to Amarah, find *Leillu*, and keep himself alive in the wilds of Val Sharis.

Yet Lathri's words still echoed in his mind.

Emonos.

Did she mean the sword, or him?

He looked around. There was enough snow here. Plenty of snow, in fact, and it wasn't as if people often travelled along the road.

He'd felt so righteous when he'd slain the Varkain who'd ambushed him. That felt like a lifetime ago.

And yet, he'd been able to take down Mateli—his greatest enemy—and he hadn't even needed the sword to do that.

Palom scratched his chin.

He was enough.

Alone, he was enough.

He didn't need the sword—the sword needed him.

Watching *Leillu* hunt had calmed his mind enough to think things through, to not give in to the darkness that threatened to overwhelm him every time he closed his eyes.

He *was* enough.

Whether Lathri agreed or not.

Whether Solvi agreed or not.

It didn't matter what anyone said or thought of him.

He was done with the *Valta Forinja*.

Palom stood, pushed *Leillu* out of the way gently with the toe of his boot, and held the Valta Forinja in front of him.

The sword was his legacy.

The result of a lifetime's dreaming.

All that he had left of Anahrik.

But it held him back, he could see that now.

With a roar, Palom drove the sword tip-first into the icy ground—the blade stabbing deep—until only the hilt remained.

He panted, suddenly sweating.

Leillu jumped at his ferocity, but then leaped forward a moment later, sniffing around the hilt of the blade and clawing at it.

'Leave it, *Leillu*,' Palom said. 'It is *emonos*.'

*

Palom had never been to Gal Etra before, but it was much the same as any Ittallan town on the outskirts. Nothing like the bustle of Taban Yul or Cora Keb, Gal Etra was a logging town more akin to Feoras Sol.

They mostly had their heads down, keeping to themselves as they cut and hauled and heaved tree trunks from the forest to where they processed them in town.

At first, no-one gave him a second look—he was just another Ittallan passing through on his way north—but once one realised who he was, the whole town seemed to drop what they were doing to crowd him. They were fascinated by his dragon, and *Leillu* scrambled up his legs to sit on his shoulder.

He was certain their behaviour was much the same as anyone else's in Taban Yul, yet somehow, he didn't mind them as much.

'Palom, you saved my son!' One old woman said, crying with happiness. 'Please, whatever you need, if I can give it to you, I will! Food, clothes, gifts for your family.'

He was taken aback by her fierce generosity.

'Can you tell me how far to Tum Metsa?' Palom asked.

‘Walking in this snow? It could take you a week at least!’ She said. ‘But as a tiger? Keep a good pace and you’ll be there in two days.’

‘Thank you,’ he said, bowing his head.

‘Rest here. The weather is terrible, and we have plenty of room in the inn, or you’d be welcome to stay with anyone here.’

‘You are kind, but I am meeting a friend in Tum Metsa. I need to be there soon.’

‘Lucky friend,’ another Ittallan said, as the old woman led Palom and a growing crowd through the town.

‘After everything that happened in Taban Yul.’ Another voice muttered.

‘I can’t believe there’s a Varkain in charge of things. Look what he’s doing! Burning half the city down.’

‘Burning Taban Yul?’ Palom asked, zoning in on a few words.

‘Yes. King Sapora unleashed a dragon on the city. He was attacked, and he retaliated.’

‘Who attacked him?’ Palom’s legs trembled.

No, Lathri.

It couldn’t be her.

She wouldn’t be silly enough to charge the palace… would she?

‘No-one knows. Sapora arrested everyone he didn’t kill. I’m sure we’ll get another runner with an update soon.’

He needed to get back down to Taban Yul.

Or was he being paranoid again?

Lathri wouldn't be the only person in Taban Yul who didn't agree with Sapora's rule, and her group of allies wouldn't be the only ones who could attack him…?

His stomach churned as he wavered between dropping everything to race back to Taban Yul or pressing on now that he was only a couple of days from Tum Metsa.

Leillu spread its wings as it yawned, then snuggled into his shoulder, wrapping its tail around his neck.

He couldn't give in to paranoia.

Lathri might not be in any trouble at all, and he'd have wasted time by travelling back to the capital.

On the other hand, if she did need help and he was at the northern-most town in Val Sharis, he'd never forgive himself.

He supposed Lathri had Voulhrik, Aetos, and Kylos around her. She'd probably have grown her ranks since he'd left the city, too.

She'd wanted him to stand by her, but she hadn't wanted his help. She never had, even when they were young.

Palom sniffed. He'd already made his decision, really.

He simply needed to talk himself into it.

Palom gently scratched the top of *Leillu*'s head as he looked out onto the vast ice fields. Only ice and trees separated Gal Etra with Tum Metsa.

Fields and fields of nothing.

And yet…on the horizon, in Tum Metsa, his old friends waited.

Amarah.

And Kohl—though Palom wasn't sure how he felt towards the Arillian now.

'*Leillu*, it is long way to travel. I hope you are ready for this journey.'

The residents of Gal Etra saw him off, everyone jostling with each other for a chance to watch Palom pass through.

He was grateful for their kindness and hospitality, and if he'd not been pressed for time, Palom would have gladly stayed in their town for a few days.

But he had to get to Amarah.

And he hoped he was making the right decision.

With a sniff, Palom tapped into his *meraki* and transformed.

It felt easier than it had been, like slipping on a favourite pair of boots.

He couldn't explain it—had the *Valta Forinja* been holding him back so much for so long?

He'd been a fool, if it had, and wished he'd listened to Lathri sooner.

Palom shivered as the wind caught his fur. *Leillu* clutched on as always, and he looked back to Gal Etra, amazed at how many people had come out into the freezing cold to watch him.

For all his power and strength, he'd been blind to the darkness that had gripped him.

It still gripped him—there was no way to shake a shadow that big—but at least he knew it was there.

At least he'd stopped feeding it.

Getting rid of the sword was something he should have done weeks ago. If he'd been stronger—mentally stronger—he may not have been so dependent on it.

But he'd been caught up in everything.

Too afraid of failure.

Too wrapped up in grief and loss and pain.

He charged through the trees, powered on by an inner strength he'd forgotten he had.

During the fight with Mateli, he'd tapped into the edges of it—driven on by raw emotion—but this was not some surge of energy that would fade with adrenaline.

Palom felt alive in a way he could hardly remember. Since before the death of his brother, he supposed. Two decades of grief and guilt carried around in his chest.

His paws careened him across the snow faster than ever before. Perhaps even faster than Anahrik could have flown.

He'd failed Anahrik in life. Palom wouldn't fail him in death. He'd live the life he was supposed to, driven by his own ambitions and desires, not out of a fear of failure.

Of not being good enough.

He kicked up snow, the trees a blur on either side as he ran between them. He focussed on the small pinpricks of pain as *Leillu's* claws dug in.

Wolves hunted here, it seemed. The air was thick with their scent, and he didn't want to encounter any while he hurried to Tum Metsa. When they appeared in the trees ahead, he darted off to the side, and gave them a wide berth.

Palom came to a stop in a particularly thick clump of trees, crouching down as he caught his breath and waited for them to pass.

The biggest led them in a straight line, occasionally putting his muzzle to the ground, the others yapping at one another.

Wondering how far he was from Tum Metsa, Palom glanced around for a way sign, but found nothing.

He spotted an old bronze sign nailed into a tree, which read: *Karekis*.

Some old Ittallan, perhaps?

The woods were full of loners and nomads who lived in the trees and rarely ventured out. To think he'd been close to living that lifestyle, too.

Once he was sure the wolves had gone, Palom continued on, though at not such a break-neck speed. He had to conserve some energy after all.

A large warship flew overhead, and Palom glanced up to watch as it passed. It reminded him of Amarah, and their travels with Moroda and the others. The memories were positive, his heart light as he remembered their journey together.

The friendship that had developed.

He would help Amarah bring Moroda back.

Leillu chirped and shifted its grip.

If Palom could smile, he would have. He didn't have to be afraid anymore—he wasn't alone.

End

THANK YOU SO MUCH FOR READING!

If you enjoyed reading *Palom*, please could you take a minute to leave a review on Amazon and Goodreads?

Reviews are crucial for indie authors like me, and even a couple of lines can make a huge difference!

I hope to publish book three in the series, *Amarah*, in 2019, which continues the story as the sky pirate joins old allies in Linaria's greatest treasure hunt. There's plenty of magic, legends, and of course—dragons!

If you can't wait to get back into the World of Linaria, sign up to my mailing list and you'll be the first to hear news, announcements, and special offers.

You'll receive a high-res digital map of Linaria just for signing up!
www.llmcneil.com/contact

I'm also on Goodreads, Twitter, and Facebook if you'd like to follow me on social media!